Deception on Margin

Gregg J. Haugland

PublishAmerica
Baltimore

© 2003 by Gregg Haugland.
All rights reserved. No part of this book may be reproduced in any form without written permission from the publishers, except by a reviewer who may quote brief passages in a review to be printed in a newspaper or magazine.

First printing

ISBN: 1-59286-493-7
PUBLISHED BY PUBLISHAMERICA BOOK PUBLISHERS
www.publishamerica.com
Baltimore

Printed in the United States of America

Dedication

For Cindy, who always believed this could be done.

For John and Joan, whose faith in me has never wavered.

For Kelly and Britt, the two brightest points in my universe.

Prologue

There was very little light in the suite. At one end a TV projected a flickering bluish cast over the sitting area, images of CNBC playing out unwatched, stock ticker moving relentlessly across the bottom of the screen. The sound was on, louder than would normally be needed for someone watching the program to listen comfortably, loud enough for someone standing outside the door to hear the muffled sounds. The fashionably attired anchorwoman interviewed a not so well dressed analyst who warned of the impending impact of the Fed Chairman's upcoming address to the New York Press Club, while at the same time shamelessly peddling the virtues of his own favorite stocks.

At the other end of the suite a laptop sat open on the dining table. Random fractal images generated by the screensaver danced across the wall toward the bathroom and the door to the hotel hallway. The laptop itself was unremarkable, a state-of-the-art system offered by any number of vendors, the familiar "Intel Inside" logo displayed just above the keyboard.

The mirrored door to the closet stood partially open. Inside were two conservative suits, a sports coat, neatly tailored slacks and four dress shirts still in their transparent wrapping provided by the hotel dry-cleaners. A hanger draped with brightly colored ties hung above a pile of workout clothes tossed unceremoniously on the floor, partially covering a new pair of Nikes. Two pairs of dress shoes, one black, one brown added to the collection of what would be the wardrobe of any well dressed traveling businessman.

The only other sign of occupancy was the remnants of a room-service breakfast. A brown tray sat on the table, well away from the laptop, on it a plate of mostly consumed scrambled eggs, toast and traces of grease left over from a couple of pork sausages. A half glass of orange juice and a white coffeepot sat closer to the computer, the coffee cup nowhere to be seen.

Outside the heavy drawn drapes, the intensifying heat of the mid-day sunshine shone relentlessly against the windows. The blue sky of the

Dallas afternoon was unblemished by clouds and summer day pollution, light winds constantly dispersing the hazing effects of the weekday traffic. A black stretch limousine pulled into the entrance to the Adolphus Hotel, glided under the canopy and stopped in front of the doors as the bellman smartly marched out to assist the arriving guests.

Back inside the room, the screen-saver flicked off and was replaced by a screen for InterAmerica trading services. Then another window popped up on the screen, the words 'Automatic Phone Services' set in the middle, the program status bar indicating the percent complete slowly filling in below. At the bottom right corner of the window a phone icon appeared as the speakers inside the computer hummed, and the sound of a dial tone filled the room. After a moment the familiar 'da da dot du da' of touch-tone dialing emitted from the speakers, followed by several rings. There was a click, and the tinny sound of a woman's voice emitted from the speakers.

"Welcome to InterAmerica automated trading services. Please use your touch-tone phone to select one of the following options: Press one to submit a trade, press two for account…"

A third window popped up and displayed a small face, tape recorder and slide bars for volume and tone levels. The blip of a phone key interrupted the digital recording coming from InterAmerica.

"Voice recorded trading. After the tone, please clearly state your name, account number, pin number and the nature of your trade. To ensure accuracy of your request, please repeat the trade instructions twice, then hang up. This trade will be digitally recorded."

The TV, still on across the room switched to a Pepsi commercial, momentarily adding a bit of humanity to the empty room. On the screen, the tape recorder icon began to spin as the speakers came to life again.

"This is Fred Simpson. Account number 434-554-8982. Pin number 445564. I wish to issue a sell stop for Bandwidth Networks, symbol BWDT at 102. Repeat. Fred Simpson. Account number 434-554-8982. Pin number 445564. Sell stop on Bandwidth Networks, symbol BWDT at 102. Thank you"

The speakers clicked again, followed by the sound of the telephone hanging up. The window with the tape recorder disappeared from the screen and the speakers once again fell silent. In the bottom right corner of the screen the time display indicated 1:27 PM.

Chapter One

He paused just outside the massive supermarket and surveyed the parking lot one last time. He smiled as his heart pumped almost audibly in his chest and the adrenaline surged through his veins. Dressed in blue sweat pants, long sleeve workout shirt and Nikes, Fred Simpson (a.k.a. John Anderson, Richard Williams, Stuart Jones) walked confidently through the invisible wall of air that pushed down through the 24-hour entrance to the store. With styled brown hair and striking brown eyes he blended in well with the shoppers already about their business. The upscale surroundings boasted a large number of professionals who worked in and lived around the Denver Tech Center, and it was not uncommon to see patrons dressed in anything from sports bras to business suits. The neighborhood affluence was always a prime selection criterion for his targets.

He walked into the soup aisle and headed toward the back of the store, the generic plastic shopping bag in his hand swinging as he moved past the stacks of Campbell's soups. He ran the scenario one last time through his mind as he approached the deli, then turned toward the back hallway where the offices and restrooms were located. He knew exactly where he was headed, the store layout carefully mapped and studied on a trip to Denver two weeks before.

He reminded himself of how easy it had been to determine store schedule despite the security measures implemented. A few days watching the daily transfer of money from the office to an armored transport truck was usually sufficient. A significant amount of cash moved through stores like this one, never less than a hundred grand a day, and the relatively safe location far from high crime areas caused management and employees to be complacent about security.

He glanced around briefly and slipped into the men's room. Determining he was alone he entered a stall, then closed and locked the door behind him. He checked the contents of the bag he had meticulously packed before his flight that morning from Dallas. On the bottom loafers, brown socks, tan Dockers, a white golf shirt and light sweater. Next, a canvas bag big enough to contain the bundles of fives, tens and twenties, (the fifties and hundreds never took much room) that he would soon liberate from the store. On top lay a brown wig and a moustache.

Finally tucked in the side was the gun. It was a Glock, gleaming gray-black under the fluorescent lights. The heft and weight distribution made the piece easy to handle, though he had no intention of killing anyone. The weapon was a studio prop he had acquired several years ago during a period of time when he traveled to LA.

He removed the wig and placed it over his short hair, then slipped the mustache over his lip like he'd been a makeup artist for years. He emerged from the stall and looked at himself in the mirror, making only a minor adjustment to his disguise. The image of a man with curly brown hair and moustache pleased him, and he felt exhilarated by the transformation. He was John Anderson now, professional thief.

"Ready John?" Fred said to the reflection. The man in the mirror didn't say anything, just nodded.

He looked at his watch. 12:20 - Showtime.

Liza Fitzgerald slowly pushed the cart along the aisle and unfolded the grocery list again. The paper was wrinkled from handling and torn where she had creased it before she left home. Her aged neck creaked a bit as she glanced down at the contents of the cart, a single can of Campbell's chicken broth, a box of toothpicks and some breadsticks, then looked back at her list. The list was blank of course - she couldn't read or write - but it was a comfort to have it along.

As she approached the deli Liza spotted Sam the butcher behind the counter slicing a ham into a neat pile. Sam was her favorite person in the store and he always gave her a taste of one of the many items on display. Often the sample was the only meat she had for several days.

"Hello Sam," Liza said as she approached the glass protecting the wares.

Sam, a portly fiftyish man with thinning hair that protruded from underneath a King Foodmart baseball cap smiled back. "Hello Liza, how's my girl today?"

Absently brushing at the front her sweater, long ago matted into tiny balls from continuous wear, she replied, "I'm fine Sam... just doing a little shopping, Lordy yes."

"And a fine job of it too," Sam said and smiled with only a glance at the cart.

Liza came into the store almost every day. She didn't have any money, and could never buy anything, but the management and staff of the store had grown accustomed to her presence, and as long as she didn't bother anyone she was tolerated. When she finally left, one of the bag boys retrieved her cart and replaced all the items contained within back on the shelves. Her blank shopping list often stayed behind.

"Would you like to try the turkey today Liza? It's peppered and is very good."

"Lordy, yes please, Sam," Liza replied, ignoring the rumble deep in her stomach. She moved closer to the glass and watched as Sam pulled a tissue from a box below the counter and placed a few slices on it. Liza reached out to take the turkey, careful not to appear too anxious. Smelling the turkey, she smiled back at Sam, slipped a portion to her mouth and chewed it slowly, savoring the taste of the tender piece.

"Oh Lordy, that is good Sam." She folded the tissue over and carefully slid the package into a side pocket of her matted sweater. "I may just be back for more of that."

"You just let me know dear," Sam replied with a wink.

She trudged slowly towards the back of the store; one hand on the cart, the other occasionally reaching into her pocket to ensure her meal was still there. She would leave soon by the doors next to the back office entrance, her cart left out of the way in an empty aisle. Just a little more shopping to do she said to herself and controlled the urge to break off another savory piece of the turkey. She pulled the ragged paper from her other pocket and continued on.

Margaret Hawkins was pissed. She drummed her fingers on the steering wheel of her white Lexus and watched as the light once again turned from green, to yellow, to red. Up ahead she could see the flashing white and blue lights of two Denver police cars, one in the middle of the road, the other parked along the curb. Three cops were busy questioning the drivers of two cars involved in a minor fender-bender, oblivious to the traffic jam they caused.

Margaret absently fingered the hem of her tailored tan suit and glanced at her watch yet another time. She was almost late for lunch at one of the trendy new restaurants that continually opened in the Tech Center. Her companions would understand though; they would be there for hours anyway, visiting over a long lunch and a few carefully sipped glasses of white wine.

After what seemed an eternity the left lane finally opened. When the light turned green she pulled forward past the wreck on the right. Once clear of the blockage her foot pressed down, the powerful Lexus responding to the pressure on the gas pedal. With hopes she wouldn't be too late she ignored the speed limit, rationalizing that all the cops were behind her. Up ahead the taller office towers of the Tech Center came into view. She glanced down at her watch again and smiled. She was not even fashionably late.

Liza sighed, sad that it was time to leave. Shuffling towards the back of the store she abandoned her shopping cart along the wall where it wouldn't be in anyone's way. She glanced back ruefully at the contents and hoped that someday she might actually be able to shop in the store, head held high, basket filled with many wonderful items, proudly standing in line for the checkout counter.

She walked through the hallway by the offices towards the back door. The sign said *Authorized Use Only* but no one had ever questioned her use of the exit. She looked around and pushed the door open, squinting as she slipped quietly out into the afternoon sunlight and headed down the alley past the back of the store.

John took a deep breath and stepped into the hall. The door to the outside was just closing but that didn't bother him at all. He moved confidently down the hall and stopped in front of the door marked *OFFICE*. He pulled the sunglasses from his left pocket and slid them onto his face. Holding his right hand in the pocket with the gun, he lifted the sack and knocked on the door with the familiar "dot dot da dot dot, dot dot" cadence.

After a moment he heard footsteps behind the door, then a quiet, "Yes?"

John moved his gun hand over his mouth and sneezed loudly twice. He paused, then in a nasally voice shouted, "Kleenex, quick!"

The door opening slightly followed the sound of a lock unlatching; the partial face of a middle aged black woman visible between the door and the frame. John pulled the Glock away from his face, shoved it into the gap, and pointed it at the surprised woman's head. A screech escaped from her lips as he lowered his shoulder and pushed the door in. The woman's eyes widened as he quickly moved into the room, his back against the door as it closed behind him.

"Quiet now," he said and leveled the Glock at the woman's midsection. "Over against the wall." Frozen, she continued to stare, her eyes riveted on the gun, huge breasts heaving against the tight red King Foodmart uniform.

"Now!" he barked and waved the gun hand towards the far side of the room. The woman, trembling, a "please no" forming at her lips slowly slipped towards the wall, feet moving from side to side like she was performing a line dance. He glanced around and located the second occupant, a thirtyish man sitting at a long table in front of the safe. He too was mesmerized by the sudden intrusion into the room, hands frozen above the stacks of partially counted bills in front of him.

John glared at him, eyes hidden by the mirrored glasses and ordered, "Get up."

The man's hands rose tentatively and he stood up.

"What's your name?" John demanded.

"Uh... David."

"OK David, I want you to walk over to your buddy there," John said, gesturing with his head towards the woman.

David, cheap black dress pants too short for his legs and white shirt slowly began edging towards her.

"That's it David. Nobody's gonna get hurt here,"

Pointing the gun at the both of them, John said, "OK David, now put your arms around sweetness there and give her a very big hug."

With obvious trepidation David lifted his arms, slid them under the woman's arms and around her bulk to her back.

"You too sugar. Give your friend David a big friendly squeeze."

The woman lifted her arms up and placed them around David, nestling him onto her ample bosom. John moved purposefully around the table, then not taking his eyes off the pair across the room he pulled the canvas bag out of the plastic sack and opened it on the table. He began with the thin stacks of hundred dollar bills, and neatly placed them in the bag as the timer in his head calculated the time. About a minute he thought as he turned his attention to the fifties and twenties, the more frequently used bills slightly harder to arrange inside.

The pair, still hugging yet trying not to touch each other watched silently, their mouths agape. John spoke softly again. "That's it you two... I know you'd like to get to know each other better, so if you behave yourselves I'm sure you will live to do so."

He glanced down at the sack now nearly filled with stacks of larger bills and turned his attention to the bulkier piles of tens, and fives. Mentally calculating the take so far he gathered up the tens and dropped them into the top of the sack. Then considering the quickly diminishing returns, he grabbed both sacks with one hand and returned his full attention to the pair by the wall.

"Steady now," he said, and began to work his way back across the room toward the door, gun still pointed at the trembling employees.

"I'd like you both to do some counting for me," he said. "Why don't you see if you can make it to a thousand. You start David."

Puzzled, David looked at him.

John reached for the door handle and said, "Duh... I think you start with one there buddy."

"One." David said after some hesitation.

"Now you sweetness."

"T...two," said the woman, stammering with fear.

"Three?" David asked, as if questioning the sequence.

John smiled. "That's it you guys... now don't move till you hit a thousand or I'll be back." He reached for the knob, turned it and slowly pulled the door open.

"Four."

"Five."

John leaned his head out the door, quickly glancing down the empty hallway and wondered to himself how far they would actually count before they came to their senses. Then with no one around he eased his way out the door and quietly closed it behind him.

Liza, her legs protesting a little, finally approached the end of the long building. On her left was a large blue dumpster, the words *WASTE MANAGEMENT* stenciled in faded white letters on its battered side. She always checked around the sides for sacks discarded by shoppers from the food establishments in the strip center surrounding the grocery store. Sometimes the bags contained a few remaining bites of a roast beef or turkey roll scrunched inside a plastic wrapper. Occasionally she found bagels too, though she didn't really like the stale hardness on her decaying teeth. Lordy yes she thought, my poor old gums.

She felt guilty and ashamed about grubbing for food like this, but rationalized it by the gnawing in her stomach. "Only take bags that look fresh," she said to herself. "None that old Mr. Rat might have been snooping in." She spied a crushed sack and leaned over, her back protesting. The dank smell of Mexican wafted out as she opened it, the remains of a burrito smeared in the tissue at the bottom. It looked fresh enough for her, untouched by the street critters she thought. "I'll just keep this little bag and think about it," said to herself as she prepared to go wait for the bus.

Margaret didn't let up on the gas as she continued down the street, smiling as the light in the intersection beyond the strip center turned green. A large truck rumbled toward her as she changed to the inside lane and steered the Lexus around a slower car on her right. Still concerned about being late, her foot pressed harder on the accelerator. She recognized the back of the supermarket ahead and thought a grocery stop might come in handy after lunch. She mentally started a shopping list, picturing her fridge, and tried to think of items to pick up when she stopped back after lunch. More than a little distracted, she drove faster.

John moved quickly down the alley past the length of the store towards the street ahead. The Glock was safely tucked in the canvas bag with the cash, his change of clothes in the other sack swinging beside him. He turned his head and glanced over his shoulder back along the alley, relieved to see no one had emerged from the back of the building. He failed to see the old woman, hand clenched around a grungy sack step out from behind the blue dumpster. He crashed into her, and they both fell to the cement, a 'whoof' forced from her chest as he sprawled on top of her. Surprised, he stared into her wrinkled face, her startled brown eyes locked on his.

Liza screamed, her first instinct to fight off the attacker. Arms flailing she began to push at the man suddenly thrust upon her, the food bag flapping as a blow caught the side of his head.

John was caught completely off guard. The canvas bag with the money slipped from his grasp and a few of the loose bills spilled from the open top. Composing himself he pushed back, and lifted himself off the old lady and struggled to his knees.

"I'm so sorry," he said, unable to think of anything else to say.

"Get away from me you monster," Liza yelled from the ground, arms still waving, and kicked her feet at him. "Get away!" she shrieked again.

He looked down and without thinking he reached out to help her.

"Heelllppp!" she cried, sure he was about to strike her and take away her prized food. She stared at him, and noticed that his brown hair had fallen to the side of his head, and a small but prominent birthmark was visible on his neck below his left ear. The fear gripped her as his face etched permanently into her mind.

John quickly regained his composure, adjusted the skewed wig and gathered the sack handles back into his hands. He ignored the old woman as he stood up and considered his options. Disregarding his original plan of moving casually up the street, he decided to work his way across the street to the park.

Liza screamed again as he moved past her, one of the sacks banging into her head as she rose. Knocked flat again she rolled over on her stomach and watched as the man began to flee.

Intent only on the park across the way, John crossed the sidewalk and ran into the street. He took several long strides before he checked the lanes to his left. Far too late, the approaching truck blared its horn at him as the grill suddenly loomed up in his face. Momentarily stunned, he froze, and stared up through the glass of the cab as the driver, who equally surprised yanked the steering wheel to the left. John jumped back as the rumpled fender of the truck just missed him and veered away. A rush of hot diesel laden air pushed against him. There was a violent thump as the front left tire struck the cement and brick median that marked the entrance to the alley from the street. He watched as the silver side of the truck flashed in front of him and he heard the sound of the contents shift, disbelieving that he was reading the panel as it moved by.

Student Movers - Test Us for Quality he read as he heard the whump of the other tire strike the median. Unable to move, he watched as the truck barreled into the oncoming lane of traffic and directly in front of a white Lexus.

The explosion of sound nearly knocked him over as the Lexus plowed into the front grill of the truck. The screeching of tires was mixed with the loud sound of metal grinding and twisting as the momentum of the truck crushed the hood of the Lexus, windshield imploding, and pushed it sideways across the street. A second car, following close behind the

Lexus slammed into the side of the crushed vehicle.

Suddenly the vehicles stopped. John's heart pounded in his chest. He stood in the middle of the road, unable to comprehend what had just happened. He jumped again as a horn blared and another car squealed to a halt next to him.

"Shit," he said as he crossed over the median and slowly moved around the back of the truck, unable to pull his eyes from the wreck of the two cars in front of it.

"Shit!" he said, louder this time.

A steady hissing escaped from the front of the truck as he watched the door of the cab open and a jean covered leg pop out. He looked up the street; cars now stopped beside and in back of the wreck, and began to move slowly across the empty lane. Eyes still fixated on the carnage he crossed the street and up onto the sidewalk. He hesitated for a moment as he heard voices from people getting out of their cars.

"Somebody call an ambulance."

"Who's got a cell phone?"

"There's a woman badly hurt here."

His stomach in his throat, John quickly turned away from the street and began to walk down the hill and into the park.

Liza groaned and turned over on her side, stunned and still afraid of the man who had senselessly attacked her. Her concern quickly shifted to her food prize until she realized the bag was still clutched in her hand. Eyes wide in disbelief, she noticed the ten-dollar bills that littered the alley next to her. Oh Lordy Lordy, she said to herself and ignored her creaking joints as she reached for the money. As her fingers closed about the first of the bills, she heard a tremendous crash in the background. Her hand jerked back. Then another huge crash filled the air.

"Oh Lordy," she said aloud. She looked up the alley. The massive collision filled her eyes as she was drawn towards the street. Suddenly she turned and stared at the money on the ground. "Oh my, my," she said, "He paid me, yes he did."

She hesitated for a moment, then reached again towards the bills on the ground.

"For my trouble," she said, "He attacked me and paid me, Lordy yes."

She quickly gathered up the cash and pushed it into the pocket of her sweater, squishing the turkey placed there moments ago. She hadn't seen money like that in years. Her heart raced as she began her slow shuffle back up the alley. She glanced at the wreck briefly, but couldn't comprehend what had happened. As she walked she kept her hand in her pocket, clenching the bills, and wondered how much money it was.

"Three hundred fifty two," David said.
"Three hundred fifty three...." Sweetness said.

Margaret Hawkins was doomed long before they could get her out of the car.

Chapter Two

The conference room buzzed with activity, but Marshall Hawkins ignored the people in attendance, choosing instead to relax a little before his weekly staff meeting. He occasionally glanced at the agenda on the table in front of him, but his thoughts were turned inward, content for the moment to let others posture before he assumed control.

He looked up for a moment to see if anyone was watching him and surveyed the room. It was unremarkable, typical of those found in any newer office building. An oak table surrounded by twelve comfortable but not expansive chairs dominated the center. Two of the walls were covered with white boards, several of which contained diagrams and flow charts, others with carefully written bullet items on sales performance and budgetary actions. In the middle of the table sat a spaceship like phone unit for conference calls, complete with two little satellites speakers attached by ribbed black cords.

Marsh mused as he rocked back and forth in his chair. He'd been considering taking a week off, the company he founded now running smoothly and he badly needed a diversion. He silently looked at his two senior managers and rated them. Joe Davos, a capable second in command would surely be able to handle any critical business decisions. Recruited from PriceWaterhouse, he had proven not only to be the technical architect and visionary the firm needed, but had also impressed Marsh with his contribution to the business operations of the growing consulting firm. Sheila Parker, a feisty forty-year-old head of sales also needed no help. Though Marsh recruited most new clients, his reputation and personality still opened the doors; Sheila handled the negotiations and cut the final deals. He trusted them both explicitly and rewarded them generously with increasing percentages of the firm he had founded and still held majority ownership.

The problem was what to do with his time off. He had worked seventy and eighty-hour weeks when he built the company, vacations limited to a day squeezed in here and there, mostly structured around business meetings with clients and industry executives. Golf at Hilton Head, a short cruise associated with the IPO of a major telecommunications company and a keynote address at an industry conference provided some relief, but the hidden agenda was always business. He hadn't totally relaxed in three years.

Money wasn't an issue either. At thirty-four he was more than comfortable. His personal income from the firm was growing steadily, and careful investments had made him at least paper millionaire. Though single, handsome and well dressed he seemed to find little time for feminine companionship. It had been two years since his last permanent relationship had crumbled, a painful victim of the stress and long demanding hours required to start his company.

"Marsh?" Sheila inquired.

He pulled himself back from his reverie, leaned forward and unconsciously took control. "Sorry, let's get started. Please sit down everyone," Marsh said and waited for the group to settle down.

Marsh placed his hands on the table and addressed the group. "First, I'd like to review last month's sales figures." He tossed a look to Shiela, who on cue opened a leather notebook and removed several packets of stapled papers. She was distributing the presentation to those seated around the table when the door to the conference room opened and interrupted the meeting. Mary, the office manager and Marsh's executive assistant pushed her head in sheepishly. Marsh, eyes narrowed, frowned at the intrusion.

"Yes Mary, what is it?"

"Um... there's a phone call for you."

The weekly meetings were important to Marsh, and it wasn't often that he could get everyone together. His face betrayed his annoyance at the disruption.

"Whoever it is, we're busy. Take a message and I'll call them back."

Mary squirmed a little, absently brushing her hair from her forehead and hesitated. "I think its important Marsh." She looked around the room, obviously not wanting to be there.

"For Christ's sake who is it Mary?"

All eyes in the room turned and looked at her, still half-hidden by the door.

"It's the Denver Police Department. It's about your mother."

Will Carter was munching slowly on over cooked french fries when the call came in. Jesus he said to himself, they interrupted my lunch again. Probably a bunch of damn high school kids sitting on some old lady's Mercedes. He pulled the phone from his coat pocket and held the instrument to his ear.

"Carter," he said, more at the phone then into it. He absentmindedly picked up another crispy fry, then froze midway as he listened.

"Wait, say that over. Is it an accident or a robbery?"

He held the phone in front of his face and looked at it inquisitively, then listened again. "Damn girl, get it straight." His brow wrinkled slightly and the grin faded from his lips. Shit, he said to himself, then addressed the phone again. "I'll just get over there and find out myself."

He clicked the call to an end, slid the phone back inside his tailored jacket and stared longingly at the remaining fries. Too bad he thought, then adjusted his Garcia tie as he got up from the table, deposited the tray on the trash receptacle and walked towards the exit. He pushed open the door of the Burger King and stepped into the mid-day sunshine, squinting as he pulled his shades out of his pocket and slipped them over his deep brown eyes. He couldn't make sense of the call he just received, the dispatcher relaying the details of a robbery at the King Foodmart up the street, then going on about an accident at the same location.

Will had moved quickly up the ranks of the Denver Police Department, his career launched as one of the best in his academy class and highest ranked black cadet. As a rookie he distinguished himself in the grueling physical conditioning as well as the mental and philosophical side of the training, and accepted his first assignment in the rough inner-city neighborhood north of downtown Denver without question. He made himself fit into the tough hoods, dealing easily with the gangs and drug trade even though he had grown up in a prosperous family well out in the sprawling suburbs. An athlete and scholar in high school, he had breezed quickly through college attending the close-to-home University of Denver, double majoring in Criminal Psychology and Sociology. He had always wanted to be a cop, even though his parents had wanted him to enroll in the Business School. He was close to his family though, and his parents had proudly accepted his position in life.

As his car approached the area of the alleged incidents, the traffic ahead slowed to a stop. He looked over his shoulder, wheeled the car up over the curb and drove the last ten yards over the grass to a parking lot of one of the office buildings on the edge of the Tech Center. He quickly got out of his car, crossed into the street and walked swiftly between the stalled cars. He pulled out his phone, slid the cursor down a list of names until he reached the entry for 'Dispatch'. Punching the talk button on the cell, he lifted the phone to his ear and waited for the response as he walked.

"Dispatch, yes Detective Carter?" the female voice on the other end inquired.

"I'm on foot, a few blocks from the scene, or scenes. Who is on site and who do I contact first?"

The phone finally responded. "Sergeant Kalorky is on the accident scene with three units and two ambulances. Two more units are positioned at the robbery scene behind the King Foodmart."

"Great, that's nice to hear dispatch, where the hell am I supposed to go?"

He frowned at the lack of response. Finally the phone squawked, "Uh, we will get back to you on that Detective Carter."

Will pulled the phone away from his ear and glared at it, then spoke again. "Well make it snappy, I'm almost there."

Jesus H. Christ he muttered to himself and clicked off the phone. He continued up the gradual hill and tried to imagine what the hell was going on. He finally reached the intersection near the shopping center where the grocery store was located. All traffic was hopelessly knotted. He could see the accident now, the back of a truck at an angle in the wrong side of the street, one of the cars scrunched and pushed aside to the left. The phone jangled in his hand and he paused briefly to activate it, then lifted it to his ear.

"Carter."

"Will, this is Captain Adams," a brusque voice said.

"What the hell is going on Captain?"

"It's still a bit confused there Will."

No shit Will thought. He continued forward and increased his pace.

"As best we have been able to determine, there was a robbery in the King Foodmart. Apparently the perp ran down the alley in the back and out into the street which caused the accident. We believe one woman was killed at the scene."

"Yes sir," Will said, waiting.

"I want you to proceed to the accident scene first, find out what you can, then get the robbery investigation started. We need some information about the suspect."

"Yes sir, do we have a location on him?"

"No Will, he apparently just slipped away after the accident. Notify the teams at the accident that you are taking charge, make sure they have the scene under control, then get your ass down to the store."

He was used to the Captain's language, but shit he thought, this must be bad.

"Yes sir, I'm approaching the accident scene now."

"Call me back directly on my cell phone. I want a preliminary report in 15 minutes."

"Yes sir. I'm on it now." He looked around, suppressed the feeling of dread in his stomach and scanned the area for Sergeant Kalorky.

John was breathing hard as he moved over the grass and down into a shallow depression in the center of the park that led to the small stream. Not good he thought, what the hell happened? In his previous eleven robberies, each performed in a different city across the country; he never attracted attention to himself. He stepped around a railing and approached a small red steel and stone footbridge that crossed the shallow creek. He was sweating and the dampness trickled down his back and soaked his shirt as he pressed on over the bridge. He scanned the other side of the park, then glanced nervously over his shoulder. With no sign of pursuit he tried to control his breathing and moved more casually up the grass toward the office buildings looming into the blue sky ahead.

The park was fairly crowded as office workers finished their bag lunches and returned to work. He hoped he would appear to be just another face in the park, but was concerned about the large number of witnesses that might remember him or the distinctive sacks in his hands. As he approached the boulevard a stream of cars passed before him, the lunchtime traffic still heavy. He waited for the light at the intersection to retard the flow, then quickly crossed the street, passing close behind the last of the cars as it sped by.

The tenseness in his stomach unabated, he began to think through his next movements. One of the office towers ahead would provide brief sanctuary he thought, enough time to change into the other set clothes he carried in the bag. The tall blue tower of the Hyatt a block away caught his attention and he immediately changed his plans. There were always taxis at hotels and he could make a quick change and be at the airport in 45 minutes. He altered course and headed for the hotel, feeling totally conspicuous as he walked.

Relieved at the sight of two taxis patiently waiting for fares by the entrance, he pushed through the revolving door and entered the lobby of the hotel. Again he searched for a restroom, wanting to swiftly shed the identity of John the Thief. He crossed to the backside of the lobby, trotted down the short set of stairs that led to the conference and ballrooms. He hesitated, looked at the people clustered around the pay phones and tried to locate the facilities. Finally, he said to himself as he spotted the brownish door marked MEN just behind the phone bank. He forced himself to walk calmly across the carpeted hall, leaned his shoulder into the door and pushed it aside as he entered. He ignored the two men washing their hands, moved quickly to the last stall, opened the door and stepped in.

Marsh was devastated. Waves of uncertainty washed over him, his stomach in knots as he rode pensively in Sheila's car. What the hell had happened? The police had refused to provide any details over the phone despite his vehement protestations. Thoughts of the fate of his mother filled him with dread as Sheila efficiently guided her red Porsche down University Avenue. Out of the corner of his eye he noticed her glance briefly at him, then look back to the road. He closed his eyes and the conversation with the police played over and over again in his mind.

"Mr. Marshall Hawkins?" the indistinct male voice had said through the phone.

"Yes, this is he," Marsh had replied.

"This is the Denver Police Department. Are you the son of a...", the voice paused, "a Margaret Hawkins?"

"Yes, what is it?" A pang of fear suddenly shot through him.

"There has been an accident sir, your mother was involved. She's been taken to University Hospital."

He froze, a dozen questions quickly filling his head. "What happened? Where is she? How is she?" Marsh asked frantically.

"I'm sorry sir, I have no details. But you should get to the hospital as soon as possible."

"My God, can't you tell me anything? Is she okay?"

"Sir, I'm sorry, I can't provide you with any more information."

Marsh hung up the phone, not believing the conversation. Joe came out of the conference room, a concerned look on his face.

"What's wrong Marsh?" he said.

"It's mother, something about an accident. They wouldn't fucking tell me anything," Marsh managed to say, his voice strained and the muscles in his face taut. "I've got to get to the hospital."

The others, emerging from the meeting joined them, all starting to question him at once. He stared briefly at them, but ignored their queries and started for the door. "I've got to go."

Joe stepped towards him, taking his arm, "I'll go along," he said, "Let me drive you."

Marsh looked back and pulled his arm away, not seeing the obvious concern on everyone's faces.

"No, I'm going alone," he said. "Thanks... but I've got to go."

Sheila, pressed forward and practically shoved Joe out of the way. "Bullshit," she said. "I'm going with you, and I'm going to drive."

"No..." Marsh stammered and took a hesitant step backwards.

Sheila reached out, firmly grasped Marsh by the arm and turned her head toward the others. "Mary, get my purse," she said, then spoke in a softer tone. "Quickly please."

She faced Marsh again and held both his arms gently with her hands. "Marsh, we will go down together. Whatever has happened I'll be there with you."

It was the last thing that Marsh remembered clearly. He turned and stared blankly out the window, his thoughts again consumed with his mother. They had dinner together the other night at Del Frisco's, a steak house near where he lived and one of their favorite dinner spots. She had seemed so alive and happy then, just the two of them enjoying dinner like old friends. They had grown even closer since his father had died five years ago. An unforeseen heart attack claimed him early, and it had taken his mother more than a few years to regain her lust for life. Another bolt of fear shot through him as he waited to arrive at the hospital.

A few agonizing minutes later the hospital complex appeared in front of them. Sheila reached over and pressed his arm.

"Marsh, we're almost there."

He turned and looked at her, eyes searching hers, a pained look distorting his face.

"OK."

"I'm going to drop you off at the emergency exit and park the car. I'll find you inside all right?"

Marsh nodded meekly, turned from her and stared blankly through the windshield. The Porsche sped down the street toward a large blue EMERGENCY sign that indicated the appropriate driveway to enter. Downshifting, Sheila wielded the car into the circular driveway and pulled up to the glass doors marking the entrance. She reached over and squeezed his hand tightly as he opened the door and pushed his legs out.

"I'll be right in," she said to his back as he exited the car. She watched nervously for a moment through the passenger window as he walked away and didn't look back.

Sergeant Kalorky leaned back against the front of the squad car, radio in one hand, cell phone in the other. "About time you got here," he said as he stepped away from the car, his broad belly spilling over the leather belt holding his gun and nightstick.

Will smiled as he approached. He liked Kalorky, they had actually done some street time together back when he was still in uniform.

"You guys in suits," Kalorky continued. "Just because you don't wear blues anymore you think you can just waltz in any old time."

"Good to see you too Sarge," Will said with a faint smile, then continued more seriously. "Tell me what you got here."

Kalorky tipped his head toward the truck and walked as they surveyed the scene. "The truck was headed northbound in the left lane. The Lexus," he said and motioned with his hand at the crushed vehicle still pinned under the front of the truck, "was coming south, also in the left lane. It was more than likely speeding a bit. The Pontiac over there was in the center lane a little behind the Lexus."

They halted their stroll and looked over at the wreck buried in the front of the truck.

"The driver of the truck says some guy just bolted off the sidewalk directly in front of him. He says he reacted without thinking and yanked the wheel to the side to keep from hitting the guy. He bounced up and over the median, and by the time he hit the brakes the Lexus was already toast."

"The Pontiac was also in the wrong place at the wrong time. It plowed into the truck and the Lexus as they spun over to the center lane. Judging from the skid marks it looks like the guy at least had time to hit the brakes.

Probably saved his life."

Will paused for a second. A small crowd of people had gathered to watch the scene with morbid curiosity. The sweet fresh smell of the cut grass he had walked through earlier had been replaced by the stink of oil and gasoline. He started to speak to the sergeant, but was distracted by the sound of the ambulance engine turning over. He watched as one of the paramedics closed the back door and rushed around to the passenger side door, hand trailing along side of the orange and white vehicle. It pulled away quickly, red lights beginning to flash as it headed up the street.

"Who's that?" Will said, gesturing with his head.

"That's the Pontiac. Back injury mostly. Like I said, he was lucky."

"And the Lexus?"

"A woman, late fifties probably, though it was hard to tell. I'm guessing she's a DOA," Kalorky replied. "They hauled her up to University a while ago."

Will started back towards the patrol car and the sergeant followed.

"How's the truck driver doing?" Will asked.

"He's pretty shaken up, but more from what happened than any injuries. He's in the back of the squad car. You wanna talk to him now?"

"Sure. Get him out of the car though, I want him out in the open air. Hopefully he will feel good enough to give me some decent information."

"You got it Detective." Kalorky continued on toward the blue and white patrol car. After a few steps he stopped and turned back. "Will?"

"Ya Sarge?"

"So what's going on? Why did we get a bunch of calls about the grocery store too?"

Will thought for a moment and tried to make sense out of the still sketchy pieces of the puzzle. "The King Foodmart was knocked over just minutes before the accident. The theory is that the perp caused this little diversion here as he beat feet out of the store."

The Sergeant looked at Will, his eyebrows raised slightly then shook his head slowly without comment.

Will understood. "Give me two minutes with the trucker, then I've got to head over to the store. They're probably going ape-shit in there by now. You keep in charge here, and get a team out to talk to the bystanders. See if you can dig up anyone who saw this disaster happen. What we really need now is anyone who can ID the guy."

Will turned and walked toward the truck, examining the Lexus as he passed by. Most of the front end and engine had been pressed back into the front seat. The passenger side door had crumpled and the car was shorter by at least two feet. As he looked through the shattered windshield he could see the steering column pushed almost completely to the driver's seat. It was a wonder they even got the poor woman out of the car. His eyes moved to the front of the truck. It was a ten wheeler, about half the size of a semi but all one unit. The damage to the front of the truck was apparent, but not significant. The Lexus never stood a chance he thought.

"Will?" Kalorky interrupted.

Will spun around and looked at the truck driver accompanying the sergeant. He was dressed in somewhat grimy jeans and a red plaid shirt with a white T-shirt visible beneath at the open collar. His hair, brown and graying was pulled back in a long ponytail. He looked about fifty but was probably younger.

"Will, this is Dan Robbins, the driver of the truck."

Will stepped forward and reached out his hand. "Hello Dan. I know you are a little shaken up right now, but I would like to ask you a few questions, all right?"

Robbins extended his arm and gripped Will's hand tentatively. Will, noticed his nervousness and briefly thought that probably the only time this guy had dealt with cops before was on drug busts. Robbins nodded to him slowly.

"The sergeant here will get a full statement from you in a minute. But right now I'm more interested in the man who jumped in front of your truck. Can you tell me anything about him?"

"Uh ya, sure. I was driving up the street here," Robbins gestured, "I guess I was looking ahead mostly when all of a sudden this dude was right in front of me. It was weird, kind of like he just appeared. You know, like the X-files or something. I was almost on top of him so I gave the wheel a good crankin'. I missed the dude but the truck, she bounced over there, then the cars started piling into me."

Robbins paused, looking at Will.

"Did you get a good look at the man?"

"Ya, he was looking right at me. Was about six feet or so I think. Hard to tell from up in the cab. White guy too. Brown hair, mustache. Umm... he was wearing what looked like a running suit or something – you know like those joggers wear?"

"What color was it?"

"Blue I think. Mebbe some white on top."

"Age?"

"Mmm... younger then me, and I'm forty-five. I'd say more like you."

"One more thing Mr. Robbins. Was he carrying anything?"

"Ya, two bags. One in each hand – you know with handles and shit."

"Thank you for your help Mr. Robbins," Will said and turned to Kalorky. "Sarge, take Mr. Robbins and get a full statement, and more important, get a wider search of the area started. Blue jogging suit – two bags. I'd like to see if we can nab this guy before he splits from the area."

"Yes sir," said Kalorky, already leading the trucker back to the patrol car.

Will set off toward the back of the grocery store and tried to focus on how to proceed with the robbery investigation. He moved quickly past a blue dumpster set next to the back of the building and pulled the cell phone out of his pocket. He quickly moved the cursor down until he had the Captain's number in the tiny window. Pressing the talk button he lifted the phone to his ear and waited through a few rings until the Captain answered.

"Yes Will, what have you got?"

"I've just left the accident scene sir, and am almost at the store. It's my guess that the guy who robbed the store made a bad getaway and ended up smack in front of the truck, which in turn caused the accident."

"Any chance we can catch this guy?" the Captain asked.

"I've got patrol checking the crowd, but it all happened so fast. Hopefully we will have better luck with the store employees on getting some kind of ID."

"Keep on this one Will, the shit's going to hit the fan over this. If what you say about the guy who robbed the store causing the accident is true, the DA's going to want a homicide investigation."

Will winced at the thought. Ever since Jon Benet and Columbine every Police Department in Colorado was sensitive about publicity regarding ongoing investigations, especially murder ones.

"Yes, sir. I'll follow up at the robbery scene, then return to the station and file a preliminary report." He hung up the phone without waiting for a reply and wondered what the hell he would find out next.

Fred leaned his head back against the blue velour of the top of the bench seat in the back of the taxi, his closed eyes still hidden by his sunglasses. One of his hands absently pressed against his temple trying to quell the low throb of a headache, an unpleasant reminder of the massive amount of adrenaline that had pulsed through his body during the escape. His other arm casually rested over the canvas sack now containing only the money and the Glock. He tried to appear like any other afternoon traveler on the way to the airport, and hoped that his lack of luggage at the hotel had not attracted too much attention. But that's ridiculous he said to himself. So soon after the theft there would be no reason for him to stand out more than any of the other people looking for a cab. Besides, he thought, between the grocery store and the incredible accident that followed, the police must be in a state of total confusion. In the few minutes it had taken him to get this far, he doubted very much that any sort of organized pursuit would have started. His continued rationalizations eased his paranoid feeling somewhat as he looked for details he might have missed, mistakes that might initiate a trail to him.

In the stall of the restroom, he had quickly changed out of the sweat suit and sneakers and into his casual clothes. Carefully restacking the bills in the canvas sack and secreting the Glock inside the bundles, he emerged from the stall and checked his appearance in the mirror. His tightly cropped blonde hair looked almost white from the lights above the mirror.

"Welcome back Fred," he said to his own image in the mirror.

He reached down into the silver receptacle built into the wall, moved aside the residual trash and pushed the running suit, shoes, wig and moustache deep into the bottom of the bin. That's more than enough of John for a while.

From there, heart still beating fast in his chest, he quickly left the restroom and retraced his steps across the still busy lobby to the doors. The taxi was simple. A maroon uniformed attendant whistled, and one of the waiting cabs quickly pulled up from its perch at the side of the circular drive.

"DIA," he said simply to the driver, a broadly smiling thin Asian man with a large gap between his yellowed front teeth. The driver tried to make small talk, barely intelligible through a thick accent. He ignored the man who finally gave up with a shrug and returned to the task of piloting the vehicle.

In the distance, Fred could now make out the white spires of the terminal through the side window as the cab motored over the access way. He glanced at the meter fixed to the dashboard and quickly estimated the fare and tip for the ride. He reached around and patted the right rear pocket of his slacks. Relieved that his wallet was still where he had placed it earlier that morning, he pulled it out and extracted two twenties and a ten. A good tip, but not too much to attract attention he thought. Keeping the cash in his hand, he rolled down the window, the fresh air washing over him as he stared out. The mountains were visible through the slight haze, white tips of snow on the peaks still visible despite the early summer month. As the cab rounded the ramp and pulled up onto the long concourse, the driver turned with a question on his face.

Without waiting, Fred said "Alaska Air". The driver bobbed his head several times and wheeled the vehicle past the single and double-parked vehicles dispersing passengers and luggage. He glanced at his watch. His flight back to Dallas was on American, the requested airline stop given the driver just another precaution. Probabilities he said to himself. The departure time originally planned still gave him plenty of time to retrieve his stored garment bag, stow the money and Glock inside and check it as luggage. All this despite the timing mess up caused by the accident and flight from the store. He wasn't worried though. American flights out of Denver to Dallas were a dime a dozen.

As the cab pulled up and stopped at the curb, Fred leaned forward and handed the driver the money. "Keep it," he said.

"Ah sank you," the driver replied, his head bobbing again.

Fred grabbed the canvas sack, opened the door and headed into the terminal.

Will, lifted the yellow police line tape, stepped under and noticed an armored truck parked off in the distance, two guys leaning against it smoking.

The uniformed officer standing by the open door said, "Hey Will."

Will pulled his badge out of his pocket, moved the lapel of his jacket aside and slid it open faced into the pocket of his light blue shirt. "Hey Art, how's it going?"

The cop laughed then replied, "A little confused in there."

"I can imagine."

He left the man to guard the door and walked down the barren cement brick hallway to the office. He gathered his thoughts as he strode confidently into the room and quickly surveyed the scene. Across to the left below the windows were a group store employees who chatted nervously among themselves. Ignoring them for the moment, he proceeded over to the two cops standing near a table by the open safe.

"Hey guys," Will said, his tone strong and commanding their attention. "What do we have so far?"

Both officers turned towards him, the plump fortyish woman speaking first.

"Hi Will. Well it seems as though a man just came in and managed to help himself to a boatload of cash."

"He just walked in?"

"No, he knocked first, and the sister over there opened the door for him."

"Jesus, what did he say?"

"Well he apparently sneezed a few times."

"Sneezed?" Will said incredulously, "What's up with that?"

Laughing a little, the other cop, a short white man with military style hair added, "Ya. She said she heard sneezes and figured it must be her manager. Apparently the guy has allergies."

"Christ," Will said, "It takes all kinds. Was the guy armed?"

"He had a handgun. Nobody here could tell the make though. They were both too scared."

"Who was in here when it happened?"

"The woman over there and the thin guy. He's the head cashier. He was counting the cash when the perp came in. The daily money transfer you know."

"Ah, that explains the armor parked outside."

Both cops nodded.

"And it also shows that this must have been a planned hit - not just some guy walking in off the street."

Will turned toward the table and safe. A man in plain clothes and gloves was carefully spreading a thin layer of dust over the edge of the table and the remaining pile of bills. Will ignored the murmurs from the fidgeting bunch of employees behind him and walked over to the table, resisting the impulse to rub his finger in the dust.

"Anything Mark?"

Without leaving his knees, the man checking for prints looked up. "Sure lots of prints so far Will, but I doubt they mean much. All the guy had to do was scoop up the cash. Unless he leaned against the table these prints are most likely from employees".

"I'm sure. Well run 'em anyway alright?"

"No problem Will. You know I live for this stuff," Mark said, a slight grin pushing up the corners of his mouth.

Will smiled and gestured toward the two cops. "Let's go meet the troops."

The three walked over to the employees, who quieted and turned toward them simultaneously. Looking over the group, Will noted the woman and the thin guy who were part of the robbery, then looked at the other two. One was about forty, as well dressed as possible in what passed for store clothes, the other about thirty, attired the same way but not quite as presentable. On each was a store nametag, one indicated 'Arthur Jones' and the word 'Store Manager' below. The other read 'Greg Suzanne', 'Assistant Store Manager'. The whole damn gang Will thought to himself as he approached them.

"I'm Detective Will Carter. Who wants to start?"

Confused, the employees looked at each other. Will waited patiently, wondering who would step up to the plate.

"Uh, I'm Arthur Jones, the Store Manager," he said, then hesitated. "This is the first time we have been robbed and I don't quite know where to begin."

"Let's start at the beginning," Will prompted and looked at the black woman and the thin guy. "You both were in the room, right? What are your names?"

"Yes sir," the woman replied cautiously. "Martha Aberdeen sir. I was filing the weekly store receipts in the cabinet over there when I heard a knock at the door."

Will waited.

"I asked who was there..." Martha said and looked nervously over at the manager, obviously worried about her role in opening the door. Seeing no apparent reaction she continued.

"I just heard sneezes. I thought it was Mr. Jones. He's always sneezing."

They all turned towards Jones as he sneezed, his timing perfect. Sheepishly he pulled a handkerchief from his pocket and wiped his nose.

"I opened the door, just a little, and the man pointed a gun at me and pushed the door open. I was so scared I didn't know what to do." She fidgeted while one hand smoothed her store dress in front. "I can't remember it too clearly but he told me to get over against the wall and stay there. I just did it."

All eyes of the group locked on Martha as she recounted the story, probably for about the tenth time Will thought.

"Do you remember what he looked like? How he was dressed?"

"He was about your size, but white. Kind of brown curly hair. He had a blue sweat suit or something on."

"Moustache?"

Pausing for a moment, Martha thought, "I think so. I'm not sure."

The thin employee piped up. "He had a mustache."

Will looked at the speaker. "And you are?"

"David Carter sir, Head Cashier," he replied, standing a little straighter.

"Nice name David," Will said, and his lips creased into a faint smile. "What did you see?"

"Well I wasn't paying much attention when I heard the knock. I knew Martha would get the door and I didn't want to lose count. It was getting close to pickup time and I wanted to be ready."

Thinking for a minute, Will said, "Was this a regularly scheduled pick-up for you?"

Jones, the manager interrupted, "Yes, every day we count the money and transfer it all to the bank. For safe keeping."

Will resisted the impulse to interject another witty remark. "How much money?" he asked instead.

"Usually about a hundred thousand," Jones replied, then looked over at the cashier.

"Uh, at least ninety-two thousand. That's what I had counted when the man came in. I hadn't counted all the ones and fives yet."

"Well he seems to have left that anyway. Anything in the safe?"

"No, just papers and payroll information, no cash. The man looked in there but didn't take anything."

"Ok, then what happened?"

"Well, he made us stand together, right about here," the woman replied. "He told us to put our arms around each other."

The cashier silently nodded in agreement, obviously a little embarrassed. Will waited.

"We did," the black woman continued. "He began to take all the money, putting it into a bag he was carrying."

"One bag?" Will asked.

"Ya, just one. But he had another bag with him. It looked just like one of our store bags. Plastic, not paper."

Will smiled to himself. Jeez a straight-line a minute he thought irreverently. "Then what?"

The cashier looked at Martha, then continued. "When he had taken the money he started to leave. He told us to hug each other and start counting."

"Hug and count?"

"I said one, then Martha said two," the cashier said and glanced over at her. "We just kept counting. He said to count to a thousand or he would come back and kill us."

Jesus he said again to himself, quite the character this thief. "And how far did you get?" Will asked, curious.

"We were at about four hundred something when Greg came in. We stopped then," he said, almost proudly.

Hoping to add to the conversation, Greg, the assistant manager added, "Four hundred and thirty-two." The others looked at him, incredulous. He shrugged back.

Will pondered for a minute. "Ok that's it for now. Thank you all - we will take formal statements in a while, OK?"

They all nodded in unison.

Will walked away and left them standing there without further instructions. Deciding to get back to the office, he retraced his steps down the hall and walked back to his car. He'd fill in the Captain on the way.

The small waiting room where Marsh sat, head in hands, was a soft blue. It was the color that psychologists had determined would be the most soothing for despairing relatives and loved ones. He hadn't noticed.

Marsh barely remembered how he got there. After leaving Sheila's Porsche, he had run into the Emergency Room lobby frantically looking for someone to help him. Rudely pushing past a young man helping what could have been his grandfather, he leaned over the counter and pleaded for information. A smiling woman in a nurse's uniform patiently inquired through the computer on the counter for the status of one Margaret Hawkins.

"Are you a relative?" she asked with little emotion in her voice, years of experience dealing with distraught visitors numbing her to Marsh's obvious distress.

"Yes ma'am. Hawkins, Marshall Hawkins. I'm her son."

After what had seemed to be an unbearable length of time, she replied. "We need you to go to Waiting Room A, Mr. Hawkins."

"What's that, where's that?"

She turned towards him, smiling softly, not betraying any information that she may have gleaned from the screen. She pointed to her left past the edge of the counter and reception wall and said, "Around the corner, down the hall past the drinking fountain. Second door on the right."

"What's there?"

"It's a waiting area Mr. Hawkins. A doctor will see you there."

Reluctantly he had turned and walked towards the hallway, ignoring a man with a patch over his eye that brushed unsteadily against his side.

"Marsh?" a soft voice said and he snapped back to the present, face lifting from his hands.

Looking up at Sheila he was unable to speak, his knotted stomach the only feeling he noticed. Sheila sat down on the edge of a chair, leaned over and gently took one of his hands in hers.

"Is there any news yet?" she asked, her face full of questions.

"No, I don't know anything. I was just told to wait here."

Marsh's thoughts drifted back in time, picturing the day when he and his sister had moved Mom out of the family house and into a condo in southern Denver. It had been a stressful day, emotions flooding them all as they finally shed the home that had been the family residence for more than twenty years. With the passing of their dad, the house had become too much for mom, empty with only memories of their happy family. He and Susan hoped moving her to a condo would bring some closure to his death and let her start out on her own again. Suze, he said to himself, his wandering thoughts turning to his younger sister living in Minneapolis. What am I going to tell her?

Sheila looked up as a younger woman dressed in hospital blues stepped into the room. The woman, a surgical mask pushed down around her throat, looked over the brown clipboard held in one hand as she walked toward them. "Mr. Hawkins?" she asked as she stopped

A pang shot through his stomach as he pulled his hand from Shiela's, and jumped up from the seat.

"Yes? I'm Marshall Hawkins," he said, his eyes riveted on the doctor.

She moved closer to him, voice softer in an attempt to provide some semblance of privacy in the open room.

"I'm sorry…"

A feeling of dread exploded within him. "What is it?" he stammered.

The doctor glanced at Sheila, then forced herself to look back at Marsh.

"I'm really sorry. There was nothing we could do."

Marsh's jaw dropped open as Sheila quickly stood up to join him, her arms moving through his.

"Her injuries from the accident were too severe," the doctor continued. "She died before we could get her to the hospital."

Despair overpowering him, he pulled free from Sheila's grasp and collapsed back in the chair.

Chapter Three

Fred entered the terminal and finally relaxed as his pre-flight routine settled back to normal. It took him a few minutes to cross the tented concourse of the expansive DIA terminal, blending in with the hundreds of other travelers on an early Monday afternoon. He casually worked his way across the granite floors toward an alcove and rows of lockers where that morning he had stored his garment bag, empty at the time. He removed the flat key from his wallet and opened one of the oversized lockers. Unconsciously he glanced over his shoulder before he removed the garment bag, then stepped away and headed once again for the restrooms located in the center of the structure.

He whistled softly to himself as he walked. He took pride in his accomplishments, and later that evening he would check the news over the Internet for stories of his efforts. The websites of the local newspapers usually carried something of his exploits, but they more often than not buried them somewhere in the back pages. This time would be different he thought and he imagined the headline. 'ROBBERY CRASH AT DENVER SUPERMARKET' would be appropriate. He smiled at his wit as he avoided a group of chatting travelers and turned toward the restrooms. He followed the circular passageways around, unconcerned now about the number of men and children using the restroom.

Smiling in anonymity, he watched as another man about his age exited a stall carrying an unremarkable garment bag and briefcase, just as he did. He nodded politely and smiled as the man passed, targeted the stall just vacated and pushed his way in before the blue door swung shut. Setting both articles down on either side of the stool, he pushed the door shut with his butt, then turned and locked it.

He flopped the seat down with a thud, pulled up the garment bag, unzipped it and spread it from the top of the toilet to the bottom of the seat. The sturdy bag had been specially crafted for him after the first robbery and he considered it a good luck charm. Instead of the usual open area reserved for shirts and suits, the bag had a set of eight built in zip pockets, two across, four on the top half and four on the bottom half of the fold. He opened the canvas bag, removed the unbundled bills and carefully arranged the cash inside the pockets. Conscious not to over pack, he filled three pockets before his fingers closed around the Glock. The gun he placed in the fourth pocket in the top section of the bag, then stored the bundles of twenties, fifties and hundreds securely in the bottom section. He picked up the canvas sack, placed it neatly over the bottom section and folded the bag. Satisfied, he grasped the handle and exited the stall.

It was a short walk back to the American counters. He entered the belted rat cage of the check-in line and nonchalantly assumed his place behind a small group of passengers who waited in front of him. When it was finally his turn, he picked up his bag and walked across to the counter. He dropped his bag on the silver platform to the side and smiled politely at the woman behind the computer terminal.

"Hi there," he said as he reached into his pocket and removed his wallet.

"Good afternoon sir," she replied, dressed as expected in an American agent's uniform. "Destination?"

"Dallas," he said.

She waited as he flipped open his wallet and pulled out a Minnesota driver's license. He checked briefly to ensure it was the correct one, then handed it across the counter. "John Anderson, E-ticket," he added.

She looked down at it, then up to his face, routinely checking the picture against his appearance. She handed it back to him and her hands moved to the keyboard in front of the terminal on the counter. He slipped the ID back into his wallet, replaced the wallet in his pocket, then leaned forward, his arms on the counter as she typed.

"Yes, Mr. Anderson. Flight 262 departing for Dallas at 3:03 p.m."

She smiled at him as the whir of the printer below the counter spit out a boarding pass. "One bag to check?"

"That's it."

It took only a few more keystrokes to produce the tags for his luggage. "Gate 42 sir, concourse C."

"Are we on time today?" he asked as he took the ticket folder from her hand.

"Yes sir," she replied as she lifted the garment bag and swung it to the moving belt behind her.

DECEPTION ON MARGIN

"That's good news," he said when she turned around. "Have a nice day," he added as he left the counter and walked toward the center of the terminal. Checking his bag was always the last hurdle to overcome. He knew that even a random X-ray check of his bag would probably not reveal the hardened plastic Glock, but it was one more opportunity to be apprehended. His smile broadened as he checked his watch and headed off toward the underground train and the concourse beyond.

Will sat at his desk, idly drummed his fingers on the imitation wood top and tried to decide his next course of action. He had used the drive time back from the store to fill in the Captain, but unfortunately the report he delivered didn't have much substance. He shuffled the printout of the accident report delivered by Kalorky via email in his hands. It contained sketchy details and logistics regarding the accident and injuries, but nothing more than he had already learned in his brief conversation with the truck driver at the scene. The report also recapped the results of canvassing the area for witnesses. The one bright spot there was that one woman had been located who didn't really see the accident, but claimed to have been accosted by a running man near the scene. He was still waiting for her to show up at the station,

He tried to place himself in the mind of the thief. On foot and somewhat identifiable, what would I do. Did I have a car available? If so, where would I have parked it? The robbery had obviously been planned, so some thought must have been given to the getaway process. He mentally reconstructed the scene, imagining himself leaving the store and running down the alley in the back. Toward the street he thought - what was there? Across Yosemite was the park that stretched for a few blocks at the east end of the Tech Center. To the north, houses, the high school and a strip center a few blocks beyond. To the south, the front end of the shopping center. Any number of places to stash a car and discreetly drive away. The accident must have changed things he thought, but how?

He reconsidered the information about the old woman. Why would I attack an old lady in the alley if I was trying to flee the scene? This made no sense whatsoever, but the coincidence of a robbery, accident and mugging all at the same time didn't either.

Who am I? I'm a white guy, thirties. Pretty calm about walking into a store with a gun and making off with a boatload of cash. Where do I go with that kind of money? Why do I dash into the street in front of a truck?

Something clicked there for a second and he leaned forward to his desk, concentrating. Something happens, the woman sees me and I panic. I don't run either direction up and down the street, I run into it. Either I don't have a car handy, or I'm way cool and decide to leave it and head into the park. Come back and get the car later? Maybe, but I'm still leaving on foot and have to go somewhere. How? I can't hang around the park with two bags, and I don't want to stash the cash anywhere. Closing his eyes, he imagined being in the park. What's ahead? Buildings, restaurants, hotels.

He sat up with a start, a plan coalescing, and reached for the phone. He jumped when it rang before his hand reached it and he paused before picking it up.

"Carter," he said, slightly annoyed at the untimely interruption to his thought process.

"This is Patterson sir," the voice on the other end said. "We have the woman from the accident waiting in the lobby for you."

"OK, keep her there. I'll be out to get her in a minute."

Will jumped up from his chair, ignored the jacket draped over the back and headed down the hallway away from lobby toward the far end of the building where the uniforms had an open work area. Nodding absently at various hi's and hello's as he progressed down the hall, he searched for the Sergeant as he entered the large room. He spotted the man sitting at his desk and he walked over to him quickly.

"Sarge," he said, interrupting what seemed to be a casual conversation between the Sergeant and another uniformed woman officer. They both turned and looked at him.

"Hey Will, did you get my email?" Kalorky asked as he looked up from his messy desk.

"Uh, yea, thanks, I did," Will said, "but I need some more help."

The woman nodded to the Sergeant and turned away. "I'll catch you later Sarge," she said over her shoulder.

Ignoring her, Will said, "Do you still have the units covering the accident area?"

"Of course. Three of them."

"Great. Get them on the horn and have them check out the restaurants and hotels. Have them talk to anyone working near the doors. You know, hostesses, bellhops, those guys."

"Sure Will, but…" Kalorky started to say, a little puzzled.

DECEPTION ON MARGIN

Without hesitating Will continued, "I don't think this guy has wheels, so he has to get out of there somehow, maybe a taxi. Get somebody to contact RTD and find out about the bus schedules in the area also."

"OK Will, I think I've got somebody who can follow-up on that. The units can hit the restaurants and hotels. RTD is gonna take a while though."

"I understand, but Sarge," he said, authority creeping into his voice, "the Captain wants results on this, and fast."

Kalorky looked at him, the implication not lost. "Ok Will, I'll let you know as soon as I get anything. Where will you be?"

Grateful for the response Will said, "I'm not going anywhere for a while, but if I'm not at my desk call me on my cell."

He turned and began to walk away, then added sincerely, "I owe you for this one Sarge. I'll buy you a few beers."

Laughing, Kalorky replied, "Ya, you suits always say that, but when do I ever collect? Especially from you. Where's a rising star like you gonna take poor white trash like me?"

"I's gonna buy you some pork and grits," he replied. "Fo sure." He turned from the man and walked back toward his own office, his mind already focused on the woman witness.

Liza had no idea what she was doing at the PO-lice department and she was scared. Her hand stuffed into her pocket, she gripped the bills she had not shown anyone, crumpling them between her grimy fingers. The bag with her tasty Mexican treats was still clutched in the other hand. Lordy yes, I didn't do anything wrong she said to herself. That man hit me first he did. He owed me this money.

She looked around the lobby area, shifting her old butt every once in a while on the hard plastic chair. Her experience with cops was limited. They had often been visitors to the shelter where she lived, sometimes bringing in drunks from the street, sometimes coming in and taking people away. Since the folks they took away rarely came back, she did not have a good feeling about being with any of them.

The PO-lice had been talking to everyone standing around the auto crash, and she had tried unsuccessfully to slink away from them. When caught, they asked her if she had seen anyone, something about a running man carrying bags. She didn't really understand or know what they wanted, but she did manage to say something about a man who had

41

knocked her flat and tried to steal her food. He hurt her she told them, hoping they would leave her alone. Instead they had taken her to one of their cars, put her inside and told her to wait. The back seat of the car had been gentle on her old back, softer than the rigid bus chairs. She couldn't remember the last time she had actually been in a car.

After a while a white man with big white stripes on his arms had gotten in the front seat and asked her all kinds of questions. He said his name was Sergeant K-something. The name meant nothing, but she did know what a Sergeant was. The Salvation Army had sergeants. She had clutched her food treasure to her chest and tried to make sense of what the man wanted, but scared, she could only tell him about the bad man that hit her. After a moment the sergeant told her they were going to take her downtown for a little while. Downtown was what the bus driver always said when she boarded a bus home, and she had relaxed a bit. She had almost enjoyed the ride in the car when they took her away.

But then they brought her here she thought. Lordy yes this wasn't the shelter. My oh my no. She pressed her knees together a little, hidden under the long gray and streaked skirt. She did have to make a little water she thought, feeling a little pressure down there, but she was still too scared to say anything. Instead she just sat there, not knowing what else to do.

Will returned to his desk quickly, anxious to see the woman who waited out front. He composed himself and briefly hoped that she would be able to provide him with more details of the crimes. Standing beside his desk, he reached down, picked up the phone and punched in the extension of the front desk. "Bring her in," he said.

He looked over to one of the walls, spotted an unused chair by one of the chalkboards and walked over to retrieve it. He was placing it in front of his desk when the officer brought her in. He looked up, completely taken by surprise. The old black woman was totally disheveled. Oh jeez, he said to himself, is she homeless or what? Maintaining his outward composure he walked over to her and smiled softly.

"Will, this is Liza," the officer said to him.

Liza just stood there, obviously nervous, startled at the sound of her own name.

"Hello Liza, my name is Detective Will Carter," he said and extended his hand. When he noticed she had some sort of bag clutched in one hand

and the other hand in her pocket he changed his mind. He motioned to the chair instead and said, "Please sit down."

"I'll take it from here, thanks," he added as he looked up, dismissing the officer. He slowly walked back around his desk, reconsidering his strategy, then noticed she was still standing. "Please, sit down Liza and tell me how was it you happened to be at the King Foodmart today?"

"I was shopping," she said, eyes locked on his face.

"And do you shop there often?"

"You're a black man."

"Well, yes Liza," he said, surprised.

She looked at him quietly, then said, "Are you in charge here?"

"Well yes Liza, I suppose I am. Not of everything of course, but in charge of the investigation."

She looked puzzled at his reply and said nothing.

"Do you know why you are here Liza?"

"Lordy no," she said. "Those other men asked me questions, then put me in a car. They took me here, not the shelter, no."

This may take a while he thought, and felt a pang of sympathy for the old woman. "Is that where you live? The shelter?"

"Lordy yes, the shelter. Home."

"Have you lived there long Liza?"

She struggled with a question for a minute, eyes questioning. "It's where I live. I lived in an apartment once before. That was home."

"How do you get to the store Liza?"

She perked up a little at the question, "Why the bus of course. They take me down to the store almost every day. Nice men drive the bus."

"And how do you pay for the bus rides?"

She seemed to struggle with that as well. "Oh, you mean the colored paper that I show the driver when I get on the bus? They give us those at the shelter."

"And you take the bus to the store, right Liza? To shop?"

"Yes, almost every day, even in the rain Lordy yes."

"And you were shopping today?"

"Why yes, of course. I went through the whole store, shopped I did. Sam the butcher let me sample the turkey. It was very good today."

He looked at her carefully, seeing the grimy bag in her hand. She was beginning to open up now and he wanted to keep her talking. "Is that what you have in the bag Liza? Turkey?"

She pulled the bag up to her chest and held it there. Will thought she looked a little embarrassed.

"What's in the bag Liza?" he repeated.

She looked down at it. "It's... it's my dinner. I got it at the store."

"May I see it?" he asked, noticing for the first time the label of a Mexican restaurant on the side.

She hesitated and looked at him, then slowly extended her arm and the bag toward him. He pushed up out of his chair and reached for the bag. She watched him closely as he unrolled the top and looked inside. A wave of stale burrito remains assaulted his nostrils. He closed it back up, leaned over and returned it to her. She clutched at it again.

"Where did you get your dinner Liza?"

Hesitating, she looked around, obviously embarrassed now. She looked down at her lap and meekly said, "Behind the store by the big blue box."

Intrigued by her description, he remembered the dumpster at the back of the store. Continuing patiently he said, "The dumpster in the alley?"

"Yes, I stop there when I leave the store. Sometimes I find things there. Bags of food that people have left for me. Lordy yes but not those dirty ones that ol' Mr. Rat has eaten on. No sirree. That's where the man hurt me, tried to take my food."

Will sat up straight in his chair. "What man hurt you Liza?"

She sat there and thought for a moment, forehead and eyes wrinkled in a thousand time lines.

"I had just gotten my dinner when he ran into me. Lordy yes. Pushed me down and was on top of me."

Will waited for her to continue, watching closely but saying nothing.

"I hit at him, tried to get him off me. But he stayed there, his hair all funny."

"What was so funny about his hair Liza?"

"It was down over the side of his head. It moved when I tried to hit at him."

OK, a wig he thought to himself. So much for the color of his hair. "Did you see what was under his hair Liza?"

Liza just looked at him, obviously not understanding the question. Worried about interrupting the flow he said, "What happened next?"

"He looked at me. I could see his face close to me Lordy yes. I was scairt of him."

A glimmer of hope surged inside him and he continued quickly. "Do you remember his face Liza? Could you recognize him? Describe him?"

"Well, he was a white boy, a young'n I think. He had a mark on his neck, right here" she said, pointing to a spot low on her neck below her ear.

Wondering why the two at the store hadn't said anything he asked, "Like a birthmark?"

"Yes, a God's mark it was," she said clearly. "Then he got off me and said he was sorry. He paid me he did."

"He paid you?"

Liza squirmed a little on her chair, moving her hand in her pocket. Realizing that her hand had been in her pocket the whole time they had talked, Will continued. "What's in your pocket Liza?"

She looked at him, then slowly pulled her arm and hand up. A crumpled fistful of ten-dollar bills emerged from her pocket, one falling to the floor.

"May I see that Liza?"

"It's money," she said and carefully placed it on the desk in front of her.

"Yes it is Liza. Did he give it to you?" Will asked as he leaned over and gathered up the pile.

Liza's eyes never left the bills. "He left it for me. He ran away and left the money behind."

Will straightened the bills into a small stack, counted eighty dollars and considered whether to test them for fingerprints.

"And then?" he asked instead.

"He had two sacks with him. He ran away. I was still so scared, but then I saw the money he left for me so I took it."

Will considered the old woman quietly as another wave of sympathy washed over him. He placed the money back down on the desk and wondered what to do with it.

"Do you know how much money this is Liza?"

She looked at him, her face tilted and eyebrows rising. "It's shopping money, Lordy yes. You can buy things, food, with money."

He got up, walked around the front of the desk and bent down to retrieve the single bill that had fallen to the floor. Gently placing his hand on her shoulder, he paused for a second, considering.

"Well Liza," he said as he returned to his chair. "This money belongs to the store. The man stole it from there."

Liza looked up, her eyes fully widened and mouth agape. "He stole the money from the store? Lordy that's bad."

"Yes it is Liza, and I need to give it back to them."

Liza looked down at the money and her shoulders drooped. She didn't say anything.

He looked at her and smiled gently, a surge of compassion spreading over him. He separated the bills into two piles and set half aside, then handed the rest back to her.

"But you know Liza, the store and the police want to thank you for your help. You can keep this, as a reward."

She beamed at him and grinned through crooked teeth. "Then I can keep it? I don't want no bad money. Lordy no."

He laughed out loud, feeling very good about his decision despite the impropriety. "No Liza, it's not bad money. It's all yours."

She hesitated, then leaned forward and carefully took the bills from his outstretched hand. "Lordy yes, good money. Shopping money," she said, a huge smile on her face as she shoved the bills back into her pocket.

Will considered what he had learned so far and decided that he had troubled the woman enough for today. He smiled at her. "Liza, thank you very much for your help today."

She smiled back, "Help? Did I help?"

"Yes Liza, very much. Do you want to go back to the shelter now?"

"In a car?"

Will couldn't help but laugh and said, "Yes Liza, in a car if you want."

She gazed at the bills in her hand and said, "Lordy yes, in a car. I can go shopping tomorrow." Then shifting slowly in her seat, her face saddened.

Will noticed the change and asked, "What is it Liza?"

Embarrassed now, she looked around sheepishly and replied, "Well, before I leave, could I?"

Will rose from his seat and walked over to her, gently held her arm and helped her up. "Do you need to use the restroom Liza?"

"Lordy yes. These old bones can't go too long without making a little water," she said and laughed at him. She relaxed in his grip, eyes sparkling.

"Come on girl, I'll show you the way then."

Will slid his arm through hers and slowly escorted her out of the office and down the hall.

Marsh sat in the living room in an overstuffed easy chair. He faced the sliding doors to the balcony, the eleventh floor concrete ledge towering above the busy street below. A soft breeze spilled in through the screen, the sounds of traffic the only noise in the room.

He took a sip from the tumbler, then set it down on the table at his side. As he got up from the chair he stretched and walked toward the wall, his eyes roving slowly over the pictures proudly displayed above the leather couch. There was a family portrait, taken about the time Suze had graduated from college. She must have been about twenty-two at the time he thought, pretty like her mother. He was standing next to his father, still a proud man despite his age. It was his mother's face, however, that held his attention. She was a striking woman, her full hair flowing over her shoulders onto a simple blue dress made elegant simply by her wearing it. Her face was strong, but even in the picture he could see the laughter that never left her eyes. Another wave of grief washed over him, but he was unable to take his eyes from the picture.

He'd returned to his condo over several hours ago. Sheila had driven him there, constantly at his side since the hospital. He vaguely remembered the events that transpired since the young doctor had delivered the news of his mother. Sheila had immediately taken charge he realized, and he was surprised by his helplessness. It was all he could do to maintain his composure, sitting numbly in the waiting room. She had left him there with stern instructions to stay put, her determination masking her own grief. He had no idea how long she was gone, but finally she returned to gather him up and take him out of the hospital.

"We're leaving now Marsh," she said gently as her arms reached down to help him from the chair.

"But..." was all he managed to say, unable to formulate any thought of what to do next.

"I've taken care of what needs to be done for now. Come on, we need to leave the hospital... get out of here," she insisted.

They left the hospital and just walked, her arm in his, not saying a word as he mindlessly pressed one foot forward after the other. They had traversed the sidewalk to the end of the long block and turned the corner before she said anything more.

"Marsh?" she said softly and looked at him, her arm hooked through his. He stared at her, but didn't respond.

"I've made arrangements with the admissions desk to hold your..." she started, unable to think of the words. "To keep her until tomorrow."

Marsh's knees bent as an unbearable image of his mother, lying on a slab, covered by a sheet swept over him. Sheila gripped his arm and held it firmly as they both stopped in the middle of the sidewalk.

"Jesus," he said, the word lodged in his tight throat and he doubled over as his stomach knotted up completely. She had pulled him forward, her own eyes damp and blinking as they had started to walk again.

She drove them silently back to his condominium, its downtown location only minutes from the hospital. Moments later they were both seated at the glass dining room table.

"Marsh... I can't stay too long. I should get back to the office and update the others. They are waiting to hear from us."

He looked at her, eyes focused for the first time since they left the hospital. "I'll call them," he said and started to get up from the dining room chair.

"No," she said firmly. Then, softer she continued. "I'll call them from the car. I want to get back to make sure things are still running."

"How could this happen?" he managed to say. "We just had dinner the other night."

"Marsh," she said, a touch more authority in her voice. "You need to be alone for a while and accept what happened. Think it through."

He got up from the chair and ran a hand through his hair. "I know," he said, a little control returning to his voice. "I'll be all right here. Go ahead." He helped her up and almost smiled. Then he practically pushed her out the door and said, "Thank you Sheila, thank you very much."

Without an argument she allowed herself to be escorted through the door, turning back to look at him as he opened it. Not knowing what else to say, she leaned up and kissed him on the cheek.

"I'll call you later, OK?" she managed to say as she stepped into the hall.

"Yes," he said, then she was gone.

That was an hour ago, and since then he allowed himself to simply sit and remember, trying to bring back as many thoughts of his mother as he could. He felt no guilt at doing nothing for that long, an unusual occurrence for a man as driven toward productivity as he was. He savored the time, sometimes smiling, sometimes grieving as the memories of his mother washed over him. He cried only once when the memory of his father's funeral entered his mind. He could picture his mother standing in the grass at the cemetery, attired in a long black dress and veil, tears welling up in her eyes as the pastor's words echoed over them. "... and though he has departed, he will never be forgotten. For his spirit remains in our memories. His love in our hearts. His laughter in our souls. May he rest in peace with God." He had cried then also, his grief as great for the pain he could see in his mother as it was for the loss of his father.

He stood and stretched, the fatigue associated with hours of inactivity unfamiliar to his athletic body. I've got to call Suze he thought and realized he had procrastinated for too long. He crossed the room and reached down to pick up the portable handset from its cradle on the end table. He sat back down in the easy chair, stared at the phone and tried to come up with the right words to say. Reluctantly he punched in the numbers of his sister's home. The phone responded with a ringing sound then a click as the answering service kicked in.

"Hello," his sister's voice echoed in his ear and his heart jumped as shafts of anxiety shot through him. Before he could say anything it continued. "You have reached 612-555-3223. Sorry I'm not here to take your call. Please leave a message and I will return your call as soon as possible."

A misplaced feeling of relief replaced the anxiety, then he felt guilty at only postponing the inevitable.

"Suze, this is Marsh," he said, starting strong. "I'm at home. Please call me as soon as you can..." then struggling to maintain his control he added, "Please Suze, it's important."

He pressed the end call button and dropped his hand and phone to his lap, not waiting for the connection to terminate. He realized that he had not eaten lunch during the staff meeting, but felt no urge to do so. The thought of the office triggered a sudden sense of guilt about leaving his business without contact all afternoon. He sighed, knowing that everyone had gone home for the evening, the guilt increasing as he wondered how they had managed without him. He was startled as the phone whirred in his hand.

Mustering the courage to face Suze, he pressed talk and raised the receiver to his ear.

"Hello?"

"Marsh, it's Sheila. How are you doing?"

Feeling both relieved and guilty again he said, "I'm fine." The platitude sounded hollow as he spoke. "Where are you?" he added quickly.

"I'm still at the office," she said. "There was... there was a lot to do."

His thoughts raced as he said, "Does everyone know?"

"Yes Marsh, they are all so sorry. They want to know how to help."

He thought for a moment, then replied, "The best thing they can do is to keep going. Keep working."

"That's what I told them, but it wasn't a very productive afternoon. It was like a tomb around here. Everyone is so sad. Mary and I have cleared your schedule for the week. We don't want to see you here at all. We can contact you if we need to, or if there is some sort emergency. We can have a conference call tomorrow afternoon if we need to."

His mind turned toward the details of his mother's passing and the arrangements that would need to be made. It would take some time he thought, the funeral, the house. He felt his breath rush out sharply as he remembered his mother's body at the hospital.

"Sheila, what did you arrange at the hospital?" he asked, then heard her hesitate.

"They will... hold her until tomorrow. You need to have the funeral home arrange to pick her up."

"Jesus," was all he could say, the phone dropping a little from his ear.

"Marsh?" he heard, the handset distant.

"Yes, I'm here. I'll call you in the morning."

"Are you alright?"

"I'm OK, I'm fine," he said and noted the concern drifting into her voice.

"Would you like me to come over? Have you had dinner?"

He paused for a second, "No, uh no. I've got to wait for Suze to call. I haven't been able to reach her."

"I could pick something up and bring it over..."

"No Sheila, but thanks. Thanks for everything."

There was an uneasy moment, as neither knew what to say.

"OK Marsh, take care of yourself. Call me if you need someone, anytime."

"I will Sheila, thanks again. I'll call you in the morning."

"Bye," she said.

Feeling guilty, not knowing what else to say he simply said, "Bye."

He hung up the phone, got out of the chair and wandered around the apartment, thinking. The funeral home would be his first call in the morning, the same one they had used for dad. He was heading for the kitchen when the phone rang again. His thoughts interrupted, the anxiety quickly returned as he realized it must be Suze returning his call. He ignored the white phone hanging on the kitchen wall and returned to the living room. He let the phone ring three times before he picked it up.

"Hello," he said, his stomach twisting.

"Marsh, it's Susan. I just got home and your message sounded so serious. Is everything OK?" she said. Her voice betrayed a touch of nervousness.

He pictured his younger sister on the other end and didn't know where to begin. "No Suze, it's mom..." he said, his voicing trembling.

"Mom? What's wrong? Is she alright?" she said frantically.

He struggled to sound calm as he leaned on the back of the chair and steadied himself. "No Suze, there was an accident. She's d..." He hesitated again. "She was killed in an accident today."

He felt the grief overcome him again, and unable to think of what else to say he waited for a minute. He heard her catch her breath, then begin to sob into the phone.

"Suze? Susan?"

"Oh God Marsh, mom..."

His heart breaking he spoke again, "When can you get out here Suze? How soon can you come?"

Her crying grew louder, and he had a hard time understanding her. Remembering that he already had time to deal with the situation, he let her grief spill out. Finally he said gently, "Susan, when can you be here?"

"I don't know Marsh... tonight?" she asked.

"No Suze, not tonight, it's too late and there is nothing you can do." The words sounded harsh as soon as he uttered them. "Tomorrow. Can you catch a plane first thing in the morning?"

"I don't know... yes of course. I'll get there as soon as I can. Oh God Marsh what happened?"

The realization that he hadn't even attempted to find out the details of the accident shook him completely. His knees buckled and he sank down into the chair. "I don't know yet Susan," he said, racked with guilt over his failure to ascertain anything concerning his mother's death. "We will know more tomorrow. For now just try and get here."

"I will. I'll call you as soon as I can," she replied, the grief still filling her voice. "And Marsh?"

"Yes?"

"I love you."

"I love you too Suze," he said and hung up the phone. The conversation had left him empty, a feeling that he should have said more, comforted her more. There was so much left unsaid he thought, but there was nothing he could do about it now.

Chapter Four

Fred sat quietly in the boarding area near the gate and watched the passengers slowly file past the attendant collecting boarding passes, confident he had completed another successful getaway. He always waited until just before the gates closed to board the plane. He didn't mind waiting inside the jet, however, in the very unlikely event someone had tracked him to the airport he would be trapped there, the possibility of escape virtually nil. He glanced down the long window lined concourse and thought there wasn't much chance of escape here either, but the percentages were at least a little more in his favor, and he was a man who played percentages. He felt a slight twinge of excitement as percentages reminded him of tomorrow and the trip to Vegas. But that was tomorrow, and he still needed to complete the current day's schedule.

He waited a few more minutes, then glanced across the now empty rows of seats toward the open door of the jetway. The attendant was alone and he decided to board. He removed the boarding pass from his pocket, walked past the seats and stepped up to her, slipping the card into the slot of the silver box beside her. Moments later he completed the trip through the plane and located his spot in row 25, an aisle seat almost at the back of the jet. An elderly couple already occupied the window and center positions and he smiled politely at them, then leaned his head back against the headrest and closed his eyes. He dozed off almost immediately and didn't stir again until well into the flight.

He forced himself awake when the attendants started the in-flight service, his three dollars exchanged for a Bud. He took a long pull on the almost warm beer and his mind drifted back to the afternoon's theft. He rarely thought about his exploits once they were completed, except of course when he checked the news online. This time was different however. It was the first time that events hadn't gone exactly as planned, and that bothered him a little. Now safely on a plane a few hundred miles away he had little concern of being caught, it was the lack of perfection that bothered him. Although the altercation with the old woman was purely an accident, it was still a mistake and he didn't like slip-ups. Worse yet was the wreck that he caused by running into the street. Once the robbery and crash were tied together, and he was sure they would be, the publicity and police scrutiny generated would be more intense than usual.

He thought for a moment and tried to imagine any conceivable way they could trace him to the crime. By the time the police even got any sort of investigation going he would be in another state, and another person. He was a man with many identities and had four distinct personas thief, gambler, thug and day trader. He was a chameleon by nature, and able to shift between any of them with ease.

He was used to change of course. He had grown up in a normal family - at least as normal as any he had experience with. His father had been very successful, a computer professional always commuting to far off cities. When an opportunity presented itself, a new company in a new city, the position was accepted without regard to the turmoil caused by uprooting the family and moving. He had always been popular and accepted wherever they landed, new friends quickly replacing those left behind and forgotten. Throughout school he had always been an 'A' student, or close to it, the occasional 'B' showing up only when he put forth no effort at all. He knew he had been given an IQ test early in life, but his parents refused to discuss it with him, treating him exactly like his younger sister and brother. As he grew older, he realized that others did not possess his mental abilities, and he thanked his parents for not revealing the difference between himself and others. But his intelligence was hardly limited to intellectual prowess. It was his uncanny ability to learn that paved the way to his success. He adjusted to any situation immediately, picking out clues and learning from simple phrases or even body language, often extrapolating knowledge from seemingly unrelated facts. Of course he wasn't always correct, but his confidence and demeanor often overrode the doubts of others. He absorbed information instantly and never, ever made the same mistake twice.

He took another long pull from the beer, musing about his identities. Thief, he thought. How did I become one? How did anyone become one? He had never been short of money. After breezing through college, earning both a business and a computer science degree, he had followed his father's footsteps and joined the firm his dad was currently consulting with. Computers had always fascinated him and the combination of their elegant simplicity and his strong personality had made him instantly successful. Rising up through a series of technical positions, he collected knowledge like a sponge, his people skills quickly moving him into ever increasing roles of management and responsibility. He changed jobs and companies often, like many others in his field, and by thirty he was a respected executive. At thirty-two he was given the "opportunity" to resign from the Vice President's position he occupied - the CEO and himself not agreeing on the strategic direction of the organization. The offer was six months salary and benefits, and he had left his office that afternoon. It was the last time he had actually been gainfully employed.

It was while traveling for work that he began to carve out the role as a thief. It was so simple to be anywhere in the country, an hour to the airport, a couple of hours on a plane. He moved from city to city with the same ease that most people went to work. What cemented his plan was a show he watched on television one night. He had been in a hotel room, he didn't even remember where, the TV on for background noise while he worked. An NBC news series was being broadcast, the segment covering brazen thieves who robbed convenience stores with little fear of being apprehended. He had been fascinated, ignoring his work as the show described the entire process, complete with store videotapes of the heists. Positioning themselves inside the small stores, one or more thieves distracted clerks and store managers, while a single individual crept behind the deserted counter and emptied the cash registers and safe. Amounts up to four thousand dollars were reported. He couldn't imagine himself knocking over 7-11's however, and he begun to consider bigger and more lucrative targets.

He hadn't then set out to be the next Jesse James, but subsequently devoted many free hours to the planning stages of his new career. Like anything else he undertook, he had wanted to do it well, and didn't mind the prospect that it would take him a few years to prepare. For about two full years he researched when he had the time, coming up with then discarding ideas of how he would accomplish the perfect crime. During this period however he never actually executed one. He lacked the one element that drove so many others to the real thing, motivation. He realized, looking back, that he had been fantasizing, constructing an identity to add excitement to what had become a successful but ever increasingly routine lifestyle.

A single event changed all that. The evening had started out as a simple date with Susan, the woman he had been dating for just a few weeks at the time. She was younger than him, mid-twenties, pretty, intelligent and a great body. Of course so were all the women that he went out with, or at least the pretty and great body part, but he found himself enjoying her company more and more. They had met one evening in a bar frequented by young professionals in downtown Minneapolis. Her wit and humor had easily frustrated his attempts at seduction without being rude or dismissive, and he had left with only her phone number. After a week or so he called her, and this time she had accepted his invitation without hesitation. The sexual tension aside, they had a wonderful time together and their personalities instantly meshed. Though neither seemed to desire any sort of permanent relationship, they began spending a lot of time together.

That evening they had been at the Haberdashery, a downtown bar/restaurant famous for its barrels of salted-in-the shell peanuts. They were on their second glass of wine, debating about what to do about dinner when she had spotted a friend of hers. Waving him over, she had introduced him as Arthur Petersen, explaining that they had been friends during school at the 'U'.

The conversation had flowed easily, especially after the third glass of wine, and he had been intrigued by Art's discussion of his newfound hobby. Art was a stockbroker by trade, with Dean Witter, but had been exploring the radical practice of day trading. Day trading he explained was the technique of buying and selling stocks in an extremely short period of time, sometimes hours or even minutes, using a large capital investment to take advantage of small fluctuations in a stock's price. The impact of computerized trading had revolutionized the way people on the inside were moving stocks. There were any number of brokerage houses that offered online investment tools, complete with real-time quotes, analytical tools and virtually instant trades. It was possible to make a fortune just sitting at home with your PC, Art had bragged.

The concept of merging computers and stock trading instantly fascinated him and he had pressed Art for more details despite Susan's obvious displeasure at being the third wheel in the group.

"OK, say Oracle's at 53," Art had started. "You put in an order to buy 2000 shares, 1000 of them on margin. You sit back and watch the ticker, waiting for your time to sell."

Doing the math quickly Fred said, "But that's over a hundred grand."

"Yup, but fifty of it is on margin, borrowed from the house."

"They let you do that?" Susan had interjected, trying to get back into the conversation.

"Sure, if you have enough cash in your account to cover it," Art said, acknowledging her. "Like I said, it's a capital intensive game. So you watch, Oracle goes up an eighth, then a quarter. You decide when you want to get out. A quarter of a point now is five hundred bucks remember so you need to decide what's greedy and what's not."

Fred had been captivated, his mind racing with the possibilities. "So when do you sell?"

"Whenever you want. It's your game. Let's say then you decide to get out at 54, so you put in a sell order at that price. Then you need to keep track of the order status, to see if it gets executed. But Oracle is still bouncing around, now about fifty-three and a half. It jumps to fifty three and seven eighths but your sell still doesn't execute, then the price starts to drop, you cancel the first order and try a sell at 53 and five eighths. Bang, that goes through and you just made twelve hundred and fifty bucks. Not bad for an hour or so."

"Jesus," Fred said, still lost in thought at the possibilities.

"But what happens if the stock goes down?" Susan had asked, her conservative nature showing through.

"Well the best way to deal with that is to put in a sell stop as soon as you buy." Noticing the confusion, he continued to explain. "A sell stop is an order to dump if the stock hits a set price on the way down, when it's dropping. In this case say 52 and a half. If you were wrong, the most you lose is a thousand. As soon as you buy you also put in an order to sell on the downside. Hopefully though you don't have to use it."

"How do you choose what to buy?" Fred asked.

"Ah there's the rub. Even though you are online, news gets to the public much later than the real traders on the exchange floor. You need to know what you are doing, know about the companies you choose to trade in. The big boys are all into technology and energy stocks. They have the biggest volatility." Art continued, almost lecturing now. "You know the big swings in technology stocks these days? Day traders. It's where the big bucks are."

"Well why not just buy it and keep it?" Susan had asked, again the conservative.

"Then it wouldn't be called day trading." Fred responded, already grasping the huge implications.

The rest of the evening had been somewhat subdued, Fred lost in thought and not paying much attention to Susan. Art had departed and they had settled on a simple dinner of burgers, not leaving the Haberdashery. She had been a little upset at his lack of attention and he was surprised that he felt bad about it, his feelings towards her obviously stronger than he had realized.

But he had almost been reborn that night. It was the first month of his six-month "retirement" and was already bored. His new exposure to day trading immediately consumed him, and he devoted his days to learning more. He had about a hundred and fifty grand in the bank, built up over ten years of high salaries, wise investing and few major expenses. Over the next couple of months he had dabbled in the art, acquiring a new powerful home computer system dedicated to his market activities. He was still on salary after all and was less concerned with making a lot of money than becoming an expert in the craft. He had a few successes and setbacks, sometimes only making one real trade a week.

His relationship with Susan also continued to grow, the difference in their ages not an issue, and they found themselves seeing each other constantly. Although neither of them pressed for any firm commitments, they had become a couple of sorts, often spending weekends away together and sharing each other's places.

It was a bad day in the market that again spurred a change. Tempted by the large gains he was seeing in his practice portfolio, now pushing a half a million dollars, greed began to set in and he wanted the big gains to follow in real life. Selecting a telecommunications stock he had been following closely, he opened a large position unaware that the FCC was holding a policy hearing that day. Negative comments by the commission's head caught the market by surprise and all telco stocks took a beating. He lost nearly twenty grand of real money before he caught his error. Vowing never to make that mistake again he realized he needed more cash, and his long incubating plans of being a thief had resurfaced. He had finally found the motive he lacked, hard cash, to provide the ability to day trade in ever-larger amounts.

The landing announcement interrupted his reverie as the plane began its gradual descent into Dallas. He stretched and cleared his thoughts. There were a few more things to finish before he could call today's activity successful. He glanced at his watch and adjusted it back to

Central Daylight time. It was 5:30.

Will was still at his desk long after everyone had gone. He had utilized the time waiting for a call back from Kalorky to clean up his desk, answer a few emails and generally clear his plate for the case at hand. He had a whole lot of questions and not many answers. He was trying to make sense of the whole series of events when the phone rang and snapped him back.

"Will, it's Kalorky. I'm over at the Hyatt. How soon can you get here?"

"I'm on my way," he said, already getting up out of his chair.

The trip over to the Tech Center only took a few minutes. The Hyatt loomed above him as he turned from the street into the long driveway, the circular tower rising up into the evening sun. He spotted two white squad cars parked in the drive, left the car in the driveway and covered the last few yards to the entrance in long purposeful strides. The sergeant was on the other side of the portico and he quickly eased past the guests and staff, the overhanging structure briefly blocking out the setting sun. Kalorky was talking with a couple of uniforms off to the side. A bellhop in uniform and a tiny oriental man sat on the bench quietly. Noticing Will approach, the sergeant walked toward him.

"Nice of you to keep me from dinner Will," Kalorky said, eyes laughing. "Abrahms and Wetters here have found something for you."

Will's eyes traveled to the two young cops standing there. "Hey guys, thanks for helping out," he said, shaking both their hands.

"Hello sir, anytime," Wetters replied.

Will sensed nervous movement from the civilians behind him on the bench, but ignored it. "What do we have gentlemen?"

Kalorky responded immediately, "Good call on the search parameters Will. Abrahms and Wetters here visited a few of the restaurants across the street before coming here. The bellman over there," he said, nodding towards the bench, "was just getting off duty. He remembers a guy coming across the parking lot and over to the hotel. I think maybe it's your perp."

"And the other guy?"

"Cab driver. He picked up a fare here. Wetters tracked him down from the call logs."

"Great. Now we're getting somewhere," he said and turned quickly from the three cops and toward the two men on the bench.

"Hello," he said as he approached, motioning for them to stay seated. The oriental jumped up anyway.

"Why you keep me from work?" he said, accent thick and excited.

"I'm sorry sir, this will only take a minute. We just need some information. I would really appreciate it if you can help us," Will said, addressing the cabby.

The man's head bobbed a little and he sat back down. Will then spoke to the bellman. "What did you see sir?" he asked politely.

The bellman leaned forward. He was young Will noticed, maybe a college student on a summer job. His long tan arms stuck out a little too far from the sleeves of his red uniform.

"Well it was just after lunch and it was slow for a moment. I noticed this guy in a blue jogging suit coming across the lot from the building over there. He wasn't running or anything, just carrying two bags."

"What did they look like?" Will asked.

"One was white cloth, kind of full. The other looked like a grocery bag. I didn't pay too much attention, but it did strike me a little odd that he would be coming from the lot over there, then go right into the hotel."

"White canvas bag, two handles," the cabby said suddenly. Will and the bellman both looked at the driver.

"Yea, that's it, two cloth handles on the canvas sack."

"What did he look like?" Will asked, and hoped it was the perp.

The bellman replied first. "Well when he went in, he had curly brown hair, not too long and a moustache. About six feet. Average kind of guy."

The driver started to speak but Will interrupted him. "What do you mean when he went in?"

"Well, when he came out, he had very short hair, blonde or brown I think. It was hard to tell. And no moustache. I only recognized him because of the canvas sack. It was about ten minutes after he went in. At least I thought it was the same guy. He was dressed in pants and a sweater."

The cabby joined in and said, "Yes that's him. Sunglasses."

"He came out, asked me for a cab and I whistled at the line. A guest was pulling up so I didn't spend a lot of time with him."

"He only had one bag with him?" Will asked.

"Just the canvas sack. That's why I wondered if it was the same guy, but then I got busy and forgot about it 'till you guys showed up."

"One sack," the little man added, head still bobbing.

Will turned abruptly to the officers behind him. "Hey guys," he said. "It looks like our man might have dumped something inside the hotel. Can you go in and check it out? Plastic bag, a running suit, maybe a wig." He watched as Abrahms and Wetters moved towards the entrance and nodded a quick thanks as they moved by. Kalorky strolled over and joined Will by the bench.

Will addressed the driver again. "The same man with the canvas sack? You picked him up?"

"Ah, yes sir," the little man replied. "He go to airport."

"Who is this guy anyway?" the bellman asked, interrupting Will.

"Watch the news tonight kid," Kalorky said.

"DIA?" Will asked.

"Ah yes. DIA. No luggage, just bag."

As a sinking feeling built up in his stomach Will asked, "What time?"

"No traffic - nice ride. About one o'clock. He say nothing all way."

"Where did you drop him? What airline?" Will asked impatiently.

"Awraska."

"Damn," Will said. "The fucking airport." He thought for a moment, then addressed Kalorky. "Sarge, see if you can get a list of flights for Alaska, no wait," he said, reconsidering, "get a list of all flights after, say 2:30." He glanced at his watch and noted the time. Shit he could be anywhere by now he thought.

He turned back to the two sitting there. "Do you think either of you could describe him? Do you remember his face?"

The bellman spoke first. "I suppose. I might recognize him if I saw him again, but I really didn't pay too much attention. He was just another guy."

Will looked at the oriental man, waiting. The man shrugged his shoulders. "Whrite guy."

"Ok gentlemen, that's it. Thank you for your help," he said to both, dismissing them. "We'll be in touch alright?"

They nodded and got up from the bench. Will watched them walk away, his hopes dashed. He turned to Kalorky. "Sarge, even with a list, what are the odds we can check about a hundred flights for a white guy getting on a plane?"

"Slim to none Will."

"Ya, that's what I thought."

Disappointed, he wondered what to do next. He looked at Kalorky and slapped him and the back. "Thanks for the help. At least we know where he's not."

Kalorky looked at him, a puzzled look on his face.

"We know he's not in Denver, Sarge."

Chapter Five

Sara McGloughin had a boob job. She regretted it now, but at thirty-five she had long since stopped worrying about the decision. She sat quietly in the news control center and stared up at the monitors that continuously screened broadcasts of the Denver channels and cable news networks. She still had her suit coat on. Rarely at work did she dress in a way that would call attention to her figure. She was a beautiful woman - long flowing blonde hair, trim and athletic and sharp model-like facial features. But nature had forgotten about her chest and in an effort to improve herself she had, at twenty-three, decided to do something about it.

She had been a graduate of the UCLA School of Journalism, an aspiring writer and communications specialist with dreams of breaking into network TV. Despite her excellent grades and intelligence, she was convinced that it took more for a woman to get ahead, and she had been willing to use every edge she could. She knew that working her way up through the ranks would require work outside the studio where more bodily exposure was not uncommon. Her strategy seemed to work for a while. At her first job in Sacramento, with the last place local network, she had parlayed her striking features into more and more airtime. Covering breaking stories, reporting on public service events, even attending the city's social affairs she became a fixture on the screen, but never at a desk in front of the camera. From there she moved to Austin, a bigger and more visible station, then on to Houston and finally San Francisco. She was always respected, her journalism training produced excellent work, and she was once nominated for a California broadcasting award for her coverage of embezzling activities in the Oakland Public Assistance program. But other than spot appearances on screen, she never made the transition from reporter to broadcaster. After a tumultuous and failed marriage to an investment banker, she had left the Bay Area and returned to her native Colorado. Resigned to the fact that she was not destined to be on the air, she rededicated her career toward investigative journalism. In retrospect she wondered where the dream of being a famous face came from anyway. She never really blamed her breasts for not allowing her to been seen in the nation's nightly broadcasts.

The six o'clock news was showing on the four screens dedicated to local stations, the sound from each muted but audible in jumbled unison. The second story on her own station, KDEN, caught her attention and she grabbed the black remote control that sat on the counter several chairs away. She clicked up the volume, drowning out the other stations and leaned forward, ignoring a puzzled look from one of the technicians on the floor below. An American-Indian woman in a conservative brown suit was recanting the story.

"…spectacular accident just outside the Denver Technology Center today has reportedly claimed the life of at least one victim. The crash has unofficially been linked to a robbery that occurred at a King Foodmart grocery store nearby."

The image changed as the director switched cameras from a slight angle shot to a closer frontal face view. Nice work, she mentally praised the director - add a little sincerity to the story.

"No reports have been released by the Denver Police Department at the time of this broadcast. However, KDEN has learned that a lone white male entered the store at around 12:30 p.m. today, and escaped with an undisclosed amount of money. His flight from the scene apparently caused the accident in which the as yet unidentified woman was killed."

She grabbed her purse, fumbling with it as the image changed again. The shot showed the two co-anchors, the second a slightly graying fiftyish male in a conversational view. The woman anchor shuffled a paper for effect and turned toward the man.

"Terrible tragedy it seems Tom."

Completing the segue he looked at her and replied, "Yes Anita, and we will have more coverage on this breaking story tonight at ten."

She ignored the rest of broadcast, pushed with her feet and sent the roller chair over the tiled floor and past the long table toward a phone at the end. She grabbed the receiver with one hand, the other latching onto the table to stop her movement, then quickly dialed the extension of the news desk.

"News desk," she heard a staff member respond.

"Get me Howard!" she shouted into the phone, ready to deliver a tirade at the station's News Director. She fumed for a second, holding the

DECEPTION ON MARGIN

handset close to her ear, one foot tapping on the floor.

"Barnes," a calm voice said after a moment.

She launched into him immediately. "Damn it Howard, why wasn't I included on the Tech Center robbery thing? If this isn't an investigative story then I don't know what the hell is." Getting even angrier she said, "Whom did you put on this story anyway?"

It took a moment for the response, as if Barnes was mentally counting to five. "You're on it," he said. "What do you have so far?

"Jesus Howard."

"Maybe if you'd pick up your messages or answer your phone Sara, you could be a little more on top of things."

She relaxed her grip on the receiver, rebuked, then remembered her comatose cell phone. "Uh, sorry Howard, my cell's dead again," she said, wincing at the excuse. "What do we have so far?"

"Basically nada. Most of what's been reported we picked up off the radio. I'd like a little more substance for ten."

"Gotcha. Who do we have on the inside?" she asked, already building a strategy.

"Nobody yet. I suggest you use that investigative reporter charm of yours to get us something. And fast."

"Right Howard," she said and dropped the phone. She got up out of the chair, unconsciously closing her jacket and headed out of the control center.

By the time she reached her desk she had a plan. She sat down in her chair and located the mouse sitting under a pile of wire flashes. The movement flicked off the screen saver and she brought up her personal address book. Scrolling down she selected a name and clicked it, another window showing the number she needed. She dialed the direct line into police dispatch, hoping that Rita was on the boards. She could picture the woman - a middle aged mom who had been working the phones at the PD for years. Sara bumped into her often while covering crime stories and had always struck up friendly conversations, taking the time to learn a little about her life.

"Southeast Dispatch," a woman said.

Sara perked up at the familiar voice. "Rita, this is Sara McGloughin at KDEN. Can you talk?" She hoped so, recalling that the incoming calls were always recorded.

"Why hello Sara, hang on a second."

Sara was put on hold and noticed that there was no elevator music playing while she waited.

The phone clicked back on. "Sorry Sara, it's been a bit hectic around here," the woman at dispatch said after a minute.

"I can imagine," Sara said. Then encouraging Rita, she inquired, "Big day at the Tech Center?"

Rita laughed, "Phone's been ringing off the hook dear."

Sara smiled and probed a bit more. "Rita, any chance you could tell me who's handling the King Foodmart robbery?" She shifted in her chair, anticipation tingling through her as she slid closer to the edge.

"I don't see why not. Detective Carter is on that I'm pretty sure."

Sara racked her brain for a moment, trying to remember the man. Failing to she said, "I don't think I'm acquainted with him Rita."

"He's the nice young black detective here at Southeast. Will Carter."

Noting the name on a sheet of scratch paper she inquired, "Any chance you could connect me to his extension?"

"Of course, the Police Department is a public service organization you know."

Quickly, and wanting to keep up her good relations Sara added, "And how are the kids Rita?"

"Just fine Sara, can't keep up with them these days. Teenagers you know. I'll connect you now," she said, her voice instantly replaced by the phone ringing again.

Sara waited, hoping but not expecting an answer. At least I know who's in charge she said to herself. The phone rang a few times and she briefly considered who to call next when it picked up.

"Carter."

Surprised, she put on her best professional voice. "Detective Carter, this is Sara McGloughin at KDEN news.

"Yes Ms. McGloughin. What can I do for you?"

Her notepad and pen ready she started. "It is our information that you have been placed in charge of the investigation of the robbery at the King Foodmart this afternoon," she said, then without waiting for a reply, "and also that this incident has contributed to the death of several innocent bystanders." She baited him with the last statement, hoping it would force him to reveal something.

"Yes," he said, "and no."

"Yes, you are in charge of the investigation?"

"That is correct."

"And no, several innocent people have not been killed?"

"That is also correct."

She smiled and continued probing, not at all frustrated by his evasion. "Can you confirm that there were fatalities associated with the crash?"

"Yes, there was a single fatality caused by the accident."

"And was the accident a direct result of the robbery?"

"The robbery and the accident occurred in the vicinity of each other, at approximately the same time. It is an ongoing investigative effort of the Police Department to determine whether the two incidents are related."

Pretty cool character this one, she thought. "And the results of that investigation have yielded what results?"

"We will have a statement regarding the incident, or incidents, at a press conference tomorrow morning at ten am."

"And that is the official position of the Police Department at this time?"

"We will not be releasing any further information until tomorrow," he said, little trace of emotion in his voice and offering nothing.

"You are aware that reports on the evening news broadcasts have already linked the robbery and the accident, and that one fatality has occurred as a result."

"Yes, the department is well aware of what is being reported."

"And you do not wish to comment on these reports?"

"As I have said Ms. McGloughin, results of our efforts will be fully disclosed tomorrow morning."

Feigning closure, she said politely, "Thank you very much for the information Detective Carter."

"You are welcome Ms. McGloughin."

The instincts that had made her a good reporter kicked in. Before he could hang up the phone she took a chance. "Will?"

"Yes Ms. McGloughin?"

"Please Will, call me Sara. I understand your reluctance to release any information outside official channels, but hey, I'm just a poor working girl here. Can't you help me out?" she said, adding her best little girl laugh.

"Oh I see... Sara. Look, I appreciate your position but I really can't comment any more."

Undaunted, but pleased at his softening, she continued, "Will, you know what's going to happen. This was a big event, and the news shows are going to want to lead with it or at least play it up at ten. The less information you give out now, the more misinformation will be broadcast on the news. Speculation will abound and your job tomorrow at the press conference will be twice as difficult."

She paused for a moment, letting this sink in. "I'm an investigative reporter, and a damn good one. Other news channels have investigative reporters. Everyone is going to be poking into this you know."

"And I suppose that if I provide you with some details you will share it equally with all these other news channels?"

Ouch she thought, but she sensed an opening. "Come on now Will, a girl has to make her mark. What can you give me? I promise we will report it sensibly and not compromise your position at all."

"OK Sara, ask me some questions and I'll be as honest as I can." Then after a short pause he added, "However this is off the record until tomorrow morning. I don't want my name, or anyone at the department linked to this. This is the proverbial unnamed source. If I see myself on the news I'm gonna be real pissed."

Yes, she said, making a fist and pulling her arm back. "Can I at least name you as the officer in charge?"

"Sure," he replied, "Do you need help with the spelling of my name?"

"No, I think I can handle that," she said, and laughed. "Are the two incidents in fact related?"

"Yes, we have eye witnesses that confirm the thief caused the accident as he was leaving the store. We are at the time assuming it was unintentional."

"And the victims of the accident, what are their conditions?"

"One fatality, a woman, late fifties. One male, hospitalized, stable condition. One male, treated and released."

"Identities?"

"Not until tomorrow Sara."

"Didn't think so." She considered the option of tracking down the man in the hospital, but decided it wouldn't be of any use before ten.

She changed track and said, "Can you disclose any information about the robbery itself?"

He seemed to choose his words carefully before replied, "The suspect entered the offices of the store, held two employees hostage and escaped with an undisclosed amount of money."

"Was it an armed robbery?"

"Yes."

"Was anyone harmed during the theft?"

"No."

"So it was a single thief, working alone?"

"Yes."

"What information do you have regarding the suspect? Do you have any positive leads on the individual?"

"He is white, mid-thirties, short blonde hair, about six feet and average build."

Laughing she said, "Will, that describes about a quarter of the male population of Colorado."

"Yes, unfortunately it does."

"And do you have any leads?"

"We have tracked his movements from the scene and are following up with several more witnesses. That's all I can say at this time."

Sensing she had gotten about as much as she was going to get, she closed. "Anything else you can tell me Will?"

"Only that this event has the full attention of the Denver Police Department. We are dedicating a significant amount of resources toward swift resolution of the incident."

"Mmm... I'm sure of that." She wanted to keep her new found contact on friendly ground and added, "Will, can you meet with me tomorrow?"

"I don't see why not Ms. McGloughin. Officially of course, and after the conference."

Noting the change in his tone she added, "Thanks Will. I appreciate your candor, and your help."

"My pleasure Ms. McGloughin. Now I'm sure you need to be off to share with your competitors the information you managed to pry out of me."

She noted the friendly sarcasm in his voice and laughed again. I like this guy, she thought. "Of course, immediately." Then, wondering how the station should bill the story she added, "Detective Carter, is this an exclusive story?"

"Only if no other reporter manages to track me down," he said, but she couldn't tell if he was kidding or not.

"I'm looking forward to meeting you tomorrow then."

"Tomorrow," he replied.

She heard him hang up the phone and mentally summarized the conversation, then glanced down over the few notes she had made. She returned to her keyboard and redrafted them. There was something more to this she thought. She emailed the summary to the writer's desk and added the footnote 'Exclusive' in bold at the bottom. She hoped it was true. She then picked up the phone and dialed her boss's direct extension, knowing he was still at his desk.

"Barnes," he replied immediately.

"Jeez Howard, don't you have a life?" she asked, teasing him about his unrelenting work habits.

"No more than you Sara. What's up?"

"I've got the story for ten," she said. "I just emailed it to the writers and copied you."

"I know, it just popped into my box but I haven't read it. What's the deal?"

The wonders of email she thought, how did we get along without it? She quickly summarized the conversation with Carter, embellishing a little where she thought she could get away with it.

"What's this 'exclusive' shit?" he asked.

"So far I'm the only one to reach him."

"That's hardly exclusive Sara, anyone can get to him before tomorrow."

"But not before the news tonight."

"Mmm… Good point. And?"

"There's something else going on here Howard. He wasn't telling me something."

"Did you expect him to?"

"No, it's not that. I just have this feeling that there is something missing that's all."

"So what do you want me to do?" he asked.

She could smell it she thought her body was tingling all over with excitement. Deciding immediately to go all out she said, "I want to run with this. I think we have a shot at a good investigation here. Do the station some good you know?"

"I'll reserve judgment on that until after the press conference tomorrow. Until then it's all yours."

"Great," she said. "I'll see you after I meet with Carter."

"Do you want a film crew for the briefing?"

"Couldn't hurt. I liked the guy. He might make for some good footage." Then, without knowing why she added, "He's apparently black."

"Apparently? All right, arrange it with the desk. I'll see you tomorrow."

She hung up the phone and checked her watch. It was getting late and she was tired, but her mind refused to stop. She wondered about how to frame the story. Professional robbery and thief, or the human interest angle? The family of the woman she decided as she cleaned up her desk. I'll start there tomorrow.

Will sat for a while, recounting the conversation with the reporter. Mission accomplished he thought. He had every intention of briefing the press fully at the conference tomorrow, but the opportunity to stifle rumors by "leaking" information to the press had presented itself and he had taken advantage of it. He doubted the reporter even suspected his motives. Sara McGloughin happened to be the first reporter to get in touch with him, but he would have manipulated whoever got to him first in the same way. He didn't actually think that she would share the information with her competitors, but that didn't really matter. By the time the early broadcasts aired and the newspapers hit the street the details would have circulated sufficiently and he would have the control he needed at the press conference.

He picked up the phone while he scanned the internal directory for the Public Relations Department. Dialing the extension he wondered who was on duty tonight.

"PR, this is Sarah," came the reply after a single ring.

He laughed at the coincidence, recalling the woman who worked in the organization dedicated towards keeping the name of the Denver PD in good standing. She was younger than he, a fellow DU graduate and incredibly effective at her job.

"Hello, Ms. Robbins," he said, "this is Detective Carter."

"Why Detective Carter, how can the PR Department assist you tonight? A little publicity perhaps?" she said, a trace of laughter in her voice. "You know we like to keep big strong men like you in the public's eye."

"As a matter of fact, you can. You know the incident at the Tech

Center this afternoon? The robbery and accident?"

"I'd hardly be a responsible PR woman if I didn't. We've had our share of calls this afternoon from the media."

"What has been the official position so far?"

"Well I didn't get on until six so I didn't handle many of the calls. It did come up at our staff meeting tonight though. Standard procedure, no comment."

"Wonderful," he said, suddenly grateful that he hadn't been the target of more inquiries.

"Is this your gig?"

"Yup. And I need you to do a few things for me OK?"

"Sure Will, what do you need?"

He gathered his thoughts for a moment. "First, I would like to issue a blanket statement regarding the incident. Send it to all the usual media suspects, news wires, etc. Would you like me to run through it now, or do you want me to whip up an email?"

"Now is fine Will. I assume you trust my note-taking ability?"

"Absolutely Sarah," he said with confidence.

He quickly summarized the details he wanted to go out. He considered his conversation with the other Sara and decided to leave the details on the victims out of the release. Giving her at least some exclusivity might come in handy later he decided.

"Do you want to see the text before I release it Will?" she asked. "I can email you a copy."

"Unless you have some specific questions I think I can trust your professional judgment."

"Fine Will, consider it done. What else?"

"I need to schedule a press conference for tomorrow morning. Ten a.m., any problems with that?"

"None at all. We keep the conference room open for such events. Sorry I won't be there though. I'm off at 3 am."

"Nice hours. Who should I work with?"

Hesitating for a second she said, "David Osterback will be on in the morning."

"OK Sarah, and thanks for your help."

He hung up the phone as she did. One more duty to perform he thought, not relishing the update call to the Captain. He glanced at his watch. He's probably at dinner. A little bad news for dessert. He reached into the pocket of his coat on the back of the chair and removed the cell phone. Flipping through the list of names, he located the entry for the Captain's cell phone. He picked up the receiver on his desk again and punched in the number, reading it from the small display on his cell.

"Captain, this is Carter," he said when the phone was answered.

"Hello Will, I presume you have an update for me," the Captain said, a statement rather than a question.

"Uh, yes sir. I hope I'm not disturbing your dinner."

"We'll see. It depends on whether this is good news or bad."

Ouch Will said to himself, but continued firmly, unconsciously straightening his shoulders. "The robbery and the accident are definitely related. A white male working alone held up the store. It was an armed robbery. A handgun."

"And the amount of the take?"

"Just under a hundred thousand dollars, sir. The store will provide us with an accurate amount in the morning."

"Was anyone injured during the actual robbery?"

"No sir."

"What caused the accident then?"

"The perp left the store through the back door. He proceeded to the west, towards Yosemite Avenue. At some point he apparently ran into an old woman and a brief scuffle ensued."

"Have you interviewed this woman?"

"Yes sir. She lives in a shelter up off Colfax. She is not exactly star witness quality. She thinks she might be able to identify him, but from our conversation I learned he was probably disguised at the time. At least a wig and false moustache."

He waited for a response, then continued anyway. "The altercation must have surprised him. It was then that he ran into the street and directly in the path of a large truck. The truck swerved across the median striking the car of a woman heading southbound. Another car, also southbound and following close collided with the truck and the first car."

"Fatalities?"

"The woman in the first car was a DOA at University. The second car driver is stable and the truck driver was shaken up but not injured. He verified the woman's description of the suspect, including the fact that he was carrying two bags. We assume that one was filled with the stolen money."

"What's the ID on the woman who was killed?"

Will paused for a second, using the mouse to bring up the accident report from Kalorky on his computer. "One Margaret Hawkins, white, 57, widow, Denver resident. Close relatives include a son Marshall in Denver and a daughter Susan in Minneapolis."

"Have you contacted the son yet?"

"No sir. He was notified through official channels - like any other accident. I didn't see the necessity to reveal the link to the robbery at this time." He added, "I plan to contact him tomorrow."

"All right. Were you able to track the suspect?"

"He left the scene of the accident immediately. No one there was able to provide any more details. We picked up his trail by canvassing the hotels and restaurants in the area. He was spotted by a bellman at the Hyatt who remembers a man fitting the description entering the hotel, then leaving a few minutes later, minus the wig, moustache and one of the bags. A team is searching the hotel now to try and locate the second bag."

"Then what?"

Will stiffened and delivered the bad news. "He caught a taxi to the airport sir. He was dropped off about 2 p.m.."

"So, what you are saying detective, is that our suspect is now probably hundreds or thousands of miles away, and we have no real means of tracking him down."

"Yes sir, that's what it looks like."

"Shit," the Captain said.

Despite himself Will winced, but in an effort to keep the conversation moving he added, "Sir, this looks like a well planned and professionally executed theft. The accident was just an unfortunate mistake."

"Yes, it does. And that makes our work all the more difficult. What's the next step? And by the way, this did make a big splash on the news tonight."

"Yes sir, I know. I have personally spoken with one news station, and revealed enough information to keep the rumors down. I issued a preliminary statement through PR. It should be going out as we speak. I have also scheduled a press conference tomorrow at ten, but unfortunately we won't have much more concrete information to disclose."

He waited as the Captain paused for a moment. "Tell me Will, what is your honest opinion on the outlook?"

He decided to be completely candid regardless of the consequences. "Sir, this guy knew exactly what he was doing. And unless we get a break from fingerprints at the scene or from the missing bag, both of which are doubtful, I think he is long gone."

"That's my opinion too. Not going to make anyone very happy though." Then, changing the subject a little the Captain said, "And the woman's death?"

Knowing exactly what the Captain implied Will answered immediately. "A death during, or as the result of the commission of a crime sir. A homicide."

"Yes it is Will. Thank you for the update. Please brief me again after the press conference tomorrow, or sooner if you have any more details."

"Yes sir." he said and hung up the phone, all thoughts about any sort of pleasant evening now firmly banished from his mind.

Chapter Six

Fred had a few remaining butterflies in his stomach as he came down the escalator and walked into the baggage claim area. He was one of the last to leave the jet, biding his time in the back, making casual conversation with a flight attendant as they watched the passengers struggle with carry-on items in the overhead compartments. He never really got nervous until well after leaving the plane, the walk from the gate to the baggage claim area always longer than he remembered. He couldn't help thinking about a possible reception by the police when he claimed his bag, and wondered what he would do if it were to happen. He tried to dismiss the thoughts as nonsense, but they always seemed to lurk at the edge of his mind.

His heart skipped a beat when he noticed a man in a plain gray suit staring at him. He locked eyes momentarily with the man, then nodded in recognition as he realized it was the passenger who had occupied the seat across the aisle from him. The klaxon sounded, startling him, and a red light in the center of the carousel began to flash. He scanned the area once again, becoming more confident that no one was paying the slightest bit of attention to him. The belt began to move and he counted six black garment bags in the first ten pieces of luggage that emerged from the opening in the wall and traveled slowly down the path. It was one of the reasons he chose generic black for his bag, one that blended in with dozens of others that dropped onto the carousel. He could instantly recognize his bag from a distance, but one of his fears was that someone would inadvertently mistake it for their own and snatch it away.

Only a few more minutes he told himself, then was surprised to see his own bag slide onto the belt, partially covered by a blue Nike duffel. Not able to help it, his heart began to race and an anxious feeling dropped into the pit of his stomach, his eyes now locked on the bag as it slowly passed in front of the watching passengers. He realized he was holding his breath, and forced himself to breathe, exhaling audibly though no one was close enough to hear him. His eyes suddenly opened wide as a young woman, smartly dressed in a blue skirt and red silk top leaned forward, pushed the duffel aside and grasped the handle of his bag. Frozen for a moment, he could only watch as she pulled it up and examined the brand as it continued to move along the belt. She almost bumped into a couple of kids standing next to her before she realized her error and unceremoniously dropped it back to the belt, the bag now hanging partially towards the floor. Fred decided to act and strode quickly across the carpet, pushing his way past a young couple holding hands and latched on to the handle. Muttering an 'excuse me' to the startled pair he rescued the bag and quickly turned away, eyes locked on the door.

    The bag was heavier than he remembered and he felt Goosebumps rise on his neck as walked across the commons. His back felt like a huge target as he walked, and he fought the urge to turn around to see who might be following. Trying hard to control his pace, he imagined the pressure of the point of a gun shoved in the small of his back, strong arms pinning his own to his side. The muscles in his butt tightened his steps stiffer as he neared the door. He avoided two older women shuffling towards the door at the same time and rushed out onto the street, the outer set of doors opening with a whoosh as he approached.

    The heat of a late Texas summer afternoon felt like a wet wall, the humid air doing little to dry the beads of sweat he felt on his forehead and down his spine. He turned quickly towards the ground transportation area and looked ahead at the line of cabs waiting to pick up fares along the curb. Seeing no one in line, he bypassed the ropes used to contain a larger crowd and nodded at the huge black man leaning against the dispatch cage. The dispatcher, tight curly gray and black beard, biceps bulging out from under a plain brown shirt eyed him suspiciously, then pulled the stub of a cigar from his mouth with one hand as he whistled for the next taxi through yellow tobacco stained teeth. Fred turned his back to him and waited as the blue and white cab glided up and stopped. Ignoring the trunk popping up, he opened the right rear door and tossed the garment bag across the seat, then followed it in and closed the door behind him. Thankfully, the cab was cooler than the outside air, the air conditioner blasting away in the front seat. He pulled his shades from his pants pocket and slid them down over his eyes as he watched the driver get back into the front seat.

    "Where to mon?" the cabby asked, looking at him in the mirror, black hair in wildly splaying dreadlocks knotted with small blue beads.

    "Downtown," Fred said, then looked away. "Renaissance Tower."

The man nodded, needing no further instructions. Fred felt a surge of power as the car quickly accelerated and he settled back, almost slumping in the soft seat. Totally ignoring the driver he relaxed, feeling the adrenaline seep out of his system, his stomach slowly returning to normal. Surprisingly, he felt a little drowsy and began to nod off, his hand absently moving towards the garment bag next to him on the seat, resting on top of it. An image of the silver side of the truck flashing past him filled his mind and he jerked forward, arms reflexively pushing in front of him to keep it away. Startled by the near dream he sat up, not wishing to fall asleep on the last leg of his journey.

He smiled a little, the bag full of cash resting comfortably under his arm. At least ninety grand he thought, it would make a nice infusion into his portfolio. He also knew it was foolish to think that he could go on robbing grocery stores indefinitely. Although he had been a careful and organized thief, the incident in Denver had been a sobering experience. He was surprised at the twinge of regret that passed through him as he considered retiring the Glock and canvas bag for good, savoring the switch in his identities to thief. He did get a rush from his operations around the country, and he likened the experience to other adrenaline junkies. Some guys jump off tall buildings and cliffs with parachutes, others drive racecars he thought. For one day every month or so he was a thief. It had been almost a year since he resurrected his plans to rob stores, the need for more money then fueling his intense desire to day trade in ever increasing amounts. Day trading was also a huge rush for him, thousands of dollars riding on the blip of the stock ticker. He considered himself addicted to it. Obviously he thought smiling to himself. Jesus, I hold people up at gunpoint to get cash. Just a little higher class than street junkies looking for their next fix.

The taxi slowed a bit as the traffic coalesced and he glanced into the rear view mirror at the face of the driver. The cabby turned and looked back at him, hair wriggling like a collection of black worms on his head. "Roosh hour," he said with a huge grin. "Sorry mon."

Fred nodded without saying anything, the singsong words from the driver betraying his origins in the Bahamas or Caribbean. He loved the Caribbean - the clear aqua-blue waters were paradise. It was only three months ago that he and Susan had spent a long weekend there, getting away from the drab in-between winter spring weather of Minneapolis, basking in the sunshine of the islands. For Fred though the escape had also been business. The fall months had been a huge boom in the market and he had fared incredibly well, more successful than he had originally imagined. While Susan had languished on the beach, he had used the trip to the Grand Caymans to open an offshore account, transferring almost four million dollars to the safe haven of the banks there, the start of his retirement fund. He smiled as he remembered the tiny bright yellow thong bikini he had bought for Susan in a trendy hotel boutique. This is nothing more than a couple of Band-Aids she exclaimed when he gave it to her, but the exotic atmosphere of the islands eventually won out and she soon was wearing it shamelessly. She was a beautiful woman he thought as he recalled the wisps of fabric barely concealing her trim frame. I've got to call her tonight he vowed, missing her already.

He looked at his watch, not really concerned about the time, more out of habit and returned to his self-examination. Denver had been number twelve he thought. Twelve times he had entered a store and confronted the unsuspecting office employees. Well eleven times anyway. The one botched job in Oklahoma City where the employees wouldn't let him into the office still bothered him. He had memorized them and ticked them off in his mind: Chicago, Boston, D.C., Philadelphia, St. Louis were the first five, the summer and fall months allowing him access to anywhere in the country. But he soon realized that the larger metropolitan areas, especially the east coast, made for a more complex getaway, and as more inclement weather approached he had turned to less populous and more hospitable climes. OK City, Memphis, Sacramento, Orlando, San Jose, Reno and now Denver - an even dozen he thought. He had refined the process significantly since the first couple of attempts. Rather than basing his operations in Minneapolis, the last ten had all been staged from Dallas, the busy airport providing quick access from anywhere in the country. Although he doubted he would ever need it, his cover had been meticulously established at the Adolphus. He was a known client, a successful investor coming to the city regularly for conferences and meetings with venture capital firms. He had cultured his familiarity with the hotel employees, taking the time to learn names and be generous, but not lavish, with his gratuities. His computer had completed the ruse, dialing out unattended during the day while he traveled to his targets, establishing a phone record of his apparent presence in the hotel room. He had educated the staff in the need for his privacy, day trading activities from his hotel room requiring no interruptions, and they had embraced his somewhat eccentric habits willingly. He again glanced at his watch, anxious and eager to execute the final steps of his plan.

He rode the rest of the way downtown fully confident of another successful trip. He reached into his pocket as the cab pulled to a stop in front of the main entrance to the Ren Center, pulling out a packet of bills held together by a money clip, a gold plated likeness of a hundred dollar bill that Susan had given him for Christmas. Peeling away the fare he paid the driver without comment, grabbed his garment bag and exited the cab curbside, the heat once again assaulting him.

Joining a crowd of workers at the corner, he moved cheerfully down the avenue, nodding politely as he passed others on the sidewalk, casually peering into the windows of shops lining the street. It was only two blocks until he turned left a street away from the front of the Adolphus. He entered the building through unmarked glass doors and traversed down the empty corridor for about a hundred yards. Making several corners in the light blue brick passageway he approached an unmarked set of brown doors and pushed through. The friendly smell of the Adolphus greeted his nostrils as he stepped onto the plush carpet and into a little used hallway at the back of the hotel, deep in the center of the block.

He met no one on the trip to his room. The ornate door was just as he had left it early that morning, the 'Do Not Disturb' sign hanging conspicuously from the knob. He could hear the muted sounds of the TV projecting through the door as he pulled the card-key from his wallet and activated the lock, kicking the door open wide with his foot as he strode in. He tossed the garment bag nonchalantly on the plush couch and stepped to the windows, pulled open the drapes to let the evening sunshine fill the room.

Attending to business, he sat down at the table and grabbed the mouse, the screen saver flicking off at the movement. He first checked the automated phone log, noting that all three calls he had scheduled for the day had successfully occurred. Then he stepped over towards the couch, picking up the handset of one of the room phones on the end table, smugly looking at the garment bag cushions. Another profitable day he thought to himself as he punched the speed-dial button for housekeeping. They answered on the third ring.

"Yes, this is Fred Simpson in room 1004. I'm afraid I've been in the room all day and could use some help. Would it be possible for you to send someone up to clean the room?" he asked.

Housekeeping obliged and he walked back to the table, gathered up the tray and the dishes and carried them to the door. Gingerly balancing the tray with one hand he opened the door and placed it on the floor in the hall. He started to close the door again before he remembered the sign, and reached his hand around without looking to retrieve it. Hanging it on the inside knob he started back, pulling off his shirt as he walked. Dressing silently in a clean set of workout clothes he looked around the room as he prepared for a run. He was a little tired and briefly considered skipping his daily exercise, but it was important to his cover he thought, and he needed to get out of the room for housekeeping anyway. He grabbed the garment bag by the handle and placed it in the closet against the wall, closing the glass doors behind it. He stretched again, loosening up his legs and back for the run while he considered trying to reach Susan. Later he decided sliding the keystrip into his shorts pocket and left the room.

Fred was drenched by the time he returned to the hotel, now entering conspicuously by the front doors. He nodded at one of the bellman that had often shuttled him around in one of the hotel vans.

"Evening Mark," he said, checking the nametag on the man's chest to make sure he got the name correct.

"Hi Mr. Simpson," the youth replied, quickly moving towards the doors to open them for him. "Have a good workout?"

Fred paused for the courtesy; his gray t-shirt plastered to his chest and back with sweat. "Too hot for me Mark. I'm getting too old for this shit," he replied as the door opened, his breathing still heavy.

"You look like you're in pretty good shape to me sir."

Fred turned over his shoulder as he stepped through the door. "Good plan Mark, always flatter a good tipper," he laughed.

"Yes sir, always," the youth replied with a smile.

Fred walked into the lobby area tired but feeling better after completing his run. The cool air washed over him as he made his way towards the desk. He ignored a disdainful glance from an elegantly dressed couple, and leaned up against the counter like he owned the place, watching as a plump but smartly dressed clerk checked in a fellow businessman. He nodded briefly in recognition, in no hurry as his breathing finally slowed. Drake, the head clerk emerged from the office behind the counter carrying a small clipboard in his hand.

"Hey Drake," Fred said, catching the clerks eye.

The man, about his own age and handsomely attired in a sharply tailored black suit and colorful but not flamboyant tie smiled and stepped toward him. "Good evening Mr. Simpson," he said with a customer service smile.

"Jeez Drake, how long have I been staying here. Call me Fred."

"Of course Mr. Simpson. You look a bit bushed."

Fred looked up and down over his workout clothes. "Ya well I've been cooped up in the room all day. Thought I'd better get some exercise before I turned into a vegetable. Besides," he added, "housekeeping was probably getting grumpy with me. I know they like to run a tight ship."

"Yes sir. They were concerned about being able to service the room."

Fred noted again the amazing service at the hotel. "They are on top of things. I called them before my run, and hopefully the room has been made up by now."

"I'm sure it has been attended to. If not, give me a call and I'll take care of it."

Fred smiled and started away from the counter, then turned back. "Drake, I'm checking out tomorrow, but I'll be back again in two weeks."

Immediately turning to business Drake asked, "Yes, I remember. Do you know the dates yet sir?"

"Not yet, but I'll let you know personally. If I don't see you tomorrow, thank you again for another excellent stay."

"Thank you sir. Have a good evening," Drake replied, only a faint smile at the compliment.

"You too Drake, take care," Fred said, satisfied at the final completion of his daylong masquerade.

He whistled to himself as he entered the room, happy to see the freshly made bed and tidy look. I love it when a plan comes together he thought. He quickly undressed, turned on the shower and stepped into the oversized tiled confines, letting the hot water drench over him. The water seemed to wash away any remains of the stress of the day and he realized he was very happy. Jeez I love my job he thought. I wonder what all the little people are doing today. The thought triggered a song in his head, and he whistled the tune of 'I Wonder What the King is Doing Tonight' from Camelot as he adjusted the water colder, the stinging spray totally refreshing him.

Half humming, half singing the words to the song he grabbed an oversized fluffy towel to dry himself, then wiped away the steamy dampness from the mirror, mockingly flexing his muscles and expanding his chest. At about six-one he managed to keep his weight at 180 without too much effort, but he needed the daily runs. Then the reflection wavered and he blinked, momentarily seeing a grinning apparition. He shook his head and the image cleared the sight of his naked body instead reviving memories of Susan in bed. He felt a longing in his loins as he walked out of the bathroom, toweling down his back as he stepped over towards the couch. Could I be falling for her? Conceding my bachelor life to her he thought, and realized as he wrapped the towel around his waist and sat down, that he didn't mind. The TV was still droning on in the background, but he ignored it, instead picking up the phone and dialed her number from memory. He tried to remember her Monday schedule but couldn't. The phone rang several times, each ring unanswered. He waited, hoping to talk to her, but was disappointed.

Her digital voice echoed in his ear. "You have reached 612-555-3223. Sorry I'm not here to take your call. Please leave a message and I will return your call as soon as possible."

Drat he said to himself, wanting to share his good mood.

"Susan, hey baby it's me. It's about seven here. Sorry I missed you but I'm sure you're out having fun somewhere." He paused for a second, trying not to ramble too much. "I'm gonna head out for a steak in a minute - had a good day here though. I'll be back by eight-thirty or nine. Why don't you give me a call when you get back? I'll be working online later so call me on my cell, OK? Miss you. Bye."

He hung up the phone and glanced in the mirror above the dresser. This time his reflection had completely changed. His face was unshaven and rough with a two-day-old beard. His hair was almost spiked and seemed longer. The eyes were darkened below in faint circles and pierced into him as he looked.

"Still pining over the goody two two-shoes in Minneapolis Fred?" the image asked.

Fred didn't reply, just stared back silently. He couldn't control the faint anticipation rising up in him.

"That's right Fred. Las Vegas is calling us. And you know what that means. We have so much more fun in Vegas, don't we? So much more than Susan could ever dream about providing. I really don't know what you see in her."

Fred continued to stare back without uttering a word.

A slight, yet evil smile turned up the corners of the man in the mirror's mouth. "And you know, I'm getting a little tired of this once a month shit. I think we are going to have to step up the pace a little, don't you?"

Finally Fred shook his head and the reflection changed. He rubbed his hands over his face trying to forget what he had seen, but as he turned away he couldn't ignore the excitement that still burned in him.

Dinner was uneventful, but the steak was excellent. He treated himself to a nice bottle of cabernet, a fragrant '95 Cakebread Cellars vintage that blended wonderfully with the twelve-ounce New York Strip. He overindulged in the wine, relaxing at the table well after finishing his meal to have one final glass - leaving the bottle only a third full.

As he walked back to the hotel the evening turned to fully dark. He cursed himself for a moment, realizing that he had forgotten his cell phone in the room, and hoped that Susan hadn't tried to call him yet. The remainder of the walk back he planned the rest of his night. He had some work in front of him, some reading and online research to take care of, though he noticed he wasn't exactly motivated to tackle it. Must be the big dinner he thought to himself. He also wanted to check the Denver papers for some news of the afternoon, curious to see what kind of press his little escapade had generated. He whistled to himself as he ticked off one last task. Packing and confirming his flight to Las Vegas tomorrow. Vegas he thought, was the best part of his life of crime. Tomorrow he would fly to the City of Sin and launder his freshly obtained cash at the tables. Richard the gambler persona was the one he enjoyed the most, and he limited it to once a month. He realized that day trading was also gambling, for much higher stakes. But it was so impersonal and technical, nothing like standing over a craps table, money riding, dice in hand. Being a thief was an even bigger gamble of course, but he refused to think of it that way, not wanting to even consider the consequences of losing that game. The tables were his favorite, and he relished his trips where he legitimized his haul from the grocery stores. He loved it so much he kept his urges well in check, staying away from casinos except after one of his thefts.

The suite was dark when he got there, except for the TV on across the room. He never turned off the set when he stayed in hotels, the background noise providing a certain type of companionship for him. He kicked off his shoes and settled down in front of the computer, establishing his online connection with ATT. He decided to humor himself and check the Denver news first. Guessing at the URL he keyed 'www.denverpost.com' into the address window and was immediately rewarded with a switch to the paper's web site. Ya gotta love people with intelligent web-site names he said to himself as the screen refreshed with choices. He selected a likely suspect, the 'Tomorrows News' link and clicked on it, a small window with a few headlines displayed underlined in blue. The first item in the list immediately caught his attention: "Tech Center Robbery/Crash Claims One Life," it read. His heart skipped a beat at the reference to a death, and he clicked on the link. A facsimile image of a newspaper column appeared in black and white on the screen. A sinking feeling came over him as he read:

Tech Center Robbery/Crash Claims One Life

Tragedy struck Monday in the normally docile atmosphere of the Denver Technological Center. An armed man held King Foodmart employees at gunpoint at noon Monday, robbing the back office and escaping with an as-yet-undisclosed amount of money. No store workers were harmed in the theft at the southeast Denver location on Yosemite and Belleview. However, while fleeing the scene, the suspect apparently caused a major accident on Yosemite Avenue, killing at least one woman. The crash snarled traffic in the Tech Center area for hours while Denver Police investigated the double incident.

The Denver Police have released no formal statements about the crime at this time. A press conference has been scheduled for Tuesday morning at 10 am. The suspect described as a white male, short blonde hair, about six feet and athletic build was seen leaving the scene on foot carrying two bags. Anyone with information regarding the crime should contact the Denver Police Department immediately. (Full story in Tuesday's morning edition)

Fred leaned back in his chair, stunned. He couldn't believe his actions had actually killed someone. He quickly re-read the story, hoping it would change. He recalled the spectacular wreck and wondered who the woman was. The elated feeling he had enjoyed all evening had vanished, replaced by a sobering feeling of dread. He never meant for anyone to get hurt, and his stomach ached at the thought of this nameless woman, probably someone's wife or mother being snuffed out this afternoon. His dread intensified as he realized that this was no longer any simple robbery. The Denver Police had some serious motivation to try and track him down.

His cell phone whirred on the table next to the computer and he picked it up, recognizing Susan's number displayed on the tiny screen. He took a deep breath and tried to calm himself.

"Hey Susan," he said, inserting a little cheer into his voice.

"Oh God, Fred," was all she managed to get out.

Quickly forgetting the story he said, "Susan, what's wrong? What happened?" He heard nothing but sobs and he tried again. "Susan?"

"Oh God Fred, I wish you were here..." she said, voice trembling. "It's mom, my mother."

"What about your mother Susan?" he said.

"I just got off the phone with Marsh," she struggled to say. "Mom's been killed in a car accident."

Fred's stomach felt like a dagger was twisting in it. Marsh, her brother in Denver. "Oh Jesus Susan, what happened?" he said, incredulous, the coincidence too much to believe, implications washing over him.

"I don't know. It was an accident. Marsh couldn't tell me anything. What am I going to do?"

He sat helpless with the phone in his hand, unable to reply. Could it really have been Susan's mother? Finally, he said, "I wish I was there with you honey..." It sounded cold and insincere.

"I'm flying to Denver tomorrow... can you come?" she pleaded.

He thought of his schedule, torn between wanting to see her and the bag full of cash in the closet. The decision turned him cold inside. "I've got to go to Vegas tomorrow, but I can be there on Wednesday," was all he could say.

She seemed soothed. "I'll call you tomorrow when I get to Marsh's, OK?" she said.

"OK babe. I'll be waiting," he added.

"Fred?" she asked.

"Yes hon?"

"I love you…"

Fred was overwhelmed at the first utterance of the words from her.

"I love you too," he found himself saying.

Chapter Seven

The sun was intense on his back, the heavy starched collar of his crisp white shirt digging into his skin as if it was two sizes to small. His hand reached to the back of his neck as he walked and tried to relieve the pressure, but he was unable to insert his fingers beneath the material. He moved faster over the grass now, sweat dripping down his back, breath ragged as he trudged. He could see the road just ahead and tried once more to pick up the pace.

The grass turned softer below him, the weight of his body pushed his feet into the ground and covered the bottom of his loafers every time he stepped. He looked off to the left. The road had only one wide lane with blood red stripes on either side of the black pavement. The stripes stretched away from him, leading like ruby lasers towards the line of smoke belching trucks he could see approaching. He picked his knees up higher with each step, but his feet now seemed to be sticking into the ground. He tried to count the huge trucks as he pushed forward, but the sun glinted off their mirrored sides, blinding his eyes like silver darts every time he focused on one. He could hear and feel the deep rumbling of the monstrous vehicles as they drew closer.

He was breathing heavily now, and his chest heaved underneath his shirt, the starch coating his skin like sticky paste. He thought he heard something, a voice maybe, and looked off to the right. A single white car was approaching in the distance. His stomach twisted as the car came into focus. He recognized his mother's white Lexus and tried to break into a run, but the ground now covered the tops of his shoes every time he stepped. A long blast from an air-horn yanked his attention away and he looked again to his left. They were coming faster now, the column of trucks stretching off into the distance, trucks as far as he could see.

He waved his arms as he plowed forward. "Mom!" he yelled, the effort stinging his raw throat. "MOM STOP!" he screamed again. The Lexus was getting closer, coming faster as he redoubled his efforts to reach the road. The driver's side window was open and he could see the silhouette of his mother, wind blowing her hair back as she drove. He didn't need to look back at the trucks; he could feel the sound of them reverberating through every bone in his body.

"MOM!" he screamed again. He had almost reached the road, but each time he stepped the ground covered his feet up to his ankles. The effort to pull each foot free was immense and the muscles in his thighs and calves burned with each step. He could see her clearly now. She was smiling; beautiful features distinct as she turned towards him.

"Hi Marsh!" she yelled at him over sound of the wind blowing through the car window. "Just going to lunch dear," she said, her hand waving.

"No Mom, DON'T," he managed to get out. He was just a few yards from the edge of the road, but his legs had sunk in deeper, the ground sucking at his feet.

The trucks were almost on top of them, the howling of their engines raising goosebumps on his spine. He struggled one last time with his legs, but they were now trapped in the ground and he fell forward, catching himself on his hands as he looked up.

The trucks and the Lexus were almost on top of each other, racing forward. The roaring was immense, drowning out all other sounds. The Lexus passed close and he looked as his mother, still waving, looking at him rather than ahead towards the massive column speeding towards her.

"Mom..." he gasped under his breath.

She smiled at him again. He couldn't hear the words over the din but could clearly read her lips. "I love you Marsh," she said, her face radiant.

Marsh sat suddenly up in bed and felt the tears streaming down his face. "I love you too Mom," he said to himself, the dream still vivid. He sat there for a moment in the dark and let the grief spill out, sobbing a little while he tried to calm his breathing.

He looked over towards the clock. The pale green digital display showed 5:27 and he decided to get up. He stepped out of the silk boxers he used for pajamas, dressed silently in his workout clothes and grabbed his Nikes without putting them on.

His condominium was way too large for a bachelor, but a real-estate agent, whom he happened to be bedding at the time, convinced him that it was a good investment. She hadn't been wrong on that point, the price of the condo steadily rising long after she had disappeared from his life. He had three bedrooms and two and a half baths. The bedroom at the end of the hall he converted into an office, and it was there that his company had been incubated. It also contained a treadmill and a large-screen TV, seldom watched, not wanting to clutter up his living room with the distracting device.

Reaching the office, he sat on the edge of the small couch in the room and sighed as he struggled to pull his shoes on. He wasn't feeling that motivated to run, but sticking to his routine would be good for him he thought. He stepped onto the black running surface and leaned down to stretch his thigh and calf muscles. A half-full water bottle was set in a holder on the side of the control panel and he pulled it out, wetting his mouth before starting. He also grabbed the remote and clicked on the TV, changing the channel from CNN to a local station.

He was about ten minutes into his run and beginning to loosen up when the broadcast caught his attention. He hit the pause button on the treadmill's panel and leaned against it as the course black ribbon slowly ground to a halt beneath his feet. He watched intently as the local news team, a younger black man and a middle-aged white woman filled the screen. He clicked the control again and turned up the volume.

"And there are no additional details on the robbery accident yesterday in the Tech Center," the man in a dark suit reported. He turned on the segue to the woman sitting next to him.

"That's right John. The Denver Police are still not releasing information on either the robbery at the King Foodmart store in southeast Denver, or the tragic accident that occurred immediately following the crime." Her face betrayed no trace of emotion. "As we reported yesterday, there is an apparent link between the armed theft at the store and the accident that occurred on Yosemite Avenue, reportedly claiming the life of at least one Denver woman."

Marsh was shocked as he stood there, not able to believe that the story had anything to do with his mother's death.

The camera switched back to the man. "Channel 4 News will be on the scene at police headquarters at ten am this morning when a news conference is scheduled. We will have full details following the session. In other news this morning…"

Stunned Marsh ignored the rest of the broadcast. If this was Mom why wasn't he informed about any of this? The police had told him that there was an accident, but he had neglected getting any more details after leaving the hospital. And what did a robbery have to do with anything anyway? His shock was replaced by anger as he stepped off the treadmill.

Suddenly the phone rang, interrupting his thoughts. He glanced at the old-fashioned clock sitting on top of one of the bookcases and wondered who it could be. He walked over to the desk and sat down in the large leather gray rocking chair and lifted the phone. "Hello?" he said.

"Marsh, it's me," Susan said. "I couldn't sleep Marsh. I just lay in bed tossing and turning all night, crying."

"Me too Suse. When are you coming?"

"I almost took a six am flight, but I need to clear up a few things at work first. Most of the flights are full, but I did get on United that gets me to Denver at three. Can you pick me up?"

"Of course I will," he said, scrambling in the drawer for a pen and piece of paper. "What's your flight?"

She hesitated for a second, obviously looking for her own notes. "It's United 223, arriving at 3:07."

"I'll be waiting in the terminal where the trains come in."

"Marsh?" she asked, then paused.

"Yes Suse?"

"Do you... know anything more?"

He hesitated for a moment, not wanting to jump to any conclusions and certainly not wanting to talk about it over the phone. "No," he said and hoped he wasn't lying. "But I will know more when I pick you up, OK?"

"All right. I'll see you this afternoon."

"I'll be there, bye," he said and hung up the phone.

Marsh leaned back in the chair and wondered what to do next as his thoughts returned to the accident. Was it really Mom that was on the news? Why hadn't anyone contacted him? A slow flame of anger began to ignite inside him. He pushed up from the chair, his T-shirt sticking to the back of the cushion as he rose. Deciding to scrap the rest of his workout, he walked back into the kitchen looking for some coffee. He was at a loss. Who do I contact about this? Maybe call the police department directly? Another thought occurred to him and he began to formulate a plan of action.

Steven Race, the lawyer who been counsel for the company should be able to help. Steve had been a buddy at CU and they had known each other for years. He would need to contact Steve anyway, to handle the affairs of Mom's estate, and the attorney would know what to do. He looked at the time displayed on the microwave. Jesus, it's only six, too early to call anyone he thought. He started the coffee and walked back into the living room, opened the doors to the balcony and stepped out. The mountains in the distance were purple and gray, not yet fully illuminated by the sun rising behind his building to the east. The balcony again triggered thoughts of his mother, and this time he relished them, the pain not quite so deep, replaced by more of a longing and a sense of loss. It was a beautiful morning and Mom would have loved being here.

He left the doors open and returned inside, allowing the freshness to seep into the room. A shower could wait for a minute he thought, feeling comfortable in his shorts and now wide-awake. He dialed Sheila's number from memory, cringing as the phone rang, ready with an apology for the early intrusion.

"Hello?"

"Hey there. I didn't wake you did I?"

"Marsh?" Sheila said, obviously a little groggy. "Are you OK?"

"Well, I didn't sleep too well," he said, the nightmare flashing by quickly, "but life goes on and I need to get to work."

"Marsh I told you we don't want to see you there. You have enough to worry about," she scolded.

"I know, I know," he said, "but my car is there, remember? I thought I would stop in, talk to everyone for a moment and clean up my desk a little. Can you pick me up?"

"Sure, OK, but that's it, then we are kicking you out. I can be at your place by a little after seven. I'll call you from the car when I'm almost there and meet you downstairs."

"Great, and thanks Sheila," he said, hoping the appreciation showed through in his voice.

Marsh set down the phone and headed towards the kitchen for some coffee. He needed to deal with the legal issues and the funeral arrangements he thought, but procrastinated a little. He decided to call his lawyer, knowing he would get voice mail at this time of the morning. As expected he got a recording, surprised that it was a direct line to Steve. Gathering his thoughts, Marsh said calmly, "Steve, this is Marsh." Then, bluntly, he continued. "My mother was killed in an accident yesterday and we need to initiate whatever actions are required to settle the estate. It's early Tuesday morning and I wanted to get to you as soon as possible." He paused for a second, starting to choke up a little. "Uh, I'll be, uh… running around today so try and get me on my cell phone."

He thought about the newscast he decided to confide in his friend, not really knowing how to phrase it. "Also Steve, I don't know if you have seen the news reports this morning. Something about a robbery and accident at the Tech Center yesterday. The police haven't given me any details on the... accident... yet, and I'm a little concerned. The news story said a woman was involved and I'm worried that that it might have been Mom, but I don't know anything." He was rambling now but forced the rest out. "I don't understand what is going on here but I'm not very happy about it. Can you tell me what to do? What my recourse is in this? Anyway, call me as soon as you can. Thanks."

He set the phone back down as the feeling of anger re-ignited in his chest. God damn it, he thought, why hadn't anyone told me anything? He sat there for a moment, wanting to know more, hating the helpless feeling the lack of information cast over him.

Will arrived at his desk before six and spent the next hour making notes on a yellow legal pad about the robbery and accident. He summarized everything he knew about both incidents, chronologically, attaching the names of witnesses with each key point along the way. He stretched a little in his chair and flexed his fingers. He wanted every known fact at his fingertips when he presented the details at the conference that morning.

He hadn't slept well, his mind consumed with reviewing everything he had learned so far, examining it over and over again, looking for that little detail or scrap of information he might have missed. Twice in the middle of the night he had pulled himself out of bed and made notes for today, reminders of items he could not forget to do. The first was to contact the deceased's son and get his approval for releasing his mother's name during the briefing. The second was to make sure he got an accurate dollar count of the take from the store. The first task he was not looking forward to. Talking to loved ones about a loss of a family member was unpleasant at best. In this case, when they were sure to be a topic of conversation in a press conference he knew he would meet with hostility.

He didn't have much information to present, and the reporters, hungry for any kind of story would probably be as interested as much in who he was as they were in the incident. He had chosen a charcoal-gray suit, double breasted and white shirt. He didn't want to look like an undertaker, but did concede toward his fashion sense and had chosen a colorful, but not flamboyant blue, gray and red tie. He briefly wondered if the event was still big enough news to land him some airtime on any of the local broadcasts.

It was almost seven he thought and wondered if it was too early to contact the son. He turned to the computer and brought up the information the department had access to about the Hawkins' family, telling himself he wasn't really stalling as he scanned the screen for details. Of course there wasn't much there, just standard public domain biographical data, mostly obtained from the Colorado DMV. He thought about tapping into a few of the other databases he could use as a member of the police force: the IRS, Colorado Department of Revenue, and credit bureaus, but decided the intrusion was unwarranted and bordered on an invasion of privacy.

Reluctantly, he picked up the phone and dialed the number of Marsh Hawkins still displayed on his screen. He waited as the phone rang, wondering how the conversation would go.

"Hello?" a man's voice said after three rings.

"May I speak with Marshall Hawkins please?" he said, starting with a neutral tone.

"Speaking."

Steadying himself, he said as professionally as he could, "Mr. Hawkins, this is Detective Will Carter at the Denver Police Department." Then without hesitation he said firmly, "I'm sorry to intrude this early in the morning, but I wanted to speak with you in regard to the accident involving your mother yesterday."

There was a pause at the other end of the phone and Will briefly wondered about the man he was talking to. What would his reaction be?

"Tell me detective, has my mother's death been the subject of the news stories that are filling the airwaves this morning?"

Will sensed the animosity in Marsh's voice and immediately decided to tread carefully. "Yes sir, I'm afraid it was. You see sir…"

Marsh interrupted him immediately, and in a harsh voice continued, "And am I supposed to believe that this is normal police procedure in circumstances like this? When citizens wake up in the morning and have to speculate whether or not a loved one is the subject of sensationalist TV news stories, and I presume the newspapers as well?"

"No sir, it is not normal police procedure," Will said. "But…"

"I see detective," Marsh said sharply. "And what is normal police procedure in situations like this?"

Will gathered his thoughts, completely sympathetic towards the man and not surprised by the hostility he was showing. "Mr. Hawkins, please let me try and clarify the situation. But first, on behalf of the Denver Police Department, I would like to express my sympathy on your mother's passing." Hearing no response he continued. "The accident was handled by the Police Department in accordance with standard traffic incident procedures. It was only when a link was discovered between the robbery and the accident that the news media assumed a more intensive reporting stance, which is of course totally out of our control. Both the robbery and the accident investigation are under my personal supervision, and, it was I who released the information to the news media last night. By no means was this done with any intention of causing you and your family any additional grief. Your mother's identity is known only to myself and to the officers who investigated the accident yesterday. My disclosure of the information last night was done, in essence, to protect you from wild speculation and unfounded reporting of the incident by the press."

Will paused for a moment, letting the information sink in, and hoped for a response that would dictate his next statements.

"And when were you planning on informing my family about our involvement in this media circus?" Marsh inquired.

"Sir, I did not contact you yesterday because to be honest we didn't have many facts in our possession until later last night. At the time I did not want to intrude on your bereavement at such a late hour and so soon after the accident. It was a judgement call on my part and I sincerely apologize if I acted incorrectly."

"I see Detective," Marsh said, his voice still angry. "And what are the next steps here? I heard on the news something about a press conference this morning. Am I supposed to wait until the noon news to find out anything more?"

"Absolutely not Mr. Hawkins," Will said, finally sensing an opening. "What I would like is for you to meet with me this morning, before the conference, so I can completely share all the information we have regarding the incident yesterday. You have my assurance sir, that other than my direct superiors you will be the first person to be informed of all the facts at our immediate disposal."

"That's very nice Detective, but not very comforting. Then what happens?"

"If you are satisfied, I would like to get your consent on releasing what we have to the media. It is the only way to keep rumors and speculation under control."

"And if I refuse to consent?"

"Then I will only comment on information that relates directly to the robbery and the accident, but not reveal your mother's identity. I would point out, however, that the press can and will find out about your mother. I assure you that being up front with the details is by far the safest road to travel."

Will hesitated a moment, allowing Marsh to consider the situation, then decided to take a risk and a firm approach. "Let me explain something Mr. Hawkins. The matter of your mother's unfortunate death will be public record in accordance with Colorado motoring laws. I do not have to reveal anything at the briefing, but that will only forestall the inevitable. What I am offering you, and I am under no legal obligation to do so, is the chance for you, as a private citizen and a victim in this matter, to learn all the details first. I am sympathetic and I would like to have the opportunity to share what we know with you, in hopes that any further exposure relating to you and your family will be minimized."

Will waited and hoped that his offer would be accepted. He really did have some feelings for the man's situation, and would need his cooperation once the investigation began.

"All right Detective Carter," Marsh finally responded. "You have my attention although I'm not at all pleased with the circumstances. When and where would you like to meet?"

Encouraged, Will responded immediately. "If you could meet me in my office at nine it would be very helpful. I have a lot of preparation for the press conference and I want to give it my full attention. Is that possible for you?"

"I don't see why not. And you are located where?" Marsh asked, the irritation still obvious in his tone.

"At the Southeast Precinct. Just go to the main reception area and ask for me, Will Carter and I will make sure you are expected. And thank you Mr. Hawkins for your cooperation in this matter. As I said before, you have my deepest sympathy."

"I'll see you at nine."

Will hung up the phone, relieved that the conversation was over and it had gone as well as it did. He was a little surprised at himself though, and wondered why he had offered to take the man so fully into his confidence. It was a sympathy reaction he thought, but something else was bothering him. He had good instincts and trusted them implicitly, but there was more to this situation than was immediately apparent. Deciding that he had made the right decision, he ignored the nagging feeling and returned to his preparations. He had about an hour and a half before Mr. Hawkins would arrive.

Marsh sat back in his chair and tried to make sense out of what had just happened. The detective seemed to be sincere, but he was confused by the complexity of the situation. Why all the fuss? Why hadn't he just simply been informed of the details over the phone? He obviously didn't have a lot of experience in situations like this, but the detective was right on one point - he was being given special consideration for some reason. Confused and still angry he was now more determined than ever to get to all the details of the story.

He found himself pacing the living room like a caged animal; his mind wandering so fast he wasn't really concentrating on anything, hating the waiting. Finally, the phone rang and he practically ran across the room to pick it up. The connection was less than clear. It sounded like the caller was standing in a rushing shower near a construction zone.

"Marsh, I'm almost there." It was Sheila and he could barely understand her.

"I'm coming down Sheila," he practically shouted into the phone, then slammed it down and hoped she had heard him over the static.

The trip down to the street took only a moment, but it seemed like hours. He pushed his way out of the glass doors, breathing a little faster than normal as he scanned the street for the Porsche. He spotted the little car stopped at a light up the block, stepped over to the curb and willed the light blocking its way to change. A few seconds later the Porsche slid to a stop in front of him and he grabbed the handle, yanked the door open and jumped into the car. "Good morning Sheila," he said in a voice distant, still wrought with uncertainty as he shut the door tightly. "Thanks for coming."

She looked at him, face full of questions, not attempting to drive the car away. "Hello Marsh..." she said, but didn't continue.

He returned her gaze for moment, but said nothing. Finally, the silence overpowering, she turned her head toward the outside rear-view mirror, checked for cars and accelerated away from the curb, sliding the Porsche into a hole in the traffic. They drove in silence for a while as Sheila concentrated on navigating the car through the stoplights and out of downtown. Marsh just looked ahead through the windshield. He remained silent until they were well into the commute.

"Sheila?" Marsh said finally and turned toward her, feeling the need to clear the air between them.

She turned her head, the corners of her mouth pushing up a fraction, her brown eyes still somber. "I understand Marsh. It's OK if you don't want to talk."

She shifted her attention back to the road as a column of brake lights lit up in front of them, the Porsche braking rather abruptly. "Oops, maybe I should concentrate on driving anyway," she said and smiled.

Marsh let a short laugh escape him. "Thanks for fetching me," he said, watching her nod in acknowledgement as she continued to focus on the road. Then suddenly needing to placate his curiosity he added, "Did you see the paper this morning?"

"I glanced at the front page, but I was somewhat rushed," she said, still concentrating forward. Then, she turned quickly towards him, a look of sudden realization sweeping over her face. "Oh my God, Marsh… was that… I didn't…"

"I'm afraid so. I actually haven't seen the papers yet either, but it was all over the news."

"Jesus Marsh, I don't know what to say," she said, torn between looking at him and keeping her eyes on the road.

"I don't know what to make of it all Sheila, it's still sinking in," he said. Then, after a pause he continued, "I talked with a detective at the Denver Police this morning. I got a vague explanation, but it's all so mysterious. I'm supposed to meet with him at nine this morning."

Neither said anything for a moment, the traffic thinning enough for Sheila to accelerate close to the speed limit. He found himself not wanting to talk about it further, but for Sheila's benefit he said, "Can we wait until we get to work? I'd like to talk to everyone at once."

"Of course," she replied as a new look of concern settled over her face.

They rode in silence the rest of the way to the office. As they pulled into a parking spot she reached out and touched his arm gently, looking at his face for some indication of his thoughts. He smiled for a moment, at the gesture, but said nothing.

The office was already busy despite the still early hour. Marsh could see a few employees down the hall towards the cubicles in the larger open space towards the back. They seemed to stop in their tracks as his presence was discovered, one of the younger female programmers waving toward him, then bringing her hand down quickly, her embarrassment at the gesture obvious. Mary looked at them over the short wall of her cubicle outside his office as they approached. She also looked uncomfortable, but the confident personality that had made Marsh a natural leader took over.

"Good morning Mary," he said and smiled warmly at her.

She hesitated for a moment, her eyes moving back and forth from Marsh to Sheila, then rose from behind her desk and ran over to him, wrapping her arms around him.

Marsh squeezed her silently for a moment and then pushed her back a little, saddened at the sight of a single tear building in her mascara. "Mary," he said softly, "please let everyone who's here know I want to have a brief meeting in the main conference room in about ten minutes, OK?"

She wiped the moisture from her eye and straightened her skirt. "All right Marsh," she said, moving back towards her desk.

Marsh, a little overcome by the emotion his friends displayed quickly stepped in the direction of his corner office, wishing to avoid any other contact for a moment. He walked inside and closed the door behind him slowly. He crossed past the glass conference table to his oak desk, the soft leather chair rocking a bit as he sat down. The weight of all his responsibilities seemed to push him down into the chair and he succumbed to it for a moment, leaning back and rubbing his hands up over his face and into his short hair. His stomach knotted as he tried to sort out his priorities, conscious of the time constraints imposed by his need to get to the meeting at the police station. The message waiting light on his phone was blinking but he ignored it, moving instead to his computer and logging on. He brought up his email and was immediately overwhelmed at the number of messages waiting for his attention. He scanned the subject list and counted at least twenty sympathy notes, many of them from his staff. Mary and Sheila must have sent out a note to the employees he surmised, and he was grateful for their thoroughness. I must send out a note myself he thought, realizing that just handling the emails would take hours. Deciding to deal with it later, maybe from home, he instead pulled his briefcase from the side of his desk and opened it, then removed his personal organizer. He flipped through the pages until he located the entry for the call he was already dreading. He found it under the 'G's - Green Hills Funeral home, Charles Stevens - Director. Wishing he could do anything else at this moment he picked up the phone and dialed the number.

It took about fifteen minutes to complete the arrangements, the memory of his loss renewed, but also relieved at the completion of the task. He logged off the computer, vowing again to respond to emails from home, stood up, and stared out the large windows over the office park outside. He took a deep breath, crossed back through the office and headed for the conference room.

The room was filled when he stepped through the door and it surprised him for a moment, the chair at the head of the conference table empty and waiting. The murmured conversations abruptly ceased as he walked to the other side of the room. There were about twenty of his employees crowding into the space, some in jeans, others more business casual. He walked around to the back of his chair and stood behind it, deciding to address the group on foot. He looked out over the group with a sense of pride before he started. "Jeez who's watching the phones?" he said lightly, rewarded by a couple of uneasy smiles passing over the faces.

Putting on the casual but professional air he continued. "I just want to say a few words this morning. First, let me express my thanks to all of you for your thoughts. I haven't responded to emails yet but I will as soon as I can." He leaned down on the chair for a minute, trying to make the group as comfortable as possible. "As you know, my mother was killed in an accident yesterday. It's going to be a difficult few days for me and I would like to ask all of you for your help and cooperation. I expect to see business as usual during this period, beside, I'm not really sure what I do around here anyway." He waited, relieved to hear a chuckle or two from some of the younger people. Joe and Sheila however were silent.

"There is unfortunately an added complication to the matter. For those of you who actually read the newspaper or watch the news you may have seen a story regarding an... incident... at the King Foodmart yesterday." Many of the group snapped to attention, a few others looked confused. He continued, trying to keep the explanation as simple as possible. "There was a robbery and subsequent accident at the store, and yes, it was my mother that was involved. It hasn't been announced to the public yet, and frankly I don't have many of the details myself. There is a press conference this morning that I will be attending where the police are going to hopefully explain everything. I will share the results with you as soon as I can. In the meantime, I need you to help out. There is a good chance the press will be calling here, looking for angles to the story. It is imperative that no one answer any questions regarding my family or our company."

He waited until the murmurs and whispered exclamations died out. "If you do get a call, or someone approaches you, please use your best judgement on how to deflect any questions. If nothing else just hang up. Better yet transfer the call to Sheila," he said and looked down at her. She nodded back at him, accepting the responsibility without question. "If anyone can deal with the sharks she can."

He smiled a little and stood up straight, relieved at being able to get through the meeting without breaking up. "OK, that's about it. Please, the best thing you can do for all of us is to keep at your jobs. I want to say how proud I am of all of you - at how your hard work has made us a successful organization. Please keep up it up."

He noticed that everyone was a little unsure of what to do next and decided to add a little more closure to the meeting. "If anyone feels the need to talk to me personally, that's OK too, but not today. I'll let you know when my schedule returns to normal. Sheila, Mary and Joe can you stay for a moment?"

Joe stood up and took the lead. Turning to the group he said, "OK everyone back to work." He looked at Marsh and nodded as the people slowly began to file out of the conference room, the muted conversations starting as they exited. "Lunch today Marsh?"

Marsh thought for a moment. He couldn't ignore all his responsibilities and could use his friend's support. "Sure, but I don't know when. I'll call you after the press conference."

"I'll keep the calendar open," he said, then added, "I'm so sorry Marsh."

The room cleared, leaving the four of them alone.

"OK everyone, this is the program. I don't want any of this to impact business. I know you are all concerned and sympathetic, but now is when I need you to be as attentive to the company's needs as possible. I've got my cell phone so don't hesitate to call. Mary, Susan is flying in today from Minneapolis. It's a United flight and I don't have the number handy, but it gets in just after three. I'm picking her up but check on it for me and let me know if there are any delays. Sheila, Joe, I know my schedule has been cleared, but if a client needs attention I want to know about it."

He looked at all of them individually, grateful to see their acceptance of his marching orders, hoping that he was maintaining control of the situation. "I'm leaving now for the press conference. Back to work everyone."

They rose and began to file out, Joe and Mary already deep in conversation. Sheila hesitated for a moment, then walked over and hugged him. He was startled at the sudden gesture and hugged her back, her perfume sweet and somewhat alluring. Surprised at his sudden urge to kiss her he let go quickly, blaming the thought on his heightened emotions. She looked up in his face and stared deep in his eyes, and he knew she wouldn't refuse the advance.

"I'll be OK," he said.

Chapter Eight

Sara was at the station early, digging through newspapers and reviewing videotapes of the morning broadcasts. She had been disappointed at the press release the detective had issued - just after they had talked she concluded. But he had not released everything she thought smugly; he had given her more. KDEN had been the only station to actually report on the number, sex and condition of the accident victims. It was a small concession of course, but their story was the most comprehensive and she was proud of that. She recalled the promise by Carter to meet with her privately after the briefing and hoped that she was still the only one he confided in personally.

She rose from her desk and walked over to the break room, taking her cold coffee cup with her. She adjusted her knee-length gray skirt as she moved conscious as usual about her appearance. She had dressed carefully that morning, selecting a conservative suit, light blue blouse and pulling her long hair back into a tight knot. The blonde tail made her look younger, but the tradeoff was more of a voluptuous look and she didn't need that image this morning. She nodded at one of the newsroom writers who was also refilling a cup and waited for him to move away. Why a press conference she thought. The news was somewhat of a sensation, but it would quickly fade to obscurity with the next breaking story. It must be important to the police to get the facts straight she mused, her gut feelings again sensing an investigative opportunity.

Her legs ached a bit as she walked back towards her desk; the muscles still a little fatigued from her 6:15 a.m. aerobics class. On the upside of her thirties, her health and good looks were something she cherished and was determined not to let either slide even a bit. Sitting on the edge of her desk she silently reviewed her plan for the conference. There was only one question she really needed to have resolved, what was so important about this case? Of course maybe I'm blowing this all out of proportion she thought. Maybe there really is nothing earth-shaking to this story. But she hoped not. The last year had been spent investigating routine stories and she longed to find something she could really sink her teeth into, something that demanded her full capabilities and talents. A story she could prove herself with.

She sat back in her chair, turned her attention to her computer and decided to do some probing. Starting with the robbery, she instructed the search engine to bring up the details on the King Foodmart corporation. A list of topics appeared in a window on the screen and she quickly browsed through the subjects. It was mostly standard business stuff - quarterly reports, new store construction, a Wyoming food store chain acquisition, a labor dispute story - nothing that caught her attention as being relevant. She refined the search to include the keyword 'crime' and submitted it. The list was shortened to just a few items almost immediately and she felt a glimmer of hope. The first, however, turned out to be a piece by a newspaper on shoplifting in Colorado, with only a passing reference to grocery stores and the King Foodmart chain. The others of course were multiple references to yesterday's incident, one for each of the Denver papers, and they only contained links back to the stories she had already read. She marveled briefly at the power of the search engine which gave her access to thousands of news media events from all over the world, feeling a bit frustrated by her rudimental knowledge of how to put it to good use.

She sighed and again changed the request, this time to grocery stores and crime. The request took a moment to process and she tapped the pen on the desk as she waited. Finally a window appeared on the screen, indicating that 22,354 items had been found. 'Did she want to narrow the search parameters?' the message prompted, and she again cursed her lack of skill with the tool. She got up and paced behind her desk, impatient for the conference to begin. She hated the down time her job often dealt her, a feeling that she should be doing more foremost in her mind. She briefly considered calling Detective Carter again, but dismissed that thought also, knowing he would tell her nothing more before the conference. It did give her an idea though. She sat back down, ignoring the feeling of prying as she instructed the computer to find out everything it could about one Detective Will Carter of the Denver Police Department.

While the computers at KDEN where working behind his back, Will sat at his desk, confident that he was fully prepared for his presentation. It was a little before nine and he was waiting for Marshall Hawkins to arrive. He had second thoughts about the meeting and wondered if it was a good idea to share everything with the man. He pondered the dilemma a little, weighing the pros and cons. The only downside he thought was having the man intimately involved in the details of the investigation. Would he want to be continually apprised of the status of the case and scream bloody murder if no progress was shown? The last thing he needed right now was a loose cannon citizen who would cause waves, especially with the press. On the other hand, the robbery aside, the department was treating the woman's death as a homicide, and that meant getting results. If there was one thing the department, the Captain and the Mayor in particular hated it was open homicide cases. He knew the pressure would be on to solve the case, even if it was immediately attributable to an accident. Crime statistics mattered and the legacy of Jon Benet lived on. He would need Mr. Hawkins to be on his side he decided, and hoped he was a reasonable man.

The phone buzzed, breaking his concentration, and he quickly picked up the receiver. "Carter," he said. Then after a pause, "Right. Please have someone escort Mr. Hawkins back."

He stood up, absently straightened his tie and decided not to put on his suit jacket. He was still trying to conjure up a mental picture of the man when an officer appeared at the door, Mr. Hawkins in tow. Carter looked him over quickly and tried to gage him from outward appearance. He was about his own age, casually dressed in light brown slacks and blue dress shirt. He held himself with an air of self-assurance and Will was momentarily relieved. At least it's not some street bum he thought. He moved from behind his desk and walked towards him, hand extended.

"Mr. Hawkins, I'm Detective Will Carter. Thank you for coming."

They stood quietly for a moment, appraising each other. Finally, Will broke the silence. "Please sit down," Will said, and motioned to a chair. "Can I get you some coffee? Something to drink?"

"No, thank you I'm fine," Marsh replied, face set in stone as he sat in the chair.

Will sat down at the same time, then leaned forward over the desk, a look of sincerity on his face. "I want to again express my condolences about your mother. And I realize that this is probably not a very pleasant experience for you."

"That's quite an understatement Detective," Marsh said, his own face betraying a trace of anger.

Taking the rebuke in stride, Will continued, trying to remain positive.

"Please, call me Will. I would like this to be as informal as possible. May I call you Marshall?"

"Marsh is fine," he replied, his arms crossed defensively in front of his chest as he sat back in the chair.

Will used the next ten minutes to recount the details of the robbery and crash fully, using the situation to practice his presentation for the news conference. He left out nothing, continually watching Marsh's face for any significant reaction. He was comfortable with the facts so far and had no trouble with his summary, never once referring to the notes he had meticulously prepared earlier. He noted that Marsh was quiet the entire time, but seemed to concentrate on each word. When he had finished, he leaned back in his chair and waited for a response, unable to read the man's reaction.

"That's a nice story detective, but why are you telling me all this?" Marsh said, anger beginning to seep from behind his calm mask.

Will struggled to maintain control of the conversation. "As I told you Marsh, I wanted you to know the complete details of what happened."

"And now that I am informed, what is it I am supposed to do?"

"Well first, I wanted to get your permission to release your mother's name at the conference."

"I really don't see what difference that makes at this point Detective. It's going to come out sooner or later anyway," Marsh snapped.

Will's patience began to wear with the tension of the situation. "Then I have your consent?" he asked, his own harshness oozing into his words despite his best intentions.

"Sure, why not? Make my mother part of your little media circus."

Will glared at the man. "That's not fair Mr. Hawkins, I'm not the bad guy here. If anything I'm trying to help you."

"I'm a little confused at your definition of help. My mother is dead, and the subject of newspaper articles and TV news. How is this helping?"

Will took a deep breath and sat back, trying to contain his own emotions. "Believe me, I understand your frustration. But a crime has been committed here and it's my job to find out who did it."

Marsh interrupted, "And my mother was killed in an accident. I'm not a stupid man detective, what is it you are not telling me?"

Surprised at Marsh's perceptiveness, Will decided to lay all the cards on the table. "Marsh," he said slowly, "I don't believe you are a stupid man. In fact I'm hoping you are intelligent enough to comprehend the situation. Unfortunately because of the robbery, your mother was killed in an accident - an accident that is directly attributable to the commission of a crime. In the eyes of the law this links both incidents directly together. In short, the man who robbed the store is not only a thief, but a murderer."

Will watched as Marsh seemed to sink into the chair, proud and defiant shoulders now slumping a little. "So you see Marsh, I have a bit of a dilemma on my hands. To be honest, the point of the press conference is to make all the details of yesterday perfectly clear to the media. The fact that your mother's death is technically a homicide does not need to be played all over the news. In fact, it's the complete opposite that the department wants. We would like nothing more than to have this incident quickly fade from the public eye, allowing us to conduct our investigation without scrutiny from every reporter who would glamorize the story. That, we believe, is in your best interest and ours, and why I asked you to come here today."

"Uh, could I get that glass of water now detective?" Marsh said.

"Of course Marsh," Will said, leaving the man to ponder the situation, sensing the change in his attitude. By the time he returned with a paper cup of tepid water Marsh still hadn't moved.

"Are you all right Marsh?"

"I'm sorry Det... Will. I'm afraid I don't know what to say."

Will looked at him, all previous hostility replaced with a feeling of sympathy. "I'm sorry I was so blunt Marsh. I guess I could have been a bit more delicate."

"No, I'm the one who is sorry," Marsh said. He suddenly looked genuinely embarrassed. "I understand now. How can I help?"

"You already have, by coming here and listening to me. I honestly am trying to make this as easy as possible for everyone involved."

"Let me get this straight Will. You are going to tell all to the press, try to diffuse the media attention by disclosing everything, hoping that they will be placated into dismissing the story as yesterday's news. Is that right?"

"That's the plan Marsh."

"And in doing so, you think that you will have a much easier chance of continuing with your investigation, free of scrutiny by the media. By downplaying, or covering up the homicide aspects, it will be treated as just another robbery."

Will winced at the remark. "I don't think cover-up is a fair choice of words Marsh. We aren't covering anything up. When we do catch the thief, we will also have apprehended the murderer, so to speak. I just don't see the need to treat this as a homicide and attract any more attention than is necessary. There is absolutely no upside to doing that."

Marsh appeared to consider it for a moment. "I'm not disagreeing with you Will, and I'm really grateful that you have been honest with me here. I have no desire to tarnish the memory of my mother by treating this as anything but an accident. You have my cooperation in that matter and I will do anything I can to help. But you haven't told me everything have you?"

Will was taken back by the insight of the man, and struggled momentarily with how much to reveal. He found himself liking Marsh and hoped he could trust him.

"No Marsh, I haven't. I will tell you that I used you to practice my presentation, to see how you would react. I was hoping that you would accept everything that I have said, and would be content to hear any new developments as they came along. It's the way I want the press to react."

"I understand that. And so far it looks like you have done an excellent job. But there's something else isn't there?"

Will sighed, a sinking feeling washing over him. "Everything I have related is honest and complete - except for one small detail at the end of the story."

Marsh looked at him puzzled, but a knot was beginning to form at the bottom of his stomach. "What's that?"

"The bellman and the taxi driver. They provided us with a very good description of the man, and we will soon have a composite sketch we can use for identification purposes..." he said, trailing off.

"Then what's the problem?"

"The destination. I didn't say anything about where the thief was dropped off."

Marsh just looked at him, waiting.

"It was the airport. DIA," Will said, his enthusiasm at the success of the conversation deflated.

"So he's gone."

Will leaned forward again, looking Marsh directly in the eyes. "From all indications, this was a well organized and professionally done theft. The accident seems to be nothing more than a last minute slip-up. Totally unplanned."

"And your chances of tracking down and apprehending the man?"
"Unless we get some sort of lucky break? Slim to none."

Sara had arrived early at the conference room, partially because she couldn't wait any longer, partially because she hated to walk alone into a room mostly full of men. She self-consciously pulled her suit coat around her chest, deciding to sit about three rows back from the front.

The conference room was large, and looked like it could seat about a hundred people. There was ample space along either side for camera setup, and she could see two of the network crews setting up for a full-coverage film session. They were local and she wasn't surprised, this wasn't a big enough story to warrant coverage by the national networks. She craned her neck around and looked for her own cameraman, hoping he wouldn't be late. She hadn't felt the need for a lot of footage and told Howard a shoulder mount video unit would be sufficient for a few seconds of airtime, if the story warranted it.

She turned back and studied the setup. At the front of the room was a single podium with microphone, oak she thought, and a six-foot white board set behind it and to the right. There was a diagram already drawn on it and she recognized the outline of the King Foodmart store, the alley and the Yosemite Avenue running down the side. There was a red 'X' placed in what she assumed was the office location in the store, a line running across the board through the alley, and another larger red 'X' in the street.

Looking around again she watched the participants file into the room. It was not going to be much of a crowd today she thought the usual number of journalists obligingly covering the story. She wondered again at her instinct about this being a real story. She waved politely at a few of the reporters she recognized, and then a lone man sitting almost in the back caught her attention. Dressed in slacks and collared shirt he looked out of place among the suits and the jean-clad technicians. She found herself staring at him, wondering who he was when he looked back at her, their eyes locking briefly. He was handsome, but looked tired, almost as if he didn't want to be there. He nodded almost imperceptibly at her before turning away.

"Sara?" The voice startled her. She turned and looked at her video man whom she hadn't noticed cross the room.

"Oh, Kerry hi. I'm glad you made it," she said looking up at him, scraggly beard and wild long hair as unkempt as ever.

He was lugging a video unit by the top handle in one hand, the lighting unit connected by a black curly cable in the other. "I live for this stuff," he said. "Where do you want me?"

Not able to tell if he was being facetious or not she motioned to the side of the room opposite the rival network operations. "Set up over there, about even with the first row. Concentrate mostly on the speaker's face. If he has any presence at all I want to be able to use it on the air. Also make sure you get full coverage if he goes to the board. Shots like that at least have a little action to them."

"You got it babe," he said, grinning as he started off.

She winced at the comment but let it slide for a moment. "Kerry," she said, getting his attention back. "Make sure you get a few shots of the other camera crews. If this turns out to be a big story we can use it to look like we had major coverage here."

He smiled at the ruse appreciatively and started away again.

She let him take a few steps before calling out to him. "And Kerry," she said, then flashed her most radiant smile. "Don't call me babe." She turned away from him, cutting off any further interaction.

Sara picked out Detective Carter as he entered the room through a side door with two uniformed officers and another suit she didn't recognize. He had a presence to him, a confident manner that showed he was in charge despite his rather young age. She watched attentively as he walked across the front of the room, oblivious to the murmuring crowd in front of him. Then, she didn't know why, she turned back and looked at the man sitting well back from the rest of the occupants. He was leaning forward, elbows on his knees, face in his hands.

"Good morning everyone. Thank you for coming," Will said without hesitation. "I'm Detective Will Carter of the Denver Police Department. I hope that I can keep this briefing short. I'm sure you all have bigger stories to cover."

There was a polite chatter of laughter from the audience and Sara was impressed at how quickly he seemed to engage their attention.

For the next fifteen minutes she paid close attention, watching the speaker's body language and presentation. She took no notes, listening closely for any discrepancies in the story.

Finally, the crisp presentation complete, Will stepped back from the

DECEPTION ON MARGIN

microphone and scanned the audience for a response. "That's our full summary at this point, and now if you have any questions…" he added, and it seemed like he wanted badly to get off the stage.

Sara watched as a hand shot up from a younger man with a notepad in the front row. The detective simply pointed at him.

"Detective Carter, can you tell us how much money was taken from the store?"

"Due to insurance restrictions, the King Foodmart corporation is not releasing the exact amount. It was somewhat less than a hundred thousand dollars."

"And how much was recovered?" the man asked quickly.

"About forty dollars in tens," Will said, ignoring a few snickers from the audience. "It is also being tested for fingerprints."

A middle aged black woman in a cream colored suit stood up immediately. Sara recognized her as an on-camera reporter from a rival station. The reporter nodded briefly at her camera crew, then focused on Carter. Sara was somewhat disgusted at the obvious grandstand play for the cameras.

"Cathy Wells, KCDL TV. Can you please tell us if you have a positive identification of the suspect or, if not, where the suspect was dropped off by the cab?"

Sara was a not bit surprised at the question. She looked back at Carter, who for the first time seemed a bit uncomfortable.

"At this point we do not have a positive ID. As for the location I'm afraid I can't answer that question in order to preserve the integrity of the investigation. Once again thank you for your attendance at this briefing." He left the podium quickly and headed for the door at the side of the room.

Sara sat for a moment, trying to make sense of his response to the last question. She wasn't quite sure why he hadn't answered it, but once again the little alarm bells went off in her head. The camera lights were flicking off as she walked over towards Kerry who was packing up his camera at the side of the room. "Did you get everything OK?" she said.

"Piece of cake. I'm not so sure if this is major story material though."

Wondering herself she said, "Me neither. Thanks for your help Kerry. I'll see you at the station later to go over the footage."

"You got it babe," he said again, grinning mischievously.

She was tempted to rap him one, but was distracted by the mysterious man from the back of the room passing by.

"Excuse me," he said, squeezing close to her, avoiding the camera on the floor.

She looked at his face. "No problem," she said twisting away, then watched as he left through the same door as the detective. "I gotta run Kerry."

"Later," Kerry said to her back.

She moved off toward the door hoping to catch Detective Carter for her promised meeting. As she left the room and entered the hallway she spotted Carter and the other man deep in conversation by the water fountain a few yards away. Never one to be shy she walked up and addressed them both.

"Excuse me for interrupting Detective Carter. I'm Sara McGloughin from KDEN TV. You promised me some time this morning?" She stood there firmly, holding her ground. The two men looked at each other, then Will turned and responded politely. "Of course Ms. McGloughin, I thought I recognized you at the briefing."

She was confused; she hadn't met the man before. "You did? How?"

"You weren't taking notes or recording the meeting. You seemed to be the only one paying attention," he said with a touch of humor in his voice. "I assumed it was you."

"Oh."

Will faced his companion as if looking for approval. A look of silent consent passed between them.

"Ms. McGloughin, this is Marshal Hawkins."

She reached her hand out slowly, offering it to Marsh. "Hello, nice to... um, I'm sorry for your loss Mr. Hawkins. I assume you are related..." She stuttered a bit, uncharacteristically at a loss for words, cursing herself for not being better prepared.

"Thank you Ms. McGloughin, nice to meet you," he said, gently shaking her hand.

There was an uncomfortable silence for a moment before Marsh spoke again. "Will, I'll call you later all right? I have some business to attend to."

"Thanks again Marsh, I'll be in touch."

Sara was surprised at the familiarity between the two and wondered how they knew each other. Marsh nodded politely at her and walked away. She cursed herself again for letting him leave before discovering

DECEPTION ON MARGIN

more.

"OK Ms. McGloughin, you have my attention. Is there something I didn't cover in the briefing?"

"Please, it's Sara," she said, regaining her professional demeanor. "I was wondering Detective, why the press conference? Why is this event getting so much public attention?"

He seemed to ready himself for the response. "Actually Sara, it's not the department that wanted the publicity. But since the story was prominently featured on the news and in the papers, in fairness to the victims we felt it necessary to make sure all the facts in the case were known. We did not want to have any unwarranted speculation of the incident."

The answer seemed a little to well rehearsed and she probed a little further. "Tell me Detective, why did you evade the last question regarding the taxi?"

He smiled at her, all traces of his earlier discomfort erased from his face. "I wouldn't exactly say I evaded the question. It was my decision not to release the location in order for us to examine all possibilities regarding the whereabouts of the suspect without outside interference."

She interpreted the reference to press involvement immediately, then took a shot in the dark. "May I assume then that you have somewhat, er, lost the trail at that point?"

He didn't hesitate. "You may assume anything you like Ms. McGloughin, but rest assured we are diligently following up leads."

She examined his face carefully, searching for any information in his expression. Seeing nothing there she switched topics. "And your friend Mr. Hawkins?"

"Mr. Hawkins is the son of the deceased. I felt we owed him an explanation of the cause of his mother's death. It was his decision to sit through the press conference."

"I see," she said, mentally making a note to try and contact the man. She extended her hand, and he shook it firmly. "Thank you for your time Detective, and I appreciate your candor both last night and today."

"My pleasure Sara. Please feel free to call me anytime. As you can see we are trying to be as cooperative as we can with the press," he said, hesitating for a moment, then walked away.

Sara just stood there, watching him leave. She was impressed by the man. Very capable. But there was something more to find out. Hopefully

I'm not clutching at straws and trying to build a story where there isn't one she thought. She decided to return to the station to complete her report, then, maybe, try and contact Mr. Hawkins to hear his side of the story.

Chapter Nine

Fred didn't sleep well, and that surprised him. He was normally a very early riser, his automatic clock kicking in around 4:30. That morning, however, he was up by 3:30, after a restless half-hearted attempt at sleep. Even the soft droning of the air-conditioner had bothered him and he had shut it off despite the heat outside.

Two thoughts had kept him awake, and the death of Margaret Hawkins had been at the root of both. Once the shock of learning that the accident had killed somebody - Susan's mother for Christ's sake - had sunk in he couldn't stop examining his career as a thief. He was coldly detached from the turn of events, reviewing the implications from a probability standpoint. He had inadvertently raised the bar on the diligence with which law enforcement agencies might be pursuing him. Up until now his thefts in a dozen cities were isolated events, and he had been comfortable with his assumption that the investigations would soon wither and die, the lack of any hard information leading nowhere. Denver, however, had changed all that. The most recent robbery had caused a front-page splash and it would keep people's attention for a while. Of course he was still sure that he would never be traced to the crime, but he had never really thought about the time when he would retire, putting away the John Anderson personae for good. The money aside, he liked being a thief.

The second thought that troubled him even more was the end of the conversation with Susan, the part where she had said I love you and he had responded in kind. Her voice and his had repeated over and over in his mind, and he couldn't come to grips with his feelings. Did he really love her? It wasn't that he did or did not, he was unsure if he really understood what it meant or if he was capable of it. Could he actually just be Fred, only Fred, day trader, successful businessman? Could he continue to open up and share his life with another person? A woman?

Arrrgh, he thought to himself, shaking the remainder of his interrupted sleep from his head as he slid out of bed, walked over to the TV and flipped it on. He turned away from it before it focused the background noise of a cooking infomercial on CNBC filling the suite. He debated going for another run, thinking the physical exertion would help clear his thoughts, but at 3:30 in the morning he decided he didn't really need to be jogging the streets in downtown Dallas. Besides, he had work to do that morning.

His mood changed as soon as he pulled the black garment bag from the closet, opened it and spread it across the couch. He loved this little duty, once again surprised that the events of the night before had caused him to postpone it. He slowly unzipped each of the little pockets, removed the bills and carried them in stacks over to the table where his laptop sat. The bundles felt almost heavy in his hand, and twice he stopped to flip through them, watching the portraits flash past. Once he even smelled a bundle, the scent of hard cash most distinctive. There were fifty one-hundred dollar bills in his hand he thought, five thousand dollars, and he marveled at how it affected him. He traded ten times that amount without blinking an eye, but that money was not tangible like this. Real money he thought, could be spent, flaunted, and gambled with. He liked the feel of real money in his hand, and the upcoming trip to Vegas popped into his thoughts, a flash of anticipation spreading over him.

It took him about ten minutes to count and rebundle the money. The exact take was $94, 445. A nice haul he thought to himself - a little above average for his appointments. Ninety thousand of the dollars he carefully repacked into the garment bag. The other four grand plus he dropped into the desk drawer, some spending money and his stake for the craps tables, and other pleasures.

Feeling even better he sat down at his computer to start the day, beginning with an update to his career totals. He maintained a simple spreadsheet, not meant for anything except a personal reminder of his exploits. His eyes quickly flicked over the numbers, the zeros across the row designating Oklahoma City standing out. He debated about deleting the reminder of the failed attempt, but as usual decided not to. Inserting a row just above the bottom he typed in 'Denver' and '94445'. The sheet dutifully recalculated his totals, his take to date over a million dollars.

Taking the time to revel in the figures, he tried to calculate how much money the million dollars had become. He didn't track the growth of the monthly robbery proceeds, though he often thought he should. The last year in the stock market had been explosive in profits, at least for him, and his uncanny ability as a day trader had rewarded him with huge gains.

Besides the four and a half million in the Caymans, he had a million in his active trading account and another three million in various money market funds.

Almost eight million dollars, in a year. When was enough, enough? Uncharacteristically he had not set a timeframe for his exploits. He was just getting good at what he did and had hardly considered retirement. But he had the money now to do whatever he wanted, keep active at day trading, even buy a company and run it. He scrunched his bare feet into the plush carpet and leaned back in his chair. Could he really be happy just as Fred he wondered again. He would have to consider it carefully he thought, then pushed the dilemma away. Time to make some money he thought to himself.

It was almost four am, and the segment 'Today's Business' was starting on CNBC. He turned the TV on the small swivel base, squeaking as it moved, so he could see it from the table where his laptop was. Yawning a little he returned to his computer and brought up his email. He had about forty messages to plow through, most of them computer generated from the search engines he had constantly querying the financial world, keyed specifically to news related to technology and biotech corporations. It took more than an hour to digest the information. He never took notes, relying instead on his memory for general details, carefully saving each mail by indexed topics if he needed to retrieve specific information. There were announcements of two IPO's, a rare event these days, but neither of the two companies interested him and he filed away the mails. Four companies were announcing earnings, two of which he had traded in before. For each of those he brought up analysts summaries of the companies. He had subscription access to the major firms on Wall Street, Goldman, DLJ, Credit Suisse and others. It wasn't cheap, but the cost was insignificant to the amount of money he traded. He looked over the whisper numbers for both companies - the earnings and profits the analysts were forecasting prior to the actual release of the numbers by the corporations themselves. Nothing there roused his investment interest, and he filed those as well.

He got up from the chair and paced a little, thoughts about Susan resurfacing. I should call her he thought as he crossed past the disheveled bed and pulled the curtains open. The city was dead outside his window, the sky a pinkish color as the sun, still below the horizon, threatened to rise. He opened the window and leaned out into the morning air. It was quiet, save for a few background noises that filtered out of a city no matter what the hour. The temperature outside was about the same as inside his suite so he left the window open and picked up the phone next to the bed. He continued to stare out the window as he sat down and ordered breakfast.

For the next half-hour he studied the market performances from yesterday. It had been a lackluster day on Wall Street he determined the DOW down a little, the NASDAQ up about 10 points. The week before had seen about a 100 point total rise in the NASDAQ composite but the momentum had not carried over the weekend. He mostly ignored the DOW components, viewing the old and venerable measure a slow-moving dinosaur compared to the technology laden NASDAQ index. That was where the action was, the up and down price volatility the key to his profession.

There was a knock at the door, and he quickly pulled a t-shirt over his shorts. A fiftyish man in black pants, white shirt and some sort of flowered vest had his breakfast tray perched on his hand up over his shoulder. Fred stepped aside as the man entered the room and deposited the tray on the table, well away from the computer. He followed him, took the check from the tray and signed it, leaving a substantial tip. Maybe I should have given him a stock tip he mused. Or even better the location of a good grocery store. His good humor and mood pleased him, Susan and the tragedy unfolding in Denver the farthest thing from his mind.

He sat back down and attacked his breakfast, finished it quickly and poured a cup of hot coffee. He listened to the stream of reports from the TV and tried to get a feel for which way the market would be moving. He was a momentum player, buying into rising market, selling into dropping ones. Like any good day trader he didn't care about the stocks he bought and sold. All he was concerned with was price fluctuations, his buying power allowing him to establish positions of thousands of shares, then quickly turn them over for an instant profit. By six he had a general strategy in mind. There was no real positive news to be found nothing to give either index a big lift. It would be a down day he surmised, probably slowly at first, then gaining in speed as jittery managers pulled money out of the market. He never traded in the last hour of the day. Too many unpredictable computerized programs dominated that activity.

He finished another cup of coffee and gathered the remains of his breakfast, leaving the coffee on the table and carried the tray out the door. There was no complimentary copy of <u>USA Today</u> in the hall and he smiled. The Adolphus was definitely not a Holiday Inn.

He walked back into the bathroom and turned on the shower, letting the steam rise in the bathroom as he brushed his teeth. He looked at his reflection in the mirror, his stubble of a beard portraying a rougher image. It wavered again, suddenly becoming much more unkempt.

"Time to go good buddy," the man in the mirror said.

Fred just stared for a moment.

"Come on, come on. You can trade any old day. You know there must be an earlier flight."

Fred shook his head and the vision cleared. He skipped shaving, pulled off his shorts and t-shirt and stepped into the hot shower. It refreshed him, the apparition from moments ago lost as he reviewed the coming day. He had about four hours to trade before his flight to Sin City, the anticipation once again surging over him.

By six he settled down to watch CNBC intently, still attired in just his shorts after the shower, now on his third cup of coffee. He was getting anxious for the day to begin, and listened to the broadcast without moving from his chair. At seven, market trading began through Instinet and he focused his attention on the ticker parading across the bottom of the screen. He knew the symbols of most of the stocks shown, and the general price range of the stocks. It was still an hour and a half before the major markets opened, but the pre-market activity would help to confirm or deny his intuition.

His cell phone rang, and he picked it up. The display showed Susan's home number as the caller and he realized he had again totally pushed all concerns of her from his mind. He pressed the talk button and brought the phone to his ear.

"Susan?" he said softly.

"Fred, hi..." she said.

"How are you babe? Are you doing OK?" he asked, and hoped the concern would be credible.

"I've had better nights - not much sleep. I wish you were here," she said with a touch of sadness.

"I wish I was too. I miss you. What are your plans?"

"I'm flying to Denver at noon. Marsh is picking me up. Are you coming?" she asked, almost pleading.

"I have a flight in tomorrow, from Vegas. I should be there in the afternoon."

"Can't you come today? I really could use the company."

A pang of guilt shot through him as he realized he didn't want to skip the trip to Vegas. It didn't take much for him to lie though. "I really can't, Susan, I have some business to clean up that I can't skip." She was silent for a moment and he offered, "Besides, you should spend some time with Marsh alone. You two should be together without me tonight."

"Maybe you're right. It might be good for us."

He felt relieved and continued, pouncing on the reprieve. "Yes it would, but I'll be there tomorrow all right? We can spend all the time together you want."

She hesitated, "Fred, it's about last night. What I said."

He wondered what she would say and felt even guiltier. "What is it?"

"I think I meant it Fred," she said.

He was getting in deeper he thought, but covered. "I think I meant it too."

"I can't wait to see you, please hurry," she pleaded again.

"I'm so sorry about everything babe. I'm sorry it had to be like this."

"I know. Me too."

He didn't know what to say next. "I'll call you tonight, before dinner. Will you have your cell phone?"

"Yes, of course. I'll be waiting."

"Later, then. Have a good trip," he said, and the words sounded foolish considering the situation.

"I will," she said, almost automatic in the response. "I love you," she added.

He hesitated again, then added, "I love you too, bye."

He set down the phone and leaned back in his chair, and coldly analyzed his feelings. It had been so easy to talk to her, to drop into the loving Fred mode. Christ, you just killed her mother and it doesn't seem to bother you a bit. He got up, walked back to the open window and looked out at the city. Rush hour was in full force and he listened to the sounds of the traffic. So many people out there, people that knew nothing about him. He closed the window on his thoughts and returned to his computer.

By nine-thirty he was up over six grand. His guess had been right about the market direction, the NASDAQ slowly dropping on slow news. He had shorted two major telco companies at the opening, to the tune of three thousand shares each. Both stocks were languishing, mired in the mess of their impending merger. He had watched telecommunications stocks flounder all morning, a stock ticker covering just that sector of the market continuously displaying prices on his screen.

Shorting was the practice of selling stocks before you owned them, essentially borrowing the shares from the brokerage firm. On down days like today it was how he made money, watching as the price slowly dropped, waiting for the right price to buy them back, repaying the investment firms and keeping the profits between the buying and selling price - despite the fact it was done in the wrong order. One of the telcos had dropped almost a point and a half when he issued the buy order, netting over four thousand dollars. Fifteen minutes later the other one had lost a point and he bought that back too. Another three grand in his pocket.

It seemed too easy he thought, six grand was a quarter years wages for millions of the people in the country, and he had made that in about ninety minutes. Of course it helped to have a million dollars to play with, allowing him the luxury of buying huge blocks of a stock, even minor fluctuations in the price gaining or losing hundreds and thousands of dollars. He wasn't always right though, but he took the wins with the losses without emotion - calculated risks that for him proved more successful than most.

He was debating about calling it a day, nothing much else attracting his attention when one of his bots popped an alert on the screen. His online trading software designed specifically for day traders had features called software robots, or bots for short, which the user customized to seek out information that was freely available over the net. These little programs ran unattended inside his computer, analyzed data that he had instructed them to watch, and automatically sent him messages when pre-defined situations occurred. This one informed him of a significant drop in the price of a recent hardware IPO, Handheld Accessories. He was familiar with the stock, it was a spin-off of a larger computer maker who wanted to separate its traditional PC line from the more volatile mobile computer market. It debuted on the street last week, marginally successful, as most stocks even remotely associated with the internet were these days. The stock had risen from 24 to about 30 on opening day, speculators running the price up to a level that didn't surprise him but still defied logic. He quickly brought up a five-day chart on the stock and reviewed the activity since the IPO. It had held the price through the end of the week, mostly because gains in the NASDAQ through Friday kept all stocks up, the buyers significantly outnumbering the sellers. But yesterday it had started to slide, losing about two points. Today it was already down almost six points; the bot picking up on the twenty- percent drop in value.

He quickly accessed the analyst's comments on the stock, only two of which carried any coverage. It was new he surmised, and even though the parent company was well tracked, the other firms had yet to issue any opinion. Both analysts had issued strong buy recommendations for the spin-off, probably because they had underwritten the IPO and had large positions in it. Curious, he opened a window and instructed his software to track the trades as they happened. He leaned forward and watched the ticker display the activity.

22 5/8 (2), 22 1/2 (2), 22 5/8, 22 3/8 (5), 22 3/8...

The numbers in parenthesis indicated trades in thousands of shares and he was intrigued. The big blocks were mostly at a lower price than the previous trade so people were indeed bailing. Even at this level the big players, the brokerage firms and the fund managers had already made a bundle and they could sell without a conscience, able to brag about their market prowess. It was the little guys who were getting hurt. It was these uninformed folks who had bought the stock when it was eight points higher, at the end of IPO day, and well after the big players had already divided up most of the pie.

Already ahead for the day, he decided he couldn't pass up the opportunity. He opened a trade window and issued a short sell at 23 for twenty thousand shares. It was executed almost immediately, his offer out a little higher than the market price. He calculated quickly and decided that his downside risk should be about fifteen thousand, about double the money he had already made. If he was wrong, he'd hold until it went back up through 25 and only lose about ten grand on the day.

He stood up, nothing to do but wait and keep an eye on the ticker. He was excited now and rush of adrenaline filled him, conversations earlier in the day once again banished from his thoughts. For fifteen minutes he watched as the price hovered around 23. He wondered if he had jumped in too late, and whether to get out with only a few thousand dollar loss. The TV caught his attention as the reporter stood in front of the NASDAQ board, showing the top volume leaders. The usual suspects were there, Microsoft, CISCO, Intel, all showing modest losses. Handheld got a special mention though, the announcer commenting on the large percentage loss. He looked back at the ticker, relieved to see the prices edge lower again. That had gotten someone's attention he mused. The selling blocks were getting larger and suddenly he was ahead again. On a whim he issued another offer to sell for ten thousand shares, this time at 22. This order took a moment to fill, a good sign showing there were fewer people willing to buy at that price. He was in at an average of about 22 5/8, his short position valued at well over six hundred grand. The price flattened out again as he watched, and then somebody unloaded twenty thousand shares at 22. Bingo he said to himself, knowing that would trigger the rest of the players to continue to sell. He issued a bid to buy thirty thousand shares at 21 7/8 and fired it off. All he had to do now is wait.

He walked over to the closet, selected a tan pair of Dockers and started to get dressed, humming 'We're in the Money'. He was confident now, his instincts sure he was right again. He dressed quickly, but kept an eye on the computer screen. While putting on his belt, the trade window updated. He walked back to confirm what he already knew had happened. He bought thirty thousand shares at 21 7/8, reaping a profit of over twenty thousand dollars. That made his total for the day about twenty-six grand. He wondered briefly how far it would drop, how much money he could have made. Never have second thoughts he said to himself; it had been a good trade.

Time to head out he thought. Another twinge of excitement began to build in his belly as he shut down the computer and meticulously packed his belongings, CNBC still talking to him in the background. He folded the moneybag up and set it by the door. He next gathered up his dirty laundry, workout clothes, socks and underwear and stuffed them into a laundry bag from the closet. He squeezed these into his other garment bag with half of his shirts, pants and suits. Into a smaller suitcase he folded the rest of his wardrobe and placed the Glock between several layers of pants. He set both items by the door and turned to his computer. It took about five minutes to shut down the laptop, gather up the speakers and pack everything into his oversize computer briefcase. Peeling off four hundred plus from the wad of cash in the drawer, he placed the other four thousand in a back pocket of the top half of the case. He looked around the suite carefully, examining the room for any forgotten items. Satisfied he left the room, door open and waited for the bellman.

There was a short line for checkout and Fred waited patiently, looking around the lobby. Fresh flowers had been set out again, and he reveled in the luxury of the setting. I should bring Susan here he thought; she would love this place. He took a step forward as two elderly women, one with a small mink around her neck stepped away from the counter. He was surprised at the gentle thought that crept into his mind, and he again wondered about his motives. He noticed, however, that a bellman was hovering next to him, and he shifted back to reality, glanced at the gold tag and addressed the man by name.

"Thomas, I can watch the bags. Why don't you store the small black one there for me. I won't be back for a while so put it in a safe place, OK?"

The bellman nodded, reached down and easily retrieved the nearly empty luggage and started off to the back. The Glock should be safe here he thought, no need to transport it all over the country. Besides he wouldn't be using it for a while.

It was his turn, and he stepped up to the marble counter and leaned on it. "Hi Sally, Fred Simpson, 1004 checking out," he said.

She busied herself at the computer for a moment, the printer to the side starting to spit out his bill.

"Was everything excellent during your stay Mr. Simpson?" she asked politely.

"Yes, quite nice, as usual."

She slid the bill across the counter to him and he picked it up. Not really concerned about the totals, he did check to make sure his phone calls from yesterday had been accurately logged on the receipt. Satisfied he folded it up and handed it back to her.

Thomas had returned from his task and stood attentively, but respectfully to the side. Fred nodded at him, picked up the credit card bill and signed it with a flourish. She picked it up, tore off his copy and stapled it to his statement.

"Thank you for staying at the Adolphus sir," she said, customer service oozing, and handed him the bill.

DECEPTION ON MARGIN

"Thank you for having me Sally," he said, wondering if she would catch the implication. He was in a good mood now, and turned back to the bellman.

"Come Thomas, let us be away. My limo awaits," he said, and briskly walked towards the glass doors. Thomas retrieved the rest of the luggage and followed him outside, the late morning air already stifling. The limo was parked a little to the side and he stepped over to it, nodding at the driver leaning against the side of the door smoking a cigarette. The chauffeur leaned into the car and popped the trunk. Thomas quickly stepped over and loaded his three bags carefully into the cavernous trunk.

"Your claim check sir," Thomas said, hand extended with a small peach colored ticket between his fingers.

Fred pulled the wad of bills from his pocket and stripped off a ten-spot. "Thank you my good man," he said, taking the check as he handed the bellman the tip. "Take care now."

"Thank you sir," Thomas said, and he rushed over to open the back door.

Fred slid in, the smell of the leather seats over powering the blandness of the air conditioner. It was cool inside, and he settled back and relaxed.

"To the airport, and don't spare the horses," he said to the driver.

"Airline sir?"

"United," Fred answered, the excitement building in him. As the car accelerated from the hotel he pulled his wallet from his pocket and slipped the claim check in. He grinned as he took out a plastic card with his picture and examined it; a New York driver's license issued in the name of Richard Williams. Nice photo he thought.

Chapter Ten

Marsh set his nearly empty glass of Killian's Red Ale next to the off-white plate that contained a few unfinished bites of a hamburger, green pickle spear untouched. The luncheon conversation with Sheila and Joe had been hesitant from the beginning. Marsh had not offered any details, the others hadn't asked. That had changed with his sudden revelation, and his two friends now stared at him, incredulous.

"Mom was murdered," he had said out of the blue. He wasn't quite sure why he phrased it that way, but the anger at the situation still burned inside. Sheila was about to go to the restroom but instead sat down abruptly. Joe practically dropped his beer. A waiter in dark slacks and an open necked tuxedo shirt appeared at the table to bus the dishes, but Marsh chased him away with a glance. It was past the end of the lunch hour and the tables around them were no longer occupied.

"What?" Sheila managed to say.

He turned for a moment and gazed out the window of the eatery at the small park set in the middle of a half circle of three and four story office buildings. A flock of geese lifted from the water that surrounded a gushing fountain and circled away, their honking unheard through the windows.

"The accident," he said, as if pausing for effect, "should never have happened."

"You mean it was planned?" Joe said, glass still in the air.

"No, it's not that. It's just that the accident was caused by the man who robbed the grocery store... while he was escaping."

"So?" asked Sheila. "What does that mean?"

"Maybe I'd better start at the beginning."

"Please do," Sheila said firmly, almost indignant that she had been left out of the know.

"I don't need to go into the details of the robbery, that's beside the point. What is relevant is that the thief, while escaping from the store apparently panicked. He ran out into the street in front of a truck. The truck swerved to avoid him and..."

Marsh stopped as the memories flooded back. His friends got the picture without needing him to finish the scenario. Sheila reached over and placed a hand on his arm.

"No, it's OK Sheila, I have to get through this. I've got to tell Suse anyway. Mom was driving down here, probably to meet some friends for lunch. She did that often, but I guess we'll never know." He paused for a moment, choked up at the last thought. "The truck crossed the median and rammed right into her."

"Oh my God," Sheila said. She had her hand on his arm and squeezed it slightly. Joe didn't say anything but watched Marsh's face closely.

"It was a bad accident. There was not much anyone could do... for Mom that is. Apparently there was a tremendous amount of confusion. The guy, the thief that is, just walked away."

"So the truck didn't hit him," Joe said, more of a statement than a question.

"No, he ran off into the park that's close by. He was in a disguise I guess, and somewhere along the way he changed clothes, took off a wig and mustache. The police traced him to the Hyatt where he just got into a cab."

"So where did the cab take him?" Sheila asked.

"That's the problem. He went to DIA."

Joe jumped in. "To the airport? Did he get on a plane?"

"Nobody knows. The police assume he did. Why else would he go there?"

There was a moment of silence as they both assimilated the information. Joe was the first to respond. "Marsh, they don't really know anything about this guy do they? Who he is? Where he went?"

"The police detective was brutally honest on that point. He said the robbery was professionally done. The accident just happened. Mom was at the wrong place at the wrong time. Unless they get some kind of a break they don't have a lot of hope of catching him."

"But Marsh," Sheila interrupted, "you said Margaret was murdered. It still sounds like an accident to me."

"Well according to the detective, the accident was a direct result of the crime. It was part of it. He said that makes what happened technically a homicide." He stopped for a second and looked at them both, eyes pleading. "It's so stupid, senseless. Some guy robs a grocery store and Mom is dead. I couldn't believe it when I was sitting there, in the police station. It was like I was watching a TV show or something. All the cops around and this detective just rattled off the details. He talked about guns and money and disguises and getaways and..." He stopped, choked up and turned away from them both, the napkin he clenched pulled up to his face. "How am I going to tell Suse?" he said to the window.

The waiter approached the table again, this time a bit more timidly. Marsh nodded to him, grateful for the interruption to the conversation. They were all silent while the young man, oblivious to the situation efficiently cleared the table.

"Can I get you folks anything else?" the waiter asked.

"Just the check please," Sheila responded quickly, hoping to chase him away, relieved when he left.

Finally, Marsh said, "I'm sorry... I don't mean to burden you with all this."

Both Joe and Sheila started to talk at the same time. Sheila won. "Don't be ridiculous Marsh, you are not burdening us with anything. We want to help." Then she added softly, "We all were close to Margaret, she was part of our family too."

"What can we do Marsh?" Joe asked.

Marsh calmed himself, grateful for their support. He was lucky he thought to have such good friends. "There is not much to do but wait. The press conference this morning was just a show by the police department. They wanted to downplay the homicide aspects of the case. As you know there was a lot of media attention yesterday and this morning, and they didn't want a lot of speculation in the case. That's why the detective talked to me personally. The bottom line is they don't want anyone to know there is not much chance of solving the crime or catching the guy."

Joe picked up the implications immediately. "Oh, I get it, another unsolved murder. Bad publicity." Marsh seemed to jump at the word murder and Joe was instantly sorry at his blunt assessment. "I'm sorry Marsh. I didn't mean it that way."

Marsh recovered quickly. "It's OK Joe, I know what you mean. When I was at the police station I had the same thoughts. I was angry and I practically accused the man of a cover-up. I was wrong though, what they did this morning is really in our best interests. The detective was a good man; I rather liked the guy. We don't need to have this in the news every day. I would much rather treat it like an accident myself. I don't know what else to do."

The waiter returned with a small folder, the check inside and placed it in front of Marsh. Sheila quickly grabbed it away.

"I'll take this if you don't mind," she said harshly. The waiter was startled and moved away quickly. She turned to Marsh and said, "It never fails. Just because I have bigger breasts, everyone assumes that I can't pay for a god damned meal."

Joe's mouth dropped open and he looked at Marsh, not knowing what to expect.

Marsh stared at her for a second, and then laughed. "Shit Sheila," he said, the tension in his stomach lifting. Joe, relieved, started to chuckle as well and shook his head at her.

"Well it's true," she said with a mock indignant look. "You know how embarrassing it is to be wining and dining a big client, and he ends up with the check?"

"It must be horrible. A damn tragedy," Joe added.

Marsh laughed so hard he had tears in his eyes, not able to tell if they were from laughing or from his pent up grief. He didn't care though, it was the first time he had smiled since yesterday. "Thanks Sheila, I needed that."

She flashed a smile at them both, twinkles in her eyes. "Just don't get any ideas. Now if you will both excuse me I am long overdue for the trip to the ladies room." She pushed back from the table and walked away. "And no talking about me behind my back," she declared over her shoulder.

Marsh reached to finish the last of his beer, then, deciding it was too warm picked up a glass of water instead. Joe looked at him, hoping to keep the mood upbeat. "You wanna go get drunk? Scope out some babes?"

"Thanks Joe, I think I'll pass this time. I've got to pick up Suse at the airport this afternoon." He glanced at his watch and checked the time, his mood sobering a little as he wondered how he would talk to her. "We should talk business for a while anyway."

They waited in silence until Sheila returned. "Well?" she asked.

"Well we didn't exactly talk about you Sheila," Marsh started, then nodded across the table. "But Joe here did suggest we blow off the rest of the day and go bar hopping, maybe pick up some chicks."

"I see. And of course I'm not invited," she said, sitting back down primly.

Marsh laughed again. "Well no…"

"Don't know if you would exactly fit in," Joe added.

"Come on guys. Get a grip. I could be bait. Help lure the unsuspecting ladies in. You know, the subtle approach."

"OK, OK, enough. I've got to get to the airport and we should discuss some things," Marsh said, trying to get his friends under control, but again grateful for their honest compassion. "It's going to be a tough couple of days. Anything big on our plate that we need to deal with?"

Sheila spoke first. "Not anything Joe and I can't deal with. We have been getting a lot of calls though, as the word gets out. I can't imagine what your email looks like."

"I know, I'll probably try and deal with that tonight from home."

"I think the employees are a little unsettled Marsh," Joe said. "You know they all look up to you so much. Their fearless leader so to speak. My project meeting this morning was less than focused."

"How was my little speech this morning? Did it hurt or help?"

"I thought it was good," Sheila added.

Joe continued, "You know most of the folks are pretty young. I think it took them all by surprise."

"Mmm… I suppose so. Well, I guess we will just have to deal with that as best we can. I'm not disappearing you know. I'm meeting with the funeral director tomorrow morning. I'm going to request that the services be early Friday afternoon. Do you see any problems there?"

"Of course not Marsh, whatever you decide is best," Sheila said.

"If I may make a suggestion?" Joe said.

"Sure, what?"

"I think that at least a few of them will want to attend the funeral, if they are invited that is. You know, Mary, Saffer, Hector, the ones who have been around a while. Probably others as well. Maybe we should kind of close down in the afternoon, make it optional. With the weird hours these guys work Friday afternoons are pretty low key anyway."

Sheila leaned forward and looked at Marsh. "I think that's a good idea too. It would kind of bring closure to the situation."

He considered for a moment, then decided. "Ok, that's probably all right. Let's not just turn it into a holiday. Sheila can you handle the details?" She nodded at him and he turned to Joe. "Joe you retain control and give everyone on staff your approval. A little formality should keep everyone in check." He stopped for a moment, somewhat amazed by how easy it was to slip back into business mode.

"I hadn't thought about the funeral though. I guess it will be open to everyone who wants to come. We'll have some sort of gathering after I suppose. I'm not sure where though."

"I'd like to volunteer Marsh," Sheila said, her face sincere. "At my place. It's not huge but it's big enough."

"I can't ask you to do that Sheila."

"No, I want to. I really do. You know how close I was to Margaret. I would be honored to have it. I've got a light schedule on Friday and I'll take the morning off. Maybe Susan could come over to help me get ready. I'd like to see her. We could talk - you know, girl to girl."

Marsh was touched and he felt the tears well up in his eyes again. "That's very gracious Sheila, really." He picked up the napkin again, wiped his eyes and looked at them both. "Thanks very much, both of you."

"Hey, what are friends for?" Joe said softly.

"It's all settled then," Sheila said.

The silence was broken by the sound of a cell phone. Everyone glanced around automatically and wondered whose it was.

"I turned mine off," Sheila remembered.

"Me too," Joe added.

"Must be me then," Marsh said and lifted his back to pull the phone from his pocket. He glanced at the face and then powered it off, ignoring the call. "Sorry, just my lawyer," he said.

"We should get back to work," Sheila said and glanced over to Joe.

Joe got up immediately. "Absolutely. Since Marsh here doesn't want to have any fun this afternoon we might as well get back to the farm."

Sheila opened the folder and signed the check, then got up with Joe. They both stopped and looked at him.

"I'll be ok… really… and thanks again. Somebody call me tonight alright?"

"You got it boss," Joe said and they walked away.

Marsh sat there for a moment and stared out the window, for some reason wanting to be alone. He thought about returning Steve's call. The restaurant was empty and he could talk freely, but he procrastinated, deciding instead to call from the car.

Half an hour later Marsh was almost to the airport. He picked up his cell phone from the seat next to him, retrieved the missed call list and selected redial when he located Steve's number. He put the phone into the mounting on the center panel and activated the car speakers and microphone. The phone ringing filled the car for a moment.

"Steven Race."

"Steve, its Marsh. Sorry I missed you earlier," Marsh said, both hands on the wheel.

"Not a problem buddy. I'm sure you have a lot on your mind. I'm sorry about your mother. I wish this could be more of a social call."

"Thanks, I understand. I'm dealing with it. I presume you got my call this morning?"

"Yes, and I can't say I really like messages like that first thing in the morning. Not the best way to start my day."

Marsh noticed a small flash of red in the car and looked in the rearview mirror. A police car was speeding towards him in the left lane, lights flashing. He instinctively pulled his foot from the accelerator and glanced at the speedometer. The car ignored him and roared by on his left side. It triggered memories of the station that morning and he realized he was holding his breath.

"Marsh? You there?"

"Uh, yea, sorry. I'm in the car and got a little distracted," he said and exhaled.

"Just keep it on the road. OK, first things first. As far as your mother's estate goes everything seems to be in order. I went over the will this morning and..." the voice paused for a moment. "You OK to talk about this now?" Steve asked.

"Sure. It's alright. I'd actually like to get it over with."

"Good. Margaret named you as executor, but I'll handle everything for you except signatures."

Marsh interrupted, "Great Steve, I appreciate that."

"Not a problem. She left everything to you and Susan, to be divided evenly, except for a bequest to her church in the amount of twelve thousand dollars. To sum it up that leaves the house, personal possessions, investment accounts including an IRA, and savings. The good news is that there is a substantial amount of money there, much of it from your father's insurance. Oh yeah, and her insurance too. I forgot about that but I assume you and Susan are the beneficiaries of that also. The bad news is that the government is going to get a big chunk of it unless we do something to avoid it."

Marsh thought for a moment as he changed lanes to avoid an old station wagon plodding along. He didn't need the money, but he wanted Suse to be comfortable. "Options?"

"I haven't worked them out yet, didn't want to spend the time until I heard from you. Do you want to keep the condo? That's the big decision."

He thought for a moment. Maybe Suse will want to move back. She could take it. He changed lanes again as another faster moving car moved up behind him. Would she want to come back to Colorado?

"Jesus I don't know Steve. I really haven't thought about it. Why don't you work out the options and let me know."

"OK, give me a day."

"But Steve," Marsh added, "I don't want this to drag on. Whatever you come up with make it as clean and short as possible."

"Right, but that is going to cost you some."

"Probably not nearly as much as your fees, Steve," Marsh said half seriously.

"Ouch. Now, it's about the other matter you mentioned. I've seen the papers this morning and I understand your concern. Are you looking for some sort of legal action here?"

Marsh quickly summarized the events of the morning as he worked his way into the terminal complex. "I'm going to lose you in a second. I'm almost at the parking garage."

"It's a hell of a story Marsh, but legally the police behaved as they should have. I don't think we have any recourse."

"I know, I didn't have all the facts this morning and I was angry and upset. I don't see any reason now not to let the cops do whatever it is they are going to do. They actually seem to be handling it quite well."

"I agree but now that I know the facts I'll keep an eye on it. Anything else?"

"No, and thanks again Steve for your help," Marsh said sincerely.

"I'm at your service. By the way Marsh, when's the funeral? I'd like to come if I may."

"Of course, it's Friday afternoon. Please come. I'll let you know the specifics tomorrow."

"And I'll have some options for you by then. Just call me when you are ready. Take care."

"Bye Steve," Marsh said as he pulled the phone up and tossed it back on the seat.

The conversation was over just in time. He pulled into the multi-storied parking structure and circled slowly for a while looking for a spot. He still had at least a half an hour before Suse's flight arrived and was not really concerned about the time, but he did want to meet her as she came up from the trains. Finally, he spotted an open space and wheeled the Lexus in, shut off the engine and sat there in the semi-darkness. He was a little overwhelmed. So much had happened in the last twenty-four hours, and he had very little time to reflect on it all. He got out of the car, reaching back at the last minute for his phone and walked across the lot, full of cars but devoid of people, his footsteps producing lonely echoes as he stepped in the silence.

The main terminal however was far from empty. At nearly three o'clock it was packed with travelers. As he walked over the granite floors he looked up towards the canopy, stopping for a second as much to avoid running into people as to admire the top of the building. Heavy white canvas spires rose stories above the floor below, the two leveled terminal area dwarfed by the height of the roof. He stood there for a moment, an anonymous figure alone among so many people. Suddenly a man brushed by him carrying a canvas sack in one hand. His heart stopped for a moment and the thought of the thief overwhelmed him. It was yesterday, he thought - Jesus, get a grip. He watched the man walk casually through the crowd, sadly realizing how easy it had been for his mother's killer to slip away.

Now more anxious than ever to see Suse he walked to the end of the terminal towards security and stopped to check the status of her arrival on the long row of monitors that listed every flight for the day. He never really paid attention to how many there were, when he traveled he was only concerned about his own trip. Out of curiosity he started counting the entries on the departure screens. Hundreds of them he thought, and realized the futility of any search. No wonder the police had treated the airport as a dead end.

He returned to the waiting area above the trains, unable to proceed all the way to the gate since 9/11. He sat down on a small retaining wall by the fountain to catch his breath and realized he had been clutching his phone in his hand the whole time, the instrument now covered with sweat. He tried to recall the last time he had seen Suse - March, he thought. He had been at a symposium in Chicago and at the last minute had changed his plans and stopped in the Twin Cities. They had a long dinner and talked for hours, about her work, how much she loved Minneapolis but missed the mountains. She was happy to see him, but disappointed that he wouldn't be able to meet her now steady boyfriend. Fred, he recalled, had been in Dallas on a business trip.

Impatient, he drummed his fingers on the speckled granite tiles. He absently wiped the grime from the face of the phone, then decided that checking his voice mail would kill some time. The reception in the terminal was weak, but acceptable, and he had to push the small phone hard up against his ear to hear. He had seventeen new messages. He sighed as he screened them, listening only for a moment to determine the caller, then hitting the pound key to skip the message. He was not really interested in talking to anyone right now, but wanted to make sure he didn't miss anything important. There were a few routine business calls, but most of the messages were from friends, presumably to leave their condolences. He had almost worked through the list when one message caught his attention. It was that reporter from the television station he thought, and he felt somewhat annoyed by her calling him. Her voice sounded a little muted, not at all like he remembered.

"Hello Mr. Hawkins, this is Sara McGloughin of KDEN TV. If you recall we met at the Police Station this morning. I'd like to apologize if I said anything disrespectful, I'm afraid I wasn't expecting to meet you. I wanted to offer my respects again, this time a little more sincerely. I was also was wondering if you would like to meet with me. Perhaps tomorrow if that's not too early or intruding. Anyway, my number is 303-555-4345. It's my cell phone so please call me at any time. And again, I'm sorry for your loss. Good bye."

The speech ended and Marsh hung up the phone before he realized he had cut off the rest of the messages. He expected something from the press, but the call from the woman at the station still surprised him. He thought Will pretty much diffused the situation in the conference, and he wondered what she wanted. Some damn fool background story he thought - just what he needed. Despite his annoyance, he was a somewhat intrigued. Maybe she knew something he speculated. He pushed the thought away as ridiculous, then noticed another rush of passengers coming up from the trains below.

His heart raced as he stood up and arched his head above the others waiting and scanned the crowd for her. He had to keep stepping out of the way of the disembarking travelers as he inched his way towards the exit.

"Suse!" he yelled when he saw her, and waved. A few people gave him a curious look as they filed past, the rest writing him off as another impatient family member.

"Marsh!" she yelled over the top of the people in front of her and waved back. She was lovelier than ever he thought as she slowly came into view. My little sister. She was dressed in rather tight jeans, a simple white top and a light blue sweater tied by the arms around her neck, body of the sweater invisible behind her back. She pushed passed the last few people and flew into his arms. They squeezed each other tightly.

"Oh Marsh, I'm so glad to see you," she said into his shoulder.

He pushed her away for a moment and kissed her cheek softly. "And I am very glad to see you too Suse." He looked at her, tears in both their eyes and hugged her again hard.

There were a few murmurs from exiting passengers, obviously perturbed about the couple clutching each other in the walkway. Marsh ignored them, but pulled her to the side, then wrapped his arms around her again. They stood there and both cried for a long time.

Finally, he pushed her away, held her at arms length by the shoulders and looked her over.

"You look better than ever Suse."

"Oh, stop it Marsh," she said and rubbed her red eyes. "I'm a mess."

"Well a beautiful mess then. I'm so happy you are here now."

She began to cry again and his heart sagged. Attempting to relieve the tension a little he said lightly, "No luggage?"

"I checked it all. I didn't know how long…" Then, a laugh blended in with the tears and she said, "I seem to have significantly overpacked."

"It's good to see you smile Suse. I was so worried about you. Come on, let's get out of here. The airport gives me the creeps."

He took her hand and led her away toward the escalators that led to baggage claim, ignoring her curious glance at his last comment. He was in no hurry now, content to stand motionless on the belt while more impatient travelers pushed past them. He was reminded of the times when they were much younger, when she was a little girl, and he would lead her everywhere holding her hand.

"Marsh?" she asked quietly, looking up at his face.

"Not now Suse. We can talk all we want later."

The wait at baggage claim took about fifteen minutes, and they only exchanged a few pleasantries and comments about the airport. When her luggage arrived Marsh offered a snide remark about the volumes she had packed, and Susan defended her possessions by telling him she had no idea what she needed. By the time they had crossed the parking structure he could tell she was impatient, but still refrained from saying anything. She stopped suddenly as they approached the car, the flashing of the lights and beep from the security system attracting her attention.

"What's the matter Suse?" he said, still holding her bulky luggage in each hand.

"Mom had a Lexus too didn't she?"

"Yes, I bought it for her when I got mine," he replied. Tears began to form in her eyes again and he dropped the bags and reached out to hold her.

"I can't believe she's gone Marsh," she said.

"I know. Let's go home."

Chapter Eleven

Richard Williams was excited and invigorated as he walked out of the jetway into the circular gate area at the end of the long concourse of McCarran International Airport. Thoughts of Susan or the robbery in Denver or Margaret Hawkins had completely disappeared from his radar screen. The computer case in his hand felt lighter, buoyed by his anticipation as he dropped down another escalator into baggage claim. He waited patiently for his luggage, and loved the excitement that surged through his veins. His hand absently rubbed the rough beard that already formed on his face.

It took only about ten minutes for his two bags to show up, now completely unconcerned that anyone was watching. He retrieved them casually, then struggled a bit with the three bags as he walked out of the claim area and stepped through the sliding doors onto the street. The desert heat assaulted him as he took his place in the taxi queue. He didn't care at all.

When he finally made it to the front of the line, a frazzled old man with crooked teeth hopped out of the cab and reached for his luggage. Richard grabbed the computer case prudently and watched the cabby throw the remaining bags into the open trunk with little regard to their fragility. He climbed into the back of the taxi and opened the window despite the temperature outside.

"Downtown. Four Queens," he said as the driver slid back into his seat. "And take me up the strip," he added.

"That's the long way, and a lot slower. Cost you more," the man replied, accent unknown, as he looked back over the seat.

"I know," Richard said and looked out the window, cutting off further interaction with the driver.

It took a few minutes to wind their way out of the airport. He relaxed in the back seat, despite the drum beat in his chest, head tilted back on the cracked leather headrest. He rode quietly, like a tourist, as the car turned left onto Tropicana and headed for Las Vegas Boulevard. He hummed softly and enjoyed the ride despite the snail's pace they made. As the taxi approached the Strip, the number of cars on the street and people on the sidewalk increased exponentially. He reveled in the sights like a little kid, knowing it was just a predecessor to the full night he had ahead, then satisfied with his little tour he powered up the window, the driver giving him a glance of appreciation in the rear view mirror. He was anxious now to get downtown and check into the hotel. It wasn't the first time he had performed this ritual though; in fact the last six times he visited he had started his trip this way.

It took another fifteen minutes to negotiate the last few miles of the wide boulevard to Fremont Street, the heart of downtown. The cab couldn't drop him in front of the hotel; the street years ago converted into a vast pedestrian promenade. The taxi instead drove up Casino Center, pulled into the side of the hotel/casino complex and parked in the small circular drive. Richard paid the old man, tipping him well for the tour and hopped out of the car with his computer case. A young bellgirl dutifully retrieved the rest of his bags from the trunk and followed him into the reception center of the hotel. He gave her a few bucks and shooed her away, content to handle his own luggage from there. As usual there was a crowd of people queued up to check in. He waited, reveling in the commotion around the lobby and toward the casino area, taking in the sounds and smells of the small but busy hotel.

He registered under the name of Richard Williams and paid in advance in cash, enough to cover the room and any incidental expenses. It took another few minutes to take the elevator up and traverse down the red and gold carpeted hallway to his door. He slid the plastic key into the slot and pushed his way into the mini-suite. It was tastefully furnished, a large bathroom just inside the door to the left, king-sized bed and dresser in the front area, a couch, TV, easy chairs and bar across the room by the window that opened to the plaza below.

He set about his business immediately, proceeding first to the large safe in the closet. He opened it and set the electronic combination to the digits in his birthday backwards. The ninety thousand in cash he retrieved from the suitcase and stacked it in the bottom of safe neatly, pausing for a second to admire the bills. From his computer case he retrieved the other four grand and pushed it into his pocket, ready for the craps table. He also stashed away his wallet and all his ID's, and kept only the Richard William's NY driver's license in his possession. Satisfied he closed the safe and locked it, a single tug once on the small

DECEPTION ON MARGIN

handle for assurance. Finally he emptied the clothes from his other garment bag, and placed them as neatly as possible in the closet and drawers of the dresser.

Housekeeping chores completed he crossed the room, picked up his PDA from the computer case and opened the mini-bar. He removed two small bottles of Chivas, which he poured into a glass from the tray on the counter. He grabbed the remote and flicked on the TV as he sat down on the couch, the background noise of the hotel channel mindless but comforting. The scotch warmed his throat as he sipped it, and he stretched out to put his feet up on the coffee table, now totally relaxed in the comfort of the suite. This is way too much fun to only do once a month, he thought. "I'll have to talk to Fred about that," he said to the ceiling and leaned his head back on the couch. Then suddenly he jumped up and walked to the mirror, drink in hand, as he stared into it. The silent but well manicured Fred stared back at him.

"Did you get that Fred ol' buddy? You guys have all the fun and I only get once a month."

The face in the mirror looked back silently.

Richard laughed and brushed Fred away with a wave of his drink hand. "Fuck you," he said to the empty room, "I've got calls to make."

He returned to the couch, powered up his PDA and summoned his personal phone directory. Setting the little computer on the table, he picked up the phone and dialed the number displayed. It was a voice pager and he waited for the beep to leave his message.

"This is Richard Dallas. It's Tuesday at around 2. I'm at the Queens in room 654," he said then, hung up the phone. He took another gulp of scotch, felt it burn as it dropped down his throat and smiled to himself at the use of a code name to disguise what was already an alias. "Let's make a drug deal," he conceded. Flipping through the PDA again he located the second number, pressed the alternate line on the phone and dialed. What would we do without pagers?

He waited for the tone and spoke, this time with a bit more fun in his voice. "Hey there, hope I didn't wake you. It's Richard Dallas and I'm in town tonight. The Four Queens, room 654. Call me."

He hung up the phone, got up and walked to the window. Something inside told him to switch the TV channel to CNBC, but he ignored the impulse and stared out the window instead. The street below was like a circus, hundreds of pedestrians surrounded by vendors, kiosks, and street entertainment of all kinds. The lights raced through the canopy above, the myriad of colors hypnotizing, the sounds from the huge speakers that pulsed music over the street barely audible, but certainly felt.

The phone rang quietly and he briefly wondered who got back to him first. Who cares he thought and picked up the receiver.

"Hello?"

"Hey baby," a sultry voice responded. "Looking for some action tonight?"

"Hello Crystal. Later tonight OK with you?"

"Anytime is good for us sugar," she replied.

He laughed at the innuendo. "I'm sure it is. Main bar at the Queens at midnight."

"We'll be there. Bye baby," she said, her voice trailing off.

"One down," he said to himself and finished off his scotch, a slight buzz filling his head. He walked back to the mini-bar and pulled out another, the last of the Chivas he noted, twisted off the metal cap and emptied the bottle into his glass. He sat back down to enjoy it, picked up the remote and flipped through the channels mindlessly for a few minutes.

"I need to take a leak," he said out loud. The scotch was taking effect and he was content with his own company. The lights were bright in the bathroom when he flipped them on, and his reflection stared back at him in the mirror. "Very handsome, you stud," he said to it, happy with the rugged unshaven look. The phone rang just as he finished and he zipped up quickly, then walked back across the suite to the phone on the table, ignoring the one next to the bed.

"Hello?"

"It's Rico. Forty-five minutes at the bar."

"Drinks are a buck and a half there," Richard said.

"Right."

He hung up the phone and once again the disguised reference to the deal amused him. "I love it when a plan comes together," he said, and laughed out loud.

He tapped one pocket, the hundred dollar bills tucked in nicely. Reaching in the other he checked for his ID, and counted another couple hundred plus left over. "I'm ready," he said and headed for the door.

For the next forty minutes he wandered around the street under the canopy, denying his urge to head for a craps table. It was hot, but the mist that floated down from above, evaporating before it hit the street level, had a slight cooling effect. It was a great place to people watch he mused, and enjoyed the growing effects of the scotch as he walked. He noticed a liquor store and stopped in briefly to pick up a bottle of cognac, Remy Martin, which he carried out in a white plastic sack. It was forty-five minutes exactly when he sat down at the main bar at the Four Queens.

The old bartender served him a scotch and inquired if he wanted to play the dollar poker machines built into the bar in front of him. He declined politely and paid for the drink, a rare occurrence in the casino. He sipped the scotch and spun around on the stool as a loud cheer from a craps table across the casino attracted his attention.

"Table must be hot," he said to himself and wished he was shooting.

"Dallas," a sharp voice came from the side.

He turned and looked at the short Mexican man, about five six and short dark hair. Nothing but muscles rippled out from underneath the white tank top.

"Have a drink?" Richard asked quietly.

"Why not?" the man said and looked at the bartender. "Tequila."

The old man tipped a shot glass on top of the poker machine and filled it with white liquid, slopping a little on the glass. Rico slowly reached into the black pouch secured around his waist, pulled out a small packet and palmed it. Richard pulled a hundred and fifty dollars from his pocket, folded it once and set it on the bar between them. Rico picked up the shooter and threw it down, then grabbed a cocktail napkin from a small black tray on the bar and wiped his mouth. He slipped the packet inside the napkin as he wrinkled it and tossed it nonchalantly in front of Richard.

"Thanks amigo," Rico said as he got off the stool. His hand swept the bills off the bar as he walked away.

"See you next time," Richard replied and shoved the crushed napkin into his pocket. He waited patiently for a moment and finished his drink, then gathered up the cognac, left a five on the bar and headed for the elevators. He rode up to his floor and quickly walked down the hall and into his suite. He pulled the Remy from the sack and set it down on the dresser, gathered three glasses from the bar and set them down next to the bottle. He removed the napkin from his pocket, extracted the packet and tossed it down next to the bottle. Smiling to himself he dumped the napkin and the bag into the trash can.

He looked in the mirror above the dresser for a moment, and saw only himself. "Time to play," he said and left the room.

Susan and Marsh talked little on the trip from the airport, despite her occasional inquisitive glances at him. He struggled with how to tell her the story, and wondered how she would take it. By the time they were inside his home he was tired, even though it was still early in the afternoon.

"I'll put these in the guest room Suse," he said, glad to be rid of the heavy bags. "Why don't you unpack and then we'll talk, OK?"

When he returned into the open room he saw Susan in front of the pictures on the wall, fists clenched and pulled up under her neck. There were tears in her eyes again as he walked over and stepped behind her. He slid his arms around her waist and held her tightly.

"Good pictures."

"So many memories Marsh."

They stood there for a moment, eyes tracing over the portraits and collages on the wall. Neither one spoke. Finally, Susan pushed away and walked toward the guestroom.

"Are we going anywhere?" she asked as she turned quietly toward him.

"Um, hadn't thought about it. Not for a while at least," he replied. "Why?"

"I thought I might change, relax for a bit. It's been a long day."

"No, that's fine. Good idea."

She disappeared down the hall and he walked over to the kitchen, suddenly thirsty. "Do you want something to drink? Iced tea maybe?" he yelled through the wall.

"Sounds great," she yelled back.

From inside the fridge he retrieved a large pitcher of tea and filled two glasses. Holding both in one hand carefully he traversed back through the room to the balcony, opened the sliding glass doors and screen and walked out. He set her tea on the small table and took a big gulp from his own.

It was another beautiful day he thought. The sounds of the city filtered up toward him, the sweating glass cold and wet in his hand. He stood still for a moment, mind at ease, until he heard her behind him. She was dressed for summer, white shorts and simple blue top, hair pulled back behind her head with a teal wrap.

"You look great Suse," he said. His eyes moved back to hers.

"Thanks, I try. I'm working out a lot - aerobics mostly..." she said but trailed off, eyes locked on the mountains in the distance.

"Mmm..." he said. He sat down in one of the chairs and pushed with his legs to lean back. Susan sat down in the other and picked up her glass. After a moment she looked at him, face serious.

"Enough stalling now Marsh, what's going on?"

It took him about fifteen minutes to go through the details. He started hesitatingly at first, then the story gushed out of him. She said nothing, but listened intently. Her eyes alternated from his face to the mountains, occasionally taking a small sip from her tea. When he finally finished they both sat quietly for a moment. She looked somber, but was not crying.

"It's so sad Marsh," she said, her voice barely a whisper.

He looked at her, surprised at her neutral reaction.

"I mean it's so pointless. So random."

He waited, but didn't respond.

She turned and stared at him. "Do you believe God had a plan for this? That this is all part of a bigger picture we don't understand? I've been going to church occasionally," she said. "Stephanie, a friend of mine from work and I found a nice little church in the suburbs, not too far away. It's not like what we went to as kids. It's kind of progressive, most of the people there are my age or a little older. They have a band, well not a band but a piano, guitars, a drummer. You know not just a stuffy pipe organ. The music is modern, uplifting."

He looked over at her. He hadn't been to church in years, the pressures of the business and his busy schedule always seemed more important.

"Do you remember what it was like when we were young Marsh? I used to hate going to church. I did anything I could to avoid going to Sunday School." She smiled a little, remembering. "You know I used to sneak into Mom and Dad's room early Sunday morning. I would crawl across the floor in my pajamas hoping they wouldn't wake up. I must have been ten or twelve and you were already old enough so Mom wouldn't make you go. I would reach up and try and turn off their alarm clock. I thought if they overslept I wouldn't have to go."

He laughed a little, the image of a little girl in pink jammies slinking across the floor filling him. He could picture their bedroom in the old house perfectly.

"Now I like going," she continued. "The pastor there gives such great sermons. They really mean something to me. They are not bible thumping save your soul or else messages, but real life situations. Things that really affect the way you live."

"I can't remember the last time I went to church," he said with some guilt.

"Well next time you are in town I'll take you to mine. It would do you some good you know."

"Probably so."

"Where are we going to have the service Marsh?"

"At Mom's church I suppose, I hadn't thought of it. I guess we need to notify them too," he said. He sighed, reminded of another detail that slipped through the cracks.

"I'll do it, I'd like to. By the way, what else can I do while I'm here? There must be a million things to take care of."

He looked at her proudly. She had grown up so much he thought. Whatever happened to the little girl in pigtails that used to follow him around?

"Well, one thing for sure. Sheila wants to have everyone over to her place after the service. A little gathering. She asked to actually. She was wondering if you would like go over Friday morning and help her get ready."

"Friday?"

"Oh yeah. I'm meeting with the funeral director tomorrow morning. I'm going to set the service for Friday afternoon. You should make sure the church is OK with that."

"Fine. I'd like that. How is Sheila anyway? Are you and she…" she asked, a mischievous smile pushing up the corners of her lips.

He laughed a little. "No nosy, we are not anything."

She laughed with him, eyes twinkling.

"It's good to see you laugh Suse."

"It's good to be able to laugh. So is there anyone?"

He was relieved that the conversation had lightened up a bit, and felt so happy she was there. "Sure, ton's of women. I usually have to screen my messages they call so much."

"I can just imagine."

"How about you? What's with what's his name? Fred?"

"Well..." she said.

Marsh looked at her and wondered if she was going to spring something on him.

"We are getting quite close actually. He's such a good guy. Kind, smart, a good conversationalist..." she said leading him. "And he's rich."

"Rich huh? And a good conversationalist? Every girl's dream."

She hesitated for a moment. "I think I'm in love with him."

The revelation shocked him. "What?"

"Don't look so surprised Marsh, I'm almost twenty-six you know. Most girls my age are married and making babies by now."

"But, I... I know but I didn't think..."

"He's good to me, Marsh. He's good for me."

He pondered the situation for a moment, even prouder than ever. "But you're just my little sister," he said with a grin.

"Little sister my ass. I've asked him to come to Denver Marsh."

"Oh."

"You don't mind do you? I mean I want him to be here."

"No, it's fine," he said, and somehow dreaded the next question. "Where is he going to stay?"

She looked at him firmly. "Here. With us, or me. If that's all right with you."

"Mmm..." he replied, but didn't commit. He tried to decide how he felt about that, then realized that another person, someone he didn't know, might intrude on their closeness.

"Don't be such a prude Marsh," she said, misinterpreting his silence. "You know we have been sleeping together for months."

He wasn't shocked at the revelation, but surprised at her frankness. "No, it's not that Suse. It's just that, well I was assuming it would just be the two of us, together."

"Oh," she said. "You'll really like him Marsh. He's a lot like you, you know. Maybe that's why I fell in love with him."

"I take it that compliment is meant as a bribe," he said and smiled slightly.

"I guess it was. No really, he used to be in computers too you know. Now he's just into finance, mostly day trading."

"And he's rich?"

"He's very good at it."

"When's he coming? Today?" he asked, but hoped they could spend some more time alone together.

"No, he had to go to Vegas for some business he couldn't get out of. He's flying in tomorrow if that's OK with you."

"That's fine Suse. Had this all planned out did you?"

She got out of her chair, leaned over him and gave him a hug. "Well not exactly, but I was sort of hoping."

He started to choke up and hoped she wouldn't see. "Mom would be proud of you, you know."

She squeezed him again, her eyes full of tears as well.

The casino was crowded and noisy and smoky as he walked down the two steps into the slightly sunken room. He loved it. He had a nice even buzz from the scotches and felt energized. He tapped his pocket again, the hundred dollar bills burning a hole in it. The first table on his left, the one he had heard the screaming from earlier was still jammed with people, others standing behind looking over shoulders. He liked an enthusiastic gathering, but the table was too crowded for his taste and he walked to the third in the row, one less occupied.

He stood back a few paces and judged the participants. There were six people, five of whom seemed to be playing. At the far end of the table was a man in a tan suit and mismatched tie, a brunette next to him. She wasn't paying attention to the action and he wasn't paying attention to her. Three of the others, all males were spaced out at the long side of the table. They were all older, dressed casually but not like tourists. An older woman, about fifty with a purse tucked between her feet was closest to him. The near end of the table, his favorite place, was wide open so he stepped over to it and leaned down with his forearms resting on the chip racks in front of him. He surveyed the green felt with yellow markings spread in front of him, then reached down and brushed the surface softly, almost like a caress. The red dice careened past his hand.

"Hands up sir," the stickman said.

"Sorry," he said nodded, and pulled his hands up. He looked over the four gentlemen running the table. The two chipmen, both opposite him were attired in black slacks, white shirt and orange vests. There were huge piles of colored chips stacked in front of them. The stickman dressed the same, stood next to him at the center of the table, smaller piles of chips stacked in front. The table boss in a dark suit sat quietly to the side and slightly behind him, eyes locked on the table.

The chipman opposite him, 'Dave - Reno' his gold badge read, looked at him. "Joining in sir?"

"I'll watch for a moment," Richard said.

Tan suit owned the dice. The stickman hooked them in his tool, slid them to the shooter, and deftly flipped them with the tip to a six, the current point. Tan suit picked them up and gently shook them in his hand before he tossed them down the table. They ricocheted off the little black foam pyramids that lined the inside of the table, bounced back and settled.

"Fiver, two three," stickman said.

The chipmen leaned over the table and paid a few bets with efficient clicks of stacking chips, then stood back up, almost at attention. The stickman returned the dice to tan suit effortlessly.

"Come on baby," tan suit said, and tossed the dice down the length of green.

"Seven out."

There was a slight mumble from all the players. Tan suit responded with a curse. The chipmen swept all the chips away and the dice were passed to the next player, unshaven and in jeans and a plaid shirt.

The dice rolled.

"Nine, center field."

Richard looked around at the participants, all of whom were low stakes players. It wasn't his normal table; he liked a little more crowd participation. The shouts and camaraderie of strangers all engaged in the same pursuit was half the fun, but he decided to stay for a while anyway. Things always change he thought.

Plaid shirt picked up the dice again, blowing on them. He tossed.

"Nine, winner."

"Finally," said lady, and shot an indignant look at the chipman, as if he was responsible for the cold streak.

The stickmen distributed the winnings, chips clicking. Richard decided to jump in. He pulled five hundred-dollar bills from his pocket and laid them on the table. Dave the chipman closest to him picked them up and stacked piles of green chips, twenty fives, in front of him. "Some reds please too," Richard asked. A stack of five-dollar chips instantly replaced two of the greens. He nodded at Dave, picked them up dropped them into the rack.

"Changing five hundred," Dave said without turning. The table boss silently noted the transaction.

He dropped a green on the passline.

He could feel the excitement building in him as Plaid shirt tossed the dice again.

"Six, easy six. Point is six."

He set two green chips behind his pass bet. Next he took three more greens and tossed them down in the general direction of Dave. "Twenty four inside," Richard said.

Dave went to work. He picked up the greens, changed them for three stacks of reds and dollars, twenty-four bucks each and placed them in on the numbers 5, 8 and 9. He returned three dollars to Richard and the dice flew again.

"Eight, easy eight."

"Press that," Richard said immediately, the win on his eight paying six to five, rounded to twenty-eight bucks. With the winnings Dave doubled his eight bet to forty-eight and slid four dollars back. Richard was getting into it now, the value of his wagers on the table increasing.

"Eight, hard eight," the chipman said, the number repeating.

"I'll take that," he said as he watched the table, not pressing the bet again. Dave paid him fifty-six for the eight win, his eight bet still intact. He collected the chips and set them in the tray, sorting them by color.

"Cocktails," a passing waitress said flatly, not really to anyone.

"Scotch neat, and none of that watered down bar stuff please," he said. He looked over at her and ignored the breasts pushed up the front of a skimpy dress. He tossed a red on her tray as he heard the dice roll again.

"Seven out."

"Damn, we need a shooter here," Richard said to the table. Two of the men walked away shaking their heads, hands empty. He watched the chips clear from the table, down about seventy-five on that pass alone he thought. The dice were passed to lady, who gingerly picked them up. Plaid shirt and tan suit stayed put, although the brunette with him was gone.

"Come on sugar, you a shooter?" he asked. She looked at him blankly. She's no fun he said to himself.

He dropped two greens on the pass line and hoped his optimism was infectious. He hated to bet against the shooter even if the table was cold.

"Come on shooter," tan suit said.

She squeezed the dice in her wrinkled hand and threw them, the red cubes not even reaching the end of the table. He hated that.

"Eleven," stickman said, "Pay the line."

Dave stacked two greens next to his pass bet, doubling the fifty. Richard left the chips on the pass line, betting a hundred. Lady rolled again.

"Twelve craps."

Richard lost the hundred.

And so it went. The players at the table coming and going, few winning. Richard didn't move, cemented to his place at the table. He was into his third five hundred and fifth scotch two hours later, but could barely feel the effects of the alcohol. He stretched, his legs tight and back stiff from leaning on the table. By now, Dave knew his every move, as any good table man should for a high roller. The bets flowed faster, and Richard increased them continuously, his table stakes fluctuating wildly. At six the evening crowd was rolling in from the street, the table now packed and louder as the drinks continued to flow.

He had pulled out another five bills when two college kids joined the table dressed in shorts and t-shirts. Both were very sunburned and very drunk, but they raised the spirits of the players with their exuberance and wild shouting. He needed to take a leak badly, but didn't want to miss the action. They couldn't lose, making pass after pass, whooping loudly. He bet right along with them, and laughed with every high five they gave each other whenever they won. The streak was good enough to recoup almost all his losses in a half-hour, when it abruptly came to an end, as they always do. Everyone around the table congratulated the kids, the employees that manned the table unemotional as always. The adrenaline rush from the last few minutes suddenly faded and he needed a break. Some food he thought, would be good, and realized he hadn't eaten since breakfast.

He turned to the stickman. "I need a break Dave."

Dave looked at the rack of chips. "You want to color up?"

"Ya, I'll be back, maybe after some dinner. What can you do for me?"

"Drop the chips and I'll check."

Richard stacked all his chips neatly to the side of the table, out of the way of the flying dice. After the next roll Dave quickly counted and restacked them in piles of hundreds, then stacked them again and set them aside. He left two green chips behind.

"Color change nineteen hundred," he said over his shoulder.

"Black out," the boss said, the first words he had uttered.

Dave stacked five, five and four hundred dollar chips on the table, then stacked them on the two greens in one pile, and pushed them across the felt. Richard picked the blacks up, and slid them into his pocket. The greens he tossed back and said, "For the boys Dave."

Dave nodded, this time with a smile at the tip and turned to the boss, "How about some dinner for my man here."

The boss looked up from his chair, "Are you a guest here sir?"

"Richard Williams, 654," he said. He knew the boss knew exactly how much money he had played with, and how much money he had. His room was probably already comped he thought. Anything to get him back to the table later.

"Of course Mr. Williams, no problem," the boss said. "Why don't you go up to the Palm room and have some dinner. The steaks are very good. I'll arrange it." He turned and looked back at the table, concentrating on the action.

"I'll be back Dave," Richard pledged with smile.

He spotted a restroom sign surrounded by tiny red lights and hustled toward it. The brightly-lit room contained a long counter in front of the segmented mirror, topped off with a dozen types of aftershave and cologne. He quickly relieved himself, then hands grimy from handling all the chips; he turned on the water and pumped some soap from the little container. He scrubbed and rinsed his hands thoroughly, then leaned down and splashed his face. There was a pile of soft hand towels on counter beside the sink and he grabbed one, rubbed it over his face, his beard catching on the towel as he pulled it down.

He looked at his reflection. For a moment, he couldn't focus, then his vision cleared. "Well hello again Fred," he said and smiled. The reflection looked back at him, clean-shaven, crisp blue collared shirt, not saying anything. "Ah Fred, you're missing out on all the action. You shouldn't be such a stick in the mud," Richard continued, still wiping his hands in the towel.

He leaned forward, palms on the counter, and addressed the man in the mirror. "I already told you Fred, we really need to do this more often. I mean once a month doesn't cut it anymore. I think you better talk to John, maybe set up another job in two weeks. That would give you two enough time to plan, wouldn't it?"

Fred stared back from the mirror, silent.

Richard smiled again. "Well think about it OK? I gotta run. Got places to go, tables to play, babes to see." He started to turn away, then looked back. Fred was still there.

"Oh, and don't forget old man. You are supposed to call Susan tonight, remember?"

Richard laughed harshly and left the room.

Marsh had changed into shorts and a t-shirt and gone for a long run. The exertion cleansed his thoughts and eased the grief a little. Susan had retired to the guestroom for a nap, exhausted from the lack of sleep and the long trip. Recharged when he returned, he slipped quietly into his office room and hoped he had the motivation to clear up his outstanding communications. He started with his email, logging on to the server at the office in the Tech Center. "Jesus," he said aloud, eighty-seven unread messages in the list. He took his time, answered each condolence message as best he could, at first uniquely, then found he could only say the same thing over and over again. There was some business correspondence intermingled and he forwarded them to Sheila and Joe. He attached a short note of instructions with each email.

It took well over an hour to complete the task. He got up from the desk and walked softly over the carpet and peered out the door across the hall. The door to the guestroom was partially open and he could see the bottom of Susan's bare feet at the foot of the bed. Not wanting to disturb her, he closed the door to the office slightly and returned to his chair. He pressed the speaker button on the phone and turned the volume down quickly as the dial tone filled the room. After punching in the number to his voice mail, he pulled a note pad from his briefcase, wanting to take notes on the calls he had previously skipped. As he replayed the messages he dutifully wrote down the caller and a brief remark about the content. He filled half the sheet with notes when the voice of the reporter played again.

"Hello Mr. Hawkins, this is Sara McGloughin of KDEN TV. If you recall we met at the Police Station this morning. I'd like to apologize..."

He sat back in his chair as he listened to the message play through, and wondered again if there were any hidden meanings or sinister motives behind the call.

"Who's that?" a voice came from behind him.

He turned to see Susan in the standing in the doorway, arms folded across her chest and leaning into the wall.

"Oh, hi," he said, ignoring the prompts from the service on what to do with the call. "Did I wake you up?"

"No, I did sleep for a bit but was mostly thinking about mom," she replied.

"That's good. It's a reporter from a TV station I met at the press conference this morning. She wants to meet with me for some reason."

"Are you going to?" she inquired.

"I don't know. Maybe I'll call her tomorrow and find out what she wants."

"I'm getting hungry," she said, changing the subject. "Got anything good around here?"

"I was thinking we could go out for dinner."

"You know, somehow I don't feel like going out. How about nice home-cooked meal?"

"I don't know what we have here."

"There is a store in this city isn't there? I can run out and get us something tasty."

"Sure, actually it's about two blocks away." he said, then hesitated. "A King Foodmart." Susan apparently missed the coincidence and he didn't push it.

"OK. I'll walk over there and see what they have. I could use the fresh air."

"Need some money?"

"Sheesh," she said. "Big brothers," and walked out the door.

Properly chastised he yelled after her. "Out the front door, turn left and walk down a couple of blocks. You can't miss it."

He turned back to the phone and saved the message from the reporter. He felt better now that he had cleaned up the day's activity and decided he needed some cleaning up himself. He shut down the computer and headed for a much-needed shower.

Forty-five minutes later he opened a bottle of chilled Chardonnay. He poured a glass and returned the bottle to a rack inside the refrigerator door. The sun was setting as he walked back to the balcony and he suddenly felt a little guilty about letting Susan walk through the city by herself. He was interrupted by the security intercom and felt relieved he crossed to the door and buzzed her in. Setting his glass down he walked into the hall and toward the elevators to meet her. When the doors opened she walked out, two full plastic bags hung from each hand and a purse strap over her shoulder.

"Hi," she said.

He looked at the full sacks. "Someone else coming for dinner?" he inquired with a laugh.

"No silly," she said. "I figured you probably didn't have anything for breakfast either, so I picked up some fresh fruit and yogurt."

They started back down the hall. "I usually have cold pizza for breakfast," he added.

"Pizza. A complete food group for most single males."

They were laughing when they re-entered the condo, and it felt good. Marsh picked up his glass from the end table and watched her.

"Chicken Marsela and Caesar salad OK with you?" she inquired with a glance.

"Sounds great. Want a glass of wine?"

"Sure," she said, and busied herself with the preparations.

He pulled another glass hung upside down from an overhead rack and grabbed the door to the fridge before it closed, removing the wine. He filled her glass and set it down on the counter, happy to see her busy in the kitchen. She picked it up slowly and looked at him.

"Cheers," she said softly. "To Mom."

"Cheers," he replied and tapped her glass.

They looked at each other for a moment silently, then she set her glass down and pushed him out of the kitchen. "Out, I'm busy here."

He laughed as he allowed himself to be shoved out of the way. "You know I really am a good cook."

"Yes, So I've heard. Mom told me," she said as she unwrapped the chicken breasts. "Any time you wanted to get a woman back here you turned into a real world-class chef."

"Ouch. Mom told you that?"

"Of course. She told me everything. She followed your exploits like a hawk." She smiled at him mischievously. "That is whenever she could find out anything."

The banter was interrupted by the muted sound of Beethoven's Fifth.

"What the hell is that?" he asked.

"My phone dear. It's probably Fred."

She walked around the counter to her purse and pulled the cell phone out quickly. "Hello?" she said as she held the instrument up to her ear.

"Hi, it's me?"

"Fred! Hi, how are you?"

Marsh walked back toward the balcony and gave them some privacy.

"I'm alright Susan, just a little tired," Fred said, his words not slurred but carefully formed. "Just finished a big dinner."

"When are you coming?" she asked, and thought he sounded a little strange.

"My flight is at one tomorrow. I should be finished here in the morning."

"Can't you get here any earlier?"

"I don't think so. The flights were kind of booked up. Last minute change you know."

"OK. It's just that I wish you were here," she said.

"Me too babe. It's been a long day, and I still have to deal with the people here," he said.

She changed the subject. "I talked with Marsh. He wants you to stay with us."

"Great."

"Are you OK?" she inquired, a little worried.

"I'm fine, really. It's just there is so much going on. I'll be there tomorrow afternoon and we can be together."

"Marsh is looking forward to meeting you."

"And I'm looking forward to meeting him."

He laughed a little, but it sounded forced. "Don't worry, I'll be OK. I can't wait to see you."

She hesitated for a moment. "Do you want us to pick you up?"

"No. I'll get a car and drive in. Maybe you can show me around Denver tomorrow if nothing is planned. I'll call you from the airport for directions."

"That would be nice, I don't think we have too much until Friday. The funeral is then."

"Good babe, I'll see you soon."

She wanted to talk to him more but sensed his hesitancy. "OK, can you call me later?"

"I don't know. The people here expect me to go out with them. Probably a casino of course."

"Try, OK?"

"All right, I'll try."

"Say hi to Marsh for me, and tell him thanks."

"I will. I love you Fred," she said quickly.
"I love you too Susan."
She clicked off the phone and dropped it back into her purse. He didn't sound right she thought, not like Fred. She wondered about him being in Vegas, with so much going on - it wasn't really his style. She picked up her glass and joined Marsh on the balcony. The darkening sunset amazed her.

Marsh looked at her, surprised by her somber face. "Everything OK?"
"Sure," she said and gazed out to the mountains. "It's so beautiful."
"Suse?"
"It's fine Marsh, really. He'll be here tomorrow afternoon."
"OK," he said and didn't press it. But a little worry crept over him.
"I'll get back to dinner," she said and turned away.

Richard dropped the phone down, feet up on the coffee table. The steak dinner weighed heavily in his stomach and the couch in the suite felt awfully comfortable. He wasn't about to miss any more of the evening however. He cruised over to the mirror and addressed the man without waiting. "Good job Fred. Nice touch with the 'I love you' part. Very sincere."

Fred looked back from the mirror like he was about to speak, but Richard cut him off. "OK, enough is enough. Time to go play. Up and attem."

He turned quickly from the mirror and looked in the mini-bar, resigned himself to drinking Dewers and took out two small bottles. He located the used glass on the table and emptied the scotch into it, then took a big gulp. The scotch scorched his throat as he swallowed. "Ahhh..." he said, and walked back toward the dresser. He stopped at the mirror and smiled at the reflection.

"Cheers ol' buddy," he said. He tipped the glass with a slight salute and polished off the rest of the Dewers. He was ready again.

Ten minutes later he was back in the casino. The table was full, but not crowded he noticed, the table crew still the same, the chipman Dave now on the other end. He walked over and dropped the handful of hundred dollar chips in the rack.

Dave noticed him. "How was dinner?" the chipman asked as the dice flew down the table.

"Excellent, great steak - good wine," Richard replied, the excitement of the game building in him. "But I'm ready for some action and a scotch."

"Cocktails," Dave said quietly over his shoulder. "You want a color change?" he asked.

"Yea, five hundred for now," he said and dropped five black chips to the top of the green felt. "How's the table?"

"Better now that you're here."

Richard laughed. Always PR he thought.

"Changing five," Dave said without emotion, picked up the black chips and quickly exchanged them for stacked piles of greens. The boss nodded and looked at him, but said nothing.

Richard scooped them into the tray. The point was eight, so he took three greens and tossed them down. "Inside."

Dave knew his betting style and picked them up quickly. The dice careened down the table, stopping on a six and a one.

"Seven out."

"Oops," Richard said, losing his bet before it was even distributed on the table. "Easy come…" he said.

Dave said nothing, but smiled a bit.

A cocktail waitress appeared, different girl same outfit. "Scotch, neat," Richard said to her and watched as she scribbled an unreadable marking on a white pad. He looked back and around the table. There were a lot of substantial bets being laid down and he was happy. Serious gamblers made for a better game. He set fifty on the passline and waited for the roll, dice held by a grungy old guy who resembled a beaten down prospector.

The dice landed. "Eight, easy eight."

He picked out six greens. "Inside," he said, his bets getting bigger, then put another fifty down for odds on the pass bet. "OK shooter, show us what you got," he yelled down the table, getting into it.

The dice careened off a pile of chips.

"Winner eight."

"Shooter!" Richard yelled down the table and watched as Dave piled up his winnings, chips clicking. He loved that sound.

For hours he stood there, never leaving his spot. He won some, lost more, the scotches coming faster and faster. As he steadily got drunk, he increased his bets, hoping for another big run. It never came. It was past midnight when all his chips were gone, more than fifteen hundred down again. He tapped his pocket, tempted to pull out another five hundred in cash when he realized the time.

"Well kids, it's been fun," he said, not really to anyone.

Dave was on the other side of the table again and Richard waved to him. Dave saluted with a nod as Richard walked away. He headed for the bathroom, weaving a little, and glanced over at the bar as he passed. There were two young blondes sitting together. Heads together they laughed at some private joke. He smiled, anxious to get to the bar and hurried into the restroom. After taking a long leak, he walked back to the sink and washed the chip residue from his hands. He reached for some cologne when he was done and spilled a few drops into his hand. As he splashed it over his face, he looked in the mirror. Fred was there.

He smiled. "You got your honey, I've got mine," he said cackled. Fred said nothing back.

He returned to the bar quickly, taking in the sight of the twins as he approached. They both wore very tight jean shorts, one in a blue tank top, one in yellow, neither doing much to hide what was underneath. They both had tall drinks under little umbrellas. Foo-foo drinks he laughed to himself. He was seriously drunk.

"Hello ladies," he said with a big grin and slid an arm around each as he came up behind.

"Hey baby," one said. They both turned at his touch.

"Hello Richard," the other said, and giggled, her hand sliding down the front of his pants. "Or should we call you Dick?"

"Nice to see you Crystal," he said, leaned over and kissed her on the cheek. "And you too Crystal. Call me whatever you like." He pushed one hand up yellow Crystal's side, almost reaching her full breast. "I've been meaning to ask how come you both have the same name?"

They both giggled again. "Mom was drunk when she gave birth..." yellow said.

"She thought she was seeing double," blue added without missing a beat.

"At least I won't be confused later," he said. "Shall we go? Or better yet, finish your drinks. Meet me in five minutes in my place - 654 OK?"

"Sure baby," blue said.

He hurried back to his room, humming happily to himself. He unlocked the door and entered, started towards the dresser, then set the bolt so the door wouldn't close all the way.

"Gots to be prepared," he said, the words slurred. He examined the label on the Remy as he lifted it, then opened it and took a deep whiff. The smell assaulted his nostrils. "Nice year."

He whistled as he pulled another thousand dollars from his pocket and tossed it on the dresser. The bills fluttered and spread apart. The girls were expensive, he thought, but worth every dime. From his other pocket he removed his license and left over pocket money. He emptied the cocaine from the packet onto the dresser and used the license to carve the white powder into long lines, then took a twenty from the wad of bills and curled it into a tight roll. Satisfied he took off his watch, crossed to the safe and punched in the combination, or tried to. He swayed slightly on his haunches, his fingers not completely responding, until he finally got it right. He deposited the remaining cash, watch and license inside and gazed at the money stacked there. Beautiful he said to himself and locked the safe. He got up and backed away, for some reason avoiding the mirror, when a knock came at the door.

He opened it and Crystal and Crystal bounced in. "Some treats on the dresser," he said and closed the door behind them.

"Ohhh Dick, you shouldn't have," blue cooed as she spotted the coke. She made for it quickly.

"Anything for my girls," he said.

Yellow stopped in front of him and looked in his eyes as she slowly pulled her top up and over her head. "It's a little warm in here," she said.

He reached out and filled his hands with her breasts and stared back. "Yes, and it's going to get even hotter," he said.

She pulled at the front of his pants, as she squirmed in his grip. "I hope so."

Blue had finished doing a line and she unsnapped her shorts and wriggled out of them. The tiny red thong barely covered anything. "Come over here baby, I want to show you something," she said seductively.

He stepped over, picked up a glass on the way and gulped. The cognac warmed him as he sipped and stared.

"And what's that?" he asked.

She pulled her top off also, her blonde hair flopping down over her back as she tossed it away. "Me, baby."

He set down the drink and crossed the room toward her. He heard the snorting sound of yellow behind him. It's going to be a long night he thought.

Chapter Twelve

The press conference was a complete success Will thought, and my investigation still ain't worth shit. He had heard once, but didn't know where, that if you didn't catch the perp within forty-eight hours odds were about ten to one you would never nab him. It was already Wednesday morning and his chances of catching anything other than a cold had diminished rapidly. He picked up the 8 x 11 composite sketch the bellman and the cabby had helped create. Just a damn caricature he said to himself and tossed it down again. It probably looked like about ten thousand guys in the Denver area alone, and none of them was the guy he was looking for.

He had distributed the composite at the conference, but hadn't really pushed the sketch on the media. A few of the TV stations briefly showed it during the thirty seconds the story made the noon news, interest still relatively high immediately after the briefing. But by ten last night a forest fire was burning out of control in Rocky Mountain National Park and the plight of the elk that were being forced to flee across busy highways seemed much more newsworthy. It was for the best he thought. He was sure that the man who had robbed the store and caused the death of Margaret Hawkins was nowhere near Colorado.

He wasn't used to being in hopeless situations and it didn't sit well, under-achievement being somewhat foreign to him. Now, waiting outside the Captain's office, he wondered how the man would react to the lack of progress.

"Carter, get in here," the Captain said from inside, not looking up from his desk.

Will walked in and stood almost at attention, like a rookie cop.

"Have a seat Will," the Captain added as he flipped through some papers in a white manila folder, still not looking up.

Will pulled one of the simple metal desk chairs with a small plastic seat toward him, sat down and waited quietly.

Finally the Captain shifted his attention and drew a bead on him. "OK, fill me in on the King Foodmart fiasco, and please tell me you have more than you did yesterday. By the way, I saw the news this morning and there was barely a mention of the case."

Will straightened in the chair, lips tight and his hands clenched involuntarily.

"Yes sir. It appears that the press conference yesterday had the desired effect. We disclosed everything to the media and they quickly lost interest in the story."

"Jesus, the media, go figure. Did you see that an elk got a leg broken by a bunch of tourists driving an SUV this morning? Trying to get close-up pictures? We've got a poor woman dead here, and the news shows three minutes of some fucking elk being airlifted by a helicopter."

Will suppressed a smile.

"Well the good news I guess is that we seem to be out of the spotlight on this," the Captain added.

"Yes sir, but I'm sorry to report that we still don't have much to go on."

The Captain couldn't have been more than forty-five Will thought. He was a shorter man, red hair trimmed like he just got out of the Marines, dressed every day in a white shirt and what appeared to be the same tie. A driven man almost obsessed with his job and consumed with the need for positive results from his people. He was genuinely concerned with the image the Police Department had with the community at large, and he didn't like failure.

"That Will, is not good news," The captain said.

"No sir, it's not. Let me start with forensics. We got nothing from the store. No prints, or even partials from the door, the safe, the table where the money was, nothing." He paused for a moment to think and ensure he didn't leave out any details. "We pulled the cab in also. The door handles both inside and out were completely smeared. No chance of lifting anything there either."

The Captain grunted.

"We did find the sack the perp discarded at the Hyatt. It was a simple white plastic bag, the kind you get at almost any store in the country. There was some skin oil residue but again nothing we could use in the way of prints. The clothing inside was standard workout stuff, pants and a sweatshirt, probably came from a K-Mart or something. We also recovered a few hairs from the wig, but without something to match them against, they aren't worth much.

"And a useful description?" the Captain asked. "I've seen the composite that you made up. Rather unremarkable."

"Yes sir, I know. It was put together by the driver and the bellman. It was somewhat generic I suppose."

"Bullshit generic. It looked like my brother in law for Christ's sake. And as much as I'd like to toss his ass in jail I don't think that would help much here."

"No sir," Will said, and allowed the smile to creep across his face again.

"You didn't get anything from the employees or the old lady?"

"Well, the perp was disguised at that point, and I didn't want to add to the confusion. We have spent a considerable amount of time following up on calls we received from the initial sketch release, but to be honest sir I don't believe the man is in Denver anyway. I think it's a waste of time."

The Captain's intense eyes locked on his, small wrinkles stretching across his forehead. "What was the follow-up from airport then?"

"Well, there were about forty flights leaving DIA within two hours after the man was dropped off. By the time we had the sketch ready I didn't see much point in canvassing the gate attendants or security personnel. It would have taken days to find them and round them up anyway."

The Captain leaned forward and intertwined his fingers on the desk in front of him. "So what is your expert assessment of the situation then Detective?"

Will took a deep breath, but didn't pull any punches. "Well, sir, as I said before, I think it was a well planned job, probably a professional."

"What kind of professional thief targets a grocery store? Jesus." It was more of a remark than a question.

"Anyway, I think he's long gone, and probably won't be coming back. We have no leads, no forensics and a marginal description that looks a quarter of the population that we can only show to people in town…"

"Drop it," the captain interrupted.

Will's eyes widened. "What sir? Drop what?"

The Captain leaned back in his chair and looked directly at him. "Will, you've got shit here, right? Nothing even remotely promising to pursue?"

Will nodded his head silently, unable to argue the point.

"And the media isn't paying any attention, right?"

"No sir, they seem to be focusing on other matters."

"And the victims? Are they screaming bloody murder?"

"No, I met yesterday with the son of the Hawkins woman and gave him the full story. He's not pressing us."

"Then move on. Queue it up in the open file and get back to work." The Captain suddenly looked fatigued despite the early hour. "You do have other cases to work on don't you?"

"I do sir, or course. But I thought you said the mayor would want some priority on this."

The Captain leaned forward, face concerned. "Will, I know what you are thinking, but we fight the fights we can win, and I don't see much hope of a victory here. I don't like unsolved cases anymore than you do, nor does the mayor. But statistics aside, I'm making the call now that your time could be better spent elsewhere, and I would rather show positive results more than patronizing the public with a bunch of 'ongoing investigation' crap. If you are pressed, tell them we are following up on every available lead. That's it."

Will sensed the dismissal and stood up. "Yes sir."

"And Will," the Captain added. "Since you have already brought this Hawkins guy into your confidence, you better appraise him of the situation. I don't want to have him going ballistic because he thinks we are covering anything up. Convince him it's in his best interest to drop the whole deal and get on with his life, all right?"

Will looked at him, and understood immediately. He didn't like it but didn't see any other choice.

"Yes sir."

"Right. Get out of here," the Captain said and turned back to the papers on his desk.

Sara was hopping mad by the time she reached the station. Some idiot talking on a cell phone rear-ended her while she was stuck at a light and busted a taillight in her new Saab. There was no damage to the other man's car of course, the larger Ford Explorer being somewhat immune to minor collisions. However, the bastard didn't have his insurance information handy, and when she gave him her office number to call he hit on her for drinks later.

It didn't help either that the station had all but dropped the coverage on the robbery. The story she filed for the noon news yesterday had been cut in half by six last night, just mentioned at ten, and not even broadcast this morning. She took it out on the receptionist sitting quietly at a desk just inside door.

"Good morning Sara," the young woman, probably a college student, remarked when she walked in. "Did you see the pictures of that poor elk this morning? I can't believe what some people do to helpless animals." Her head tipped as she looked up at Sara, face drenched with lost puppy pity.

"Who gives a shit about some stupid cow?" Sara shouted at her as she fumbled with her purse and rummaged around for her station badge. She dropped the bag and the contents dumped out over the floor. She bent down to retrieve the spill and looked up. "Is that what you want to see on the news? Pictures of animals? Why don't you just go to the god-damned zoo?"

The receptionist looked at her, aghast. Another employee, a man dressed in jeans and an open jacket walked into the fray and started to lean down to help. She threw her compact, lipstick and an open package of Kleenex in her purse, then realized that a tampon had also fallen out. She picked it up and pointed the white tube at the guy.

"What are you looking at mister?" she said. Her aim was deadly.

The startled man put his hands up in a defensive manner and walked away, shaking his head. She stormed out of the lobby without as much as a glance at the ashen faced woman behind her.

She wrapped her hands around her coffee cup, the desk in front of her a mess. Feeling embarrassed now at the outburst she debated calling the young woman out front to apologize, choosing instead to wait until she calmed down a little. She pulled up her email list from the computer but couldn't concentrate on it; the new messages highlighted not holding her attention.

Was she really so wrong about the story she asked herself. Her instincts had come alive on Monday when she first heard of the robbery, but now it was old news. Buoyed by her anger at the situation she decided to visit her boss to find out what was really going on. She stopped at the coffee station and refilled her cup, then walked purposefully down the hall towards Howard's office, ignoring the pleasant hellos from her co-workers.

Howard was at his desk, on the phone. He glanced at her and held his hand up, two fingers extended and apart. She ignored the request and sat down in the chair across from him. She glared at him for a moment, then interrupted. "Howard," she said.

"I'll get back to you," he said into the phone, replaced it slowly in the cradle and looked at her, a father's look of patience painted on his face.

"Good morning Sara."

"Shit good morning. What happened to my story?"

"What story?"

"The King Foodmart story of course. You know the robbery? Car crash?"

He slowly and carefully formed the words. "Like I said Sara, what story?

Her jaw went slack. "What?"

"Let me ask you something Sara," he started. "That thrilling press conference you covered yesterday, you know, the one where the nice detective drew pretty pictures on the board? Besides that presentation what other earth-shattering news developments do you have on this story?"

"Well, nothing so far, but I'm checking on it."

"I see. And what is it you expect this station to air then, to inspire the public to watch our broadcasts?"

"Well certainly not elk," she replied. It wasn't going well and she straightened her shoulders defiantly.

"I'm going to share something with you, something I thought an experienced professional like you already knew. Fires are news. Helpless elk are news. A city councilman porking his secretary is news. But a two-day old robbery and a car crash is not news, not unless its Princess Di, and I doubt our fickle viewers even recall that it ever happened."

She fidgeted a bit and felt foolish. How could she have let herself get into this? She knew better than to chase after pipe dreams. "So what do you want me to do?"

"Do? What do I want you to do? I want you to do your job. I want you to drop this story like a rock and go find something that will attract and interest viewers."

Wide eyed, she still said nothing.

He rocked back in his chair and smiled at her softly. "Sara, you are a good investigative reporter, probably the best I have. I'll admit this story had some potential when it broke, but there is nothing now. It ain't news no more."

"I see your point Howard," she said, resigned. She got up from the chair and managed a smile. "I guess I better get back to work then."

"That's a good idea. Go sink those pearly whites of yours into something we can use on the air."

She ignored the remark and shuffled out, shoulders slumped. As she passed her desk she dropped off her coffee cup, then walked to the elevator and headed back to the lobby to issue a much needed apology.

Marsh rose up at the usual time that morning, his night thankfully uninterrupted by haunting dreams. He and Susan had talked through the evening, but didn't stay up late enough to watch the ten o'clock news. He went immediately to his office and closed the door to ensure he didn't disturb Suse while he worked out. He did, however, turn on the news and watched for a half an hour while he ran in place, somewhat surprised that there was no mention of Monday's events.

Winded and sweaty, he wrapped a towel around his neck and turned on the computer, then logged onto into the server at the office. The email messages continued to pile up, but not nearly at the rate they had the day before. He took his time answering them. The business ones he again forwarded to Sheila and Joe, at the end requesting they have a conference call later in the morning to go over outstanding details. It felt good to get back into the press of business. By seven thirty he had showered and shaved and was ready to face another day.

He walked into the living room and found Susan busy in the kitchen. A pot of coffee was already brewing and he smelled the aroma lingering in the kitchen. He watched her for a moment without saying anything. She looked happy he thought.

"Hey, got any coffee back there?" he said.

"Of course silly, can't you smell it?" she replied. "And some breakfast too if you are hungry. What time did you get up anyway?"

He moved to the kitchen and retrieved a cup, filled it with steaming coffee and looked at the spread on the counter. Bananas, yogurt, some sliced oranges. "Early. You call this breakfast?"

She put her hands on her hips defiantly. "Whatever. I'm going to sit outside. It's too beautiful to be indoors."

He watched her cross the room, then opened the fridge and poured a large glass of orange juice and finished it in one pass. His thirst quenched, he followed her out to the balcony, the morning air refreshing him even more than the shower. Susan had taken a seat in the chair, sunglasses on; legs pulled up beneath her.

"You look like a vacationing movie star," Marsh said.

She stared out over the railing. "I'd almost forgotten how good the weather is here. It's like this every day isn't it?"

Marsh had consciously not talked about the will last night, happy that the subject hadn't come up on its own. But now he used her comment as an opening. "Suse, I've been thinking. We need to decide what to do with Mom's house."

She took a sip from her cup and looked up at him. "What do you mean Marsh?"

"Well, we have some decisions to make about mom's estate. Part of it is what to do with the condo. I don't have all the details yet, but Steve, my lawyer is working out some options. But he said the first thing we have to decide is whether to sell it or keep it."

"Mmm... I hadn't thought about it. I guess I have been ignoring the reality associated with mom's..." She stopped, eyes hidden behind the glasses. "What do you want to do, rent it?"

"Well I was kind of hoping you might want it."

She pulled the sunglasses up and rested them on her forehead. "You mean move back to Denver?"

"Well ya, I guess so. It would be all paid for you know."

"God Marsh, I haven't even considered..."

"Suse, Mom had a lot of money left," he interrupted. "You can have it all if you want."

She set her cup down hard, coffee slopping out and glared at him. "I don't care about the fucking money. I would rather have her back."

She leaped up and stormed into the living room, leaving him stunned. She disappeared down the hall for a moment, then re-emerged, a wad of tissues crushed in one hand. She was crying openly now.

"Oh God Marsh, I'm sorry," she said as the tears dripped down both cheeks. She clutched at him.

"I'm sorry Suse, I didn't mean to upset you."

"I know. It's just that you took me by surprise." She took a tissue and wiped her eyes. The towel slipped from her head so she pulled it away and tossed it on the chair. Her damp hair curled down around her shoulders. She walked over to the railing and stared off in the distance, her back to him.

"Sure, I've thought about moving back, but not like this. I have a life now, a successful one, or at least I'd like to think so. I have friends, a home, a job, I'm building a career." She turned and looked at him, eyes puffy. "And there's Fred."

"I guess I hadn't considered. I guess I still think of you as my little sister."

She walked over to him and kissed his cheek. "And don't ever stop. But I can't even think of moving, at least not now."

The phone rang and interrupted what he was going to say. He left the matter unresolved, walked into the living room and picked up the phone. "Hello?"

"Marsh, its Will Carter."

His heart skipped a beat and he looked out toward Susan, who still stood at the rail. "Good morning Will. I didn't expect to hear from you so soon," he said, then, not missing a beat, "Do you have some news?"

"I'm afraid I do Marsh, but it's not very good. However I did promise I would keep you posted on anything I discovered."

"I see," said Marsh, and his stomach knotted a bit. "What is it?" Marsh's grip on the phone tightened, his knuckles whitening as he listened to the full explanation. He felt the anger begin to burn inside again. "Just what are you telling me Detective?"

"Marsh, what I'm saying is that despite our desire to do everything we can, we have nothing to work with."

"So you are dropping it? Canceling the investigation?" Marsh asked, incredulous.

"Of course we are not dropping it nor closing the case. It's just that we have zero information to follow up on at this point. If I had something, I would track it like a dog."

Marsh was silent and paced around the living room, phone in hand.

"Marsh, I'm sorry, I truly am. But we have nothing to go on here. Unless we get some kind of a break there is nothing more we can do."

"I'm sorry Will, but I am angry, very angry. I don't mean to direct it at you but this whole deal really pisses me off."

"I can understand that Marsh, and I wish I could say anything to give you some hope. But as I promised I am leveling with you."

"And I thank you for that. Please keep me posted if you find out anything more," Marsh replied, voice terse.

"Marsh, have you set the date for the funeral yet? I'd like to attend if I may."

Marsh was surprised at the request, but was touched by the gesture. For a moment he suppressed his anger. "It's Friday afternoon. I'll have my secretary call you with the details. And thanks for the call Will."

"I'll see you Friday then."

Marsh hung up the phone, set it down, and returned to the balcony. Over the last two days his emotions have been a veritable roller-coaster ride and he didn't like it. He was still angry inside but tried to contain it, not letting it show to Susan.

"Who was that?" Susan asked.

"It was the Detective I told you about. The bottom line is they have squat to go on. He didn't say as much but I think they are forgetting about catching the guy who did this."

Susan walked over to him and took both his hands in hers. "Maybe it's better Marsh, to let it be. We can all forget about it sooner."

He looked at her. "I don't want to forget about it Suse, forget about Mom."

"That's not what I meant Marsh," she said, her voice soothing. "It's just that maybe it's over. No reporters, no news. We can just move on."

His head snapped toward her when she mentioned reporters, but he didn't share his thoughts and gave her a hug instead.

"You're right of course," he said, then changed the subject. "I've got some things to take care of this morning. I've got to do a conference call, then meet with the funeral director at ten. What are your plans?"

"Well, I was going to call the church to make the arrangements. Then I thought I might walk around LODO for a while, visit some shops and galleries. Fred will be here later this afternoon."

"Will you be alright? By yourself for a while I mean?"

"I'll be fine Marsh. But first I'm going to get dressed."

"And I've got to make a call," he said and followed her off the balcony.

They walked down the hall, almost separately. Susan turned into the guestroom and closed the door. Marsh headed back into the office. He sat down at his desk, retrieved his notes and tried not to think he was grasping at straws. He located the number he needed and dialed it. While it rang he looked over his shoulder to make sure Susan was out of earshot. The phone rang several times.

"Sara McGloughin."

He paused for a moment, now that he had her on the phone he wasn't

exactly sure what he was going to say.
"Ms. McGloughin, it's Marsh Hawkins."
She paused. "Good morning Mr. Hawkins. Can I help you?"
He was confused a little, but pressed on. "Please, it's Marsh. You called me yesterday?"
"Oh, yes I did. But I wasn't really expecting you to call back."
"I'm sorry if this is a bad time."
"No, it's all right. I was trying to follow-up from the conference yesterday. I guess the reporter in me got a little carried away. I'm sorry if I intruded."
"Oh, I see," he said, more confused than ever. "I thought maybe you had something you wanted to talk to me about."
"Well, not really to be honest. At the time I was looking for any angle on the story."
Marsh understood instantly. "So you are dropping the story too."
"What?"
"Well the police have given up, so I guess there is no reason for the press not to."
Her voice stepped up a notch. "The police aren't doing anything?"
"Not really. I'm sorry to have troubled you Ms. McGloughin. I guess I misunderstood your intentions."
"Marsh, wait. Maybe we should get together, for lunch if you want."
"I guess I don't see the point now."
"Please, give me a chance," she pleaded. "Why don't we talk about this some more?"
He hesitated again. "Alright then, how about 11:30. Do you know the Timberline Grill in the Tech Center?"
"I'll find it. I'll see you at 11:30. And thanks for calling Marsh."
"Sure," he replied. As he hung up the phone he was unsure why he needed to pursue it himself.

The morning had passed quickly and without any surprises. Susan was up and out of the house by nine, and seemed content to spend the day alone wandering about the city. He was still worried about her, but didn't press it. The conference call was uneventful - business as usual - just as if nothing had happened Monday morning. The meeting the funeral home proceeded quickly and relatively painlessly. The efficient director, it seemed, hadn't changed in the years from his father's death. His mother's plans previously in place, it took less than a hour to make the final arrangements.

Marsh found himself at the restaurant just after eleven, half an hour early for lunch. He took a table anyway, the first to be seated in what would soon be a packed eatery. He had picked up a copy of the paper outside and perused it mindlessly, killing time. He found no mention of the robbery or accident. When he came across the obituaries he paused for a moment and wondered if he was supposed to provide some information to the publication, or would the funeral home take care of it. Another detail to attend to he thought to himself.

He was having second thoughts about the whole lunch idea when Sara walked in. The occupants of the few tables that were occupied turned and looked at her as she confidently strode past, some of the men staring openly. She was dressed conservatively in a dark blue pantsuit, light blue blouse and half-heeled shoes. Her full blonde hair bounced softly around her shoulders as she moved. Marsh was surprised, not remembering from the press conference how stunning she was. He stood up as she approached and offered his hand.

"Hello Ms. McGloughin. Thank you for coming I guess." It sounded hollow as soon as he said it, and he felt bad. She didn't seem to notice.

She took his hand firmly, then let go. "My friends call me Sara," she said. "And I think it is I who should thank you for coming."

She set her purse on the table, hesitated and sat down. Marsh politely waited for her then returned to his own seat. Neither knew what to say, then they both started at once.

"So what kind of..." he said.

"I'm not sure why...," she said simultaneously.

He laughed a little. "You first."

She smiled and said, "I'm not sure why I wanted to see you Marsh. It just seemed important to me."

He looked at her, his eyes full of questions.

"You struck a nerve when you called me this morning. I met with the news director today and he told me to drop the story. I didn't like it, but he seemed convincing at the time."

He sat back, thoughtful. "It doesn't surprise me. The police seem to have the same reaction."

"You have been speaking with Detective Carter on the matter?"

"Yes, quite a bit. He actually has been very open with me - genuinely concerned I think. We reviewed everything before the conference yesterday."

"Was there something he wasn't saying?"

He was surprised at her comment, and hesitated. The whole purpose of the briefing yesterday was to keep the media out of it, to avoid dredging up sordid details and let the matter rest. Now he was here talking to a reporter. He got a short reprieve as the waitress appeared at the table, dropping off menus. The young woman started to talk about the day's specials before Marsh interrupted her.

"Give us a few minutes, please," he said politely. She nodded and backed away.

Sara leaned forward, eyes eager. "There was something wasn't there?"

"How did you know?"

A smug smile spread over her face. She opened her purse, pulled out a business card and held it up in front of him.

"Sara McGloughin, Investigative Reporter. It's my job."

He smiled back, took the card and turned it over in his hands. "I should have known," he said. "And I was about to ask you what kind of reporter you were."

"And what kind of reporter did you think I was?" she asked. Her eyes sparkled mischievously.

"Sports? Cooking maybe?" The tension seemed to have disappeared from the table and he relaxed a bit.

"Can I be honest with you Sara?" He waited as she nodded slowly. "Yesterday I was furious with the press and the police. The first I learned of anything was on the morning news, and even then I wasn't sure it was about mother until I met with Carter. Everyone seemed to know it all before I did."

"It's not supposed to be that way Marsh."

"I know, but that's the way it happened. I even called my lawyer for Christ's sake. But then I met with Carter and calmed down a little. The press conference was staged to keep you guys off their back. My mother's death was listed as a homicide it seems."

Sara looked at him, the light bulb coming on. "Of course, I didn't even think... They wanted to keep this as low key as possible didn't they?"

"Exactly. And I thought it was in my, our family's best interest to do so. Now I'm not so sure." His face darkened a little.

"The cops don't like having an open homicide on their files. Bad publicity." Her nose and eyebrows wrinkled a little. "Which means that they don't have anything to go on. People easily forget a robbery, but a homicide is different." She stopped for a moment she noticed the expression on his face.

"Oh my God Marsh, I'm so sorry." She reached out and touched his hand softly, frowning.

"It's OK, I'm dealing with it," he said. He found himself strangely attracted to the look on her face.

"I guess I get a little carried away sometimes."

"Keep going, please. I want to hear what you think."

"OK, if you don't mind. So Carter left two things out of the briefing. First, he used the robbery to focus attention away from the accident. And second, the question at the end - the one he ducked about where the cab went. You know don't you?"

"Yes I do," he said. He wondered if he was breaking some sort of confidence by speaking about it and hesitated. What the hell he said to himself. "DIA."

She leaned back in her chair, "Of course. That makes perfect sense. The suspect goes to the airport and effectively disappears. They have nothing to go on, which means they don't have a lot of hope of ever catching the guy, do they?"

Marsh shook his head slowly. "I'm not sure why I'm telling you this Sara. The last thing I want is another media blast about my mother making the news. I can see the headlines now: 'Police Lose Killer at Airport' or something like that."

"So why did you call me Marsh? I am a reporter for God's sake."

"I don't know. I was angry. I'm still angry at the whole deal. I want the man to pay for what he did to us." He stopped, trying to calm himself, then continued. "When you called I got the impression that you might know something, anything. I was grasping at straws I guess."

She leaned closer, a look of conspiracy in her eyes. "You've put me in a tough spot here Marsh. What you just told me is news, real news, and I wouldn't be a good reporter if I didn't take the opportunity to give my station an exclusive on the revelation."

"I was hoping you wouldn't say that," he said. But the wheels were turning, and Marsh was a strategist. "I understand your position, but look at it from my point of view. I want to see the guy caught; you're an investigative reporter. Sure you could report on what I've told you here, but how big is that news? Your boss already told you to drop the story anyway. Wouldn't you rather get the bigger scoop? Catch the guy?"

Her jaw dropped. "What? How am I going to do that? Jesus, the police can't even find him."

"But they are not looking either."

"And you expect me to find him?"

"Look, I'm winging it here OK? Maybe we could do something together."

"You're serious about this aren't you?"

"I guess it is a little farfetched, and to be honest I really hadn't thought about it until now. But isn't that what you do? Investigate?"

The waitress walked up again and Marsh was relieved at the break in the conversation. God I must sound like I'm crazy he thought. What does this poor woman think of me?

"What will you have Sara, I'm buying."

She hadn't opened the menu, but looked up at the waitress. "Do you have a chicken salad?"

"Yes ma'am," the woman replied.

"Fine," Sara said.

"And I'll have the chicken sandwich," Marsh added, not referring to the menu either.

"Come here often?" Sara teased.

"First time, but who doesn't have a chicken sandwich?" he kidded. "Uh, would you like a drink or something?"

"I guess I could use one." She turned to the waitress, "White wine please."

"I'll have the same."

Sara's face turned serious as the waitress picked up the menus and departed. "Marsh, I don't know what to say here. But even if I did consider this wild scheme of yours, which I'm not seriously doing by the way, what could we possibly do?"

He laughed. "Shit Sara, you're the expert here. I'm just a computer jock."

She made that funny frowny face again and he liked it. He hoped he could trust her, or she would at least finish lunch with him.

"OK, dumb idea. Let's enjoy lunch and forget about it. God knows I've got enough to deal with the next few days," Marsh said.

They were quiet for a moment, and she fiddled with her silverware until she had all utensils exactly lined up next to her plate. "You know Marsh, ever since I got this story I've had a funny feeling about it. My reporter instincts kicking in I guess. But I still don't know what to do about it."

Marsh smiled at her, then looked away when he realized he was staring. She was so easy to talk to he had forgotten again how beautiful she was. The waitress returned with the wine and set the glasses down in front of them. He picked his up, holding it out.

"I'll make you a deal Sara. You don't write me off as a crackpot and walk out on me, and I'll give you a few days to think about it."

She laughed out loud and looked into his eyes, her own twinkling. "What kind of deal is that?"

He shrugged, still holding his glass. "Best I've got to offer I guess."

She picked up her glass and reached towards him, their glasses tinkling. "Deal," she said.

Chapter Thirteen

The heavy curtains pulled tight over the windows inside Fred's room blocked out all traces of daylight. He groaned as he rolled over in the large bed, the top sheet and covers nowhere to be seen. He was naked as he stretched, then peered in the general direction of the alarm clock on the stand next to the bed. A sharp pang blasted through his head as he turned, the blurring red digits revealed it was 8:57 am.

"Jesus," he said as he dropped his legs over the side of the bed and sat up. Another bolt of pain rocked him and he forced himself to hold his head still. The events of the previous night were unclear, and he was disturbed by the fact that he couldn't remember much of what happened. He was sure it was time to get moving though, and rose and walked towards the bathroom. The surface of the dresser had a white residue spread thinly across it and he noticed a mostly empty bottle of cognac, cork top nowhere to be found. He reached for it and wondered again, but the pungent smell of the liquid nauseated him and he quickly set it down.

The bathroom lights were way too bright which forced him to squint at himself in the mirror. His eyes were bloodshot and his mouth was parched and sticky, the rough and unshaven image reflected curiously unfamiliar. For a moment it flickered and seemed to laugh, but he pushed it away, attributing the apparition to a lack of good sound sleep. It took some effort to keep the pain in his head in check as he bent over and filled a glass with water and drained it, the cool liquid partially satisfying the dryness in his mouth.

"I need a shower," he said to no one and stepped into the tub, jumping out of the way as cold water sprayed out of the nozzle. He adjusted the temperature quickly, then languished under the heavy stream as the water massaged his stiff frame. As he cleansed himself, he tried to run through the timetable in his head. He needed to get to the bank, his business there hopefully would take only a few minutes, maybe a half an hour. His flight was around one he remembered, and maybe if he got to the airport quickly enough he could catch an earlier plane. He was suddenly anxious to get to Denver and Susan. Susan, he thought. He recalled talking to her after dinner last night, but wasn't he supposed to call her again?

Fred jumped out of the shower, grabbed an oversize towel and wrapped it around his waist without drying. The water droplets splashed to the carpet as he quickly crossed the room and grabbed the phone, dialing her cell number from memory. The phone rang and rang, Susan not picking up, until it clicked into voicemail. He was unsure what to say anyway, so he hung up the phone without leaving a message. She would see that he had called at least, her missed call list would contain a Las Vegas number. He'd try again from the airport he rationalized, when he knew what flight he would be on.

Somewhat perturbed by sleeping late he went back to the bathroom to finish cleaning up and get out of the hotel. He wondered to himself why he chose that city to launder his money when he could go practically anywhere to accomplish the task. He reached the sink and grabbed the shaving cream from his dop kit, the can making a squishing sound as he filled his fingers with white foam. He looked in the mirror as his hand reached up to spread the cream over his cheeks. He froze when he saw the face in the mirror.

"You know why you come here Fred?" the grinning man said to him. "Because it's way too much fun."

Fred just stood there, mesmerized.

"What's the matter Fred? Having some memory problems this morning? Blocking something out? Maybe it was all the scotch and cognac, ya think?" Richard laughed at him.

Fred tried to say something, but couldn't. He shook his head and tried to clear the image, but it persisted.

"Would you like me to remind you of what Crystal and Crystal did to you last night? Or would pretty little Susan not appreciate the specific details?"

"No, not Susan…" he managed to say.

"OK Fred, I'll let it slide this time. But remember our conversation last night. I don't want to wait another month. Get your ass in gear and get John to knock over another store. And tell him to try and not kill anyone this time. It attracts too much attention you know?" Richard said, the threat punctuated with a sinister laugh.

Fred forced his hand to his face and wildly spread the foam, covering his cheeks and mouth and part of his nose with white as he watched the reflection change. He shaved quickly, his heart thumping in his chest.

DECEPTION ON MARGIN

"I've got to get out of here," he said to himself, now more anxious than ever to finish his business and get on a plane. He wiped his face clean with a towel and rubbed hard to get rid of the beard he had already shaved off and the laughter that still rang in his ears. Dressing rapidly, he pulled on the last of his clean shirts and another brown pair of Dockers. He didn't notice the wrinkles in either one.

The beads of sweat had already appeared inside his shirt as he tried the safe, punching in his birthday backwards. He tugged on the handle and swore loudly when it wouldn't open. He tried three more times, on each attempt he hit the buttons a little slower, a little more carefully. Nothing. His mind was racing now - what could have happened? He stood up and wondered if he should call the management, and tried to determine what they would think when they saw the cash and multiple ID's inside. ID's he thought after a frantic moment. He rummaged through his dirty clothes until he found Richard William's driver's license and a crumpled wad of cash. He pulled the plastic piece out, tossed the bills to the floor and looked at the birth date. Kneeling back down before the safe, he glanced at the license then back to the numbers as he pressed them. He yanked the handle and the safe creaked open. He let out a sigh of relief and fell back on his butt. It was a few moments before his ragged breathing slowed.

It took Fred only about five minutes to clear the closet of his clothes, and reorganize his bags. The ID's he stored safely back in his computer case. He kept his and counted almost a thousand dollars in wrinkled cash from the floor. The rest of the cash - the ninety grand - he wrapped carefully inside a plastic laundry sack and stuffed into one of the suitcases. He was thirsty, starved and desperately needed a cup of coffee, but made no plans for breakfast. He left the room, door open, the TV on, and trudged with his luggage towards the lobby.

The cabby this time was a woman. She had very short black hair pulled straight up from the top of her head; the back shaved about three inches above the nape of her neck. Her tongue was pierced with a small silver barbell, and he learned in the first three minutes of the ride that she was ex-army and a lesbian. Fred informed her he had to make a stop to make as he loaded his bags into the back seat of the taxi, declining to store them in the trunk. She was hesitant at first, but a twenty quickly changed her mind. Now she seemed to be his best friend and wouldn't shut up. He rested his head against the back cushion, slouched down a bit, sunglasses pulled tight over his eyes.

"It was Desert Storm that convinced me that I was gay," she droned on. "I spent two months there, mostly stuck on a ship floating in the Gulf. I mean I joined the Army to fight, not sit on a dump of a transport ship. I was one of four women on board, along with about two hundred guys. I mean if a girl wanted to get laid that would be the place don't you think?"

Her mouth opened and closed widely as she chewed her gum to death. In an effort to avoid any further revelations of her past he pulled his cell phone from his computer case and dialed the Premier Desk at United. She looked at him in the mirror as she drove, apparently not bothered by his failure to participate in the conversation.

"Uh, yes," he said into the phone to the customer service agent. "I need to check on some flights please. I'm currently booked on a flight from Las Vegas to Denver at around one today, and I was wondering if there was anything available earlier."

"By the time we were deployed, the party was over. I mean we went from the boat to a camp in the middle of the goddamn desert. We sat there for two weeks, and then they put us back on the ship and sent us home. What's up with that?"

He shrugged politely. "Simpson, Fred Simpson," he said into the phone.

She was unrelenting. "You know what I did all day, every day? I cleaned my weapon. Over and over again." The cab lurched to a stop at a light, almost hitting the back of an old station wagon. "I've been in jail ya know. Desert Storm was worse."

He glanced at his watch, confirming the time. "Great, can you book me on that please? Thanks," he said and hung up the phone.

The car sped forward again and Fred hoped they would get to the bank quickly. He was tempted to let the taxi go when he got there but didn't think he had the time.

"So I came to Vegas ya know? Figured I'd be a stripper. I've got some friends that work the clubs and they make piles of money. Besides, being a lesbian I thought I wouldn't have to worry about all the guys hitting on me. That didn't work out either, so now I'm a hack. Go figure."

She chewed her gum loudly as she steered the cab into the parking lot of the bank, pulled into a handicapped spot and stopped the car. She

DECEPTION ON MARGIN

turned to look at him, arm on the back of the seat and tipped up her sunglasses. "How long you gonna be buddy?"

He lifted the suitcase on his lap, unzipped it and pulled out the plastic sack. "About fifteen minutes I think." He was concerned about leaving his luggage in the car and wondered if she would speed off with it. She must have read his mind.

"Don't worry pal, I'll be here when you get back. Got the paper right here," she said and tapped the seat, then pushed her glasses down again and turned away. He grabbed his computer case anyway and got out of the car.

The lobby of the First Bank of Nevada was cool and mostly empty when he entered. He walked quietly across the carpeted floors, the air conditioning cooling him slightly. He'd been on edge ever since the problem with the safe and he wanted to get this over with. He nodded at a receptionist seated at a wide brown desk and took his place in the roped line behind a very old man leaning on a cane and a younger man in a suit.

Fred looked around as he waited, and absently swung the plastic sack in his hand until a teller called him over. He smiled politely, set his computer down at his side and placed the sack on the counter. The man in a white shirt and brown checked tie looked up at him through thick glasses.

"May I help you sir?"

"Yes, please. I need two cashiers checks, one for..." he paused for a second as he quickly calculated random amounts, "uh, fifty three thousand and one for thirty seven thousand dollars."

The man looked at him and blinked twice slowly. Fred casually began to take the packed bills out of the sack and stacked them neatly on the counter. The teller looked at the sack without saying anything. Fred realized that a picture of the Four Queens hotel was printed on it, but decided it didn't matter much.

"Uh, one moment please," the teller said and walked away. Fred continued to place the money down into small piles but his heart raced at the man's reaction. He had just completed the task when the teller returned with a smartly dressed woman, obviously a manager of some sort.

He looked at her, a trickle of sweat forming in his armpits. "Is there a problem?"

"No sir, not at all. Morton just informed me that you wanted two cashier checks. It's customary for us to have two employees verify the amounts when there is a large amount of cash involved."

Fred smiled at her and breathed easier. "Of course. Probably happens quite a bit in this town."

"Yes sir, it does. Now, you wanted two checks, in the amount of fifty three thousand and thirty seven thousand dollars?"

"That's correct ma'am."

"I will need to see some ID please."

"Absolutely," he said. He pulled his wallet from his rear pocket, removed the license and handed it to her.

"And you would like these made out to whom?"

"In my name please."

She looked at the license, then him as she verified the picture. "Mr. Simpson, this will take a few moments. Why don't you have a seat while we prepare the checks. There will be a ten dollar charge for each."

He reached into his pocket and removed a crumpled twenty-dollar bill, smoothing it out as he set it on top of the cash.

"Thank you," he said, picked up his case and walked away.

He watched from his seat as the teller and the manager counted the money carefully, other patrons in line coming and going. Suddenly he remembered Susan, quickly reached for his cell phone and tried her number again. She answered after three rings, the connection not clear.

"Hello?"

"Susan, hi. It's me," he said. He felt self-conscious as his voice echoed across the lobby. "I can barely hear you."

"What? Is that you Fred?" she squeaked, breaking up.

"Susan?"

He got up from the seat and walked toward the front doors, hoping the reception would improve.

"I'm here. Did you call earlier?" he heard, the reception better but still a lot of background sound, like cars he thought.

"Yes, a little while ago, but I couldn't get to the phone in time. Where are you?" she asked.

He waited for a moment as the noise slowly diminished.

"That's better," she said. "Sorry, I was on the street. I'm doing some shopping and had to duck into a store to hear you."

"Hi," he said again.

"When are you coming Fred?"

"Well I'm just finishing up here, and hopefully I'm going to catch an earlier flight."

"Great, what time?"

It was nice to hear her voice he thought - she sounded good. He did a quick time check in his head. "I should land sometime around one, then I have to get a car."

"Oh good, please hurry."

"I'll tell the Captain you said to fly faster."

"Stop it silly, it's just that I want you to be here."

"And I want to be there too," he replied. He had butterflies in his stomach already he realized, and smiled. "Do we have any plans?"

"Marsh is out until this afternoon, so come straight to the condo OK?"

"Alright. I'll call you when I get the car, for directions. About one-thirty or two if we are on time."

"I'll be waiting Fred."

The manager waved at him from across the lobby so he waved back and held the phone in the air for a second. "I've gotta go babe. I'll see you soon."

He walked quickly back to the woman who waited patiently by his computer case. "Sorry," he said.

"No problem, Mr. Simpson. Your license and checks," she said and handed the items over to him.

"Thank you very much. It's been a pleasure doing business with you," he replied. The tension in his stomach suddenly disappeared, and he was whistling by the time he walked out the door into the heat. The cab was still there, the driver obscured inside the window by a newspaper. His headache had also disappeared, along with any questions about the previous night.

Susan had prowled the shops for hours, enjoying the time alone and away from family, work and most of all the reason she had been called to Denver. She walked lightly down the sidewalk, stopped to look into store windows and hummed softly to herself. Dressed for summer in light blue shorts, white golf shirt and hair in a ponytail she drew more than a few appreciative glances from the men she passed, but didn't notice them.

She turned the corner onto Larimer Street and looked down the row of restaurants, most with seating set in open fenced areas, a few with tables protruding onto the sidewalk. She was hungry, but couldn't decide what might satisfy her appetite. Finally she ignored the decision and settled for Starbucks. She strolled inside the store and purchased a latte, then found an open seat on the sidewalk near the street. She was in a good mood - better than she had any right to be - and that made her feel a little guilty. She had only been eighteen when her father died and just off to college. She recalled how badly she had adjusted to loss then. It had been a tough first year, away from home and family, she had pushed back against everyone who had tried to get close to her. It took over a year to get over his death and back to her normal happy self. Why was it different this time?

The sun was warm, almost hot but the air was dry. A light breeze that pushed her hair around forecast the usual late afternoon thunderstorm. She sipped her coffee slowly and tried to imagine moving back into her mother's condo. Colorado was tempting she admitted, but moving away from Minneapolis would be difficult. Through college and since graduation she had lived there almost eight years. Though Denver was still home, her whole adult life had been spent in Minnesota. She was also sure she was in love with Fred, but unclear on what commitments to make. She briefly wondered if Fred would be willing to come to Denver, then caught herself.

"What are you thinking?"

A young couple sitting at the table next to her turned and stared.

"Oops... sorry," she said and they looked away again. She giggled a little. God what would Fred say if he knew what I was thinking? Living together? Marriage? The thoughts swirled through her mind. She got up from her chair and started for the gate in the short wrought iron fence.

"That's enough of that girl," she said to the fence, this time not caring who heard as she stepped back onto the sidewalk. It was well past lunch and the crowds were thinning, the streets filled mostly with shoppers and tourists. She sighed, almost happy with the dilemma as she started the long hike back towards the Marsh's condo. She had only gone only a few blocks when her cell rang. There was a bus stop bench close to her so she sat down and dug in her purse for the phone.

"Fred?"

"Hey Susan, I'm here," he said. "Or at least I'm at the car rental place."

"Great hon. I was just thinking about you." She let a smile build on her face. "How soon can you get here?"

"I don't know... that depends on where here is," he laughed. "But I need to ask you something. I was going to get a convertible, but then I thought it might not be appropriate."

She considered his request for a moment. "Why not Fred? I'm sure it will be OK."

"All right, how do I get there?"

She spoke carefully and gave him the directions. It probably wasn't the quickest way to Marsh's condo, but it would get him there without problems.

"I'll be there as soon as I can."

"And I'll be waiting for you so hurry," she said. She felt the butterflies begin to build inside.

She had plenty of time to get back she thought, as she rose from the bench and started off. She hummed again and walked faster, anxious to see Fred, but enjoying the exercise and the fresh air until she approached the King Foodmart where she had shopped the night before. A sudden chill came over her this time and she pressed on, passing by the parking lot without a glance at the sprawling building. Within a few minutes she was back in the kitchen and paced as she cleaned up the remainder of breakfast mess.

"Jesus, I'm nervous," she said, but couldn't stop fidgeting. She walked into the bathroom, looked in the mirror and double-checked her appearance.

"You look fine girl," she said to the reflection, but picked up her brush and redid her hair anyway, then dabbed a touch of perfume to her wrists and neck. The phone rang in the distance and her heart skipped a beat, rushing back to the living room to answer it.

"Hawkin's residence," she said politely into the phone.

"Suse it's me. I'm glad I caught you. Are you OK?" Marsh inquired.

"Sure Marsh, of course. I'm just waiting for Fred. He should be here any minute."

"Already? I thought he wasn't coming in until later."

"He got an early flight. He was anxious to get here I suppose."

"Damn, I was hoping to be there when he arrived. I just got a call from Steve, and he wants me to drop by his office to go over the estate. Have you thought any more about the condo?"

"Actually I have, but do we need to make a decision about it now?"

"No, but the longer we delay the more he's going to charge us. I hate lawyers," he chided.

"Well if you have to say something I think we should keep it Marsh. I'm not making any commitments but selling it now would be a bit premature don't you think? I mean we can always sell it later can't we?"

"Of course," he said, and sounded optimistic. "I'll be home in about an hour and a half. Say hi to Fred for me and don't do anything I wouldn't do."

"Who, me? Wouldn't dream of it. We'll be here when you get back. I can't wait for you to meet him."

The intercom buzzed, interrupting the conversation.

"It's Fred at the door Marsh. I gotta go," she said and the butterflies returned in full force.

Susan dropped the phone in the chair and ran across the room to the intercom. It took a second to locate the correct button for entry, then she pressed it long and hard, opened the door and rushed out to the elevator. She ran her hands through her hair as she waited impatiently, reaching over to punch both the up and down buttons on the wall. The door opened and Fred stood there, beads of sweat on his forehead, luggage at his side and computer case in one hand. She looked at him, her heart racing.

"You're a mess," she said and laughed, then ran over and practically leaped into his arms.

Fred struggled to hold her, one arm pulling her close. They almost tripped over the luggage as she pushed into him. He kissed her quickly, then bent to one side, pulled her along and pressed the open button as the doors began to close.

"Can we get out of the elevator please?"

"Oh I suppose. If we have to," she conceded, but didn't let him go. He kicked a suitcase in front of the door then kissed her longer. The door slid into the bag, and opened again obediently.

"Come on," he said after a moment. He looked deep into her eyes while his hands slowly stroked her hair. They gathered up the luggage and stepped into the hall. "You didn't tell me I was going to have to walk here. My car must be three blocks away."

"Poor baby," she said. She clutched his arm tightly as they walked down the hall to the door. "I missed you so much."

"And I missed you too babe. It was a hard trip."

They crossed through the entry, dropped the baggage down then closed the door behind them. Susan pulled him close. Her hands stroked his head and she stared in his face without saying anything. Then she kissed him again, softly at first, then harder, as she pressed her body against him.

He was hesitant at first, then responded to her aggression, his hands moving across her back and down, caressing her slowly.

"Where's Marsh?" he asked softly, the words mumbled a bit between their pressing lips.

"He's not here," she said as her hands pushed over his chest, her mouth moving across his neck. She kissed and bit it gently. She brushed her lips across his ear, her breath brushing hotly into it. "Big brother won't be home for a while," she said, then took his hand and pulled him into the hallway.

He followed her willingly, suddenly aroused by her desire. Susan fell on her back onto the bed and dragged him on top of her. She kissed him fiercely, without abandon as her hands flew over his body. She pulled his shirt from his pants and slid her palms underneath.

"Make love to me Fred, now," she said, her voice deep and sensual.

Their clothes flew off as they took each other, hungrily first, then wildly, all thoughts of anything but each other banished from their minds. She was like an animal, totally surrendering to her passion, at times almost screaming at him. Never before had they been so consumed by their desire for each other, until they collapsed at their release together on top of the spread.

"Oh my God," Susan said as Fred rolled to her side. Her chest heaved from the strain.

He stroked her soft skin slowly. "Wow," he managed to say, his breath short as he looked closely at her face.

She turned and snuggled into him, their intertwined bodies damp from the exertion, her mouth pushing into his ear. "Mmm... again?" she asked quietly, her breath still ragged. "A little slower this time?"

He smiled at her, pushed her head back and kissed her nose and cheeks. "Do we have time?" he asked.

"I don't know, don't care," she said as she pulled away from him. "But I could use a shower," she laughed.

He watched as she got off the bed and walked slowly around it, her eyes locked on his the entire time. Susan stopped at the bathroom door with her back to him and turned on the lights. Then she turned slowly and her hands slid up her flat stomach to her breasts.

The grin spread quickly over her face. "Coming?"

Chapter Fourteen

"You two look awfully... clean," Marsh said, his left eyebrow raising just a notch.

Susan and Fred sat on the long couch under the wall of photos, not too close to each other. Her arm was stretched out between them, her hand resting on his knee. Fred had on a pair of light blue dress shorts, a gray Nike T-shirt, and no shoes. Susan sported a long flowing print wrap and a yellow tank top, the thin white strip of her bra visible below one of the yellow shoulder straps, her hair blown dry and flowing across the bare tops of her arms. There was a faint thump, thump in the background as the washer and dryer worked away from inside the laundry closet.

"I'm sorry Marsh," Fred said. "I didn't mean to be so casual."

"He was a mess when he got here," Susan said. She gazed at Fred momentarily and smiled devilishly, then looked back to Marsh. "I offered him a shower."

Fred's face strained for credibility. "And I hadn't packed enough for the trip to Denver. She took all my clothes and threw them in the wash," he added with a shrug.

"I see," Marsh replied as he glanced back and forth between them.

Susan giggled and looked radiant. "I couldn't very well have him meet my big brother looking like a slob."

Fred shrugged again.

Marsh had returned home from the lawyer's office feeling a bit drained. Steve had presented two different strategies to dispose of his mother's assets, and both included keeping the condo. But the meeting had weighed heavily on him, the reality of her death reinforced by poring over the financial details. He hoped to share the options with Suse that afternoon and tactfully resurface the idea of her moving back to Denver, but now that Fred had arrived it didn't seem to be the right time. He didn't want his down mood to spill over to the pair on the couch so he got up and started for the kitchen.

"I'm going to have an iced tea," he said as he walked. "Can I get you guys anything?"

"Iced tea sounds great Marsh," Fred said.

"Not for me," Susan said as she rose from the couch and looked back at Fred. "I'm going to finish cleaning up. I'll leave you two boys alone to get to know each other." She walked quickly out of the living room; the corners of her lips raised in a smug smile and disappeared down the hall.

Marsh found two tumblers in the cupboard and filled them with ice and tea from the fridge. He returned slowly and wondered how to start the conversation. He handed a glass to Fred on the couch and noticed for the first time the oval birthmark on the side of his neck. Fred rose politely and took the glass before sitting back down.

"How long have you known Suse," he said as he dropped comfortably into his favorite chair. The question felt out of place, like he was a father meeting his teenage daughter's first date.

"Suse? I thought everyone called her Susan," Fred asked.

Marsh laughed, "Everyone does, except for me. It started when we were just kids. I guess I never got out of the habit, although she used to try and convince me to do so."

"When I first met her, I called her Sue once," Fred laughed, "I thought she was going to toss a glass of wine in my face."

"It actually started when she was about six I think. Mom was trying to make her stop carrying her worn out blankie every where she went. She told Suse she was grown up now, and grown-ups didn't have blankets. Susan responded by stuffing her blanket in the garbage and hands on hips defiantly told everyone that if she was grown up, everyone should call her Susan. She never let anyone forget it."

They both laughed a little, fond memories flooding back to Marsh.

"About a year."

"What, oh."

"We've been... steady I guess for about eight months though. Even though I'm a little older than she is, it doesn't seem to make any difference. She seems to fit in well with everyone."

"Yes, she does." There was a moment of uncomfortable silence between them. "Suse said you were in computers?"

"I was, for a long time. I followed in my father's footsteps I guess. He was a consultant, traveled all the time. It seemed like we moved every year or two."

"I can relate to that, though not the moving part. I've always lived in Denver," Marsh said. He shifted forward in his chair, both hands wrapped around the glass. "What part of the computer space were you in?"

Fred leaned forward and spoke clearly. "Well Marsh, my early background starting in college was in software development, but I've pretty much given all that up now. I haven't done anything with computers for well over a year."

"Ah, Suse mentioned something about that... something about day trading?"

Fred shrugged a little. "Guilty as charged. I spend most of my days now analyzing the companies whose technologies I used to use. It's not quite as glamorous and I don't build anything anymore, but the hours are whatever I want and the pay is great - that is if you are any good at it."

"From what I've read, day trading is a somewhat controversial, if not down right dangerous profession. Isn't the government trying to crack down on it?"

Fred got up and stretched a little, then walked over to the screen doors and looked out for a moment. "Jeez Marsh, this is an unbelievable view," he said as he turned back. "You know I've been through Denver changing planes countless times, and have flown over the mountains a lot, but I've never really looked at them like this."

"Yes, it's pretty incredible, but like anything you get used to it though. Mom used to love to sit out on the balcony, just watching the sunset." Marsh said softly.

"Oh, I'm sorry," Fred said. He turned back and faced Marsh, "I guess I kind of forgot to express my condolences Marsh."

Marsh waved his hand towards him and brushed away the remark, the melting ice cubes tinkled softly in the glass. "Thanks, but it's all right. To be honest I'm getting rather tired of all the sympathy conversation. You were talking about day trading. I'm interested. Maybe I could use a change of professions too," Marsh said and laughed.

"Do you mind if we move outside?"

"Sure, not at all," Marsh said as he got up from his leather chair.

The sun shone brightly over the balcony and down on them, but dark thunderclouds billowed up into the blue sky to the west and the south. The air was sweet, a precursor of a late afternoon storm.

"I wouldn't give up your day job yet Marsh," Fred resumed. "Day trading is not for the faint of heart. About eighty percent of the people who try day trading fail at it - and unfortunately being a failure at trading is not like being a failure at being a fishing guide. You lose everything. Your money, your house, your life savings. That's why there has been so much public outcry on regulating it."

"How do you feel about regulation?" Marsh asked, intrigued.

"I think it's ridiculous to even consider it. I mean come on, these are grown people here who are dumb enough to think that because they have a boatload of cash and have been reading the Wall Street Journal once a week they are going to make a killing in the stock market. They dive in, put half their cash on some Internet fly-by and lose their shirts. Then, they get desperate. They've already dumped half of Aunt Mary's retirement money down the toilet so they take even larger risks, trying to get it back all at once, trades getting riskier. Within a few weeks their whole bundle is gone. Poof."

Fred leaned back, and took a sip from his glass. Marsh was fascinated. He walked over to the rail and leaned, his back to the mountains.

"So what happens to these poor fools?" Marsh asked.

"Most of them put their tails between their legs and go home, never telling their wife or dear aunt Mary that the money is gone, or worse yet, holding ten or twenty visa cards, each with a five grand balance to pay off."

"Jesus, Visa?" Marsh said and shook his head.

"You bet. Or the house, the car or anything else they could get their hands on for cash. You see Marsh, it's gambling to these folks, not a profession. They go at it with the same abandon that you or I would show at a casino on a Friday night out with the boys. They don't want to take the time to study or follow the market, or get any kind of experience. They just want to jump in and win big. That's where the regulators are taking a stance. A few of these losers, the one's who have gotten really hurt scream bloody murder. They want someone to pay for their losses."

Marsh looked at him, incredulous. "What? They play the market but want someone else to pay?"

Fred nodded his head slowly. "Sad but true. One guy in California- a classic case - filed a lawsuit against the brokerage firm. He started with about seventy-five grand, and lost it all within about two days. He claimed that the brokerage house should have been keeping track of his trades, and noticed how much money he was losing. The brokers, he said, should have seen how stupid he was and stopped him from trading. In other words, it was all their fault he was an idiot and lost all his money."

DECEPTION ON MARGIN

"Susan says you are pretty successful at trading, Fred."

"Well Marsh, I don't usually discuss my trading activity, even with Susan, although I would if she was more interested."

Marsh held his hands up, surrendering. "It's OK Fred, sorry if I was being nosy."

"No, really, it's alright. I just usually don't brag much. And of course you only get a chance to brag when you're ahead. When I left Dallas yesterday I was up over twenty-five grand."

Marsh whistled and raised one eyebrow. "I'm impressed, twenty-five thousand..." he said and set his nearly empty glass down on the small table. He leaned forward, like a young kid, one wanting to hear the details. "Is that just for the month already?"

Fred looked at him and let the suspense build a little. "No Marsh that was just for the morning" he said, his steeled features betraying little emotion.

"Jesus Fred," Marsh said and his jaw dropped half open. "You're not kidding are you?"

Fred allowed a grin to escape, and shrugged his shoulders. "I must admit it was a good day. They are not all like that," he said, then laughed. "Some days I actually lose too."

"But, how can you... I presume this wasn't just some lucky guess on a stock that won big yesterday. Was this all on paper by the way?"

Fred shook his head slowly as the smile spread wider on his face. "No, I'm a flat trader Marsh," he said. "That means I don't keep positions overnight. You start the day with your cash, make your trades and settle up at the end of the day - hopefully with more money than you had in the morning."

Marsh pondered the implications. "Wow, I didn't realize that. So you never really own anything do you?"

"Not for more than a few hours. One of the cardinal rules of day trading: Every day is a new day."

Fred stepped back away from the rail a little almost lecturing. They had been talking so much they didn't realize the sun had been obscured by the edge of the thunderclouds. A flash lit up the edge of the darker clouds off to the south, too far away to hear the thunder report.

"Most people Marsh, are buyers. They buy Disney, or International Harvester, or a mutual fund their company offers. Some even look at the paper each day to see how the market did. They are happy if it goes up, sad if it goes down. But they never really understanding the mechanics of trading, of what they are doing."

Another bolt flashed across the sky, this time a little closer. Fred nodded to the south and waved his glass, "Storm?"

Marsh got up and walked to the rail and looked out over the darkening clouds. A breeze was picking up, blowing steadily down from the mountains.

"Looks like it. It happens a lot at this time of day. May or may not get us in the city though, Marsh said. He looked over at the screen door as it opened and Susan stepped outside, a glass of white wine in her hand.

She looked them both over slowly, pleased to be the center of attention for a moment. "Well I see you two are getting along," she said. There was a smile on her face and her eyes twinkled brightly in the sun.

Fred moved closer to her. "I'm afraid I was preaching here a bit hon. You know how I get sometimes."

"Nonsense," Marsh interrupted. "Suse, you didn't tell me that Fred here was not only a successful finance guy, but a philosopher as well."

Susan stepped over and snuggled against Fred, trying not to spill the wine in her hand.

Fred a little embarrassed looked over at Marsh and shrugged under her grip. Susan leaned up and kissed him briefly, then walked over to Marsh and kissed him on the cheek as well.

"That's what I like," she said smiling triumphantly, "both my men here. Now don't take this the wrong way, but can we do something fun tonight? How about a nice long dinner with a bottle of wine or two? To remember Mom by?" she asked. "I hate to say this but if she knew we were sitting around pining over her she would kick us all out of the house."

Marsh smiled, "I think you are right Suse. Let's go out and tell old Mom stories. I'd like that."

Another bolt of lightning tore through the sky, this time close enough to briefly light up the balcony. The thunderclap was ear splitting as it followed close behind the flash.

"Oh goody," Susan said and giggled like a little girl. "I love storms. I think I'll stay out here and watch it."

"When should we go?" Fred asked and glanced at his watch. "I should at least check the markets and follow up on some messages." He looked at Marsh. "Do you have place where I could set up my laptop for a few minutes?"

"No problem Fred," Marsh replied. "I'll get you set up in my office."

They both grabbed their empty glasses and headed inside. Susan dropped down into an open chair and waited for the storm roll in across the front-range of the mountains. She turned her head a little, not really facing them.

"Fred, your clothes are clean and in on our bed," she said, then caught herself and looked at Marsh. He glanced back, not missing the reference.

She smiled back at him coyly, wiggled her fingers a little at him, and then waved him off with the glass of wine in her hand. "Go on, shoo. I'm busy relaxing here and I don't need to be bothered by your silly man thoughts."

Marsh turned and looked back across the room, "Hey Fred. Just grab your computer and I'll meet you down the hall in the office." He walked back out on the porch and laughed softly. "So this is the guy I may lose my little sister to."

"Did you like him Marsh? Did you two get along OK?" she asked, her smug smile suddenly transformed into little girl-like curiosity.

He rubbed his hand in her hair and bent over to kiss the top of her head. "We got along just fine Suse. So far I like him a lot."

Susan reached up, placed her hands on the top of her head and covered his hand. "Mom would've too I think. I wish they could have met," she said softly.

The thunder rumbled across the city in a low continuous growl. The air was still and sky darkened even more as the clouds obscured the last of the sun's rays. Suddenly, a huge flash engulfed the balcony, the lightning, a jagged pitchfork tearing across the sky not more than a half mile away. They both blinked at the light, afterimages not even faded away yet when the thunder crashed over them. The glass doors on the balcony shook for a moment then were quiet as the after echoes drifted farther away down to the south.

"Wow," Marsh managed to say. "Maybe you shouldn't be sitting out here."

"Nonsense," Susan replied with a big grin on her face. "This is great. Besides the storm will be gone by dinner."

A shout drifted out from inside the room. "Marsh, I'm going to change clothes. I'll be there in a second."

"Right," Marsh yelled over his shoulder and he pulled away from

Susan.

She grabbed his hand for a moment longer. "Say Marsh, as much as I like having the two of you all to myself, the thought of keeping both of you in line through a long dinner may be too much for even my significant social skills."

"And what are you saying little sister?"

"Well, you don't by any chance have a someone you could invite along do you?" she asked, looking at him with a big grin. "Sheila perhaps?"

He laughed and pulled his hand away. "What's up with you trying to set me up with Sheila anyway. I told you there was nothing between us besides work."

She shrugged, "Well OK then. Is there anyone else brewing inside the Hawkins bachelor pot?"

He thought for a moment, then shrugged his shoulders and put both hands out palms up. "Well, I might have someone new I could try, but I don't know if she would accept."

Susan laughed, "Of course she would, who wouldn't? Call her right now. Is she cute?"

"Cute? No Suse she is not cute. She is very attractive, quite beautiful in fact."

Susan looked at him defiantly. "She's not a bimbo is she? I'll have no bimbos at my table."

Marsh laughed louder. "I can definitely attest to the fact she is not a bimbo. Maybe I will give her a call."

"Well if she doesn't accept, let me talk to her. I'll set her straight."

"Yes ma'am," Marsh said and saluted her. "I'd better get in and get Fred set up."

"Call her Marsh, whoever she is," Susan said over her shoulder, then turned to watch the storm.

Marsh headed back from the balcony and down the hall towards the office.

Fred found a pressed pair of slacks and a clean Polo shirt in the bedroom and got dressed. As he brushed his teeth he hummed to himself happily in the bathroom. Marsh seems to be a nice enough guy he thought as he pulled a hand towel from the gold ring on the side of the sink. He cupped both hands under the hot water and leaned down to splash it on his face when he saw the reflection in the mirror. Arms frozen in mid-air, the water trickled down between his fingers. The face in the mirror was rough, unshaven and grinned evilly. The water continued to splash into the marble sink as he stared at the apparition.

"No," Fred said, his voice almost a whisper. He tore his eyes away and splashed the water onto his face hard; the droplets streaked the shoulders of his yellow shirt as some flew past. He grabbed the towel again, scrubbed his face, and tried to wipe the image away. He looked back into the mirror. The reflection hadn't changed.

"Did you tell Susan about our little threesome in Vegas yet Fred?" the man in the mirror said, then cackled, eyes wide. "I seriously doubt it. Anyway, I gotta go for a while ol' buddy, but John will be here soon."

Fred just watched, unable to speak.

"You're going to have to do most of the talking Fred. He's the strong silent type, remember?"

Richard laughed again, but the grin was gone. "Sure you do. Besides, if you need me, I'll be back. You and John work out the details. Another appointment next week - two at the latest, OK?"

Fred just nodded and dried his hands on the towel. He turned, flipped off the lights and walked out of the room.

"So why is it girls always have to sit in the back?" Susan said as she leaned forward, straining against the seat belt. The car tires splashed against the wet pavement as they turned the corner onto Wazee Street and headed north towards the stadium.

"Girls do not have to always sit in the back seat Suse, however Fred here is my guest, and I am showing him the sights," Marsh said. He glanced over at Fred and smirked.

"So you couldn't have done that with him in the back seat?"

"You know she's right Marsh," Fred added. "We did this all wrong. You and I should have taken the back seat, and we could have let Susan drive. You know, a guided tour, cute little driver, maybe one of those little black caps to cover her hair..."

"Damn Fred," Marsh said as he slapped the steering wheel. "Why didn't I think of that. I could pull over right here and we could switch."

"OK you two, stop it. Marsh, who is this mystery woman anyway? I take it I don't know her."

"No, you don't. As a matter of fact I don't know her that well either.

But I like her, and she seems to be a good conversationalist," Marsh said. He looked back at Susan in the rear view mirror and winked.

Susan laughed and leaned back in her seat. Fred looked first at Marsh, then back at Susan. "Did I miss something here?"

"No babe, you didn't. Although you might ask my brother if his date is rich."

Fred shrugged and looked out the front of the car as they pulled up to a red light, the crosswalk filled with lightly dressed shoppers and folks out for the evening. They waited in silence until the light changed, then pulled ahead. Marsh had to brake momentarily for an old woman, head wrapped in a brown scarf and using a rolled up umbrella as a cane. She glared defiantly as she crossed in front of them, oblivious to the color of the traffic light.

"I hope you are hungry Fred," Marsh said, ignoring the woman. "The food at this place is great, and the portions are huge."

"I love a good steak," Fred replied.

"Well you can get one here. It's called the Chop House, and you will see by the menu what they serve - chops. Steak chops, pork chops, lamb chops, salmon chops. You name it. Or if you are really boring you can get a salad," Marsh added and looked back at Susan.

Susan unfastened her seat belt, leaned forward again and whacked Marsh across the shoulder. "I'm not sure I like the tone of this conversation Marsh. Maybe... what's her name?"

"Sara."

"Maybe Sara and I will just go sit in the bar and see if we can find any real gentlemen who would like to have dinner with a couple of nice ladies."

Fred raised his hands in his defense. "Hey, leave me out of this. I'm just a poor tourist here."

Marsh accelerated slightly, guided the car around two couples just stepping up on the curb and pulled the Lexus into the valet stand. "OK, ride's over," he said as he opened his door and stepped out onto the old-style bricked street.

The inside of the Chop House was noisy and crowded. Fred and Susan stepped to the side as Marsh fought his way up to the reservation stand. He waited patiently for a moment until the young woman dressed in black pants and simple blue patterned shirt acknowledged him. They conferred over the transparent chart showing the table layout on the podium for a

DECEPTION ON MARGIN

moment, the area clearing a little as a waitress, arms wrapped around a stack of menus escorted a party of ten out of the confined area by the door. He thanked the hostess, then walked back to them.

"It'll only be a few minutes. I don't see any point in going to the bar and waiting there - be quicker to get a drink at the table I think."

"Works for me Marsh," Fred said.

Susan said nothing, and entertained herself by looking around the restaurant, the noise level at the door a little too intense to carry on a meaningful conversation. After a moment another college-aged woman stepped up carrying four long menus, board-like, with no folds. She nodded at them and they followed her across the first of the dining areas to a booth in the back with a good view across the room and toward the door. They settled into the old wooden booth, Fred and Susan on one side, Marsh alone on the other.

"Quite the place Marsh," Fred said as he set his menu aside and gazed out over the crowd. "And obviously very popular."

Susan handed her menu to Fred, then looked over at Marsh. "OK buddy, I've been quiet enough. Who is this woman anyway?"

Marsh smiled softly, unsure how to proceed. He had wondered over the last few hours if he invited Sara because of the deal they had made at lunch, or because he wanted to see her again. He decided honesty would be the best policy he leveled with them.

"Her name's Sara McGloughin, and she's a reporter. A TV reporter."

"What?" Susan practically shouted at him. She pushed with both hands on the side of the table and half stood up. Her eyes flashed with anger. "Marsh how could you do this to me? I wanted to have a nice dinner tonight - not wake up to see myself on the morning news."

Marsh let her calm down a moment and glanced over at Fred. His reaction was not easy to read.

"Susan, listen to me," he said, his voice even and calm. "She is not here as a reporter - well not exactly anyway. We had lunch together today and I really liked her."

"What do you mean 'not exactly'?"

"Do you remember the phone call I got yesterday? The one you asked me about? Well it was Sara, and I called her back this morning. I thought maybe she knew something."

He paused again and waited for some reaction. Fred obviously tried to stay out of the conversation as much as possible, but inched closer to

Susan. She glared at Marsh; the earlier mirth totally banished from her face.

Marsh continued, subdued. "I'm sorry Suse, I don't want this to have a negative impact on the evening. At first, she didn't even want to see me. Her boss had told her to drop the story. Just like the police, it seemed to everyone that there was nothing more anyone could do." Marsh then looked over at Fred and thought for a moment before continuing. "Oh Jeez Fred, you probably don't have any idea what we are talking about do you?"

A waiter stepped over towards the table, waiting patiently. All three of them turned, then looked up, necks craning. He was thin, and extremely tall, probably at least six-ten. His skinny fingers were wrapped around a small pad of paper, and looked to be about as long as Susan's fore arm.

"Drinks anyone?" he asked with a smile, eyes twinkling, obviously comfortable with the first impression his height created.

"Wine for me, white," Susan managed.

"Me also," Fred added.

Marsh took control. "I'll have a scotch and water, and why don't you bring us the wine list."

"Sure, be right back with that for you," the man said and strode off, reminding Marsh of an egret stretching its long legs through deep water.

Marsh looked back at the two of them, as if to say 'where were we?' Fred resumed the conversation. "I've got most of the picture Marsh. Susan has given me some of the details, and I read a few stories over the Internet. But why a reporter?"

"Like I said, at first I thought she was just another nosy journalist looking for a story. But the more I talked with her, the more down to earth she seemed." He looked sheepishly at the two of them. "I kind of convinced her to help me check out a few things since the police aren't doing anything more."

"My God Marsh, you aren't going to play detective here are you? I mean can't we just let it go?" Her eyes widened and her lips trembled a little. She looked like she was going to cry.

Marsh could feel the evening slipping away and felt horrible. He looked over at Fred for some support with Susan. Fred put his arm around her and said, "Hey babe, it's OK. Marsh was just a little desperate - and who wouldn't be?" He looked back at Marsh. "I take it there is not much to go on, is there?"

"Nothing, much. And to be honest maybe I just wanted to see Sara again."

Susan perked up at the remark. "Now that's a little better. If you are going to be a gentleman about it and admit to some real emotions I will feel better." She looked around, "Where is this girl anyway?"

"She should be here soon. I kind of wanted to talk to you two alone first, so things wouldn't blurt out in the middle of our salad course." He looked over at the two of them, eyes examining Susan first, then Fred. "But look, really, let's just have a good time like we planned. I'm sure Sara is not going to interview us anyway. I practically had to beg her to come."

Susan looked at Marsh through the corner of her eyes, "You, beg? Now that I would like to see."

They all laughed and the tension eased a little as the waiter returned to the table. He set Marsh's scotch down and held out the wine list for someone to take.

"Mine, thank you," Susan said as she grabbed the list and opened the red cushioned folder, eyes flicking up and down. "Let's start with a Sauvignon Blanc, shall we hon?" she asked.

"Um sure," he replied, not really hearing. He was staring out across the room, not even looking at the list. She ignored him for a moment, and ran the tip of her finger down the list.

"The Stag's Leap '97 would be fine," she said and handed the list back to the waiter. He nodded and walked off. She turned to Fred to add something, then stopped.

"What are you staring at?" she asked, then followed his gaze across the room.

The blonde was standing in the entryway casually, trying unsuccessfully to not attract attention. She had on a slightly faded pair of jeans, stretched tight but not painted on her long legs; an oversized man's white shirt tucked neatly into the waist of her pants and a light tan jacket covered the whole ensemble. Her long hair shook vibrantly over shoulders as she turned and surveyed the room, then started gracefully toward them.

Susan shoved Fred playfully. "Put your tongue back in your mouth young man," she said. "I'm sure she is taken, as are you."

Marsh was lost in thought and missed most of the exchange, then turned to look also. Recognizing Sara immediately he stood up and waved.

"Sara, over here," Marsh said above the dining noise.

Sara followed the wave over confidently and stopped at the edge of the table. Marsh stepped to the side and allowed her slide into the booth next to him. He beamed at her. "You look great. Thanks for coming." Then he turned across the table. "Sara, this is my sister Susan, and her significant other, Fred."

Susan and Fred's faces were somewhat blank and Sara picked up on it immediately. She turned to Marsh and said, "Did I miss something?"

Marsh laughed. "Uh no," he said, and lightly touched her arm as he sat down.

"Of course not Sara," Susan said sincerely. My honey here was just about to take his foot out of his mouth."

Sara looked genuinely embarrassed and glanced down at her plate. There was a short silence at the table. "Sometimes I seem to cause that in men. I'm sorry," she said quietly.

Susan jumped in. "Sorry shit, if I looked like you I would take every advantage of it."

Sara smiled and appraised Susan carefully. "Why thank you, but you ain't no piece of trash yourself girl."

There was another moment of silence, despite the noise in the background. Sara looked at Marsh, then over at Susan. "I'm very sorry Susan, about your mother. I hope my being here, a stranger and all isn't too difficult."

"That's sweet of you. Thanks."

Marsh was about to add something, but the waiter came back with the wine, towel draped over his arm. He offered a view of the label to Susan who nodded. Sara looked up at him as he labored with the cork. Susan watched for a moment then said, "How tall are you anyway?"

He pulled the cork out with a loud 'THUNK'. "Almost six-eleven," he said as he removed one goblet from the table and poured small sip of wine.

"Do you play basketball?" Sara asked, the first one bold enough to form the question. The others looked at her. She shrugged her shoulders. "Hey I'm a reporter. What can I say?"

The man laughed a little. "I used to, but my knees were too weak for my size. Blew both of them out."

Susan nodded at him after taking a taste of the wine. "Sara? White wine?" she asked.

"Sounds wonderful," Sara said, then turned up to look at the waiter. "Sorry to hear that Stretch."

"It's OK" he said as if he had heard the nickname before. He filled three of the wine glasses from the chilled bottle. "It worked out for the best actually. I'm in first year med-school now - pediatrics."

They all laughed, and Marsh tried to picture the tall man sitting on a short stool in front of a floor full of kids.

"Specials? Or do you need a minute?" he asked as he placed the wine on the table.

Marsh looked up, "Give us a few, OK?"

"No problem, just wave me down when you need me."

Marsh looked around the table quietly for a moment, then picked up his glass. "To mom," he said quietly.

The others each picked up their glasses solemnly and extended their arms out until all four glasses converged in the center of the table.

"To mom," Susan said quietly.

They all took a sip, exchanging glances. Then Marsh pushed his glass back out and spoke again. "And also to Sara and Fred. I don't know what it is, but I can't believe we all just met today."

The foursome toasted together and the mood lightened considerably. Susan looked over at Sara and asked, "I hope you don't mind Sara, but can you tell us about reporting? I mean I don't think I've ever met a reporter before."

Sara laughed and her long hair bounced softly. "I'm just a plain old working girl."

"Are you ever on TV?" Fred asked.

"Sometimes, but not very often. I do investigative stories, which means I do all the work and some other guy gets the airtime."

"And when everything occurred, on Monday, you were investigating?" Fred continued.

Sara looked at Marsh, who sat quietly without adding anything to the discussion. "Well, unfortunately for you what happened Monday was news," she reached up and placed her hand over Marsh's arm gently. "Or to be honest it's what the executives at the station like to think is news. For our station, I did the follow-up on the robbery and the accident, interviewed the detective in charge and so on. Actually the station had pretty much dropped coverage as of this morning."

Marsh could feel where the conversation was headed, and he wasn't sure he wanted it to continue. "OK, I admit when I called Sara this morning to have lunch I was a little bit desperate. I could see that everyone was more or less ending the investigation of the accident and that pissed me off. I thought Mom deserved more."

Marsh paused for a moment and looked around the table. Everyone had turned quiet and looked back at him. Even the restaurant seemed less noisy, a random lull in conversation occurring at the tables around them. He reached over and placed his hand over Sara's.

"But actually I think I was wrong. Maybe it's best we let it go." He looked at Sara and leaned his head slightly in her direction. "Maybe I just wanted another excuse to call you."

Sara perked up, eyes dancing. "Now that's the nicest thing I think I've ever heard on a first date," she said, then turned across the table. "Is he always like this Susan? So gallant and innocent?"

Susan laughed out loud. "Gallant I'm sure. Innocent? I think not. Just don't let him steer the conversation towards food. He'll have you invited over for fettuccini in no time."

Marsh sat back and relaxed more as the two women turned the tide of the conversation. Fred looked puzzled. "Fettuccini? I like fettuccini..."

Sara squeezed Marsh's arm again, but leaned forward, face intent on Susan's. "Do tell me more, please."

Susan bent closer as well, and playfully ignored the two men at the table. "Well you see Sara, he comes on like the poor homebody type, then let's on what a gourmet chef he is. Before long you're having a nice quiet dinner at his little pad. Mom used to call me all the time - every time she found out that is." Susan looked up at Marsh, face shining. "About once a week I think."

Sara sat back, raised her hands slightly and exclaimed, "Oh my. Once a week. Think of the grocery bills."

"And not only that," Susan said, "it was the pizza he had delivered every morning for breakfast. Must have been a fortune in pepperoni alone."

Marsh waved his hands. "OK OK... that's enough." He paused for a moment and a serious expression crossed his face. "What I can't figure though is how Mom found out all the time. Do you think it was all those recipes I asked her for?"

Susan and Sara each burst out laughing as Stretch came back to the table. "Ready for specials?"

"Sure, fire'em at us" Susan said.

Marsh watched as Sara reached across the table for one of the menus while Stretch rattled off something about yellow tail in a special sauce. She sat back in her seat, a little closer to him he noticed, and squinted at the menu without looking at the waiter. Their shoulders and hips touched, and he moved against her, pressing back. She smiled again, and glanced up at Stretch as he described some extra tasty double lamb chop. Marsh found it hard to concentrate on anything but Sara. He realized his heart was beating faster, and could feel the electricity form in his shoulder where it pushed against hers. His eyes were lost in tracing the gentle contours of her face.

She turned to him, expression sensual, and he realized the table had grown quiet around him. "And what will you have Marsh?" Sara said in a soft whisper.

He hesitated a bit, fully aware that all eyes were locked on him. He recovered quickly though, and gazed deep back into Sara's eyes "Fettuccini would be nice," then he turned to the waiter, "and a pizza to go."

Fred cracked up and almost knocked over his wine glass. Susan kicked him under the table hard in his shins. Sara, however, was unfazed by the remark. She slid an arm through Marsh's, leaned sideways and kissed him quickly on the cheek. "Sorry dear, but breakfast for me is steak and eggs or nothing."

She let go of Marsh, picked up her wine glass and toasted Susan.

Susan picked up her own glass and saluted back. "You go girl," she said.

Fred, still chuckling said, "That reminds me of a joke... and I'm sure you are all old enough to hear it."

Susan turned to him. "It better be good, and dirty."

Stretch intruded. "As much as I like a good joke folks..."

Marsh and Fred deferred to the women politely and Sara started. "Salmon, Caesar, baked potato," she said without hesitation.

Marsh raised an eyebrow toward her. "Come here often?" he teased.

"First time, but who doesn't have salmon and a Caesar salad?" she fired back.

"Touché," he laughed, but couldn't stop looking at her.

"Well I'd like the lamb chops, Caesar salad and something lighter than mashed potatoes… veggies or something," Susan said.

Stretch nodded as Marsh said. "I'll have the New York Chop medium rare, Caesar, mashed potatoes."

"Make that two," Fred added.

"Fine folks, be right back with your salads," Stretch said as he gathered up the menus and walked off.

"So who wants to hear the joke?" Fred asked.

"I do," Marsh added as he finished off the last of his scotch. He picked up the bottle of wine from the table and topped off the other's glasses. "And we need more wine I think."

"Does anyone here know what a Cinderella date is?"

Susan groaned and leaned into him. "No, but knowing you I can just imagine."

"Well," Fred continued. "It's when you ask out a woman, an unbelievably gorgeous woman," he said, over emphasizing the description. "And you take her out for wonderful long dinner. Then, you bring her back to your place for a couple of hours of the wildest, most uninhibited sex you can imagine…"

He paused and looked around the table.

"And?" Susan asked impatiently.

"And… at midnight, she turns into a pizza and a six-pack."

"Ewwww… that's disgusting," Susan said. She put both hands on his shoulder and pushed him away. Marsh leaned back and laughed loudly.

Sara looked at Susan. "Now that's a typical male don't you think? Three minutes after sex and all they want to do is go to sleep."

"That's for sure. When they are trying to get you into bed they are all love and attention," Susan agreed. "But afterwards they have the attention span of a cinder block."

"Sad, but so true," Sara agreed.

"Hey, that's not fair," Marsh protested, "Sometimes I turn on the news or SportsCenter."

"Or CNBC to check the market," Fred added.

Marsh inched closer to Sara again and looked around the table. Everyone seemed so happy, so comfortable with each other. The events of the previous two days seemed to drift away. The others continued to chat rapidly as he sat there, content to just listen for a while. He felt Sara move closer to him, almost snuggling as Stretch returned with a large black tray on a silver stand with the salads. Marsh asked for another bottle of wine as the waiter skillfully placed the salads on the table, then added a grinding of fresh pepper with a flourish to each plate.

They were well into the salads when the second bottle of wine appeared, Stretch carefully filling each glass before leaving the table. Marsh waited until he left, then raising his glass once more.

"Mom, we love you," he said quietly.

They all toasted together, wine glasses meeting with soft tinks in the center of the table. Susan's face clouded over a little, but said nothing. Fred, however, had a confused if not painful look on his face. Marsh was curious but didn't inquire further.

By the time dinner arrived they had made a dent in the second bottle. The wine loosened everyone's tongues and the conversation jumped quickly from one topic to another. Fred, Marsh noticed was speaking less and less, somehow lost in thought it seemed. Dinner was outstanding as usual, and they ate mostly in silence, the generous portions of each meal demanded their complete attention. After unsuccessfully trying to demolish the huge pile of mashed potatoes on his plate, Marsh sat back with a sigh.

"I give up," he said, wiped his lips with the soft cloth napkin then tossed it over his plate.

"Way too much food," Susan added and surrendered as well, her fork clinked as she dropped it back onto her plate.

"Anyone want more wine? Or coffee?" Marsh asked and looked around the table.

"Coffee for me," Susan said.

"Yup, me too," Sara agreed.

Marsh finally spoke to Fred. "You seem awfully quiet old man. Was dinner OK?"

"Yes, it was excellent, but I've been thinking," he started.

Susan bumped him with her shoulders. "Uh oh. I hope it doesn't hurt," she added.

He was about to continue when Stretch magically appeared at the table, as if summoned by the dropping of the silverware. He looked around at the full faces. "Everything all right here?"

"Absolutely wonderful," Sara said.

"Take it away before I'm tempted to eat more," Marsh added, "and a round of coffee would be good too."

Fred pondered a little until the waiter had departed; everyone's eyes focused on him. "Well, I've been thinking about the thief, kind of treating it like a computer problem."

"Oh, Fred," Susan pleaded. "Let's not bring that up again."

"No Suse, please," Marsh said as he raised his hand, palm out. "I'd like to hear this."

"Well from what I understand, everyone is assuming that the thief was a professional, in other words this probably wasn't a one time deal."

"That's right," Marsh replied. "The accident was just a slip-up the police said."

Sara leaned forward, riveted. Susan got up quickly and dropped her napkin on the bench behind her.

"I'm not sure I want to hear this," she said. "I'm going to the little girl's room." She turned and walked away quickly.

"And the point?" Sara asked, suddenly very interested, her eyes locked on Fred's.

"Well, if this type of robbery is what the thief is into, it stands to reason he's done it before. I was thinking that we could use the Internet to search back a year or two, to try and find other incidents that match the profile from Denver, probably in other cities."

"I'm sure we could," Sara added, "but what good would that do?"

"In computer terms, it then becomes an analysis problem, a data mining exercise. Marsh knows what I mean."

Marsh looked at him. "I get it, kind of. But what data do we mine?"

"The thief got away by plane right? So airline reservations."

Sara looked back and forth between them. "You two have lost me here. What kind of computer problem?"

The wheels were spinning inside Marsh's head. He turned to Sara, trying to explain a data extraction system in layman's terms.

"Well, lets assume that every flight by every person is stored somewhere in a computer... right?"

"Sure, I guess so."

"Now, let's say we have identified five other robberies, in different cities. New York, Chicago, wherever, on five different dates. That narrows down the data to only the flight events in those cities on those specific dates."

Sara looked up, a little confused. "Events?"

Fred jumped in. "An event in computer terms is a transaction - a record of something that has happened. For example, when you make a credit card purchase, that information is stored in some company's computer. The store, the amount, the date and so on."

"Right," Marsh added. "So each flight event has a name, a date and a time associated with it. We've now narrowed down all the information to just those specific items."

"But that must be millions of records," Sara asked.

"Sure," Fred said. "But we then narrow it down even further. For instance, maybe only those that are round trips on the same day? People who fly in and fly out?"

"OK I'll buy that I guess. Then what?"

Marsh spoke quickly, on the same page as Fred. "Well, you take all those records and churn them up, looking for the same name popping up in the records for each city on each date. How many of those could there be?"

They all thought for a second.

"Not many," Marsh said.

"A few at the most," Fred added.

"Probably one," they all said at once.

"Bingo," Fred said.

"That's so simple," Marsh said.

"OK, I get it I guess. But how do you get access to all that information? Airline reservation information is confidential you know."

Fred threw his hands up. "Hey, it's just an idea. The implementation is left to the student."

They both turned and looked at Sara at the same time. "It seems to me that someone here is an investigative reporter though," Marsh added.

"Wait a minute," Sara said surprised. "You aren't thinking that I could do anything…"

"Just a thought," Marsh added as Susan walked up.

"Did I miss anything?"

"Just a couple of good ol' boys trying to take advantage of a lady," Sara said half-seriously.

"I can imagine," Susan said as she sat down. "I just hope you two men didn't spoil a great evening."

"Not at all," Marsh protested. "Consider the topic closed, for now."

"Well I don't know about you guys, but I'm stuffed and tired. I'm about ready to call it a night," Susan said.

"I agree," Marsh said and looked over at Sara, though he wasn't sure he wanted it to end yet. "I'll get the check."

"This one's on me Marsh," Fred said and reached into his pocket. "Why don't you three get the car and I'll settle up with our tall friend, wherever he is."

Marsh started to protest, but Fred cut him off. "No arguments. My treat," he said as he pulled out a wad of hundred dollar bills looked around the restaurant for a head well above all others.

Susan got up from her side of the table and stepped out lightly. Sara slid across the bench, taking Marsh's hand as she stood, and leaned in close.

"That, was the best dinner I've had in a long time," she said softly to Marsh.

"Yes, it really was," he replied. His eyes roved over her face for a moment. "Let's go get the car." He turned to Fred, who was waving now at Stretch. "We'll meet you out front."

The air was cool when they emerged from the restaurant; the street and sidewalk still a little damp. Marsh fumbled in his pockets for the claim check as Susan stepped to the side and allowed them some privacy. Marsh raised both arms, his hands holding Sara softly by the elbows.

"Do you need a ride?" he asked. He sounded like a nervous schoolboy he thought.

She gazed up in his eyes and moved closer. "No, but maybe you could walk me to my car?"

Marsh beamed at the invitation and turned around as Fred bounced lightly down the steps to join them. He inhaled deeply and stretched his arms wide as he walked.

"Jeez I love this climate. I could live here," he said.

Susan turned quickly and stared at him, a shocked expression on her face.

"What?" he asked, "Did I say something wrong?"

"No, nothing." Susan said quietly.

Marsh led Sara over to the two of them. "I'm going to walk Sara to her car. Why don't you two take the Lexus," he said as he held out the claim check.

"No problem Marsh," Fred said quickly, then reached out to take the ticket and shook his hand. Susan rushed over and gave Sara a big hug.

"God it was nice to meet you," she said. "Thanks for coming."

"I loved every minute of it," she said with a sincere smile on her face and squeezed her back. "I'll see you soon I hope."

"Yes, me too."

The Lexus pulled up quickly. The attendant hopped out, crossed to the near side of the car and opened the door. Fred stepped in front, and handed the young man the ticket and a few bucks for the trouble. Susan slid in the passenger side, waved briefly and in a moment they were gone.

"Which way?" Marsh asked, his hand on her arm.

Sara threaded her arm through his and pulled him down the street. "This way. Just a few blocks," she said as they began to walk.

They strolled silently, the late evening crowd sparse on the street as they progressed away from the stadium. After a few blocks, Marsh began to get concerned.

"You parked this far? Did you get lost or something?"

She smiled, raised her finger to his lips and pressed softly. "It's not far now." She looked up at his eyes. "Are you serious about what Fred said, about trying to track the airline records?"

He thought for a moment, lost in her face. "I don't know, really. I guess I'll have to sleep on it."

"Mmm..." she said, and moved on.

They had gone another block, past a crowded corner pub, the door open and the sounds of the night's party spilling out onto the street. She stopped in front of an old pickup truck, dented and rusted around the wheel wells, parked on the street. No one walked on the sidewalk for the length of the block.

"This is it," she said, then slid her arms up around his neck and pulled him close for a kiss. He wrapped his arms around her, their bodies meeting as their lips pressed together. The embrace lasted almost a minute as they explored each other for the first time.

Finally, she pulled back a little, her hand sliding over his face gently. "Thank you for dinner, Marshall Hawkins," she said.

The taste of the kiss lingered in his mouth as he looked deep in her eyes. "Mmm... thank you Sara McGloughin. When can we do it again?"

She smiled and kissed his lips quickly. "Anytime you want."

"Good, I want to," he said as he turned to the truck and wondered how she managed to drive it around town.

"Not that way silly," she said. She laughed and guided him back towards the building.

"But, I thought I was walking you to your car," he said, confused.

She stopped at the door of the building, turned and looked at him. "You did. This is my loft and the car's in the garage, back there," she said, pointing toward the door.

"Tease. You tricked me." He pulled her close and kissed her again.

"Yes, I did," she said after a moment. "And it worked too. Are you coming in?"

A thousand thoughts flooded his head and he couldn't decide what to do. She looked up at him patiently, eyes wide and lips in a soft smile, and waited for his response. He leaned down, smelled the faint scent of her perfume and kissed her again.

"Of course," he said as he reached for the door.

Chapter Fifteen

Fred woke up early. It was eerily dark in the bedroom, the sun not yet risen enough to provide much illumination through the drawn curtains. He rolled over and looked at Susan in the dim light, careful not to disturb her. Her hair curled down over her shoulders, hiding the soft contours of her face. He stayed there for a moment and just gazed at her, then pulled the sheet up over her bare back and rolled off the bed carefully. He stood naked next to the bed in the near darkness and stretched his arms and chest slowly. He smiled and suddenly felt content, and a little surprised. Without moving he looked over her again and wondered about his feelings and where his mind was leading him. They had nothing planned for the day, other than to spend it together and that also made him curiously happy. His usual routine of attacking the market news seemed less important for some reason, the desire for the thrill of the day's trading lost somewhere along the way.

He moved slowly towards the bathroom. Arms outstretched he groped in the darkness, then jammed his fingers suddenly against the bathroom door. Fred froze until he was sure that the sound hadn't woken Susan. He could hear her steady breathing in the darkness, and was tempted to return to bed to wrap his arms around her, and forget the reality of his situation. He was confused for the first time in his life, at least the first time he could remember. What if she knew the truth? Slowly he slid his fingers across the door until he located the knob, then wrapped his hand around it and turned it quietly. He would lose her he knew - she would never forgive him, or understand what it was like for him. He crept inside the bathroom and closed the door softly behind him, leaned into it and rested his head back against a towel hanging on a hook. I need a plan he thought.

He flipped on the light and blinked for a moment when he caught the reflection in the mirror in front of him.

"Fred," the moustached apparition said with little expression.

Fred moved forward slowly, the image of the man with curly hair tracked with him as he approached.

"Jesus."

"Kansas City," John said to him. "Next week."

For some reason Fred was not surprised.

"Not already," he said, "We just finished…"

John was silent again.

Fred rubbed his eyes hard, knuckles pressed into the sockets until the pain caused him to stop. He looked again, the vision of the silent thief suddenly replaced by the rough unshaven version of himself.

"Fred," Richard said sternly. "Getting a bit cocky aren't we?"

Fred was mesmerized at the switch and stared back. He didn't know what to say.

"Last night, at dinner. Kind of giving away the farm don't you think? I mean come on ol' buddy, if those two have any brains they will eventually be able to track down John."

"I'm just trying to help Susan," Fred responded.

"By getting us caught? How will that help Susan? She'll learn everything. She'll know what you did. She will find out you killed her mother and then were will you and your little darling be?"

Fred said nothing but stared back at the reflection.

"I see where you are going Fred. Putting the authorities onto John means no more travel. No more travel means no more trips to the grocery store. Am I right?"

"I don't need any more."

"I don't think I can live with that Fred. You've got Susan, I've got Vegas, the twins. I'm not going to give that up." Richard seemed to loom closer, piercing eyes widening.

"Yes, Susan," Fred said, ignoring the threat.

"Fred, listen to me. Don't get stupid here, you started this remember? We don't want to have to do anything drastic. You don't want Susan to get hurt do you?"

Fred's stomach dropped at the implication. "No, not Susan. She doesn't have anything to do with this!"

"Then let's take care of Kansas City next week. No screw-ups this time and nobody gets hurt. But if things get a bit tighter we may have to do something about it, won't we?"

The door pushed open slightly. Fred jumped at the intrusion, his heart lodged in his throat. He turned quickly to face the door, the mirror ripped from his sight. Susan poked her head in quietly, the dark bedroom framing her soft face in the bright light of the bathroom. She squinted a little and looked sleepy and confused.

"Are you OK honey? Whom are you talking to?" she asked, voice soft and full of dreams.

Fred moved closer to her, his body blocking the reflection in the mirror. "Uh... no one babe, did I wake you?" He reached up and traced his fingers across her cheek. "It's early, why don't you go back to bed?"

She started to push the door open. Fred spread his hands over her bare shoulders, moved toward her and forced her back out of the room slowly. He didn't want her near the others. She looked up at him and lazily lifted her arms underneath his as their bodies pressed together. She was still warm from the sheets and he eased one arm around her back, his hand caressing her soft skin. He guided her gently toward the bed as he reached back and flicked off the bathroom light. The room plunged into darkness.

"Let's go back to bed."

"Mmmm..." she said, her head against his chest as she walked backward with his steps.

Her legs touched the side of the bed. She sat down and pulled him with her, still holding him close as they both slid across the mattress. He lifted his legs and laid down on his back with one arm under her. She snuggled close, lifted one knee over the top of his legs and draped an arm across his chest. Her soft cheek pressed into the top of his chest and her breath was warm on his skin.

"Mmm... better..." she said. Her eyes closed she dropped back into sleep almost immediately.

Fred lay motionless; eyes wide open despite the darkness while his heart pounded in his chest. What was happening? His thoughts raced as his eyes adjusted to the darkness, his fingers curled in her soft hair. He would never let anything happen to Susan but he couldn't get Kansas City out of his mind.

He held her tight and didn't move for a long time.

The first thing Marsh saw when he opened his eyes was the slightly wrinkled pink pillowcase, and realized immediately it was not his. He lifted his head and looked around the dimly lit room, totally disoriented. The bathroom was not where he expected it and he blinked twice, his eyelids still coated with sleep, then craned his neck as a sound attracted his attention. Sara poked her head around the corner; the bathroom light framed her full head of hair.

"Good morning sleepy," she said, the corner of her lips extending in a tiny curl.

He groaned and dropped his head back on the pillow, pulled his hands up from under the sheets and ran them through his messy hair.

She walked slowly from the bathroom, a fluffy white robe wrapped around her body and tied in front, until she reached the bed. She sat down and rubbed a soft hand up his arm to his shoulder.

"Not having second thoughts are you?" she asked. She tipped her head and the smile disappeared.

He lifted one arm and placed his hand on top of hers, but looked up at the ceiling.

"A little guilty I think."

"Guilty?" she said and the smile returned. "At taking advantage of a poor defenseless woman?"

He pulled himself to one elbow and gazed into her eyes. God she was even more beautiful in the morning he thought.

"No, not that. I guess it's just Mom… and I should have called Suse last night."

Her mouth opened a little and she pulled away. "I'm sorry Marsh, maybe this was a bit too quick."

He was touched, and suddenly felt sorry for apparently making her feel bad. He gently grasped her wrist and pulled her down on the bed. He waited until she had reclined next to him, then leaned in and kissed her lips softly.

"No Sara, don't be sorry. I'm not. It's just that so much has happened in the last few days. I just don't know where all this is going."

"I don't either Marsh." Her bright eyes locked on his. "I hope you know this is not something I do all the time. It's just that… it just felt so right last night. It seemed like you needed me so much, and I liked that feeling."

He smiled at her. "So you brought me home? Like a helpless little puppy?"

Her head tilted and the smile faded. She pulled back again and he was suddenly concerned that he had said the wrong thing.

"Stop it. It's wasn't that."

He reached over her, his hand pushed on her shoulder and he pinned her to the bed, then leaned down and kissed her. She was passive for a moment, then returned the kiss, their lips pressed hungrily together.

"I'm sorry," he said, their lips brushing. "I didn't mean it that way. I guess my bedside manner is a little rusty."

She reached her fingers up and caressed his cheek slowly. "Maybe the bedside manner is, but the rest of your bed work is fine," she said.

He laughed, relieved, collapsed back on the bed and looked up at the ceiling again. He could see tiny traces of the texture splattered onto it like little mountains on the moon.

"Jesus Sara," he said exhaling heavily. "So much is happening. I can't even begin to think of what to do next."

She rolled over, almost on top of him, her robe parting a little and he could see the fullness of her breasts as her hand slid into his hair.

"I can think of something."

He laughed out loud as he pulled her close. "Did I tell you last night how beautiful you are?"

"No," she said as she kissed his neck. "And I'm crushed."

"Well you are very, very beautiful. But of course I was only attracted to your mind."

She bit his neck gently. "Oh, yes, I can just imagine. And I suppose you kept your eyes closed all night."

He smiled and remembered. "Well I peeked a little."

She lifted her head and kissed him, then looked deep into his eyes. "And I kept my eyes wide open all night."

He couldn't believe he was there, with her. The thoughts of everything he had to do, to take care of rushed back to him.

"What's the matter Marsh?" she said softly.

He hesitated for a moment, not able to take his eyes off her.

"Will you help me Sara?" he said.

"Help you?" she said, "With what?"

"Everything," he said and kissed her again.

Susan wrapped her robe around her, tightened the belt as she bent into the fridge and pulled out the fruit plate left over from yesterday's breakfast. She was surprised when she and Fred had finally emerged from the bedroom at not finding Marsh at home. He could have called she thought, but assumed he had spent the night with Sara. She scowled a little, and scolded herself for treating him like a little boy who came home late. It didn't help, however, when Fred took his side.

"Maybe he went to work early," Fred offered when she informed him that Marsh hadn't returned home.

"Don't be ridiculous. We would have heard him leave."

"You were sleeping. And quite soundly as I remember. Besides, I rather liked Sara. I would have gone home with her too."

Susan had just glared at him, then stormed furiously into the kitchen. Fred decided that maybe a little distance was best and went into the office to catch the rest of the CNBC morning broadcast. She munched on a piece of cantaloupe, the juices making her fingers a little sticky. Men, she thought, no consideration whatsoever. She couldn't tell if she was more pissed at Marsh or Fred.

The phone rang, and the simultaneous jangles from both the kitchen wall and the portable in the living room startled her. She grabbed another piece of fruit and ignored the closest phone, walked instead out of the kitchen and dropped into the easy chair. She finished chewing and licked her fingers before picking up the handset. Marsh could wait she thought.

"Hello," she said flatly and expected her brother's voice.

"Yes, may I speak to Marshal Hawkins please?"

She hesitated for a second.

"This is Detective Carter of the Denver Police Department calling," the voice said after a moment.

Susan recovered quickly. "Oh detective, yes. This is Susan Hawkins, Marsh's sister."

"Hello Ms. Hawkins, my condolences on your mother's passing. Is Marsh available this morning?"

Susan didn't know what to say. "Um... thank you. He's not here right now. Is there a message I could take?"

There was a pause at the other end of the phone, then she heard the sound of a key in the door. She rose quickly from the chair and turned around.

"Hang on a moment please," she said into the receiver while she watched the hall.

The door pushed in slowly and Marsh walked in, treading quietly. Susan marched across the room, scowled at him and thrust the phone towards his chest.

"It's for you," she said.

He reached for the phone and barely grabbed it as she hurried past him and down the hall.

"Good morning to you too," he said, looking after her, then lifted the phone to his head and kicked the door shut behind him.

"Hello?"

"Marsh, its Will Carter. Sorry to bother you first thing in the morning."

The detective's voice took him by surprise. He walked slowly across the room to the balcony doors and tried to gather his thoughts. Over coffee earlier he and Sara had discussed approaching Will on helping them obtain the flight information needed to try and track down the thief, but he hadn't expected to talk to him so soon.

"Uh, Will, no problem," he said. "You don't have any news for me do you?"

"No, Marsh, I'm sorry I don't. But that's not why I called. Actually I could use your help on something."

"My help? Sure I guess. What is it you need Will?" he said and slid the glass door open to let the morning air in. The sounds of the rush hour traffic drifted up from the street and he stepped back a few steps, his back turned to the outside.

"I'm not sure how to explain it. The Captain has dropped this case on me and it has to do with computers, or at least email or online activity." Will hesitated for a second, trying to figure out what to say. "Do you know anything about chat rooms Marsh?"

"Well sure, of course, but it's a big subject. What is it you want to know?"

"That's the problem. I don't know what it is I want to know. I don't even know what questions to ask. I realize that this is a bad time for you, but I was hoping, maybe next week when things calm down, that you could spare me a few minutes to explain this stuff to me. I'm afraid I'm a little over my head here. I use computers all the time at work, but never really got into the net culture much. I hope I'm not overstepping my bounds."

Marsh thought for a second as he walked over towards the kitchen and peered over the counter to see if the coffee was hot. He spied a half of a pot still sitting on the warmer and crossed back by the dining room table and around the corner, then cradled the phone in his neck as he opened the cupboard. He reached up to grab a cup and the phone slipped from his neck and crashed to the floor.

"Shit," he said out loud, then set the cup down and bent over to pick up the phone. He lifted it back up and spoke quickly into the handset. "Will, you still there?"

"Ya, I'm here. Would it be better if I called you back?" Will asked.

"No, just hang on a second."

Marsh set the phone down and poured a cup of coffee. The aroma teased his senses and his stomach growled. This was a chance, he thought, to work with the detective, maybe trade favors. He picked up the phone again as a strategy formed in his mind.

"OK, better. Just needed a cup of coffee. I'd be glad to help Will, if I can. Do you want to get together to talk about it?"

"Next week?" Will said, obviously relieved. "Maybe Monday or Tuesday when you've had a chance to settle things down a bit?"

"How about today?" Marsh replied instantly.

"Today? Sure, but, with everything else going on…"

"Actually Will, today would be better. I've got the day off and I wanted to talk to you anyway. How about lunch?"

"You business tycoons, always doing lunch. I'm just a poor civil servant you know Marsh."

"My treat Will, and I'd be happy to. Why don't we say the Timberline Grill at the Tech Center. At 11:30 if that's not too early for you."

"That's fine Marsh."

"And Will, leave plenty of time if you can. I may be bringing someone else along."

"Marsh," Will said, then paused. "This is kind of confidential. I'm not sure I should even be talking to you about it. I'm not sure how appropriate that would be."

"I understand completely Will," Marsh said and tried to appease the detective's concerns. "I'll tell the other party to meet us at noon. That should give us plenty of time to go over whatever it is you wanted to discuss in confidence. Does that work for you?"

"Sure, I guess so," Will said, still hesitant. "I guess it beats Burger King."

Marsh laughed, "Well if you'd rather choose another place."

"The Timberline sounds great. I'll see you at 11:30. And thanks Marsh."

"No problem detective. I'll see you then."

Marsh hung up the phone, picked up his coffee and took a sip. He'd have to call Sara he thought. I wonder if she can make it?

Fred walked out from the hall dressed in jogging shorts and a T-shirt, and looked in the kitchen, the surprise on his face obvious as he noticed Marsh standing there. There was a moment of silence between them, both noticeably uncomfortable with the situation.

"Good morning Marsh," Fred said first, then glanced down at his attire.

Marsh felt an immediate sense of paternal concern for his sister and realized again that this almost stranger was sleeping with Susan in his own house. The thoughts gnawed at his stomach for a second, then he pushed them aside, remembering how well he had gotten along with Fred the night before. If Susan was happy then he should be. He put on his best morning smile.

"Morning Fred. Sleep well?"

A wave of relief seemed to spread over Fred's face. He took a few steps toward the kitchen and looked at the coffee.

"Yes, very well thanks. And Marsh, thanks again for letting me stay here."

Marsh waved his coffee cup at him, brushing off the remark. "It's OK Fred, really. I guess we both seem to be a little nervous here. Java?"

"Love some."

Marsh grabbed another cup from the cupboard and filled it, the pot almost empty now. He handed it through the opening, careful not to spill any. Fred nodded as he accepted it and held it in both hands as he brought it to his lips.

They were both silent again, then Fred continued. "Marsh, I hope you don't mind, but I used your office for a while this morning to check my email and catch up on the financial news."

Marsh took another sip, then waved his cup at Fred again as he swallowed. "No problem Fred, how's the market this morning?"

"Slow, and nothing much shaking. I wasn't really into it to be honest. Guess I better take the day off."

"Must be nice," Marsh said and laughed.

Fred shrugged a little. "Well the worst thing you can do is try and trade when you are not concentrating. Besides, I've already had a good week."

Marsh remembered the conversation from yesterday. "Yes you have. What's up with Suse anyway? She seemed a bit miffed at me."

It was Fred's turn to laugh. "Miffed? I like that, though it's a bit of an understatement. I think she was worried when you didn't come home last night, or call."

"Umm..." Marsh said.

"Of course my off the cuff remark about where you probably were didn't help any. Now she's pissed at both of us."

They were both laughing softly as Susan walked around the corner, dressed in not too short cuffed blue shorts and a yellow tank top tied behind her neck. He hair was pulled back into a short ponytail at the top of her head. She stood there, hands on her hips and glared at both of them.

Marsh looked at her, surprised again at what an attractive woman she was. When did she grow up so much? He smiled and hoped she wasn't too mad.

Susan's stare intensified and shifted back and forth between them. "Having a little fun at my expense boys?"

Marsh and Fred looked at each other, then laughed again. "Uh, not really babe," Fred said

"Good morning Suse," Marsh added.

Fred extended an arm out toward her. Susan ignored it, walked quickly past and turned the corner into the kitchen. She stepped behind Marsh and spotted the empty coffee pot.

"And who poured the last cup?"

"Guilty," Marsh replied and turned around to face her. He grabbed her shoulders and leaned in to give her a kiss on the cheek. She lifted her face a little, turning to accept it politely.

"I'm sorry Suse, maybe I should have called. I'm not used to someone keeping tabs on me."

Susan grabbed the pot and dumped the remaining liquid into the sink, then busied herself with another pot. Marsh moved quickly out of the way and gave her some space.

"You men are all alike," she said into the wall, the water splashing noisily into the pot. "I really don't know why we women put up with you."

Fred walked around the counter, slid his arms around her waist from behind and nuzzled his face into her neck. "We're truly sorry babe."

She shrugged him off and turned to the coffee maker, as a small smile bent at the corner of her lips. "Well I certainly hope so."

They were silent as she completed the ritual of starting another pot of coffee brewing. Fred slipped out of the kitchen silently and joined Marsh in the dining room.

Finally she turned and looked at them over the counter. She ran a hand through her hair, but the corners of her lips lifted even more. "Look at you two, grinning like Cheshire cats. Why do I get the impression there's not a safe woman on the planet?"

They both shrugged like little boys.

"And you big brother. I'm tempted to give Sara a call, to make sure she is all right."

"Please do," Marsh replied. "She really likes you Suse."

"And I like her too Marsh, a lot. She's quite a lady. Maybe us girls should take off today, and leave you to do whatever it is guys do."

"She's really beautiful Marsh," Fred said, but noticed the look that Susan tossed at him. "Of course not nearly as beautiful as your sister," he added quickly.

"Yes, she is," Marsh said, remembering. "You know the first few times I met her I didn't really notice?"

Susan looked at them both again and suppressed a laugh. "You guys are so full of bullshit. What am I going to do with you two?"

"Take me back, please," Fred said.

"I'll never do it again," Marsh added.

"Hmph." She walked out of the kitchen and wrapped her arm around Fred. "You are forgiven," she said and kissed his neck. Then she turned and looked at Marsh. "But I'm not so sure about you. That is until I talk to Sara again."

"Ouch," Marsh replied, his hands in the air. "It was all her fault, really."

Fred pulled Susan towards the balcony and gazed outside. The sun shone brightly, and a gentle breeze blew in through the screen. "Is it always like this?" he asked as he looked out over the mountains. "I could live here," he added.

Susan pulled away and glanced back at Marsh. He shrugged, not wishing to influence the conversation.

"Yes, it's beautiful," she said. "Why don't we take a drive up into the mountains today? We don't have anything planned do we?"

"Don't think so. I'd love to go. I've only seen them from the air."

They both turned and looked at Marsh.

"You two kids go and have fun. I've got to stop by the office and check up on things, then I have a lunch meeting."

Susan raised her eyebrows a little. "Anyone we know?"

"Yes and no nosy. It's with Detective Carter and maybe Sara."

"Right. He called this morning. Is there any news?"

"No, he actually needed my help on a different matter. But I was hoping to bring up what we discussed at dinner last night."

Fred looked a bit ruffled. "You know Marsh, I was just talking off the top of my head. I don't really know if anything can be done."

"I know, I know," Marsh replied. "But it's worth a shot, don't you think? We'll talk to him and find out if it's at least feasible."

Susan looked a little concerned. "Marsh, please don't get too obsessed with this. I mean can't we just let it go?"

Marsh smiled back at them both. "Don't worry. Just a little curiosity that's all. I won't get carried away, trust me. And Fred, maybe later we could talk a little more. Go over the technical details if there is any chance of pulling this off."

Fred shifted again and swayed on his feet. "Sure Marsh, no problem," he said with a little hesitation. "Whatever you need."

"Great. I'm going to hit the shower. We can hook up later. You guys have a good day alright?"

Susan pulled at Fred's arm. "Come on lazy let's get going. We can stop at the store and get a picnic lunch."

Fred allowed himself to be led across the room, but looked at Marsh as they passed by. The situation was closing in around him, and he could hear the rumbling of voices inside his head. Now more than ever he needed a plan.

Chapter Sixteen

For the second day in a row Marsh arrived at the restaurant early, declining the hostess's suggestion and sitting at the same table as before. He nodded with recognition and a warm smile to the same waitress as she brought over the menus.

"There will be three of us today," he said, "but one won't be joining us for a while."

"No problem sir," she said politely as she set the menus across the table from him. "My name is Diane by the way. Just let me know what you need."

She paused, looking at him with a pert smile on her face. Marsh decided that no innuendo was intended and smiled back.

"Thank you Diane. The police will be here shortly. I'm sure we will all be in good hands."

The remark caught her off guard and she hesitated for a moment, then took a small step backward. Will walked up behind and stepped aside to avoid her as she receded, his hand touching her shoulder to keep from bumping into her. She jumped a little and suppressed a yelp as she turned quickly around.

"Excuse me ma'am," Will said, nodding politely as he moved toward the nearest chair.

Marsh stood up, smiled and said, "Meet Detective Carter, Diane."

"Uh, hi," she stammered, her gaze shifting back and forth between them.

"Hello Diane," Will said, a puzzled look spreading across his face.

"Diane, I'll take an iced tea please, if you would," Marsh said, then looked at Will.

"Diet Coke."

"Sure, I'll be right back," she said and hurried away.

Will extended his arm and shook Marsh's hand, then sat down. "What was that all about?"

"Just good timing on your part," Marsh said. "Nice to see you Will."

"Thanks for meeting me Marsh. Again I hope this isn't a problem."

"No, really, things are going fine. Much better than I expected." He hesitated a moment. "Well, I guess I didn't know what to expect, but things are all right considering. Susan's in town."

"Your sister, right? I spoke with her briefly on the phone."

"And her significant other. I seem to have a house full. I think once the funeral is over we can start getting back to normal. I guess there will only be one loose end to tie up."

Will tensed a little and leaned back in his chair. He looked at Marsh carefully. "Marsh, as I said, that's not why I wanted to see you."

"Relax Will, we can talk about that later. What is it you needed help with? Right now I'm all ears."

Diane came back with the drinks before Will could get started. "Do you need some time gentlemen?" she said, apparently fully recovered from her earlier discomfort.

"Thanks Diane, we need to talk for a while. I'll just flag you down if that's OK?" Marsh said.

"Take your time, enjoy," she said and walked away. She looked over her shoulder with a curious glance.

Will pulled a folded piece of paper from the inside pocket of his sports coat and set it down on the table in front of him. He paused for a moment, gathered his thoughts, and then took a sip from the Coke.

"Marsh, I've got a problem. There is a gentleman, relatively well connected and a friend of the Captain I might add, who seems to be having a problem with his daughter. She got an email the other day, a pornographic picture. His wife found it and he went ballistic. She called the Captain and demanded that we do something about it."

"Go on Will."

"Well this guy was in my office this morning and was really pissed. He won't let me talk to his wife or daughter, and to be honest I don't know what the hell he is talking about."

"I see your problem I think. You said something about chat rooms?"

"That's what the man said his daughter said when they questioned her about it. She said she had met him in a chat room. What does that mean?"

Marsh leaned back, gathering his thoughts. "You have two issues to consider here, but let's start with chat rooms first. I assume you have heard of the major online companies, AOL, Yahoo! And so on right?"

"Sure, of course."

"Good. Well one of the services they all offer is the ability for many people to talk to each other over their computers. Chat rooms are generally set up by topics, and you select the one you want to participate in. Like sports, politics, movies and so on. The bigger companies may even have hundreds of rooms set up with even more individualized subjects, baseball, Shakespeare, football playoffs, etc. And in your case, the most popular rooms generally have to do with love and sex."

"So these people get together and talk about sex?"

"You have heard of cyber-sex haven't you Will?"

"Well ya, who hasn't. I know there is a big deal about pictures online, people trying to limit access for kids from libraries and schools and stuff. But I don't get around the web much."

"Well it would make a lot more sense if I could just show you, or if you know anyone about fourteen or so I'm sure they could," Marsh said.

Will snapped his head towards Marsh, "Did you say fourteen?"

"It was just an example Will."

"This guy's daughter was fourteen," he said and shook his head slowly. "So are you saying that this girl might have been chatting with someone? Maybe became friends or something?"

"It's entirely possible. Most people sign into rooms with anonymous names - and their online personalities can be completely different than what they are in real life. There are so called 'Adult' rooms on most sites, places where you are supposed to be eighteen to get into."

"But she was only fourteen."

"Doesn't matter," Marsh said and brushed the comment away with a wave of his hand. "The restrictions on getting into such rooms are basically non-existent. A big disclaimer screen pops up, and if you actually read it, which no one does, it says by entering the room you are affirming that you actually are of legal age, and you won't be offended by the sexual content and sue anyone for what you read or say. It's about as effective as an age warning sign on a cigarette machine in Podunk, Iowa. There is no way to actually restrict who uses it."

Marsh let the information sink in for a moment, then glanced around the room and briefly wondered if he knew anyone in the restaurant. Will looked like he was getting the picture so he continued.

"Let's say that your girl signed into an adult room, 'Women Who Love to Be Tied Up' for example."

"Hold it," Will said as he reached down and took the paper from the table in front of him, unfolded it and handed it to Marsh.

Marsh glanced at it for a moment, folded it and handed it back. "OK, in your case 'Pain and Bondage'. More than likely your girl was into a room like this, pretending to be older and struck up a conversation with some guy and maybe even got into a little cyber-sex."

"Damn, I was afraid of that."

"Anyway the conversation probably got to the point where they wanted to see pictures of each other, or correspond in other ways. Somehow this guy got the girl's email address and sent her this." Marsh said, dropping his index finger onto the paper for effect.

"How would he get her email address?"

"That brings us to the other aspect of the situation. It's possible that in the girl's online profile, she had the address listed," Marsh continued. "Or, more likely she gave it to him. In either case you would be hard pressed to say this little item was unsolicited."

Will looked perplexed, then resigned himself to the situation. "So the only way to find out anything else is to talk to the daughter, and probably the wife too?"

"You got it. And if you do want to track the guy down you need his email address that is if she still has it. She probably deleted the email in which case you've got squat." Marsh pondered for a moment and thought it through. "Or maybe she has a whole list of addresses, it's what she does in her spare time. In either case I doubt there is anything illegal here. Mutual consent probably."

Marsh looked up as Diane walked by, then glanced at his watch quickly. Sara should be here soon he thought and pointed to their mostly empty glasses. Diane nodded and drifted towards another table.

Will laughed out loud. "Gee thanks Marsh, you've been so helpful, I think. Now all I've gotta do is brief the Captain, then go back and tell the guy I want to interview his wife and daughter like a couple of criminals."

Marsh laughed with him and looked around the restaurant for Sara. "Hey, I just told you how it works, and I could be all wrong about the adult room stuff. Maybe she was in a kid's room, 'Friends of Disney' or something and met some other fourteen year old who sent the picture as a joke. It could be totally innocent. But to be honest, however it works out I don't think this is a matter for the police. Sounds like mom and dad need to have a little heart-to-heart chat with their daughter."

Will brightened considerably at the thought. "That's it. I go to the Captain and explain how it works, then let him deal with his buddy.

DECEPTION ON MARGIN

Sound like an expert and dump the whole mess back in his lap. You gotta like that."

Marsh spotted Sara walking between two tables near the door and stood up as Will trailed off. She looked wonderful again, dressed in a tan summer suit with a short skirt and sky-blue blouse. Her hair cascaded down over her shoulders as she walked, and she waved demurely when she spotted him. She strode confidently over to a chair opposite Marsh and pulled it out.

"This seat taken gentlemen?" she asked coyly.

Will stood up quickly, a confused look plastered on his face. He glanced at Marsh, then back at Sara, obviously at a loss for words.

"You remember Sara McGloughin, Will," Marsh said with a smile.

"Hello again Detective," Sara said and extended her hand towards him.

Will leaned over, shook the offered hand, and bumped into the table hard enough to shake the glasses. "Sara," he nodded politely, visibly not pleased with the situation. They all sat down, and the table was quiet for a moment as Diane returned with drink refills on a tray.

"Here you go," she said. She set down each of the drinks and picked up the used glasses. "And you ma'am?" she said turning towards Sara.

"Just ice water for me thanks," Sara said, a small smile still bending the corner of her mouth.

Will looked back and forth between them again. "Why do I get the impression I've been set up here?" he said, a scowl plastered across his face.

Sara said nothing, but picked up her cloth napkin and folded it carefully over her lap. Marsh took control of the situation, leaned forward earnestly and tried to soothe the Detectives obvious tension.

"I'm really sorry to spring this on you Will," he started," but I assure you there is nothing sinister here." He nodded at Sara.

"Absolutely," Sara affirmed.

Will was not soothed at all. "And you two are working together now?"

"Let's just say we've become friends."

Will stared at him for a moment, then glanced at Sara. Her expression didn't change much, though her smile increased a little.

"Yes, friends," she added.

The implication wasn't lost on Will and it was clear he didn't like the situation. "And just what is it you needed to talk to the police about?"

Marsh put on his best negotiation face and continued softly, assuming a friendly posture. "Will, we didn't want to talk to the police, I asked you here as a friend, hopefully for some expert advice, and maybe a little help if you think it's warranted. Just bear with us OK?"

Will was still miffed, but acquiesced. "All right, I'll listen. But I've got to tell you I'm not happy about this setup." He shifted uncomfortably in his chair, and couldn't help looking back and forth between Sara and Marsh.

"I can tell you aren't happy, but rest assured we are not trying to slam anyone. In fact, we are just trying to help in our own way. Last night we had an idea, well it was actually my sister's boyfriend who came up with it. He suggested a way in which we might be able to come up with a lead on the guy who killed…" Marsh hesitated for a moment, suppressing a sudden sinking feeling in his stomach again. "The guy who robbed the store."

"This is a police matter Marsh, not something for you two to be rubbing your noses in."

Marsh ignored the rebuke and continued. "Will, just listen to me for a moment. Everyone is assuming that this guy wasn't an amateur, right?" Marsh paused for a moment as Will nodded reluctantly. "And if he was a pro, then he's probably done this sort of thing before. What if we did a little research, and came up with some other robberies that fit the pattern? A history of thefts perhaps."

Will acknowledge the possibility with a nod. "And if we could?"

Marsh looked over at Sara, who seemed to be content to sit quietly and let him do the talking. "Well, assuming that the guy does the crime the same way, getting in and out by plane, we might be able to isolate some past occurrences, maybe in different cities."

"And if we did, then what?" Will asked, still a little testy but Marsh could tell his interest was piqued.

Marsh looked over at Sara, who nodded imperceptibly. "That's kind of where we need your advice, or help Will."

Will's eyebrow shot up a little but Marsh pressed on. "Let's say that we found a few other cities where similar thefts occurred. The first step would be to contact the local Police Departments, maybe with the picture that we have of our suspect."

"And that's were I come in I presume?" Will asked.

"Well sure," Marsh said, encouraged. "Of course if you want to. I mean don't you guys share information with other jurisdictions?"

"It would be part of your official investigation, Detective," Sara interjected. "It is still open isn't it?"

Will looked at Marsh, then Sara, then burst out laughing. "Jesus you guys, you don't let up do you?"

"Just trying to help out," Sara said softly.

"OK, nothing out of bounds so far, assuming you can get a list of these so called other occurrences."

Marsh smiled. "Leave that to us Will, we wouldn't want to start anything until we were sure of what we were doing."

"Of course not Marsh," Will said, a touch of sarcasm leaking into his voice.

The conversation halted as Diane approached and stood quietly between Will and Sara.

"Hello again," Sara said as she looked up at the young woman.

"You know, ever since yesterday I have been trying to place you," Diane said. "Are you on TV or something?"

Sara looked around the table, then replied, "Occasionally."

Diane smiled, "I knew it. You know it drives me nuts when I recognize people but can't place them. Then when you are not thinking about it, it just hits you." She stood there, beaming at them, then turned to Sara. "Chicken salad, right?"

"That would be fine," Sara said.

Diane glanced over at the two men, who were both smiling at the exchange. "And for you gentlemen? If your meeting is over that is."

"Burger, bacon and Swiss, medium," Will replied,

"Works for me. I'll have the same," Marsh added.

Diane nodded and picked up the menus, hesitated and walked away.

"Good to be famous," Will said to Sara.

"It opens a few doors and gets you a chicken salad," Sara replied, a smirk spreading over her face.

"Where were we?" Marsh said.

"I think you were about to magically produce some crime scenes for me, and I was going to do my police stuff to see if they are connected," Will said. "But I'm not sure what good that will do. I assume there is something else."

"The airlines. Passenger records," Sara interjected not waiting for Marsh.

Will snapped to attention, staring at Sara. "I presume you know that the airlines treat that information as somewhat confidential?"

"Of course, but not for a big strong cop like you," Sara replied, an innocent and helpless look on her face.

Will laughed again and glanced back and forth between them. "Are you two an item, or should I just fall for that alluring look now? I've always wanted to date a celebrity." He noticed the look that shot across the table and added. "I see I missed out again. But listen, even if I could get access to the records, which I am not committing to by the way, there would be a lot of them. We are talking about a number with a lot of zeroes. It would take years for someone to look them over."

"We do have a plan Detective," Marsh said. "If we could get them electronically, I do have access to some computer resources."

"Jeez, you guys don't quit!" Will protested.

Marsh and Sara waited patiently, although Marsh found himself sliding forward to the edge of his seat.

"Assuming I can, and that's a big assumption," Will emphasized, "what do we get out of it?"

"A name Will. The name of the guy who started all of this."

"You need some sunscreen," Susan shouted over the wind and held her sunglasses on her nose as she turned and looked at Fred.

"Nonsense," Fred replied. He glanced over quickly then returned his eyes to the road. "Never use the stuff. I tan naturally."

"Not at five thousand feet you don't," Susan said smugly, then faced forward, holding her head proudly as she talked without looking at him. "First you get a little pink, then bright red. And with those John Lennon sunglasses on by tonight you will look like a raccoon."

"Hmph," Fred said.

On the back seat of the bright red convertible were a few items they had scavenged; a large and somewhat faded brown and blue blanket and a brand new picnic basket filled with goodies they had purchased at the King Foodmart just down the road from Marsh's place. Susan had felt a funny feeling as they walked in the giant grocery store but Fred didn't seem to notice. They had spent almost a half an hour in the store, taking a while to settle on the menu for the afternoon picnic. Anyone who had been watching them would have thought they were two teenagers, standing close to each other, holding hands, laughing and arguing in fun over every selection. Fred, of course, had made a beeline towards the meat counter as soon as he spotted it.

"Salami," he had said, "we have to have some hard salami, and some good rare roast beef."

Susan had wrinkled her nose a little, "What no steak?"

"Didn't see any, maybe we should ask," he replied, his face practically pushed into the glass shielding the array of meats. "Ah there's some, but it's a little rare. Am I allowed to build a fire?"

"May I suggest some thin sliced turkey, or some of this salmon?" she said politely, ignoring his sarcasm.

Fred looked at her. She had shorts and tank top on, and had added a yellow and blue scarf tied in her hair. A white long sleeved sweater was knotted around her neck, the body covering her bare back.

He smiled at her. "Um, we are going to a forest right? The woods? I think the proper sustenance in this case has to be dead animals."

"Yuck," she said as she attracted the attention of one of the butchers behind the counter.

They had ended up buying a little of everything, probably way more than they could ever eat. The same scenario played out when they found the fruit section, each with their own favorites. Susan had won the discussion over vegetables however, Fred finding almost everything equally unappetizing.

In the liquor store next door they found a nice chilled Chardonnay and a Merlot in an attempt to match all the food types they had acquired. It was packed in a red and white two-bottle cooler on the floor of the back seat; complete with a plastic corkscrew guaranteed to open at least one of the bottles before it broke.

"We will be opening the white first," she had said as she examined it.

"And if the corkscrew breaks?" he replied as he slid his arm around her.

"You're a man, open the red with your teeth."

The sun was at their backs as they headed northwest on the Boulder Turnpike. To the left were the Flatirons, a curious formation of semi-mountains that rose steeply at angles out of the ground, one side of each small peak flat like it had been sheered off. The Rockies climbed majestically behind them in the distance.

"Stephen King lived up here for a while," Fred said suddenly over the wind noise.

"I thought he lived in New England, Maine or something. That's why all his books are always set there."

"A couple weren't," he replied as he glanced in the mirror and steered the car around a slow moving truck pulling a trailer filled with lawn care equipment.

"Are you speeding? Don't get us arrested babe," she said. "Which ones?"

He bristled for a moment at the thought and looked down at the speedometer, then realized that he matched the speed limit. Anything over it was too noisy in the convertible anyway.

"What?" he said.

"Which books?"

"The Shining. One of his first."

"Oh my God I forgot. That's where we are going, to Estes Park. The real hotel is not far from there."

"Really?" Fred said and looked at her. "Maybe we should stop in and say hi. The other was The Stand, one of my favorites. It was set in Boulder and Las Vegas, an end of the world story," he continued, then his voice trailed off. Las Vegas he thought. Sin City. He looked over at her yellow tank top again and his stomach knotted up. Las Vegas, Kansas City. He shook his head trying to clear the jumble of thoughts that forced their way into his mind. His hands gripped the wheel tightly and for a moment he blanked.

"Are you listening to me?" Susan said loudly.

"What?"

"Slow down, the cops out here are nasty," she shouted over the rush of air.

He looked at the speedometer again and realized his foot had pressed into the floor. He lifted it quickly and guided the car back into the slow lane.

"Sorry," he said. "Wasn't paying attention there for a moment."

She looked over at him, the look on his face troubling her for a moment, wondering where he had been. "Just be careful," she added.

The freeway dropped into the outskirts of Boulder, passed by the University of Colorado campus and changed into a busy thoroughfare lined with restaurants, sports stores and shopping centers. He concentrated on driving and hoped it would keep his thoughts clear as they rode silently through the city. Susan was content to lean back against the headrest and look out over the door at the street activity.

"I almost came to school here," she finally said, lifting up a little. "It was either CU or Minnesota. I was torn between being somewhat close to home and the better architecture school in Minneapolis."

"CU would have been a bad choice," Fred said as he pulled up to a stop light, the relative silence comforting until another car pulled up next to them, the loud bass of a rap tune thumping from the back.

"Why's that? Boulder is a great town, and I would have been in the mountains."

Fred slid his arm over and his hand gripped hers on her lap. "But then I wouldn't have met you," he said softly.

She laughed and leaned over to kiss him on the cheek, her breasts pressing softly against his arm. "That's right. And I'd probably be sleeping with a guy with a ponytail and three mountain bikes."

Fred laughed, enjoying her closeness. "And you would be supporting him too - in his quest for oneness with nature."

She giggled and snuggled closer. "Of course my office would be the loft in our small house, and I'd wear cutoff jeans with holes in them and plaid work shirts all the time. A big deal would be designing a new log cabin."

He sped away, leaving the music behind them. "Where am I going anyway? Is it far?"

She leaned back into her seat and stared up into the blue sky. It was clear and warm, a few small puffy white clouds appearing over the mountains in the distance. "Just drive me," she said and pointed forward. "That way."

They rode again in silence as they passed through the city limits of Boulder, the highway running north along the edge of the front range, the entire metroplex of Denver spread out to the east in the distance below them on the edge of the plain. Susan seemed lost in thought somewhere and he didn't disturb her, his own mind churning with possibilities. I do love her he thought, as the wind whipped a small speck of dust into his right eye. He blinked at it a few times, then pushed his finger up under his sunglasses to rub it out. His efforts only made it worse and he pushed his shades up over his head, then turned the rearview mirror to look at his eye. The partial image flickered a bit as he adjusted it, the rough shaven face staring sternly back at him.

"Love Fred?" Richard said. "You don't know what love is."

He forgot about the speck, not able to take his eyes off the mirror.

"Time to move on Fred, we have things to do, stores to pillage. John is waiting on us."

Fred stared at the mirror as the car drifted. The front wheels slipped off the edge of the pavement onto the graveled shoulder and small stones whipped up off the speeding tires and skipped against the side of the car. Susan jerked upright as he reacted suddenly, pulling the wheel back and gently steering the car back on the highway.

"Jesus, Fred," she said, eyes wide. "Do you want me to drive?"

His heart was pounding, fingers wrapped around the wheel tightly. "No babe, sorry," he said. "I just got some dirt in my eye."

"Don't scare me like that, please," she said, a nervous look on her face. "Sometimes I wonder if you are really here with me."

"I'm here," he said and patted her bare shoulder with his hand. "Trust me, I'll always be here."

She looked at him and studied his face.

"Were you sleeping?" he asked as if to change the subject.

She hesitated, unable to shake the chill that had crept over her. "Just dozing a little I guess, thinking about Mom. She loved to come up here."

He laughed and tried to calm her. "Well if you nod off again where do I go?"

She extended her arm and pointed to the front with her hand. "We are almost to Lyons, this road ends there. Just turn left and head west. Those big things over there are mountains. Drive at them," she said and forced a smile.

"I can do that."

She continued to stare at him. "I sure hope so."

Forty-five minutes and a few thousand feet of elevation later they had passed through Estes Park, a small but thriving mountain town set in a valley at the base of the mountains rising around it. They had talked little on the way, exchanging admiring comments mostly about the scenery both lost in thought. A brown road sign indicated the boundary of Rocky Mountain National Park and the road widened into a semi-parking lot with a ranger station situated in the middle. The altitude had dropped the temperature a few degrees, but it was still warm, a pleasant breeze drifted into the car as they stopped at the booth.

"Hi there," Susan said cheerfully to the female ranger dressed in a standard brown park uniform and brimmed cap. "What a day!"

The ranger smiled and leaned out the window toward the car. "Beautiful. Day pass today?" she asked.

"Unfortunately just today," Susan replied. "Pay the nice ranger, babe."

"Three dollars sir."

Fred reached into his pocket, lifted his hips against the seatbelt and retrieved the bills, then handed them over the door. The ranger produced a light blue sticky note with the date inked in and handed it back. "Inside the front window sir. Have a nice visit."

"Thanks," he said and attached the paper inside the windshield.

Susan undid her own seat belt and leaned forward like a little kid. "We will!" she said enthusiastically. "Come on driver, let's go."

Fred was relieved at her change of mood and drove on slowly. They were at the edge of a huge meadow, blemished only by the two-lane blacktop road that snaked along the side. A steep hill covered in pine trees was on their right, and everywhere around the meadow the mountains rose gently at first, then stretched up towards the sky, the dark blue and purple peaks ragged with rocks and small spires.

Susan lifted herself, practically sitting on the back of the seat and braced herself with her arms on the top of the windshield. Fred laughed at her.

"Don't jump!" he exclaimed as he looked over at her.

She pulled the scarf from her head and shook her hair, letting it spill down over her shoulders. "Isn't it beautiful? For purple mountain's majesty..."

"What?" he asked.

"America the Beautiful silly. It's about Colorado you know," she said as she looked down at him.

"I'm not so sure about that."

"I am, I think. Colorado inspired it anyway. Besides it fits doesn't it?"

"That it does," he said as they rounded a corner, the road suddenly lined on the right side with what seemed like dozens of parked cars. He slowed down and pointed to the people that seemed to be milling about. "What's up with this?" he asked.

"Pull over for a second, right here!"

He wheeled the car into an open area on the shoulder and stopped, then looked around with a puzzled look on his face. "What?"

"Look babe," she said softly as she stared out into the meadow. An almost dry stream meandered across the middle, on either side of the creek were about twenty elk, the herd wandering about peacefully, most with their long necks pointed down, heads bent into the grass.

Susan scampered across the seat, leaned down onto Fred, wrapped her arms around his chest and rested her chin on the top of his head. "Aren't they wonderful?" she asked, her jaw bouncing onto his skull.

"Ah, wildlife," he said as he looked out. "You can tell by the number people out there taking photos."

"Stop it," she said and twisted his head toward the herd. "Where else could you see animals by the side of the road like this."

He moved his hands over hers, then leaned his head back and looked at her upside down. "You remember Minnesota don't you? Driving along farm roads, scores of animals along side?"

"Those are cows. That's different."

"Yeah I know. They give milk and taste better."

She laughed and jumped back onto her seat. "Let's go. I'm getting hungry and I want to hike up a trail before we eat."

Fred steered the car back onto the pavement and they drove on past the gathering. The road eventually left the meadow and moved deeper into the trees, gradually inclining as they cruised deeper into the mountains.

"Where are we going?" Fred asked. "Just in case I need to stop somewhere."

"I'll know it when I see it. There are hundreds of trails leading off the road. I'm just waiting for the right one."

They rounded a corner and an open space on the side of the road came into view, two cars parked on either side of a trailhead. "There!" she said. "Let's stop there."

Fred pulled the convertible into the remaining open area, the wheels shoved slightly up into the hill. Susan jumped out quickly and looked around, took a deep breath and stretched her arms. He killed the engine, got out and slid the keys into the pocket of his tan shorts.

"Let's hike up until we find a spot to eat, OK?"

"Sure, as long as its not a four hour jaunt. I'm hungry."

Susan leaned into the car, opened the basket and pulled out a six-pack of water in plastic bottles. She pulled off two, tossed the others back onto the seat and looked over at him. "You can't have enough water in the mountains. Altitude sickness you know."

"Absolutely."

She smiled at him sweetly and tucked the blanket under her arm. "I'll carry these, you get the cooler and the picnic basket." She turned and scampered up the trail, leaving him behind.

Fred hauled the items out of the car, questioning how heavy they had suddenly become. He started off to follow her, then shouted as she vanished around a corner. "Does the term Sherpa mean anything to you?"

"Come on or I'll leave you behind," he heard her say from somewhere above him behind a large rock.

"Right," he said to himself and trudged up the hill.

He caught up to her after a moment his breath already labored. She ran back and kissed him quickly on the mouth. "Come on," she said.

It was quiet as they moved along the trail, mostly climbing but sometimes dropping down as they worked their way deeper into the forest. The path was hard dirt and well worn, but smaller rocks sometimes were buried in the way and Fred had to be careful not to stumble. Overhead the breeze seemed to whistle in the treetops, the clean scent of pine strong in the air. He was happy to walk behind her and watch her slim form move gracefully along the way. After about fifteen minutes of hiking he stopped to rest. His fingers ached from gripping the wooden basket handle.

"How far are we going?" he asked, a little breathless. "You can really feel the altitude can't you?"

Her chest was heaving too as she brushed the hair out of her face. "Yes, don't you love it?"

He set the basket and the cooler down, walked over and hugged her. "I'd love it more if we could lighten up these baskets a little."

"Mmm..." she said and tilted her face up, pressing her lips against his. The kissed softly first, then a little harder, then she pulled back and smiled at him. "Come on, just a little farther - till I find the right spot."

He reluctantly let her go and stepped back to fetch the baskets. "Soon, I hope."

After a moment the trail opened over a large ravine, huge boulders and fallen trees littered down the steep bank to a small stream far below. Just in front of them a flat ledge made up of two huge cracked rocks perched over the drop to the left of the trail. Susan set the blanket and the bottles down, scampered over a dead tree trunk and walked out to the edge. She leaned over and looked down.

"You've got to see this babe, come here."

Gratefully he set the baskets down again and climbed over the tree, scraping his leg on a dead branch. He joined her on the edge of the rock and stood just behind her as the wind cooled the sweat from his face. A silent bird circled high over them without flapping its wings.

"It's like we are flying," she said out over the chasm.

He looked down, the height dizzying. "Push her," a sinister voice sounded in his head. He jumped back at the thought. "Push her over Fred, you can do it. No one will know," the voice repeated. He took a couple of steps back and almost tripped over the back of the rock.

Susan turned and smiled at him. "Scared of heights?"

He forced himself to calm down, his heart racing again. "Uh, no, just hungry. Let's go," he said quickly.

"OK," she turned and came toward him, then noticed the original part of the fallen rock above them across the trail. "Up there," she said pointing. "Let's go up there and picnic."

It took a moment, but they discovered a way up the rock, squeezing around it between pine trees. It took Fred two trips, unable to carry both the basket and the cooler and climb the hill at the same time. By the time he reached the top the second time, Susan had already spread the blanket and was unpacking the picnic. Fred plopped down beside her, grateful to be off the ledge.

"I'm starved," she said happily, separating their disparate menu selections between them. "Can you open the wine?"

Fred struggled with the plastic corkscrew, finally getting the Chardonnay open. He filled two plastic glasses as Susan held them out. For a while they drank and ate quietly, both lost in thought.

Finally Susan broke the silence. "I miss Mom Fred, I wish you could have met her, before…" she stopped for a moment, face calm. "She would have liked you so much," she added. Her hand reached out to caress his cheek.

Fred stared at her, lost in her eyes, and realized what thoughts had been nagging at him all day. "Marry me Susan," he said quietly.

Her mouth dropped open and she set the glass down without looking. "What did you say?" she stammered.

He sat up, not taking his eyes from hers. He reached down and took her hand. "I need you Susan, now more than ever. Marry me."

She squeezed his hand back and leaned closer. She looked at him long and hard, trying to understand the look in his eyes.

"Oh God, Fred," she said and moved closer to kiss him. "If you promise to love me forever," she whispered over his lips.

"Forever," he said. He pushed her back on the rock, wrapped his arm around her and kissed her hard. She moved under him, melting into his arms, her fingers pressing into his back. She moaned slightly as his hands slid up her side and over her breasts, excited at his touch.

Suddenly he pulled back slightly, their faces inches apart. "Did you pack any pillows in that picnic basket?" he asked.

She giggled a little, "I can take it if you can."

He laughed with her. "Do you think anyone will happen by?" he asked.

"Don't care," she said softly and pulled him back down on top of her.

Chapter Seventeen

At twenty-six Lebida Murphy was still a virgin. She didn't hold it personally against men - who never seemed to call her - not even just for a date. She didn't think it had anything to do with her looks, although she was a little plain she admitted to herself. And tall. And her short hair cut without bangs and parted on the side that kept falling over the front of her face so she had the annoying habit of brushing it back while talking to someone shouldn't make a difference. And she did have a mind. She was one of the best web page designers in the company. In fact, she could find her way around the web better than anyone she knew.

She stayed in her cubicle for about two hours after everyone else had gone home for the night, getting up only to refresh her cup of herbal tea every half hour or so, once fixing a cup of Raman noodles in the microwave. The request Marsh had made seemed a little curious, but she had been happy to try and help. Her heart secretly poured out to him on Tuesday morning when he had addressed the whole company. She stood in the back of the conference room close to the door, and had quickly left the room, tears in her eyes, after he informed the staff of his mother's death. Now she was determined to get some results, even though Marsh had said it would be fine if she could find anything out in the next few days. The bluish glow from her monitor filled the cubicle in the dimming office light as she sipped at her tea and waited for the search engine to come back with the next page of results.

When she had first started her inquiries, it seemed like an overwhelming task, his instructions being a bit nebulous. Try and locate as many occurrences of a grocery store being robbed by a lone gunman he had said to her in his office, his back to her as he stared out the window and paced. She had read the accounts of the accident in the paper, and saw a brief mention of it on the evening news, so she knew instantly that it had something to do with his mother. It was the first time that she met with him privately; her contact previously limited to staff meetings or project specific updates. She fidgeted in the chair in front of his large oak desk, trying to figure out something to do with her hands.

"Uh, that's a little broad for a web search, Marsh," she said, slightly nervous about the familiar use of his name. Why she didn't know, after all she had worked for him for a year and a half, and considered herself one of the company's best employees.

He laughed and sat down in his chair, rocked back and forth, and looked at her with a gentle smile on his face. "Yes, I suppose it is."

She waited, curious what he would say next. In spite of the situation she wondered what it would be like to go out with him, quickly chastising herself for such inappropriate thoughts. But why not? I'm a woman; he's just another man. It's not like he's my teacher and I'm a student or anything.

"What exactly is it you would like me to find Marsh?" she asked after a moment. She liked the way his name rolled off her lips.

"Umm... let's see. I guess what I am looking for is a list of thefts, very large grocery stores, carried out by one person. A white male."

"In Denver?" she asked and absently brushed the hair out of her face.

"Actually, no. It would be in any city other than Denver, in the US anyway."

"OK, I can do that. Anything else?"

He looked uncomfortable for a moment before he had continued. "Are you familiar with what happened on Monday?"

"Sure... I guess so," she replied, now a little uncomfortable herself, like she was prying. She brushed her hair back again, this time realizing it and willed her hands back into her lap.

"Well something like that. If you need any more details let me know."

That sounded like a dismissal and she stood up quickly, not wanting to push it any farther. "OK, I'm kind of in the middle of the Westcorp site build, but I'll get on it as soon as I can."

"Thanks Lebida, but don't let it interfere with your project work. This is a personal favor alright?"

"No problem," she said, but she could tell that it must be important to him. She hesitated and hoped that he would keep the meeting going a little longer.

"Great," he said with a smile. "I really appreciate it. Just let me know if you find anything."

That was the end of the conversation and she had left his office, later realizing he didn't tell her what to do with the information if she found out anything.

The search engine returned another list of results and she snapped back to the present. She sighed softly at the number of matches. She was beginning to get frustrated, disappointed with herself for not being able to narrow down the criteria to something a little more tangible. Of course she didn't have a lot to go on, simple keywords like 'theft', 'grocery store', 'supermarket' and so on yielding thousands of responses. It had been a slow process so far, and she had tried at least a dozen combinations of inquiries in most of the major search engines.

She debated giving up for the evening, then decided a little more research might help. She popped into the *Denver Post* website, and submitted a query on the local search function, specifying "robbery and gunman". The resulting list was much more manageable and she immediately recognized the headline from Tuesday's paper. She read the story slowly and made a few notes on a notepad that had so far remained empty except for a few flowers she doodled while surfing. There was not much to go on, and she felt saddened at the story's details, never before reading such an impartial article that dealt directly with someone she was close to. Close to? Well someone she knew anyway.

She picked up her cup, deciding on one last tea, not quite ready to admit defeat, and walked through the now deserted office towards the small kitchen area at the back. She moved slowly, glancing into each empty cubicle as she passed, the carpet covered half walls adorned with pictures and the personal possessions of her co-workers. She stopped for a moment at the work place of her team lead and leaned in when a newspaper clipping caught her attention. It was from the *San Jose Mercury News*, the headline proclaiming 'Denver Firm Lands Local Systems Deal'. It was the project she was working on, and she read the story proudly, noticing that the article barely described the project, but seemed more focused on the fact that a Denver company had won the bid over more prominent Silicon Valley firms.

She was still smiling as she rummaged through the tea box, finally selecting an orange flavored variety while her cup of water heated up in the microwave. Fittingly, the idea hit her just as the timer dinged. She grabbed the cup and hurried back to her cubicle, unwrapped the tea bag and dropped it in her cup. She then ignored the tea and pulled the keyboard toward her and began to type. Pulling up the site for Google, her favorite search engine, she worked her way down the reference section, through geography, census/population, and metro area population estimates until she got a list of the 50 largest metropolitan areas in the US. She glanced it over, then realized that she didn't know the names of the newspapers for each of the cities listed. She printed the list, then backed the pages up and summoned the News & Media section, selecting newspapers, burrowing through a few pages until she found a list of the 25 largest newspaper publications in the US. She clicked on the print button, hurried across the office to the printer and picked up the printouts. She read them as she walked back to her desk.

The *New York Times* was the first on the list. Guessing correctly at the website name she scrolled through the home page until she found the search function and entered "robbery and gunman". She groaned as the resulting list showed 233 articles, but started to scroll through them anyway, looking for anything to do with a grocery store. A few minutes later she was convinced that New York had a high crime rate, but apparently supermarkets were only the target of shoplifters and muggings. She moved on to the *LA Times*, dismayed at the primitiveness of the search engine on that site. After chasing down several false avenues, she sat back, sipped her tea, and wondered if her idea wasn't so hot after all.

Giving it another shot she contacted the site at the *Chicago Tribune*, the search engine there much more professionally done. She chose to search the archives for the last two years, once again presented with a list of over a hundred articles. She cruised through them quickly, almost missing a story that was on the bottom of the page as she scrolled by. "Daring Daylight Robbery at Suburban Supermarket" item number 48 read. Her heart skipped a beat as she glanced at the summary, then brought up the complete text.

Daring Daylight Robbery at Suburban Supermarket

The prosperous suburb of Oak Brook was the scene of a mid-day robbery yesterday at the new SuperThrift food center. A single gunman entered the offices through a back door and held the staff of three workers hostage at gunpoint while he quickly filled a canvas sack full of the previous days storereceipts, estimated at over a hundred thousand dollars. The thief then casually left the store, disappearing into the crowd at the newly developed shopping complex.

The man described as a white Caucasian in his mid-thirties, dressed in a running suit appeared calm and collected, store officials recounted. Jim Hanberg, SuperThrift Store Manager reported: "He just walked in, shoved a gun in everyone's face and walked out with the money."

The Oak Brook Police Department declined to comment on the theft, stating that they had a full description of the subject and were pursuing all possible leads...

Lebida read the story twice amazed at the similarities of the crimes. This has to be what he's looking for she thought, smiling triumphantly as she clicked on the print button. Buoyed by her success, she turned to the next paper on the list, the *Washington Post*. She cursed uncharacteristically at the delay as the website loaded slowly, anxious to initiate another search. Optimistically she queried on the keywords 'robbery gunman grocery'. The result list was small, and one item immediately stood out. "McLean Supermarket Targeted in Theft" the subject read.

"Bingo," she said out loud, then quickly retrieved the article and read it carefully. Once again the same story unfolded before her; a moustached thief simply walked into the store and relieved the stunned workers of the store's money. She printed the article, got up from her desk, and stretched her arms and back as she walked across the office again. She was hungry she thought, but on a roll. Picking up the two articles from the printer, she headed back to the kitchen and read them over again while she grabbed a Snickers from the self-pay candy box, vowing to remember to stick in some change later. She returned to her cube while she munched, retrieved a manila folder from her desk and printed the word "Marsh" carefully on the tab. She inserted the papers and tore off the top sheet of her notepad, then made some notes on a fresh page, listing the city, the date, and the details that made each occurrence seem to match the pattern. She felt energized, and fantasized briefly about how she might present her findings to Marsh.

It had been night for hours when she finally finished, the office mostly dark except for the glow from her monitor. The lights had shut off automatically at eleven, and she hadn't bothered to get up to turn them back on. She glanced at the list of publications; most crossed off with a black felt pen, but eight of them highlighted with a yellow marker. She ticked them off approvingly: Chicago, Washington DC, Boston, Philadelphia, St. Louis, San Jose, Orlando, and Sacramento. Sacramento had been the toughest to research; the Sacramento Bee not being a newspaper name that was intuitively obvious.

She compared the list of papers with her list of the largest metropolitan areas, noting that she had not checked a number of cities. It was a good start though she thought, and if Marsh wanted more she had the procedure down pat. She gathered up her notes, inserted them in the folder and placed it in the drawer below her desktop. She smiled as she brought up her email, addressed the message to Marsh and filled in the subject line as "For Your Eyes Only". She quickly wrote a short note that described what she found, and felt a twinge of excitement at the success of her clandestine operation. She wondered if maybe she might have dinner with him to disclose what she had found.

She was humming to herself as she sent the message and gathered up her things. She couldn't wait until tomorrow.

Chapter Eighteen

"We're getting married Marsh."

She had her back to him, and her feet squished into the carpet as she nervously tried to pull up the nape with her curling toes. The glass door to the balcony was open just a crack and she could feel the cool air drop down over her feet. It was a chilly morning, the clouds a uniform gray across the sky, hanging low enough over the mountains in the distance to obscure the snow-capped peaks. The lack of sunlight caused everything in between to look drab and colorless. It smelled like rain.

"What?" Marsh asked. She closed her eyes and tried to discern from his tone what his reaction was. "Who is?"

She didn't turn around. She hadn't slept much last night, her stomach in knots and her mind racing as she tried to assimilate everything that had happened in the last few days. Fred had slept soundly after their somewhat marginal performance in bed, oblivious to her tossing and turning. She had been disappointed, especially after their little romp on the mountain and the engagement. Normally their sex was passionate and unrestrained, but last night he had seemed like another person and she had been conscious for the first time of her brother sleeping closely in the room across the hall. When she did nod off, she had a disturbing dream about making love to someone else.

"Suse?"

She hadn't wanted to tell Marsh yet, but it just blurted out of her. She had fantasized of the day this would happen, always assuming she would be sitting with mom in some bright sidewalk café, having an intimate lunch together. She would wait happily until Mom noticed the ring on her finger, then they would laugh and cry together and hug each other, and exchange stories all afternoon on what would happen next in their lives. Things were so different than she had dreamed.

"Susan!"

She heard him cross the room and felt his hands slide over her shoulders, squeezing them gently as he turned her around. She looked up into his eyes for a moment, then buried her face into his shoulder and began to sob, her breath coming in halting fits, raw sounds escaping from her throat. She wrapped her arms around him, gripped his shirt and tried to hold herself up as her knees weakened and bent. He leaned his head down, rested his cheek on top of her hair and stroked her back slowly. They stayed like that for a long time.

"I don't know what to say, Suse," he finally said and gazed down into her face. "I guess congratulations are in order."

"That's it?"

He laughed. "No really Suse, I mean it." He pulled her close and gave her a big hug, then kissed her on the cheek. "It's good news." He placed his hands on her shoulders and held her at arm's length. "Really."

She took a deep breath as a broad smile spread over his face, clutching at his sincerity. A flood of emotions passed through her, and she didn't know if she was crying or laughing. "I wanted Mom to know," she said softly.

"I'm sure she knows," he said. "I'm sure she's grinning at you right now."

"God I hope so Marsh. This isn't the way I thought it would happen." She stepped back and rubbed the back of her hand over her cheek, looking at him. "I didn't know if I should tell you... Is it... Do you approve?"

He laughed again, surprised at the levity of the situation. "This is a first, you asking for my approval on anything."

She laughed with him and a feeling of relief spread over her, grateful for his humor. "I've always wanted your approval Marsh, I just never asked for it before."

"Come sit down," he said and motioned towards the couch. "Tell me all about it."

Marsh moved to one side of the coffee table and sat down on the sofa. Susan stepped around the other side but paused for a moment to look up at the family pictures on the wall, her gaze fixated on the wedding portrait of their mom and dad. She sat down close to him, half turned on the couch, legs tucked up under her robe, sitting on them.

"Well it was somewhat of a surprise," she started. "We were picnicking up on a rock. He just kind of blurted it out."

"And?" he said, eyebrows raised.

"And what?" she said with a little laugh. "I said yes. I guess I've been thinking about it for sometime, but didn't expect it to happen now." A frown settled over her face. "It's just that this week, with Mom and everything. So much is happening so fast."

Marsh reached out and touched her hand softly. "Yes it is Suse, and that's good. Mom wouldn't want us to just sit around and mope." He waited for a second, pondering. "Suse, Mom was one of the happiest people I knew. Even after Dad's death she recovered and moved on with her life. I think she would be pleased that something like this happened to help you get through this time." He nodded at the ceiling. "She's probably up there right now laughing her ass off."

Susan couldn't help laughing herself. She loved her brother she thought. "Stop it Marsh. Mom never laughed her ass off. She was always too proper."

"Not hardly. Mom could yuck it up with the best of them. You probably don't remember because you were still young, but I do. Mom and Dad used to be pretty wild in the old days."

"Somehow I can't imagine that." She looked at him. "God I miss her Marsh."

He squeezed her hand, "Me too." They both sat for a moment lost in their respective thoughts.

"So what are the details?" he said finally.

"What? Oh, I don't know, there are none yet. I guess we were both so stunned that we didn't really talk about it much."

"Stunned?"

"Well you know, it wasn't like we had been talking about this for months. I guess we should start making some plans though." She thought for a moment. "Or maybe we'll just run off to Vegas and get hitched. Save on all those big wedding expenses."

Marsh feigned a look of surprise. "What? You said he was rich. Worried about money already?"

She laughed, "Oh it's just all those details that need to be arranged. It seems like so much trouble," she teased, then a serious look covered her face. "Do you like him Marsh?"

He looked at her with a straight face. "I guess he'll do. He is a good conversationalist after all."

"Stop it."

"I like him a lot, Suse. Where is the boy anyway? Shouldn't he be back by now?"

She thought for a moment. It had been over an hour since she took one look at all his wrinkled dress shirts and had sent him packing to the closest men's store, an exclusive haberdashery Marsh frequented on the edge of LODO.

"He's probably buying out the store. It wouldn't surprise me if he came back with a couple of new suits," she said.

"I doubt it. At the place I sent him to they wouldn't dream of letting him out of the store until they had fully fitted and tailored him. That takes a couple of days you know."

'Mmm... I suppose so. I've got to get ready myself. Sheila is picking me up in a while to get things ready at her place." She rose from the couch, her fingers gently touching her face. "God I'm a mess again," she said.

"You look fine. Why don't you get ready to go. I'll be here whenever Fred gets back."

He was wandering aimlessly around the room when Susan re-emerged from the bedroom. He smiled at her as she approached, attired smartly and conservatively in a black short-sleeved dress, cut high around the neck that descending tightly around her frame to just below her knees. There were ivory buttons down the front, and she held a pair of black gloves in one hand, a black jacket was draped over her other arm.

"Do I look all right?" she asked, stopping just in front of him.

"You look perfect, and beautiful. Just as Mom would have wanted."

She smiled back at him, her face bright with no traces of the morning tears. "Thank you sir," she said and curtsied.

He walked over to her, gathered her in his arms and gave her another hug. "It seems like we have been hugging for days," he said with a smile.

"Yes, and I love it Marsh. I guess living so far apart we forget how good it is to be close," she said.

They looked at each other for a moment without saying anything, then the security buzzer interrupted them. Marsh started to walk over to the intercom, then paused and looked back over his shoulder.

"Sheila or Fred?" he asked.

"Must be Fred. Sheila shouldn't be here for a few minutes yet."

He nodded and pressed the intercom. "Hello?"

"It's me Marsh, Fred,"

"Welcome back Fred. Come on up" he said and hit the door release button.

He pulled at the door, left it ajar and walked over to the kitchen, then opened the refrigerator on the off chance he might find something to munch on. He was moving items around inside the fridge without much luck when Fred walked in the door, carrying a white paper sack with string handles in one hand, and a plastic garment bag over the other. Marsh and Susan both looked up in surprise.

"What's that?" Susan said and pointed to the garment bag.

Fred set the sack down and closed the door as Marsh walked out of the kitchen empty handed. "It's a suit my dear. You did send me to a clothing store."

"Lemme see," she said, walked over and grabbed the bag by the plastic hanger hooks protruding from the cutout at the top. She draped it over the dining room table and unzipped it, maneuvered the hangers out and held it up for approval. It was a dark black Hickey-Freeman single-breasted suit, with faint gray pinstripes about an inch apart. The pants inside were creased sharply with one inch cuffs at the bottom.

"Very nice Fred," Marsh said as he lifted the inside of the jacket and glanced at the label. "I've bought a few Hickey-Freemans there myself."

"Does it fit?" Susan asked with a smile.

"Of course it fits," Fred said, a bit puzzled. "What good would it be if it didn't fit?"

Susan shot a puzzled glance at Marsh who smiled.

"Twisted a few arms did you?" Marsh asked.

Fred shrugged. "Well, a two thousand dollar suit, a couple of new shirts, two expensive ties, and a pathetic plea about needing it immediately was an influence," he said smugly. "And a couple of hundred dollar bills for the tailor lady didn't hurt either."

Susan looked stunned at the amount, her mouth open.

"The old Russian lady with six inch fingers and gold capped teeth?" Marsh inquired.

"That's her. It was amazing how quick her schedule opened up when I explained my problem in terms she could obviously understand."

Marsh grinned. Susan moved next to Fred and slid her arms around him. "That's a lot of money babe," she said, somehow surprised that he would casually spend thousands of dollars just for clothes.

"Nonsense," Fred said, pulling her close. "It's a good suit. I needed another black one anyway."

"Well it better look like a million bucks," she said. "You were gone so long I thought you were lost."

"Am I late?"

"No, but I'm leaving as soon as Sheila gets here. We're going to get organized at her place for the gathering after the service. You and Marsh will have to get along without me."

"No problem. I'm sure I can get dressed all by myself, and Marsh and I will find something to keep us occupied."

"That's right," Marsh added. "We'll be fine."

Susan glanced at her watch, then at Fred. "Well now that you are back I'm going to wait downstairs. Maybe I can catch Sheila before she has to get out of her car." She walked to the door and Fred followed.

"Tell Sheila thanks again for me," Marsh said from across the room. "And be at the funeral home by 1:30 alright?"

"Yes big brother," she said, and raised up on her tip-toes to kiss Fred. "See you in a bit," she added. Fred opened the door for her and watched as she glanced at both of them then disappeared down the hall.

"I'm going to make another pot of coffee Fred, want some?"

"Sure Marsh," Fred replied and closed the door. There was a moment of uncomfortable silence between them as Marsh walked into the kitchen, and set about the task of brewing a fresh pot.

Fred sat down on the couch, opened the bag from the store and pulled out a tie. It was silk, dark blue with black diagonal stripes and he pulled it through his hand slowly, the soft material sliding over his fingers. He was nervous he thought, not knowing what to say now that he and Marsh were alone again. So far he had ignored the implications of the upcoming funeral, and briefly wondered if the casket would be closed at the church. He shuddered at the thought, dropped the tie on the couch and got up quickly, then walked over towards the closed glass doors to the balcony. He glanced outside at the grayness, then caught his reflection in an antique mirror hung on the side wall next to the oak bookcase. He tried to look away, but couldn't.

"We killed her Fred," the face said, lips barely moving under the brown-haired moustache.

Fred froze and his stomach churned as he felt the WHUMP of the car and the truck colliding. The unsmiling face stared at him, eyes drilling through his head.

"No," he mouthed. "You killed her."

"What's that Fred?" Marsh asked from close behind him.

Fred jumped and put a hand out to steady himself on the glass door. "Oh, sorry Marsh," he said quickly, trying to recover. Marsh held a coffee cup in each hand and looked at him curiously. Fred looked back at him, forced a smile, and wondered if Marsh heard what he said. He reached out for one of the cups, heart racing.

"Black, right?" Marsh asked, his face blank and unreadable.

"Fine, thanks," Fred said and tried not to stammer.

Fred took the coffee by the body of the cup, the hot liquid made the glass almost too hot to hold. He quickly shifted his grip to the handle. Marsh hesitated a moment, then smiled a little.

"I guess this must be a little uncomfortable for you Fred," Marsh said warmly. "Not the best of circumstances to meet your new in-laws."

Fred looked at him, confused. "I'm sorry Marsh, what?"

"Suse told me this morning," he said and extended his hand. "Congratulations and welcome to the family."

Jesus Fred said to himself, shocked. He took Marsh's hand and tried to shake it firmly. "She told you?"

"I don't think she meant to, to be honest. It just kind of came out while you were gone," Marsh said, shook then dropped Fred's hand. "You will take good care of her, won't you?"

Fred glanced to his left at the mirror, but John was gone. He looked back. "Of course Marsh," he said. "Always."

Marsh looked at him hard. "Good. She deserves the best. And you know how big brothers are."

"Yes, I do," Fred managed.

They both stood there silent for a moment. "Well I've got to check my email. Do you need to see what the market is doing, or is it another day off?" Marsh asked, a touch of humor in his voice.

"Well I suppose I should keep up, Marsh," Fred said relieved. His panic subsided and he regained a little control. "If you don't mind listening to CNBC while you work."

"No problem. I usually have the news on anyway."

They walked across the room and down the hall. Fred followed Marsh quietly. They entered the office and Marsh motioned to the couch at the back of the room. "Sit. I'll get it."

Fred sat down quietly, still gripping his cup, grateful for something to concentrate on. Marsh walked past the treadmill and turned on the TV, waiting while the picture filled in. The channel was already set to CNBC and the familiar program immediately seemed to calm him as Marsh sat down at his desk and began working on his computer. Fred paid little attention to the commentators, instead concentrating on the two tickers moving slowly across the bottom of the screen. The two streams moved at slightly different speeds and he considered that for a moment, finally deciding that some psychologist must have determined it would be hard to read if they both moved at the same pace.

"Jesus," Marsh said to the computer.

Fred tore his eyes away from the television. "What's that Marsh?"

"Umm, I don't know yet Fred," Marsh said, "Just someone doing a little research for me." Marsh stared at the screen, the message open in a little window. 'For Your Eyes Only' the subject said, and he read the message carefully.

Dear Marsh,

I worked on the 'project' we discussed last night, and found eight occurrences of the event that you were interested in. I have cities and dates documented, with accompanying news stories, but you didn't tell me what to do with them. Do you want to get together to review the results?

Lebida

Marsh was amazed. He hadn't expected anything like this and couldn't decide what to do. He glanced at his watch, noting he had a few hours before they had to leave. He started to reach for the phone, then drew back and reflected on the development. It's mother's funeral he thought, should I be doing this now? Despite a nagging feeling of guilt he couldn't think of any reason not to. He pulled out a company extension list, then reached again for the phone and dialed the office. Lebida answered on the second ring.

"Hi Lebida. I got your email this morning. I can't believe you found something already."

"Well it took a while, but once I figured out the best way to search it was a snap."

"I want to see what you have, but can you give me a quick summary?"

"Sure, hang on while I get the folder," she said.

There was a short pause, and Marsh felt his heart pound a little faster.

"Ok, here we go. What can I tell you?"

"Well, you said eight times. Where were they?"

"Sure, I've got the list right here. Chicago, DC, Boston, Phil..."

"Wait a minute, let me get something to write on." Marsh looked over his desk for anything to scribble on. He found an envelope containing his utility bill and picked up a pen laying next to the keyboard. "OK, shoot."

"Chicago, DC, Boston, Philadelphia, St. Louis, San Jose, Orlando, and Sacramento. That's not in date order though."

Marsh finished the hasty list. "That's OK," he said.

"And there maybe more, I just got a little tired last night."

"You did great Lebida, this means a lot to me." He thought for a moment. "Are you coming to the service today?"

"Of course Marsh. Do you want me to bring the folder with me?"

"Please do, and thank you so much. I really owe you one."

"How about dinner?" she asked.

Marsh wasn't tracking too well. "Sure, anything," he said absently.

"Great, I'll see you later then Marsh."

"Thanks again Lebida. Bye."

He hung up the phone, thinking she had said something else as he put the receiver down, but didn't give it a second thought. He turned to Fred.

"Remember the idea you had at dinner the other night?" Marsh asked.

Fred looked at him, confused for a second. "Oh, you mean about tracking the thief through airline reservations?"

"Yeah," Marsh said, holding up the envelope. "Well I've got eight other cities, and dates to go with them."

"Wow, that was fast. That's great Marsh. How did you get it so quickly?"

"One of my employees, who seems to know her way around the Internet," Marsh replied smiling broadly. "Now I just need to get Carter to cooperate a little."

"Carter?"

"Our friendly neighborhood police detective," Marsh said smugly.

Sheila's house was in Washington Park, a bustling neighborhood in south Denver with huge trees, detached garages and older two story houses with wooden porches. It was once filled with families and the elderly, but in the last few years it had become the target of new professional money, houses purchased and renovated by the younger crowd who disdained high rise condos and the lofts developed downtown. Wash Park itself was the center of activity, where biking, jogging, and rollerblading was the preferred mode of transportation, and dozens of volleyball games were always in progress.

They walked up the five wooden steps onto the porch that creaked a little under their weight, but was solid. The porch had been refinished a few years ago, the blue paint was still clean and fresh looking, and complemented the grayish color of the house. To the left in front of the triple windows was a weathered wooden swing hung by chains from the roof. Sheila caught Susan looking at it and smiled.

"My favorite spot," she said. "I sit out here for hours in the evening, just reading or watching the world go by."

"It's so peaceful," Susan remarked. "I could live here."

They entered the house and Susan's breath was taken away. The hardwood floors of the living room shone, despite the lack of sunshine through the windows. A restored brick fireplace dominated the room, with floor-to-ceiling cherry bookcases that covered the walls on either side. The furniture was tasteful, but not modern, and perfectly matched the subdued yellow color of the walls giving the room a warmth all its own. There were green plants everywhere, and what little wall space that didn't have brick or windows was adorned with striking original art. The dining room was situated between the living room and the kitchen, and was filled with a huge oak table, perched on two sweeping legs that swept down to the floor with curled toe-like bottoms. Six high-backed chairs surrounded it, and flowered place mats and a huge cut glass punch bowl already covered the top of the table. Piles of paper plates and silverware where stacked carefully on either side.

"It's wonderful Sheila," Susan said, unable to move from the center of the room.

Sheila beamed, "I like it," she said. "Coffee?"

"Oh, please. And do you mind if I wander around a bit? I want to see everything," Susan asked.

"Help yourself," Sheila said and headed into the kitchen.

Susan explored the rooms, stopping and admiring everything. Sheila crossed through the dining room, past a granite counter that separated the kitchen from the rest of the house. The kitchen was bright and modern, the only exception to the wooden interior of the rest of the house, though the hardwood floors extended through it to the back door. She had already prepared the brewer, flicked on the switch, then pulled a couple of mugs from a cupboard and sat down on one of the bar stools by the counter. She watched, slightly amused, as Susan wandered.

The pot gurgled as Susan returned from upstairs, and Sheila got up to fill the mugs.

"It's perfect," Susan said as she pulled over another of the stools. "I want one."

"Well it takes a little work to keep the dust out, but that's what maids are for."

They both sat down and enjoyed the quiet. "Are you doing OK?" Sheila finally asked. She reached out and touched Susan's hand.

"I think so. I mean the shock has worn off, and it's been good to be home with Marsh. He's been so upbeat, remembering all the good things about Mom," Susan said. She felt herself choke up a little. "And it's good to have Fred here."

"Fred's the man in your life?" Sheila asked, her eyebrows raised a little.

"Yes, for about a year now." Susan hesitated and set her cup down. "We're getting married."

"What? When did this all happen?"

"Uh, yesterday actually," Susan said, embarrassed eyes tilted down for a moment. "It was kind of a surprise."

"I'll say. Does Marsh know?"

"I told him this morning. It's all going so fast, Sheila, I don't know what to think about it."

"I can imagine. But if it's right it's right."

"I think it is. I really love him. But…"

"But?"

Susan hesitated, "Well just between us girls, last night when we were in bed he seemed like another person. And then I had this dream that I was married to someone else. Someone I didn't know. It kind of shook me up."

"Well that's understandable, with everything else going on."

They were quiet for a moment.

"Can I ask you something Sheila?"

"Of course."

"You and Marsh," she started. "I kind of thought that you two would, well you know."

Sheila laughed. "Well we almost did, once. But it didn't work out.

Now we are just good friends I guess. He is my boss you know."

It was Susan's turn to laugh. "I almost slept with my boss once, when I first started at work. I'm glad I didn't though. But you and Marsh are different."

"Different?" Sheila added and laughed with her. "I don't know about that. But I am surprised I haven't heard much from him in the last few days. I thought he might need someone," she hesitated, "other than you of course."

Susan didn't know what to say. "He did have a date the other night. With Fred and I."

"A date?" Sheila said. Her eyes widened and she leaned back a little.

"I guess so, for dinner," Susan said, hesitating.

Sheila said nothing.

After a moment Susan continued. "Shouldn't we get to work? What can I help with?"

Sheila brushed her hand towards Susan. "Nothing really, it's all ready. I went to the store last night, and bought everything. Then I was restless and fixed up the rest of the house." She paused, "I just thought you might like someone to talk with this morning."

"Oh," Susan smiled again. "Thank you so much, that's great. It is good to get away from the boys once in a while. You know how they are," she added, a touch of conspiracy drifting into her voice.

"Lately I can only imagine," Sheila said.

"Can I ask you something else?" Susan said.

"Sure, anything."

"Did all this," she swept her arm around, "did it cost a lot?"

Sheila looked puzzled at the question. "Well your brother pays me very well if that's what you mean."

"Mmm... he must," Susan said. She was surprised at herself, and at the question. It was the second time that day she had really thought about Fred's money.

It was getting late, and Fred had put off going into the bathroom as long as he could. He stripped to his shorts, dropped his shirt and pants on the bed without folding them, stretching slowly in his underwear. Marsh had been lost in thought for the last hour and Fred had used the time constructively, sitting in the easy chair and going over his options. He was ready for the mirror when he finally stepped into the bathroom.

"Fred baby," Richard said immediately after the light came on. "It's getting a little tense don't you think?"

Fred stared at the face, and found himself wondering why the beard never grew any longer. He said nothing.

"John seems to be doomed," Richard added.

"Not much we can do about it now." Fred found himself calmer than he expected, ready. It suddenly seemed easier to carry on a conversation than fight it. "He'll make it through Kansas City though."

"That's the spirit ol' buddy. Let's get right back into the swing of things. Got a plan do you?"

Fred was silent again, content to let Richard do most of the talking.

"Somebody is bound to get hurt now, but you know that, don't you?" Richard asked, an evil grin on his face.

"It does seem unavoidable," Fred said after a moment. He turned on the water and cupped his hands under it, then splashed it over his face. When he looked up Richard was still there.

"Guess we will have to get Stuart won't we?" Richard said, his grin wider.

"Yes, Stuart." He reached down into his dop kit for the can of shaving cream, squirting a pile into his hand. Fred smiled as he looked into the mirror; Richards face fading from view as he covered his face with the white foam. "It is time for Stuart."

Fifteen minutes later he emerged from the bathroom, refreshed from the shower. He still had the towel wrapped around his waist as he stepped into the hall and listened quietly at Marsh's room. He could hear the shower running through the door, and quickly stepped into the office. He pulled his PDA from his briefcase and located the number he needed. He didn't bother to sit as he picked up the phone and dialed. The recorded voice at the other end was brief and gruff.

"Leave a message," was all he heard.

"It's Stuart Jones," Fred said in a deeper than normal voice. "We need to meet. I'm going to need a few special things, and I'll make it worth your trouble. Sunday night, the usual place. I'll be there at nine."

He hung up the phone and quickly left the room. "I love it when a plan comes together," he said to himself.

Chapter Nineteen

The limousine was big, but not the largest Marsh had ever been in. And quiet. Susan and Fred sat across from him, facing the rear of the car. They were both subdued, held hands and stared out the windows. Marsh leaned his head back against the seat and tried to relax. It was almost over he said to himself.

The service had gone well he thought, and he was pleased by the turnout. There were many of his mother's friends in attendance, and he had felt a momentary pang of guilt about not contacting more of them personally after the accident. No one seemed to mind however, and most of the people he was even vaguely familiar with had spoken with him sympathetically as they entered the church. There was also a large contingent from the office, his coworkers occupying up three pews on one side of the center aisle. There was a smattering of other individuals paying their respects, Sara, Will Carter, Steve Race and several of his closer business associates.

At his and Susan's request, the minister was brief and kept the service confined to a short remembrance of Margaret's life, and an opening prayer. Marsh spoke next, at first somberly addressing the gathering. Although there were a lot of people present, the sanctuary was so large it still felt empty and cold. He choked up a little at the beginning, when he tried to explain to everyone who his mother was, and how much she had meant to him and his family. Susan looked up at him and smiled, nodding in encouragement so he pressed on, his voice getting stronger as he related stories of the good times they had had together. At one point, an anecdote of how Marsh had gotten lost in the woods during a camping trip had brought a hushed chuckle from everyone, and by the time he had finished many had tears in their eyes. Several of Margaret's friends also rose to speak briefly, and he was touched by how much of an impact she seemed to have had on the lives of her friends from the church. Susan hadn't said anything.

There had been a single hymn at the end, a last-minute selection chosen at the request of his mother's bible study group, the large pipe organ at the back of the sanctuary providing the musical accompaniment. His mother's friends, most members of the church sung loudly, the rest of the attendees hummed words or stared down silently.

Marsh opened his eyes and glanced across the back of the car at Susan. "Are you OK Suse?" he asked quietly.

"I'm fine Marsh," she replied, and pulled her gaze back from the window. "It's just so gray and cold out there. I wish it had been sunny."

Marsh nodded. At the cemetery it hadn't rained, but the air was damp and lifeless. The colorless sky had pressed down on them, heavy and close. There wasn't a breath of wind as they gathered about the gravesite, a gaping dark hole next to the spot where his father had been laid to rest. About half of the people joined the final words at the cemetery, most gathered in a tight circle around the site, a few milled around the edges nervously. Even the arrangements of yellow daffodils, his mother's favorite flower, had seemed subdued. The words spoken outside were also brief, but Susan had said something privately to the casket as she walked forward, then placed a bouquet of flowers over the top.

At the end, the people walked away quietly in groups of twos and threes, leaving Marsh and Susan standing alone. Fred had discreetly moved a few paces off and let them silently say their final good-byes.

And then it was done. The three of them left the site, Susan between Marsh and Fred, holding both of their hands. She stopped once to look over her shoulder, then walked a little faster and pulled them both along. She had tears streaming down her face when they reached the waiting limousine.

The car slowed, and bumped a little as it pulled into the circular drive. It came to a stop under a wooden white awning at the side of the funeral home.

"Let's go," Marsh said quietly. They bent down and got out of the car, the door opened from the outside by one of the home's staff.

Susan and Fred walked directly across the parking lot towards the Lexus, but Marsh stopped briefly to talk with the funeral director, who waited by the door.

"Thank you. I'll call you on Monday," Marsh said to the man and shook his hand firmly. "We can finalize all the details then."

"Of course sir," he replied. "At your convenience. It was a touching service," he added.

Marsh nodded and walked away.

DECEPTION ON MARGIN

The mood was much more upbeat at Sheila's. Susan walked slowly through the gathering until she reached the back of the kitchen, then pulled aside a white-laced curtain and looked out the window. The sun had tried, but not yet successfully, to push through the clouds. The green grass was lush, and down the middle of the yard were old-fashioned metal clothes lines, stretched between two rusting poles set about fifty feet apart. Sheila moved quietly behind Susan and looked over her shoulder.

"Use that a lot?" Susan asked.

"Absolutely," Sheila replied, and a smile widened across her face. "Can't you just see me out there with a blue and white checkered dress, apron and clothes pins in my mouth?"

Susan laughed quietly at the image. "It looks a bit old and unused to me."

"I prefer to think of it as an antique."

Susan turned to her and gave her a big hug. "Thanks so much for this Sheila, it's so warm and cozy here compared to the cemetery."

"My pleasure. I wanted to. Everyone needs something like this you know."

Susan nodded and looked back out the window. She had been reluctant to mix with the crowd, but suddenly felt better. A burst of sunshine shot through the clouds, the iron poles casting long shadows across the grass. Finally, she thought.

"When do I get to meet the mystery man?" Sheila asked.

"Oh God yes, I completely forgot. Let me find him."

Susan turned and scanned over the counter until she located Fred. He was politely talking to her mother's friends, and she waved and beckoned him over. He nodded and excused himself from the women and worked his way past the table toward them, a small plastic glass of punch in his hand.

"Come here babe, I want you to meet Sheila," Susan said as he approached.

He smiled broadly, switched the glass to his left hand and extended the right one. "Hello Sheila," he said, "It's a pleasure to meet you."

Sheila took his hand firmly. "And you Fred, congratulations by the way. You have quite the little package here," she said and tipped her head towards Susan.

"Stop it," Susan protested, but beamed at the compliment.

"I couldn't agree more. You are a most gracious hostess." He looked at her, eyes roaming from top to bottom. "However if my heart wasn't already captured, a woman of your beauty would have certainly caught my attention."

"Sheesh," Susan said, and shot a warning glance at him.

"My, my. And charming too," Sheila said to Susan. "Wherever did you find him?"

"Well he used to be this homely lost puppy, until I got a hold of him."

"Sad but true," Fred said to Sheila, then looked to Susan. "By the way, is there anyone you haven't told about us? Or did I miss the announcement in the paper?"

Susan slid her arm through his and moved closer. "Just a few hundred of my closest friends. Sheila here is the only reason my brother is such a success."

"I wouldn't go that far. He does help occasionally. We do have to lead him along sometimes though. Where is Marsh anyway? I've barely spoken with him yet."

Susan looked up and scanned the crowd until she spotted Marsh. He was standing by the fireplace, close to Sara. They seemed to be speaking in hushed tones and ignoring the rest of the gathering. She hesitated a moment.

"Oh, he's over there by the fireplace," she hesitated. "With Sara."

Sheila followed her look and caught sight of them. She could only see the back of the woman, long blonde hair cascading down over her black suit.

"Ahh, the date," Sheila said, not really to anyone.

"Yes," Susan added, but glanced at Sheila.

Fred looked back and forth between them. "Did I miss something?"

Sheila brightened again as she looked back at him. "Not at all," she said. "Excuse me for a moment. I should go pay my respects." She reached out and touched Susan's arm, then moved off across the room.

Marsh saw Sheila approach and backed away from Sara slightly. He reached a hand out towards her, but she moved past it and wrapped her arms around him for a tight hug. He glanced over Sheila's shoulder at Sara, who raised a curious eyebrow.

"Is everything alright Marsh?" Sheila whispered his ear. She squeezed him again then backed away, but remained close.

"Yes, it is," he said. "Thank you so much for everything. This is wonderful."

She smiled at the compliment, but didn't look at Sara.

"Sheila, this is Sara McGloughin," Marsh said, breaking the moment. "Sara, Sheila Parker, our hostess, close family friend and my head of sales."

"Hello Sheila," Sara said and shook her hand lightly. "You have a beautiful home here."

"Why thank you. It took a long time to get it back in shape, but I love it." She looked at Sara for a moment and noticed her outfit. It was a jet-black pantsuit, creased pants closely fitting over her legs down to her matching black shoes, pointed and open at the top with half-spiked heels. The jacket was short in front, longer in back tapering down over her backside, almost like a tuxedo. Her fresh shirt was gray, with black pinstripes. "I love your suit," she added. "I wish I could wear something like that."

Sara looked briefly at Marsh, then back at Sheila. "Nonsense, you would look great in this."

Marsh shifted on his feet, trying to look relaxed, not knowing exactly what to say.

Sheila laughed. "Well I could put it on, but I doubt I could wear it like that. Have you known Marsh long?"

"No, not really. We actually just met Tuesday." She looked at Marsh again. "At the press conference."

"Sara is a reporter. She's been helping... uh, we've been working on..." Marsh stammered.

Sara was unfazed. "Marsh and I have spent some time together this week," she said and placed her hand on his arm. "We seem to work well together."

"I can imagine," Sheila said, and a coy smile drifted across her face. "He is so easy to work closely with, aren't you Marsh?"

"Would anyone like some punch?" Marsh asked.

"In the early days of the company we traveled a lot. We spent many a night together on the road," Sheila added.

"And were you successful?" Sara asked, her eyes twinkling.

"I think I could use some punch," Marsh repeated and backed away.

"Yes, very much so," Sheila replied, and reached out to touch Marsh's other arm. "Don't run off dear, we're having so much fun here."

Marsh looked back and forth between them, unable to read the conversation. "Fun?" he asked. "I feel like a minnow between a couple of sharks."

Sara looked at Sheila and grinned. "Is he always like this under pressure?"

"Under pressure he's usually a lot calmer. Now he just looks like a deer in headlights."

Marsh, at a loss for words, shifted back and forth on the soles of his feet uncomfortably. "OK you two, enough entertainment at my expense. I'm trying to be civilized here."

Sheila turned back to Sara, "Are you on TV? You do look familiar."

Sara smiled, used to the question. "I get on the air occasionally now and then. Mostly now I just do investigative work. It's kind of how Marsh and I met. I was covering the story of..." she paused. "Well you know the rest."

"I don't know about the rest, but I get the idea," Sheila said mischievously. "Marsh, you're not still digging into this are you?"

Grateful for the change of subject Marsh started in. "As a matter of fact Sara and I were just talking about it. It seems we might have some new information on the thief. A list of robberies in other cities that seem to match, or that are similar to what happened here."

"My God Marsh, I don't know if that's good news or not," Sheila said. "I was hoping that this would be the end of it." She looked at Sara and Marsh questioningly, but they seemed rooted in their convictions. "OK, I don't know if this is the appropriate place to talk about it but what did you find?"

"Well it was an idea that Fred had, to look for other occurrences of the same type of theft. I had Lebida do some research for me on the Web. She came up with a list of eight other cities where a single white guy robbed a grocery store. I thought maybe we could follow up on it a little."

"We?" Sheila asked.

"Well Sara and I, for starters. And hopefully a little help from the Denver Police Department."

Sheila glanced between them, eyes narrowed. "I hope you two know what you are doing," she said softly. It sounded ominous as soon as she said it.

Lebida looked around the room and felt out of place. She had been to one funeral in her life, but didn't attend the wake afterwards. She was surprised at the mood in the house; everyone chatting and talking like it was a cocktail party. It was such a change from the emotion filled church, where she had cried a little, her heart once again pouring out to Marsh as he addressed the mourners. She had skipped the cemetery and rode instead to Sheila's place with two of her project team members. They had said a quick hello to Marsh when he arrived, then immediately left to take advantage of the Friday afternoon off for some shopping. She had stayed, waiting and wanting to talk to Marsh alone.

It wasn't like she was a stranger, about half of the people gathered were from the company, but she kept to herself. She had dressed carefully for the day, selecting a long gray skirt, plain blouse and black sweater. She had hoped it was appropriate for the occasion, but still made her look attractive. Now she was a little discouraged as she looked across the room. Marsh stood by the fireplace talking with Sheila, who looked fabulous as usual and a blonde that she didn't know who was nothing short of spectacular. She briefly debated about joining the conversation, she knew that Marsh wanted to see more of what she had found, but hesitated. She felt a little inadequate next to the two women he was already speaking with.

The folder, with the information and printouts was in the bedroom with her purse. She didn't think it would look good to be carrying it with her, and on top of that the bottom of the folder was a bit soiled where her palm sweated as she carried it into the church. She moved through the crowd, filled a glass with punch and sipped slowly, her mouth a little dry. She leaned back against the wall in the dining room and waited for her opportunity, and rehearsed what she would say.

She was momentarily distracted, chatting idly with a coworker about a project when Marsh moved away from Sheila and whoever the blonde was. She watched as he approached another man, about his age and shook his hand. Deciding it was her time, she cut the conversation with her co-worker short and pushed through the room quickly, moving up next to Marsh before he realized she was there. The other man looked up, a little surprised.

"Hi Marsh. It was a beautiful speech you made. It made me cry."

Marsh turned a bit surprised. "Oh, thank you very much Lebida"

She hesitated for a second, then hugged him suddenly. "I'm so sorry

Marsh."

Marsh was even more surprised but hugged her back hesitantly. "It's OK," he said and entangled himself from her arms. "Lebida, this is Steve Race, my attorney," he added.

"Oh, hi Steve," she said. She retreated slightly and reached out for his hand.

"Hello Lebida, nice to meet you. And this attorney was just leaving. I've got to be in Boulder tonight and I don't want to get stuck in the turnpike traffic." He turned to Marsh and said, "Marsh, next week, call me. We need to finalize a lot of things."

"I will Steve, thanks for coming."

"No problem. We will all miss Margaret." He nodded at Lebida and walked away.

Lebida shot her best smile at Marsh. "I brought the folder Marsh, but this probably isn't the greatest time," she said to him. "Maybe when we have dinner we could go over it?"

"Dinner?"

Lebida's face drooped with disappointment.

"Oh right, dinner," Marsh said, recovering. "Of course, but I would like to have it today, if that's OK." He stopped again and glanced around the room. "And there is someone else I want you to meet."

"Sure Marsh, anything," she said. She tried to put on her best smile. "Who is it?"

"Detective Carter, from the Denver Police Department."

Detective Carter of the Denver Police Department had arrived late to Sheila's house. He was paged three times during the service at the church. His cell phone was turned off, but the pager had vibrated silently in his pocket, annoying him slightly. He ignored the first two interruptions, but on the last one he discreetly pulled the instrument from his pocket and checked it to make sure it wasn't some station emergency. He wanted to turn the silly thing off but didn't risk it.

He had been the first one out of the church. During the service he had noticed he was the only black in the gathering, and he found some ironic humor in the fact that he had chosen to sit well in the back. It wasn't that he was uncomfortable with his choice, he needed to be able to make an unobtrusive getaway if need be, but he did notice a few curious stares from the older white folk who had been in the pews directly in front of the casket and podium. At some other time he might have laughed, but Marsh's eulogy had been moving, even though he was a stranger to the deceased.

He spent the next forty-five minutes on the phone, alone in his car in the parking lot, dealing with the routine calls from dispatch. He arrived at the house well after everyone else.

Now he was troubled and he kept to himself, close to the oak banister that followed the staircase from the living room upstairs. Troubled he thought, shit he was blown away. Shortly after arriving he noticed the well dressed white man in a black suit casually talking with a few of the older women by the dining room table. He had seen him before, with Marsh and who he assumed was his sister at the funeral. He was really just crowd watching until the man dropped a cocktail napkin and leaned over. The birthmark on the left side of his neck shocked him, and now he struggled with possibilities. It had to be some sort of coincidence he rationalized, but he couldn't shake the sinking feeling in the bottom of his stomach.

To make things worse, he realized what a blunder he committed with the sketch of the thief the department had released. They had all concentrated on the descriptions from the bellman and the cabby, since the perp had already shed the wig and the moustache. But somehow he left out the significant detail he learned from the old woman at the store - the birthmark she saw when the thief had fallen on top of her. God's mark she said, and he had completely forgotten about it. He cursed himself for his uncharacteristic lack of detail, and now he just tried to get Marsh's attention.

Relived, he saw Marsh work his way across the room toward him, a tall scraggly blonde in tow. He watched as she kept pushing her hair off her face.

"Marsh, hi," he said, and stretched his hand out. "A very nice service, my condolences again."

"Thanks for coming Will, really."

Will wanted badly to speak with Marsh alone, but the young woman seemed to be attached to him. He smiled at her and wondered who the hell she was.

"Will, this is Lebida Murphy," Marsh started. "She works for me, and I think she might have something you are interested in." Marsh nodded at Lebida. "Lebida, Detective Will Carter. Can you please tell him what you told me earlier?"

Lebida looked at the detective and brushed the hair from her face.

"Its OK Lebida, Will is a friend of mine. He knows what's going on."

She started slowly, and her eyes shifted back and forth between them. "Well, Marsh asked me to look for some things on the web, about robberies."

Marsh nodded at her, as if to urge her on.

"It took a while," she continued, "but I accessed the major newspaper's websites across the country, and found eight occurrences of the same sort of robbery - grocery stores - that happened over the last year or so."

Will perked up and forgot for the moment the man with the birthmark. He looked at Marsh, who nodded with a kind of 'I told you so' look.

"And you have details on all of these robberies?"

"Of course. I printed out all the articles and made notes on the dates and locations." She smiled proudly. "I did it for Marsh."

"That, is good news. Would I be able to get a copy of what you found?"

Lebida looked at Marsh, who nodded. "Sure, I guess so. Actually I have the information here now."

Will was anxious to get his hands on the details, but remembered where he was. He was torn for a moment, so much new information to process. He looked away, across the room at the man in the black suit, who was talking with Marsh's sister again, when he realized Marsh was waving at them. The couple was holding hands as they made their way through the dining room, nodding in acknowledgment to the invitation.

Jesus Will said to himself, not able to take his eyes off the man. The sketch made by the police artist didn't exactly resemble him, but they rarely did. The description however, matched perfectly. For the first time in his career Will had no idea what to do next, and struggled to disregard the coincidence. The thief was long gone he thought, and why the hell would he be here anyway? It's ridiculous he said to himself as he heard Marsh begin to make introductions.

"Suse, this is Will Carter. Will, my sister Susan."

Susan looked at him curiously, but smiled. "Hello detective. We spoke earlier, but you are not what I pictured," Susan said.

Will forced a laugh. "Don't tell me. Old white guy, raincoat and a cigar?"

"Well yes, I guess. This is my fiancée, Fred Simpson."

"Hello detective," Fred said, and a welcoming smile spread across his face. "We've heard a lot about you."

Will could only nod at him, still not able to shake the nagging thoughts.

"It was Fred's idea to search the web," Marsh added. "Oh, and Suse, Fred, this is Lebida. She's the one who did all the hard work."

"Hello," Lebida said nervously. She fidgeted with her hair again.

"Great work Lebida, Marsh tells me you found out a lot," Fred said to her.

"Well I guess so," she replied.

"Marsh, you are not going to start that now are you?" Susan said sternly. "Not here, not now."

Everyone's eyes trained on Marsh. He lowered his voice, but smiled at his sister. "Of course not. I'm sorry."

Will felt the pager go off in his pocket again. He pulled it out immediately, grateful for the interruption this time. He glanced at it, not caring what it read.

"Well, I'm sorry, but I'm still on duty, and duty seems to be calling," he said, hoping to change the subject.

"It was nice to meet you Will," Fred said. "Keep up the good work."

"Thank you for coming Will," Susan added. "It was very thoughtful of you."

"My pleasure Susan, though I wish it could have been under different circumstances," Will said back to her.

She nodded but her eyes drifted to the ground.

Will dipped his head at Lebida, then turned to Marsh. "Uh, Marsh, could I talk with you privately for a moment before I go?"

"Sure Will, I'll walk you out. Excuse us please folks," he said to the group.

They walked away, Marsh nodding to the guests as they stepped through the house. Will pushed the screen door open and moved across the porch towards the swing lost in thought. He couldn't decide on how much to say to Marsh, but was unable to put the birthmark out of his mind. He knew he couldn't speak about his concerns now, at the wake. But her fiancée for Christ's sake - he had to be wrong about this. He watched as Marsh came out the door, a few final good-byes to leaving guests.

The air felt damp and dreary as he waited, absently pushing the swing back and forth with his hand. Marsh walked up behind him.

"What's up Will? You look like you've seen a ghost."

Will turned and braced himself. Jeez I hope not he said to himself.

"We need to talk Marsh, seriously."

"Oh yeah, about the other robberies? I can get you copies of the stuff whenever you want," Marsh said. "You can do something with it can't you?"

"Sure, of course. But there is something else I just found out, but I want to check on it first. And now is not the time anyway."

Marsh looked at him, the feeling of dread crept over him. "That sounds a bit ominous Will," he said. He stared directly at the detective.

Will forced a smile. "I hope not. Listen, I'm off tomorrow, and I hope it's not an inconvenience, but maybe we could get together?"

"That's a bit quick isn't it Will?"

"I know, I know, and hopefully I'm all wrong about this. Are you going to be around tomorrow? I could stop by your place."

"Of course. If that's what you want."

"I need some time in the office first. How does eleven sound?"

"Eleven it is," Marsh said and wondered what in the hell was going on.

Will shook Marsh's hand firmly, nodded and started across the porch. He got to the steps before turning back.

"Oh, and give my congratulations to Susan and Fred. Nice couple," he said. "They live in Minnesota right?"

Marsh looked at him curiously. "Yes, Minneapolis, why?"

Will smiled. "Just wondering if I would be invited to the wedding," he said as he walked away.

Fred stared up at the ceiling, one arm behind his head on the pillow and opened his eyes wide to adjust to the darkness. He had been awake for a long time, running over all the possibilities. There was so much that could go wrong he thought. It would all have to be done exactly right.

It was the first time that he and Susan had slept together that they hadn't made love. They had tried at first he couldn't concentrate. Susan had been distracted too, nerves she apologized, from the funeral and she was worried about Marsh. He hadn't been himself all evening, and had gone to bed early. Sara had come back to the condo with them and she and Marsh had gone alone to his office, taking the folder from the girl with

DECEPTION ON MARGIN

them. Sara had left early, saying something about seeing them tomorrow.

He looked over at Susan, who had finally fallen asleep, turned on her side with her back to him. He pulled the covers back and walked slowly towards the bathroom in the dark. He stepped inside, closed the door quietly behind him and turned on the lights. He knew what to expect in the mirror this time.

The face that looked back at him was no different than his own, the scruffy irreverent Richard long gone.

"Hello Fred," Stuart said, staring out.

Fred paused, "I have a plan," Fred said to the mirror without emotion.

"I figured you would need me pretty soon," the reflection replied. "It's not that internet busybody is it?"

Fred said nothing.

"No, it's too late for that," Stuart continued. "She is inconsequential anyway. Not the cop either. It wouldn't be a good idea."

"No, not the cop. We need him."

"Well it's not Susan of course, so that only leaves one person."

"Two people actually," Fred replied.

"Of course, two people," Stuart replied, an evil grin on his face. "That's going to be a bit more difficult isn't it?"

"Like I said, I have a plan."

Chapter Twenty

"Aren't you at least going to shave babe?" Susan asked as she came out of the bathroom, rubbing a soft white towel through her hair. Fred looked up and smiled, and stopped for a moment the task of filling his suitcase with folded clothes, eyes widening slightly. She had a larger matching white towel wrapped around her waist and her firm breasts jiggled as she scrubbed her hair with the towel. He felt a stirring in his loins as he watched her.

"What?" she asked, holding still for a moment, enjoying his gaze.

"I was just thinking that if you rubbed a little harder that towel might fall off."

She looked down for a moment, then back at him, moving her hips in a circle like a hula dancer and smiled seductively. She lowered her arms, hooked a thumb into the towel at her hip and pulled her arm out in an exaggerated dropping motion. The towel slipped open and fell to the floor.

"Oops," she said.

He walked slowly around the bed, his eyes traveling slowly over all of her naked body; already sorry he had already showered and dressed. She didn't move as he approached, but shook her head hard, her still wet hair flopping over her shoulders. He reached his arms out, ready to fill his hands with her. She suddenly snapped the little towel at him, jumped back and scampered away from him over the top of the bed by the pillows, avoiding the black suitcase opened on top of it. She ended up on the other side, leaned down, and held herself up with her arms.

"Oh no you don't," she said. "We're not even married yet."

He laughed, slid his feet over the carpet and inched his way back around the bed. He put his left hand on the bed, then vaulted over the corner, rushing at her. She squealed and jumped back on the bed and crawled away from him on her hands and knees. He lunged, his hand grabbed a fleeing ankle, yanking it back and twisting slowly. She rolled as she slid back and he dove on top of her, his hands finding her wrists. He pulled her arms up over her head and pinned her down. Her breasts heaved below him as he kissed her neck, then lower across her chest and in between her breasts, taking in the fresh smell from the shower splash. She moaned softly, relaxing under his grip.

"You seem to have me at a disadvantage sir," she said to the top of his head.

He moved his face back up, kissed her lips softly at first, then harder, releasing her hands and sliding his fingers through her wet hair. After a moment he lifted his head and looked deeply into her eyes.

"I love you Susan. I hope it's always like this."

She gazed back, her hand slowly rubbing the stubble covering his cheek. "I love you too Fred, but if you want me you'll have to shave." She paused for a moment, then tipped her head up and kissed him lightly. "Are you sure you have to go back now?"

He laughed. "Yes, I do. He rolled back and looked at her as his hand slowly stroked the length of her body.

She deftly pulled her knees up, swung her legs around, dropped her feet to the other side of the bed and jumped up quickly. "Well in that case you will just have to settle for feeding me," she said, face defiant.

He sighed and sat up, his hand absently moving the clothes around in his suitcase. She retrieved both towels, walked back into the bathroom and returned to the process of fixing her hair. He got up and resumed packing. He could hear her humming to herself, and watched for a moment through the open door as she began to brush her hair.

"Susan?" he said softly.

"Yes babe?" she said, not looking at him. "Sorry already for your wretched behavior?"

"Incredibly," he said softly. "Will you love me always, no matter who I am?" he asked.

She paused, the brush halfway through her hair and looked at him, puzzled. She didn't understand the question. "Always," she said anyway.

Susan, Marsh and Fred sat at the dining room table, sipped their coffee and didn't speak much. The door to the balcony was open and the sun was shining brightly again, yesterday's gloom burning away. A single bird chirped loudly over the din of the traffic.

"Are you sure you won't come with us Marsh?" Susan asked again.

He had been flipping through the morning paper, not reading it but aware for the first time of the power of its stories. He looked up and tried to smile.

"Thanks, but no. Sara is coming over in a bit. We have some organizing to do before Will gets here."

Fred set his cup down on the flowered place mat. "Ah, the good detective. He has risen to the challenge has he?"

"I'm not sure. He hasn't seen the printouts from Lebida yet, and there is something else he wanted to talk about."

Susan reached over and touched Marsh's arm lightly. "Marsh, please tell me you won't dwell on this. I want it to be over now."

Marsh sighed and looked at her. "I can't Suse, not now that we have something to go on. Thanks to Fred."

"I didn't do much Marsh," Fred protested, "I just pointed you in the right direction."

"So, what time is your flight?" Marsh changed the subject, then looked at Susan. "I hate to say this but I'm sorry to see the boy go."

Susan smiled.

"Why thanks Marsh, really. I wish I could stay, but I've been gone too long already. I need to get back to work sometime, and I have a meeting to attend."

"Why on the weekend?" Susan asked. "Can't you put it off?"

Fred smiled. "Money talks all the time babe. I've already postponed it too long." He looked at his watch. "Well, if I'm going to feed you we better get going."

Fred rose from his chair and walked around the table. "Marsh, it's been very nice to finally meet you, but I'm so sorry for the circumstances. You don't know how sorry I am it had to be this way. I wish I knew what else to say."

Marsh gripped his hand. "You too Fred, and I'm glad you came." He looked over at Susan. "I'm happy for everything with you two."

Susan leaned closer to Marsh and stretched on her tiptoes to give him a kiss. "I'll be back in a while. Please be in a good mood when I return."

Twenty minutes later they were seated at a black wrought-iron table, in wrought-iron chairs that were a little too hard and uncomfortable on their backs. The small café only had three tables outside, and they had been lucky to get one, sitting down even before the previous occupant's mess had been cleared away. It was warm, but a breeze pushed a few small white clouds around the sky, the sun disappearing behind them every few minutes. A paper napkin blew off the table, and Susan leaned over to pick it up as the busboy started picking up the dishes.

They hadn't said much on the short drive over; each lost in their own thoughts.

"A penny for your thoughts," he said as he looked across the table at her. She was beautiful in the morning he thought, even with clothes on. She wore short white shorts again, this time with a man's blue Polo dress shirt tucked into them, a white long-sleeved sweater tied by the arms around her slim waist. She sat on it to provide a little cushion in the chair. She smiled, but he couldn't see her eyes behind her dark sunglasses.

"I don't know," she said and turned away. "Now that everything is over, I guess I was thinking about what happens next. Until now I hadn't really thought about anything but yesterday. Now tomorrow seems to be looming up on us."

"You're not changing your mind are you? About us?"

She smiled at him. "No silly, not that. It's just that it seems life is starting all over again. I feel like I've just crawled out of a deep dark hole and don't know where to go."

"When are you coming back home?"

She waited while the waiter approached, placed two sets of silverware wrapped in paper napkins down and handed them both folded plastic menus. "Coffee?" the waiter inquired.

"Sure," Fred said.

"Just ice water for me," Susan replied.

"I'll be right back for your order," the waiter said and walked away.

Susan waited until he left. "Marsh said I could have Mom's condo if I wanted it."

Through the sunglasses Fred couldn't tell if she was looking at him or not. "And leave Minneapolis?"

"Oh I don't know. It was just a thought. I forgot how much I love it here."

Fred looked around, feeling the warmth of the morning. "I could live here you know."

"Do you have a will Fred?" she asked out of the blue.

"Excuse me?"

"I've never thought about it before babe. But with mom - Marsh and I talked about it a little. She was so prepared."

"No I don't have a will. I guess I never thought about it either. Are you hoping to get rid of me?" he said and raised an eyebrow.

She laughed. "Of course not. But what happens if a bus hits me today? Or your plane crashes on the way home?"

"You can have everything I own."

She laughed again, nervously this time. She glanced at the other tables wondering if anyone was listening.

"No, I'm serious. I have a lot of money you know."

"I'm sorry. I guess this is a little morbid. And I don't care about your money."

He paused for a moment, a serious look settled over his face. "A few million in my trading accounts."

She looked up, surprised. "What?"

"Well it's nice to know you don't love me for my money." The corners of his mouth turned up as he absently folded the napkin on his plate.

"You are kidding, right?"

"Not at all," he said and leaned back in his chair, crossing his legs. "Do you remember our little trip to the Caymans?"

"How could I forget?"

"That wasn't all pleasure you know. I have another couple of million in a bank there too."

"Oh my God Fred, I didn't know."

"You didn't know your old man was rich?"

"And a good conversationalist," she said.

"What?"

She laughed the tension of the moment past. "Well I told Marsh a few days ago, when he asked about you, that you were rich and a good conversationalist. I was kidding him. I had no idea…"

The waiter approached again and Fred picked up his menu. "We should order, or I will miss my plane."

"I could live with that."

Susan was hungry, and decided on a Denver omelet, with hash browns. Fred settled for a stack of pancakes and sausage. They both ordered a large orange juice. They laughed about their appetites as the traffic roared by in the street, a few black birds bobbing and picking at whatever birds pick at on the sidewalk next to them.

"It's all yours you know," he said after a moment.

"Stop it. I'm sorry I brought it up. Let's just eat and enjoy the rest of the morning OK?"

"Sure."

She relaxed, and the conversation turned to her friends and her job. She hoped they had missed her at work, and suddenly found herself thinking how good it would be to get back. The time at breakfast went by too quickly and then he had to leave. The waiter returned with the check, and Fred placed a fifty over it, protecting it from the wind with knife.

Susan stared at the bill and found herself thinking about his money again, then pushed the thought away. She glanced up at him, feeling guilty that he might notice. Millions she repeated to herself.

"Ready?" he asked when the waiter returned his change.

"Yes, I'm ready." But for what she didn't know.

The cafe was almost empty when they left. They walked slowly down the sidewalk toward the convertible parked half way down the block. Susan felt a sudden chill as the sun was obscured again, and pulled up her sweater, slipping it around her shoulders. They stopped at the passenger side of the car.

"Getting in?" Fred asked, puzzled by her hesitation.

"It's not far, and I'll walk back," she said. "I've got some thinking to do."

"Are you sure?"

She slipped close to him and slid her arms over his shoulders. "I'm sure. You better go or you'll be late."

He held her close, looked at her for a moment, then leaned down and kissed her hard. She melted into his arms and kissed him back.

"Mmm... nice," she said.

"When will you be home?"

She thought about it carefully, just making up her mind. "Tomorrow night I think, assuming I can get a flight. You can pick me up?"

"Sure, call me OK? Just tell me when."

She kissed him again. "I love you."

"I love you too."

He walked around the car, waited for the traffic to let up and got in. She waved, stood behind and watched as he started the car. He turned and waved, then gunned the engine as pulled away. She could see him mouth goodbye again.

"Bye," she said to the back of the car.

She turned and walked in the other direction, not really noticing her surroundings. The sun came out again, and she slid her sunglasses down over her nose and moved quickly down the sidewalk. He's rich she thought, then scolded herself for the thought. But millions?

Marsh finished his third cup of coffee, got up with a sour taste in his mouth and paced around the room. Sara was reading the articles Lebida had provided, separating each on the table sorted by date. She had a cup of coffee also, but hadn't touched it since she sat down. They had talked about the information last night, but today she had really poured over it, using her reporter's instinct on the content. She was amazed by the similarities in each occurrence. She finished the last one, adjusted the others and set it in its place, then brushed her hair back over her shoulders.

"Well? What do you think now?" Marsh said from behind her.

She turned and faced him. "I can't believe it. It's like everyone is the same, only with a different date and city."

Marsh was excited. "Exactly. It has to be the same person. I can feel it." He walked over to her slowly. "OK, so what do we do next?"

"I'm not sure Marsh, but I think we need to run this by Will. I can also contact our sister stations in some of the cities, and find out who covered the stories there, and get any research about the robberies that didn't make it into the papers. There's one problem with that though."

Marsh frowned a bit. "What's that?"

Well, Chicago and Boston are big towns, and a simple robbery might not have been big enough news for TV. I'd have to find out the local paper trail."

"But you could do that?"

She smiled at him and stepped closer then slid her arms up over his. "Yes, for you. It's only a few emails to start with. It's Will I am worried about."

"Why's that? He was one who wanted to meet with us."

She took his hand and led him across the room to the balcony. They stepped outside where the wind gently tossed her hair around.

"To make any progress on this quickly, we need the airline records. That's the only way we will be sure if it's the same guy. That is assuming he used the same name each time, which is a big assumption. Otherwise all we are doing is building a bigger and bigger profile on someone who is still an unknown character."

"Mmm... I see your point."

"Hey, don't get discouraged. This takes time, and we already have more to go on than I expected."

He turned to her, pulling her close and kissed her. "Thanks."

She kissed him back, then pulled away. "What for? I haven't done anything yet."

"I wouldn't be so sure," he said, a grin plastered over his face.

"Well there is that," she said and smiled back at him. "Tell me, are you using me for my brilliant investigative skills?"

"Of course, and a few other things. And what do you get out of all this?"

"I haven't decided yet, but it looks good so far."

The intercom buzzed and Marsh walked quickly across the room, hurriedly pressing the talk button.

"Hello?"

"Marsh, it's Will," the speaker cackled.

"Come on up," he said and pressed the security button.

Sara crossed back across the room and waited by the dining room table. Marsh looked over at her, gave her a thumbs-up sign and opened the door. He fidgeted like an anxious school boy and poked his head out the door every few seconds. Will finally emerged from the elevator, looked in both directions to get his bearings before he headed down towards Marsh's condo. Marsh stepped out to meet him.

"Will, hey," he said shaking his hand firmly. "Come in please."

Will was dressed in white shorts, a sharp contrast to the chocolate color of his iron legs. His blue Polo golf shirt did little to hide the contours of his muscular chest, biceps stretching the bottom of the sleeves.

"Nice address Marsh," he said with a grin. "So this is how you yuppies live."

"Hello Will," Sara said from across the room. "Casual day?"

"Yes ma'am," he replied. "Been here long Sara?"

Marsh smiled at the innuendo and closed the door.

"How about some iced tea gentlemen?" she said, passing on a witty retort.

"Sounds good to me," Will said as he walked over to the table. He glanced at the articles spaced out on top. "Your friend has been busy Marsh," he said, and fingered the corner of one of the printouts. He pulled his gaze from the table and looked around carefully. "By the way, are Susan and Fred here?"

Marsh detected a note of concern in his voice. "They're at breakfast, then Fred's leaving for Minneapolis," he said, the anxious feeling from yesterday returning to his stomach.

"I see," Will commented, but didn't elaborate.

Marsh thought Will looked relieved, but let it slide. "We have a lot to show you Will, but I'm still worried about yesterday. What did you need to talk to me about?"

Sara came out from the kitchen with two tall glasses. She handed one to Will, then walked around Marsh and set his on the table. She sat down across from them and waited without saying anything.

Will pondered his glass for a moment, then said, "Let's go over this first. It might help me a little."

Marsh was puzzled, but conceded. "What we have here are details on eight different robberies, all grocery stores, committed in different cities all over the country. Most seem to be about a month apart, but there are holes in the dates. Lebida said she didn't complete the research though, there maybe more that we don't know about."

"Lebida," Will said. "Sounds like a sister."

Marsh ignored the comment and moved on. "In each case the suspect was a white male, and where there are descriptions each time he was about six feet, curly brown hair and a moustache."

"Convenient, and nondescript. Could be anybody. Any of you white folk that is."

"I was being serious Will," Marsh said.

Sara suppressed a smile.

"Sorry, I know. Did they catch the guy?"

"What?" Marsh asked.

"In all these cases," Will said, pushing a finger down on one of the stacks. "Any of these thefts solved?"

Sara looked at Marsh. "Sheesh, we haven't had time to check it out yet."

Will smiled and looked at them both. "In the detective business, that is what we would call a clue."

Marsh hesitated a moment, then laughed loudly. "Touché Detective. I stand corrected, with my amateur sleuthing status restored."

"Well I suppose you do need my help with something." Will pulled a chair out from the table, spun it around and sat on it backward. He picked up an article at random from the center of the table. "St. Louis."

Marsh moved to the end of the table and sat down, leaned over on his forearms and watched the detective's every move. He forced himself not to say anything, content to let Will do his own discovery. Sara was silent, her blue eyes moving back and forth between the two. Will finished the first paper and set it back in its place.

"Do you have the summary list?" Will asked.

Sara reached over to a yellow notebook page with Lebida's writing on it and handed it across the table. Will nodded at her and looked it over for a moment, then started reading the first article in the sequence. Marsh was impatient, but didn't want to interrupt. He got up from his chair and paced in the living room behind Will. It was very quiet, except for the traffic noise in the street drifting in from the balcony. Will was on the fourth article when he paused for a moment, his deep brown face thoughtful as he took a long drink from his tea. He continued reading without saying anything. Marsh could barely contain himself during the interval; his stomach in knots again. It took almost fifteen minutes.

Finally Will set the last piece down and sighed, got up and stretched his long frame. He didn't say anything as he carried his glass past Marsh and walked over to the balcony, gazing out into the street.

Marsh couldn't wait any longer. "What do you think Will?"

Will turned back. "I think you better sit down Marsh."

He waited until Marsh moved back across the room and sat down in the end chair again. Sara looked confused and reached over to place her hand on top of Marsh's. Marsh was more worried than ever.

Will came back to the dining room, and stood in front of the table like he was about to make a presentation. His presence was suddenly dominating. "I want you both to listen to me very carefully, and don't interrupt. No questions until I have finished, alright?"

Sara and Marsh looked at each other, confused but nodded silently in acknowledgement. Will took a deep breath and pressed on.

"First off, the articles speak for themselves, and I must say that I'm impressed. When we first talked of this I didn't think you would be able to find out so much so quickly. However on the off chance that you actually knew what you are doing, I spent a few hours at the station this morning, doing my own research and preparation. I went so far as to call the Captain, to inform him that I had some new developments on the case, and would be spending some additional time on it."

Marsh couldn't contain himself. "What was his reaction?"

Will smiled. "He told me I interrupted his golf game, and I better know what the fuck I was doing."

Sara smirked, but Marsh looked hopeful. She squeezed his hand again.

"I started with the airlines. They have law enforcement liaisons in their PR departments, and it looks like we will be able to get access to the records we need, assuming we know how to submit the request. The woman started spewing computer gibberish about formulating proper queries, and specifying result content. Does that make sense to you Marsh?"

Marsh lit up. "Sure, of course. It means how to construct a specific database inquiry, with the proper search and select parameters..."

Will held up his hand and stopped Marsh mid-sentence. "Gotcha, that's your department and we will get back to that later. So your idea seems to have merit, good merit. I'm actually quite optimistic about it."

Marsh looked extremely pleased, anxious for Will to continue.

"That's great news Will," Sara said, hopeful.

"Yes, it is. The other good news is that I can take all of this information, and forward it to the police departments in each of the cities. Hopefully, with a little cooperation we can supplement what we have found, and get a full picture of the suspect, maybe put together a more detailed composite."

"When can we start Will?" Marsh asked, his face brightening

Will raised his hand again. "Not so fast Marsh,"

Sara's hopeful expression disappeared instantly. "I take it Will, that you have bad news to go with the good?"

"Unfortunately yes, and I don't know how to deal with it, other than bluntly." He reached into his pocket and removed a folded white sheet of paper, opened it and held it up in front of them. "Remember this?"

Sara spoke first. "Sure Will, that's the sketch artist composite you released at the press conference. Did you get some results from it?"

"Believe it or not, I did. And from an extremely reliable source."

"From who? Where?" Sara asked.

Marsh looked confused.

"Me," the detective said without emotion.

"What?" Marsh exclaimed.

"Let me tell you first, that this picture was created from the bellman at the hotel and the cabby, after the thief had shed his disguise - the wig and the moustache. We assumed that would be the best image to publicize. Unfortunately that was a big error on my part."

"What's your point Will?" Marsh asked.

"Bear with me, please." He walked closer, dropping the sketch on the table between them. "Do you recognize this man?"

"No, not really," Marsh said.

"Like you said Will, it's pretty nondescript," Sara added.

Will looked over the table, grabbed a felt tip pen and extended the necklines below the face down a ways, then drew an oblong circle on the left side and colored it in.

"How about now?"

The room was breathlessly silent.

"Oh my God," Sara exclaimed.

Marsh looked confused for a moment, then sat back stunned.

"We failed to include this rather prominent physical feature from the description we took from Liza, the old woman at the store. The thief knocked her down and she got a very good look at him."

"Fred," Marsh said softly. "It can't be."

"My reaction exactly," Will said, then turned his chair back around and sat down.

"It has to be a coincidence," Marsh said, his thoughts turning to Susan. His stomach twisted inside him. It couldn't be he thought. "But he's been here all week, with us. Shit, it was his idea to do all this."

"It can't be him Will," Sara said, unable to take her eyes from the sketch.

"I checked with the Minneapolis police, he has no record. They have nothing on him."

Marsh was incredulous. "You checked him out?"

"He fits the description perfectly Marsh, what did you expect me to do?"

"It doesn't really look like him," Sara said, finally looking up.

"Never does, especially with two witnesses providing the details."

"Shit," Marsh said loudly. He got up from the table and walked across the room. "There has to be some sort of mistake, a look-alike."

"Where was he on Monday Marsh, do you know?" Will asked.

"Well he flew in from Vegas on Wednesday, he had a meeting there on Tuesday I know."

"Monday Marsh," Will said again.

"Dammit Will I don't know... wait a minute. Dallas. He was in Dallas Monday. He couldn't have done this. Suse would know." Marsh stopped for a second. How could he ask Suse about this? God what would she say, think? His heart was breaking at just the thought of broaching the subject. How much more could she take?

"You say he left for Minneapolis?"

"He has a flight around noon I think. What are you going to do?" He had a brief vision of Fred at the airport, being led away in handcuffs. He couldn't bear it.

"Is he a suspect Will?" Sara asked Will, a little more calmly.

"Not at the moment. Look, I'm as shocked at this as you are. But I can't just let it slide."

"Of course not. But there has to be some explanation," she said.

"I'm sure there is, but I need to find out. When is Susan getting back?"

Marsh stared at him. "Will, you can't ask Suse about this. She would be crushed. I can't put her through it now."

"The other option is to have the boys in Minneapolis pull him in for questioning. Is that what you want Marsh?"

Marsh couldn't contain himself. "I don't want any of this. I'm sorry I dug it up," he said.

"This isn't your fault Marsh," Will said, his voice calm and even. "I was the one who recognized the picture. I'm sorry as hell, but you didn't do anything."

"That's not good enough Will, she's engaged to the guy for Christ's sake."

There was the sound of a key scraping in the lock outside the door. Sara and Will looked up quickly. Marsh froze. "Shit... shit," he exclaimed.

No one moved. The door opened silently and Susan walked in, her hair slightly messed up from the wind. "Whew," she said. "That was a longer walk than I thought. Hello everyone, are we having a party?" she asked with a grin.

She took a few steps before she realized everyone was staring at her. The smile faded from her face quickly. "What?" she said, looking first at Will, then to Marsh. "What's going on?"

Will got up slowly. "Hi Susan."

Marsh walked over next to her. "Let me Will."

"I don't like the sound of that Marsh."

"Sit down Suse, please."

Susan sat in the chair at the end of the table, her face traveling to each of the others, confused. She looked over the papers lying in the table, but didn't notice the sketch.

"Was Fred in Dallas Monday?"

"Why? You're starting to scare me Marsh," she pleaded and stared into his eyes.

"Please Suse. Wasn't he in Dallas, at a meeting?"

"Sure, he called me from there. I called him back Monday night, on his cell. I told him about Mom," she said. Her voice was shaky.

"Do you know where he was on Monday, in Dallas?" Will asked softly.

She looked at him curiously. "He had meetings all day. He goes to Dallas all the time. Once a month at least."

Sara shot a look at Marsh.

"Once a month?" Will asked.

"Yes, why?"

"Just wondering."

Susan looked furious. "Will somebody please tell me what the fuck is going on here?"

Sara looked at Marsh, then reached over and took the sketch, and set it down in front of Susan. She talked softly and calmly. "Please Susan, look at this."

Susan glanced at Sara, then looked down and studied the picture. "What's that?" she pointed at the addition to the drawing. "Is that supposed to be a birthmark?"

"I added it," Will said. "Do you recognize it?"

"Of course, Fred has one. Where is this picture from?"

Sara continued slowly. "It's a police sketch artist's composite of the thief that robbed the grocery store on Monday."

"And you think... What are you saying?"

Marsh moved closer and placed his hand on her shoulder. "I'm sorry Suse, we're not saying anything. But this is a picture of the man..."

Susan sat back. "It doesn't even look like Fred," she said indignantly. "Have you all gone crazy?"

"This is an eyewitness description Susan," Will said.

"From who?" she exclaimed and grabbed the paper. She shook it violently in the air. "I want to meet him."

"It's a she," Will added, but it sounded out of place.

Susan stood up, the chair bouncing against the wall. "This is all bullshit." She turned to Marsh. "How could you do this?"

Marsh remained silent.

Susan looked at all of them, then steadied herself. "I don't know what you are thinking, but it disgusts me. Fred was in Dallas Monday, all day. He always stays at the Adolphus so check with them. I can't believe I even have to tell you that."

"The Adolphus," Will said. "Susan, I'm sorry. We don't believe this any more than you do. I'm sorry I had to bring it up, really. But I can't ignore the evidence."

"Evidence? What evidence? All you have is a fucking picture. Who is this woman anyway? I want to meet her."

Marsh was shocked. "Susan, please. This is all some sort of mistake. A wild coincidence."

"I'm sure it's nothing, really," Sara said, trying to sooth her.

"Great, then we have nothing to lose by talking to her. I want to get this cleared up now." She looked at Will. "Well Detective?"

Will looked at Marsh, questioning.

"I don't think that's a good idea Suse," Marsh said.

"Don't patronize me Marsh. Let's just do it."

Will surrendered. "Alright Susan, let me check to see if we can see her. Excuse me for a moment." He pulled his cell phone from his pocket and stepped out to the balcony. They could hear him talking, but couldn't make out the words.

"Susan," Marsh said softly and tried to figure out what to say.

"Don't say it Marsh. Not a word."

They stood silently and waited for Will. He came back in a moment, folded the cell phone and put it back in his pocket. "We can see her now."

"Fine, let's go," Susan said, her face grim. She turned her back on them and headed for the door.

They took Marsh's Lexus. Will rode in front, Susan and Sara in the back. No one said anything on the ride, the silence thick and totally uncomfortable. Marsh was in agony and could barely concentrate on the road. He ran the first stop sign just down the block from his condominium, nearly hitting another car. Will looked at him, concerned.

"Want me to drive?" he said.

Marsh just shook his head and continued on. They went east on Colfax, heading away from downtown. The busy street was marked by stoplights every few blocks and the trip seemed to take forever. The restaurants and business lining the avenue deteriorated as they drove; soon many of the buildings were boarded up and deserted. There were lots of people on the street, most just standing around in groups of three or more. Many of the buildings had people sitting or lying in the doorways, some with bottles in wrinkled brown paper bags clutched in their hands. The population was mostly black, with some Latino youths dressed in bright colors, mostly red. Marsh locked the doors as they stopped at one of the intersections. Will shot him a look but didn't say anything.

Susan looked out the window and ignored the other passengers in the car. She couldn't believe she was doing this. She had been so happy after saying goodbye to Fred. On the walk back she had begun to plan her trip home, thinking about work, her friends and starting a new life with him. The small businesses gave way to seedy bars, tattoo parlors and adult bookstores as she watched. Where were they going? She wondered, a little nervous. What would she say to him? He was going to call when he got home tonight, to make sure she was OK. She couldn't bear the thought of telling him what she was doing. This was so absurd. Her anger had subsided, barely, and she wondered if this was such a good idea. The car slowed to a stop again, and she could hear two men yelling at each other through the window. She shuddered.

"Turn right here," Will said after a moment.

Susan was relieved as they left the crowds behind them, then noticed the dilapidated houses lining the street. They were tiny, with barren yards, most with chain link fences surrounding them. She just wanted to get it over with.

"In here," Will said again, pointing to the right.

They pulled into the parking lot of a two-story brick building, the landscaping non-existent. There were only a few cars in the lot, and Marsh pulled quickly into an open parking spot. 'East Colfax Community Shelter' the faded sign read, most of the red paint faded or peeling away. They all got out of the car and looked around. Marsh looked at Sara as he closed his door.

"Let's go in," Will said as he walked quickly across the lot.

It was hot, and there was no wind. Susan felt sweaty and nervous as she walked behind Will. She noticed an old man and women sitting on the ground near the steps. They were grimy; their clothes tattered and dirty. The woman played with a small doll, the man with a scraggly beard just rocked back and forth quietly.

"What is this place?" Marsh asked as they all stopped outside the metal door.

"Homeless shelter. This is where the other folks live," Will said.

"And your eyewitness lives here?" Sara asked.

Will shrugged silently and opened the door, but walked in first and looked around. He turned and nodded, then motioned them inside. It was hotter in the building than outside, a dank sweet smell overpowering them as they entered. There was a desk to the left, a young black woman sitting quietly reading a magazine. She looked up and Will moved over to speak with her.

Marsh took Sara's hand, stepped into the middle of the room and looked around. The walls were a faded green color, two barred windows in the middle of each wall. There was a tattered couch along one side of the room, the cushions sagging into deep wells. A coffee table with a broken leg, wrapped up in duct tape was in front of it. Along the other wall was an easy chair, stained, and ripped over the back. The wooden floor was uneven and dirty; an old newspaper ripped up in one corner.

"Jesus," Marsh said. Sara and Susan moved closer together, totally uncomfortable in the heat.

Will walked back as the woman left the desk and walked up the stairs, which creaked loudly under her feet. "She'll be right down," he said.

"Who is she?" Susan asked quietly.

"A homeless woman. She takes the bus to the grocery store a couple of times a week. She spends hours there, pushing a shopping cart around. She can't buy anything of course."

"My God," Sara exclaimed.

"It's her life," Will added, and looked down at the floor.

The old woman came down the stairs slowly, placing one foot in front of the other carefully, a weathered black hand on the wall. She wore a long gray skirt and a knotted long sleeved sweater that covered a wrinkled blouse. She looked in pain as she stepped gingerly.

Will crossed the creaking floor to her. "Hello Liza, remember me? Detective Carter?"

"Lordy yes, from the PO-lice department. Are you going to arrest me?"

Will laughed softly. "No Liza, I just want you to meet some people and talk to them a bit. OK?"

"Visitors? I don't get many visitors," she said, and her face brightened. Will took her arm and led her across the floor towards the others. She hesitated, as she looked at them, obviously confused. "Are they from the PO-lice too? Only white people come here to our home... to arrest folks." She drew back a little.

Susan's heart ached and her anger had vanished completely. All the news stories and TV shows she had seen had not prepared her for the real thing. She stepped past Marsh and Sara towards the old woman.

"Hello Liza, my name is Susan," she said and gently took her hand. "It's nice to meet you."

Liza looked at Will, then at Susan. "Why hello. You're a pretty young thing aren't you now?"

Susan smiled, "Thank you Liza, you're a beautiful woman yourself. How are you today?"

Liza laughed. "Lordy these old bones are creaking." She pulled at her sweater to straighten it. "It's the heat you know, but I do love the summertime."

"Liza, do you remember being at the store? During the robbery?" Will asked.

"Rob-ber-ry?"

"Liza," Will tried again. "Do you remember when we talked, at the police station. We talked about the grocery store, and the man there?"

"The man who attacked me? Tried to get my dinner?"

Susan looked stunned. "He attacked you Liza?"

"Lordy yes, knocked me flat and jumped on top of me. I hit him." She looked at Will who nodded.

"He paid me though. He left me some money."

"Some money Liza?" Susan asked.

Liza reached into the pocket of her sweater and removed a wad of cash. It was crumpled and grimy, almost unrecognizable as bills. "Shopping money. He attacked me Lordy yes, then paid me." She looked at Will, hoping. "Are you going to take my money?"

"No Liza, it's your money, remember?"

She smiled a little. "I don't want no bad money, lands no."

"Do you remember the man who attacked you Liza?" Susan asked patiently.

"A white man. He attacked me."

Susan reached into her pocket, pulled out a picture of Fred out and showed it to her. "Is this the man Liza?"

Liza squinted, looking at it carefully, her eyes focusing slowly. "Don't think so," she said.

Susan's face brightened and she glanced triumphantly at the others.

"Are you sure Liza?" Will asked.

Liza squinted some more. "His hair was funny, falling off his head. Mustache too."

"Liza, if this picture had curly hair and a mustache, would it be him?"

Liza frowned, her brown eyes looking at each of them. It was clear she didn't understand the question.

"Liza," Will asked, "What else do you remember about him. On his neck?"

She looked up from the picture. "God's mark, lordy yes. Right here," she said and pointed to the side of her neck. "It was right in front of me."

Susan's hopes sank. "What did it look like Liza?"

"Not round, no. Stretched a little and dark. The hair was cut, yes."

Susan thought of the birthmark. Fred had always removed the hair when he shaved. She didn't know what else to say.

Will sensed what had happened. "Thank you Liza. It was nice to see you again."

Liza looked confused. "That's all? Are you leaving?"

"Yes Liza, we need to go now," Will said.

Susan looked at her sadly. "Goodbye Liza. Thank you for talking with me." She quickly walked away from the old woman.

Will nodded at the woman, back behind the desk again. She rose to get Liza. Somber, they all stepped quietly back to the door; Marsh opened it and waited for the others to step outside before he followed. The air seemed fresh as they left the building. Susan walked ahead of them towards the car, then turned suddenly.

"Call the Adolphus," she said quietly. "You'll see."

Chapter Twenty-One

Fred's flight out of DIA was later than he told Susan. He felt guilty at breakfast when he lied and said he'd better get going or he would miss his plane. In fact he didn't really want to leave at all, but he had arrangements to make. He was comfortable now with his feelings toward her, the surprise at how close he had let her get now long gone. It was a beautiful day, and his thoughts turned back to Susan's comment about keeping her mother's condominium. He briefly considered the irony of the situation. The reason he would move into the place with Susan was because he had killed her mother didn't seem out of place at all, though he did feel a little sorry for Susan

The rental car plaza was not adjacent to the terminal, and he sped off the exit marked with large green signs that indicated the rental return area. Mid-day Saturday was not primetime for returning cars, and he quickly disposed of the convertible, then rode the bus in silence to the terminal.

The United counters were equally deserted, and it didn't take long to check in for his flight. Briefcase in hand he left the counter, passed by the escalators and crossed into the main terminal complex. He admired once again the towering roof above him, amazed that it was only a few days ago that he was carrying a bag full of cash into the restrooms to make his getaway. So much had happened since Monday he thought the pattern of his life totally changed. He ignored the implications that his relationship with Susan would cause on his life as a thief, but the familiar surroundings of an airport brought it all back suddenly. He would need to stop his appointments he surmised, and the idea saddened him. John would be gone after Kansas City though, not much he could do after that. Vegas too would be history. A voice inside his head protested, but he ignored it and headed towards the security gates.

He rode the train toward Concourse B, lost in thought, and ran the plans and contingencies through his head. A lot depended on his meeting in Minneapolis, his desire to get things done quickly hinged on quick service by his contact. It would cost him he thought, but it would be worth it. For some reason money didn't seem to matter much more anyway. He got off the train and rode the escalator up to the gate level, stopping briefly to check his flight status on the monitors at the top. He had plenty of time, and he walked slowly past the numbered gates until he reached his destination in the middle of the concourse. There was a young man at the desk outside the Red Carpet Club, who looked up as he approached.

"Hi there," Fred said, nodded as he set his briefcase onto the counter, opened it and pulled out his Club card.

"Good afternoon sir," the man replied with a polite smile. "How can I help you?"

"I need to meet someone here, who is not a member. How would I do that?"

The man pulled out a pad and pen efficiently. "If you would give me his name?"

"Oh, it's not today. In fact not until Friday. I was just wondering about the procedure."

"Will you arrive first?"

"Yes."

"That's easy then. When you check in just leave his name, and we will page you inside when he arrives."

"Great, thanks," Fred said. He took his card back from the man and slipped it into his wallet. He took the briefcase and headed towards the frosted glass doors. "Have a good one," he said politely.

Fred looked around as he entered the club, small conference rooms around the outside, a bar/food counter in the middle. He walked over to the lounge area and sat down on a couch with a table and phone in front of it. The place was almost deserted, and was indistinguishable from any of the other clubs he had been in.

He was about to pick up the phone when a disturbing thought hit him. He had to register when he arrived, the ever present computer recording his visit. He pondered that for a moment, then dismissed the problem. There would be no need for anyone to search the records for his name on Friday. He opened his briefcase and pulled out his PDA, once again locating the number for his contact. He picked up the phone, and used a credit card to make the call.

"Leave a message," the gruff voice said.

"It's Stuart again," he said. "Something's come up and I need to see you tonight, not tomorrow. Same place and I'll be there at nine."

He hung up the phone and leaned back against the cushion. There wasn't much time, but meeting tonight instead of tomorrow would help. The plan was in motion and there was nothing he could do about it now.

It had been the worst afternoon of Marsh's life. The relief at getting through the week, the fact that Susan was home again, and his meeting Sara all had been shattered by events that transpired that morning. By four, he found himself on the balcony, sipping his second scotch despite the early hour. The beautiful day and the alcohol had done little to change his mood. He was unbelievably depressed.

The drive back from the shelter had taken forever, and no one had the courage to say anything about the conversation with the old woman. Sara left, determined to go over to the station to start researching the thefts they had uncovered. Marsh wanted her to stay, desperate for her company.

"You need to be with Susan, alone," she had said. "You need to talk things out, reassure her. I can't help you with that." She kissed him and stroked his cheek gently with her fingers.

"Dinner tonight, and bring Susan," she added before leaving.

He protested but she had been adamant. Will had left at the same time, and vowed to help in any way that he could. Marsh was grateful, and pinned his hopes on what the detective could find out. Will had been genuinely sorry for what had transpired, and tried to talk with Susan before she left. Susan was polite, but cold and distant. She had gone into her room when they got back and he hadn't seen her since.

He wasn't giving Fred a fair shake he rationalized. With the revelation of the birthmark, they all had immediately assumed he was the man they were looking for. But thousands of people had birthmarks, and this could just be a wild coincidence. Fred couldn't be the thief - he certainly didn't need the money - and why would he try so hard to help them? There was so much compelling evidence that Fred was innocent when he examined the situation carefully, he had to come to the conclusion that it was all a terrible mistake. A tragic mistake he thought, that had already done an incredible amount of damage.

What was Susan thinking? How was she dealing with this? His heart ached for her. She had been so happy, despite the sorrowful circumstances surrounding their mother's death. He was proud of her for how she had handled herself during the week, and Fred had seemed to provide a foundation of support and strength. They seemed so right together. He sighed and took another sip of his drink and wondered for a moment if he should fix another. He turned around, and was surprised to see Susan standing in the doorway.

"Hey, how long have you been there?"

She looked terrible. Her eyes were puffy and red, and her hair was matted on one side like she had been laying on it. Her shirt was wrinkled and barely tucked into her shorts.

"A moment," she said. She glanced down at the nearly empty glass in his hand. "I could use a drink, do you want another?"

He hesitated for only a second. "Sure, why not?"

Marsh steeled himself for the coming conversation. He had to be upbeat, optimistic. More than anything he wanted to cheer her up, and he rehearsed all of the reasons he had come up with on how it couldn't be Fred. He had almost convinced himself when she returned with the drinks.

"Sit down Suse, let's talk for a while."

She nodded, sat in the other chair and gazed out over the railing. He took a sip of his drink, which was basically devoid of water. He held up the glass to the light and looked at it.

"Trying to get me drunk?" he asked, and struggled to paint a smile on his face.

"Seems like a good idea to me."

He chuckled once. "You may be right. Are you OK?"

"No, but thanks for asking."

He sat up from his slouch and looked at her. "I've been thinking about this Suse, and we're not giving the man a fair shake. We have one coincidence to go on, and we haven't considered all of the other facts of the matter. You don't really think he's the one do you?"

She looked back at him. "Of course not, but everyone else seems to. I just don't know what to believe."

"Good, and I'm sorry we gave you the impression that we thought it was him too. It's just that Will sprung all of this on us so fast."

"But what about the woman, Liza?"

"What about her? You saw what she was like. She could barely remember where she lived for Christ's sake. She couldn't identify him; she only described the birthmark. Millions of people have birthmarks."

Susan sat up a little. "Do you really think so?"

"Suse, I admit I was swept up in the whole deal. I have been so obsessed with tracking down the guy that I let myself get carried away." His emotions, buoyed by the scotch took over. "Shit, I should have been as upset at the implication as you were. He is going to be my brother-in-law after all."

The phone rang and interrupted the conversation.

"That's Sara. She want's us to go to dinner tonight."

Susan frowned. "I don't know if I'm up for that Marsh."

He got up and patted her shoulder. "Nonsense, we can't let this get us down."

She didn't say anything when he left, but considered the offer. She had been sulking all afternoon, just lying on her bed. At first she was surprised that she was so mad at Fred for ruining her life. She didn't admit it to Marsh, but after meeting with Liza she was convinced he was the thief. During the hours of staring at the ceiling she had grown bitter, and wallowed in self-pity. The more she lay there, the more vindictive she had become. She was convinced that if he had been next to her on the bed she would have strangled him.

Now she hated herself for even considering it. She got up from the chair and walked over to the rail, then leaned into it with her arms. Yesterday she was going to marry the man, now she was afraid to talk to him. What the hell was she doing?

She walked back, picked up her drink and wondered what was taking Marsh so long. She peeked in through the doors, but could only see his back. He stood by the table; still covered with the printouts and sketch that was so damning. He was deep in conversation, but she couldn't make out the details. Finally he turned and walked back, the phone in one hand by his side.

"Where would you like to have dinner?" he asked. His face showed no trace of emotion.

She started to protest. "Marsh, I don't think I could..."

"To celebrate," he continued, and his face broke into a huge smile.

She was totally confused. "What?" she stammered.

He walked out to the balcony, took her shoulders and pushed her down into the chair.

"Believe it or not that was Will," he said, his voice elevated. "God bless the man."

"What are you talking about Marsh?"

"Like I said before, he's on our side. He felt so bad about this morning that he went back to the station. He called Dallas."

Susan's heart leapt in her chest. "And?"

"And he worked his butt off for us. He talked to the cops down there, and got them to open some doors. He called the hotel - the Adolphus - and Fred was registered there on Sunday through Tuesday. The weekend staff was on duty so he got home phone numbers for the employees who worked during the week." He stopped for a moment, caught his breath, and then took a large pull on his drink.

Her heart pounded in her chest. "Go on..." she said impatiently.

"He talked with everyone Suse. He pulled out all the stops. The desk manager remembers Fred perfectly. Apparently he's a regular guest there. They had a conversation Monday afternoon when Fred got back from a run. The bellman helped him when he checked out on Tuesday morning, and got him a limo to the airport."

Susan couldn't believe it, or say anything.

"That's not all. He had breakfast delivered to his room Monday morning, and they have phone records of several calls made throughout the day." Marsh beamed at her.

Susan leaped to her feet. "Eeeek," she screamed and jumped into his arms. They hugged each other tightly, then danced around the balcony like little kids.

"I knew it, I knew it!" she yelled into his shoulder.

They hugged some more, then Marsh pulled back. "Will is convinced, and he apologized for all the trouble he caused. He felt terrible you know."

"I can imagine. I wouldn't have wanted to talk to you about it," she agreed, laughing now.

"I told him to forget it. In fact I invited him to dinner. Is that alright?"

"Absolutely, I want to apologize to him too!"

"Oh God, I am so relieved. I can't believe it!"

A somber look suddenly filled Susan's face. Marsh looked at her, surprised.

"What's wrong Suse,"

"Oh God I feel so bad. Jesus we had all condemned him Marsh. What am I going to say to him."

Marsh smiled. "As your big brother, I suggest you say nothing. This little incident is just between us OK?"

Susan felt a little guilty but acquiesced. "Right. Let's just forget about it. In fact I'm going to call him right now."

"Let me call Sara first, and tell her. Then we'll celebrate tonight."

Marsh started to walk in to get the phone, then realized he still had it in his hand. He pointed to it and laughed. Susan went inside and practically skipped down the hall to the bathroom. She looked in the mirror at herself.

"You're a mess girl. Better not let your man see you like that."

She started to clean up, then decided a long hot shower would be better. She splashed a little water on her face and then walked back to the living room. She couldn't wait to call him.

Marsh was still grinning while he handed her the phone. "Were all set," he said. "Sara is ecstatic. She told me to give you a big hug."

Susan grabbed the phone. "Gimme that," she said and dialed Fred's cell phone number. He answered after only one ring.

"Hello, Susan?"

"How did you know it was me?"

"Duh, who else would call me from Colorado?"

She couldn't help laughing. "Oh God I miss you already. Was your flight OK?"

"Just fine babe. You sound happy - what's going on?"

"Oh nothing," she lied, the short twinge of guilt vanishing instantly.

"Mmm..." he said.

"We're having dinner tonight. Marsh and I and Sara and Will."

"Will too? Any news?"

"Nope, he has nothing to go on," she said smugly. "I guess he's just getting to be buddies with Marsh. And so is Sara from what I can tell."

"She's definitely a keeper."

"Like me?"

"Like you. Well have fun tonight. I've got a meeting too, so call me tomorrow, alright?"

"You got it. I love you babe."

"I love you too. Bye."

"Bye," she said and clicked off the phone. She turned to Marsh who had been listening shamelessly to the whole conversation.

"Let's party," she said with a smile.

The bar was called The Hole, and the name described it perfectly.

Surprisingly it wasn't in the worst part of town. It was in the West Bank, a small community of shops and bars that derived its name from the location on the Mississippi river, close to the University of Minnesota campus. The college crowd didn't frequent the establishment however, preferring the dance clubs and sports bars that were a little more upscale. This place was wedged between an old three story brick building with a laundromat and a religious book store. A small white sign with the name in black letters hung from a rusted pole over the door. Basically it was a dive.

Fred parked directly across the street, then sat quietly for a moment and looked at the establishment through the closed car window. Finally, he turned the rear-view mirror toward him and stared at the reflection. Stuart was there.

"Ready?" Fred said.

"My turn," Stuart said back.

Fred stepped out of the car into the street, felt himself change instantly, then glanced both ways as he crossed the deserted street. He pulled the bar door open and stepped inside and paused for a moment to let his eyes adjust to the darkness. It was an old place, a long dark bar of some unknown wood on one side, a row of booths on the other. At the back end was a two quarter pool table and a jukebox, which pounded out a song he didn't recognize. The floor was tiled and grimy, and it smelled like stale beer. There were few people in the place, a sad tribute to Saturday night. No one paid any attention to him as he crossed to the bar.

The bartender looked like an ex-biker, which judging from the clientele he probably was. He wore white t-shirt, stained in the armpits. His ample belly flopped down over the large leather belt in his jeans. Stuart stepped between two barstools that were bolted into the floor on silver posts and leaned onto the bar. After a moment the bartender turned from the two men at the other end or the room and looked at him, nodding in recognition as he walked over.

"Stuart, my man. Long time no see. You been in jail?" the bartender asked with a partially toothless grin.

"Hello Deke. How's it hanging?" Stuart said. He was dressed in jeans and a work shirt, his feet shod in worn yellow boots.

"Beer?" Deke asked.

"Fine. Is he here?"

"Who?" Deke said, and pulled a bottle of Bud from a cooler, opened it on a metal tap bolted into the side of the bar and placed it in front of Stuart.

Stuart knew the game. He pulled a wad of bills from his pocket, and made sure the man could see them. He stripped off a fifty and flipped it on the bar.

"He's expecting me. Call him now." He dismissed Deke by turning his back on him, then took the beer and walked across the bar to an empty booth without saying anything else. He slid in over the cracked red plastic and waited, setting his beer down without tasting it.

It had taken him a long time to find this place he remembered, though there must be dozens just like it in Minneapolis. A few months of hanging out in seedy bars, making contacts, and dropping lots of cash before he had been trusted, or at least accepted. He started slowly, cultivating his reputation as a small time thief, who sometimes made a big score. It hadn't been hard, especially when he was buying the drinks. Alcohol loosened tongues quickly, and he found it easy to spin tales, first listening to others, then making up his own.

He started by buying fake credit cards, which he claimed he needed for one of his scams. From there he worked into fake ID's, finding a talented woman who did marginal work and always needed money for drugs. He had bought several from her for about a hundred bucks each, but never used them. She was an amateur, and he didn't trust her. But she was a conduit, and he soon was in with a more professional operation. From there he got identities, the first one he had used sparingly, waiting to see what would happen. He had even gone so far as running a credit check on John pleasantly surprised at the results. Over the next few months he had obtained two more, to the tune of ten grand apiece. They had been well worth it.

He waited patiently, took a sip on his beer, then dumped the rest of it under the table. He took the empty bottle back to the bar and ordered another, with a shot of bourbon. Deke said nothing, and Stuart paid for the drinks with another fifty. He returned to the booth and emptied the shot glass on the floor under the table. It was nine-thirty five when he finally saw the man approach.

"You wanted to see me?" the man said, and catlike slid into the booth across from Stuart.

Stuart nodded. "I need a few things."

The man nodded. He was small, with black hair slicked straight back over his high forehead. He had a sharp chin and his teeth were perfect. Stuart thought he might be Asian, but it was hard to tell. He had a black suit on, with no tie.

"Talk to me," the man said, and his dark eyes drilled into Stuart's.

Stuart returned the stare, no trace of emotion on his face. "I need a gun," he said without hesitation.

"Not your style."

"Protection."

"Right. Preference?"

"Doesn't matter."

The man's expression didn't change. "Nine, then. That it?"

"The rest is harder."

"Harder is only more expensive."

Stuart paused for a moment, and took a sip on his beer. "Expensive is not an issue."

A flicker of delight showed in the man's eyes, then it was gone.

"I need reliable muscle, for an out of town job."

The man studied him. "Rough?"

"Let's just say I need to make a point."

"Umm... I know a few."

"He has to look like me."

"That would be harder."

"Harder is more expensive," Stuart repeated.

The man nodded, but a tiny smile pushed up the corners of his mouth. He started to get up.

"One more thing," Stuart added.

The man looked at him curiously for a moment then slid back down.

"Incendiary, small and remote controlled, by cell phone."

The man said nothing. The juke box changed tunes. He nodded again, almost imperceptibly. "Costly."

Stuart reached into his back pocket and pulled out a folded envelope. It bulged slightly as he set it on the table.

"For the arrangements."

The man took the envelope and slid it inside his coat pocket without looking at it.

"Tuesday," Stuart said.
"Tuesday is hard."
"And hard is expensive."
"Call me," the man said and left.

Chapter Twenty-Two

Susan groaned and rolled on her side, then reached out for Fred. Her arm flopped lifelessly onto the empty bed with a loud thud. She panicked and sat up abruptly, a sharp knife-like stabbing twisting through her head. Totally disoriented she moved her arm but below the elbow it wouldn't respond, her hand dragging a little over the sheet. She turned quickly to look at it, then the pain shot through her head again. Her arm at least now tingled a little. She groaned loudly, then reached over with her other hand and grasped the wrist of her dead arm. She could feel it in her hand, but couldn't feel her fingers wrapped around her wrist.

"Oh shit," she said.

She lifted the arm and let go feeling more than seeing it flop back down to the bed again. It was on fire more now, like thousands of tiny needles pushing into it all at once, especially down around her fingers. She giggled a little, lifted and dropped again. Thud. She leaned back down onto the pillow, slowly this time, lying on her back. She reached both arms up to the ceiling and stretched, barely able to keep her right arm from bending at the elbow and hitting her in the face. She had passed out lying on her arm she surmised triumphantly.

"You were significantly over-served last night, girl," she said to the ceiling.

Prudently, she decided not to move her head for a while.

After a moment she opened her eyes again, and let them adjust to the dimness in the room. The sheets felt rough until she realized she wasn't between them, but laying on top of the stitched bedspread. The stabbing pain had mutated into a dull throb as she looked down over her body. She had long tan pants on, with a blue silk blouse. It looked like she had slept in them, which of course she had.

"Nice outfit," she said to her toes.

She wondered if things would change much if she closed her eyes and go back to sleep, but her head hurt too much. Carefully she pulled her legs up and swung them down over the side of the bed, then bending at the waist she slowly sat up. That wasn't so hard she thought.

She got up and trudged slowly into the bathroom, somewhat relieved to see that she didn't look nearly as bad as she felt. She stripped quickly, left her clothes in a pile on the floor and gingerly lifted one leg, then the other into the tub. The water splashed over her and onto the floor until she pulled the curtain back, sealing her inside. She stayed there a long time.

A half-hour later she had her robe tied tightly around her waist and a towel wrapped around her head as she shuffled down the hall into the dining room. It was bright outside, and the sunlight streamed in from the balcony. Sara was sitting at the dining room table reading theSunday paper; a mug of coffee sat on the table in front of her.

"Well good morning," Sara said and looked up. She had one of Marsh's sweatshirts on and looked fabulous. Susan was jealous.

"If you say so," Susan replied, pulled out a chair and sat down. She put both her forearms on the table and leaned against them. The towel began to slip down off her head but she ignored it.

"I bet you could use some coffee," Sara said, the smile lost on Susan.

"Please."

Sara got up and walked into the kitchen. The sweatshirt fell below her butt, but rode high up on the back of her slim legs. Susan stared down at the table, but heard the cupboard close, then the sound of liquid splashing into a mug. She glanced up to see Sara coming back and gratefully reached out for the coffee, the cup warm in her hand.

"Well at least I got up before Marsh did," she said, noticing he wasn't there.

Sara sat back down and looked at her, a little amused. "Hardly. He was up early, working in his office. He went out for a run."

"Figures," she said. The coffee tasted good and warmed her insides. Her head was recovering thanks to the aspirin, and she strained to revive herself. She felt a little guilty, and was grateful to have someone to talk to.

"I presume we had fun last night," Susan said, but still stared down at the table.

Sara laughed. "Yes, we did."

Susan struggled to remember. They had a long dinner at the restaurant, with champagne first, then several bottles of wine, most of which she drank she recalled. Will had left them after dinner, but at her insistence they had moved on to a jazz club, where the music was loud and the dance floor crowded. She didn't remember coming home.

"I haven't stayed out that late for a long time," Sara said.

"It was late?"

"Sometime around one thirty when we got back here." Sara smiled and looked at her. "How old are you Susan? If I may ask?"

"Well I was twenty-six yesterday," she managed a laugh. "I'm not so sure now."

"Ahh to be young again."

"And foolish," Susan added. She looked at Sara and smiled. She was totally comfortable with her being there. She felt happy for Marsh. "I'm glad you're here Sara."

Sara looked surprised. "Thank you Susan, that means a lot. I'm glad to be here too."

The door opened and Marsh came in, chest heaving. He had shorts and a t-shirt on, his face and hair covered in sweat. He looked at them and smiled broadly, obviously happy to see them both there. He walked over and put his hands on Susan's shoulders, then leaned down and hugged her neck, his cheek on hers.

"Aaack..." she said. "Slimy."

Marsh laughed and pulled away. "Good morning to you too sleepy."

He stepped back, walked over to Sara and stood behind her. Sara reached her hand up over her shoulder and Marsh covered it gently.

"No hugs for me?" she said, then leaned her head back and gazed up at him. She pulled his face down.

He smiled, twisted his head and kissed her on the cheek.

"Aaack, slimy," she said looking at Susan. They both laughed. "Don't you hate it when they don't shave Susan?"

"Nothing worse."

"That's not what you said earlier," Marsh said over his shoulder as he walked into the kitchen. He opened the fridge and pulled out a carton of orange juice.

"That was different," Sara said. "I was sleeping and you surprised me."

"Mmm..." Marsh said. He got a glass from the cupboard and filled it, but left the carton on the counter. Susan and Sara were still laughing when he came back and sat down at the table, across from Susan.

"You have a flight at about two, do you think you can make it?" Marsh asked.

"At two? Why?" she asked, confused.

Marsh glanced at Sara, who smiled. "You insisted last night, that I get you a flight out. If I recall you wanted to leave at six this morning."

"Oops," Susan said. It started to come back to her. She wanted to get home, back to Fred, back to work.

"I need to get home Marsh," she said, and the smile slipped from her face. "I've been here long enough."

Marsh nodded, understanding. "Hell of a sendoff though. I will miss having you here."

"And I'll miss you too. Both of you. But it's time to get back to reality again."

It was silent around the table for a moment.

"What are you going to do Marsh?" Susan asked.

"I'm going back to work too. I've got a company to run."

"That's not what I mean."

Marsh looked at Sara, who nodded in agreement, then back to Susan. "Well I'm a little embarrassed about yesterday, but I can't let it go. I'm going to get Will the information he needs for the airlines, then see where it goes from there."

She felt nervous about the whole thing, a pang of dread shooting through her. The elation she felt yesterday when they found out about Dallas long gone. She suddenly had a bad feeling about everything. For some reason she flashed back to Fred in bed, and the feeling he was someone else.

"I wish you wouldn't Marsh,"

"I know," he said.

Chapter Twenty-Three

It was Tuesday afternoon, and to Marsh it seemed like he hadn't slept for days. He rubbed one hand wearily over his face, moved the mouse with the other centered the arrow-cursor over the icon for his personal calendar and clicked. The window opened on the monitor and he looked over the rest of the day's schedule. Thankfully, he had an hour with no commitments. He picked up the phone and dialed Mary's extension.

"Yes Marsh?" Mary asked immediately.

"Mary, no calls, no disturbances, no nothing for an hour."

"Yes sir," she said, not questioning the request.

He set down the receiver and pressed the do not disturb button on the phone. He felt guilty. He got up slowly, left his shoes under the desk, moved to each window and closed the blinds even though there was little sunlight coming in. Finally he flicked off the overhead lights, walked over to the couch and sunk into the cushions. It wasn't dark in the office but it would do.

He had read somewhere, Fortune magazine probably, about executives who took power-naps in the afternoon - short fifteen minute breaks of meditation - who claimed it did wonders for fatigue and stress. He wondered if it would work, then worried instead that if he closed his eyes he would fall asleep for a few hours. A small smile appeared on his weary face. Of course some of the problem was Sara's fault he thought, she had spent the last two nights at his place.

On Monday he had thrown himself back into work with determination that he hadn't shown since he first started the company. He had been pleasantly surprised, and a little dismayed, that the place hadn't collapsed during his week away. He attributed the success to the talent of the organization he had built, Sheila and Joe taking over many of the functions that he had once thought only he could do. He spent most of the last two days on the phone and catching up on email, still faithfully answering any of the condolence communications that continued to drift in.

Susan left Sunday afternoon, still a bit hung over. Despite her earlier enthusiasm about getting home and the revelation of Fred's innocence, she had seemed reticent, but didn't want to talk about it. At first he attributed her mood to the reality of their mother's passing resurfacing, but now he wasn't so sure. They cried together at the airport one last time before she went through security, hugging and promising not to let so much time pass before seeing each other again. He had returned to an empty home, Sara off doing whatever women do after spending the night at a man's place, and for once it seemed empty and lifeless. He realized that he missed having everyone at his place, the week filled with family and friends despite the tragic circumstances.

Of course there were other details he had to attend to. The meeting with the funeral director was a nuisance, and he signed all the papers after barely looking them over, anxious to get the past behind him. He had breakfast with Steve that morning and they had struggled for an hour over the strategy of transferring assets with a minimum of tax implications. He wanted Susan to have Mom's condominium, but Steve had argued against it, pointing out that she probably wasn't in the position to manage it from Minneapolis. Exasperated, he had finally just given Steve Power of Attorney and told him to handle it the best way he could. They could work out the details later, after Susan and Fred had set a date to be married.

Married. His thoughts had been a roller coaster on that subject, and he couldn't quite nail down his feelings on the whole deal. He wanted so much for her to be happy, and she seemed to be with Fred. That was at least until the whole birthmark issue had come up. He briefly wondered what Fred would think about the events that transpired on Saturday, and hoped that Susan would never tell him about it. He couldn't help thinking about the damage that that day must have caused in their relationship. Despite Susan's protestations, he was convinced that Susan had suspected Fred as much as he had, and that bothered him a lot. It was a trust issue now, and he was worried how much the secret she carried deep within her would affect them over time.

And then there was the thief, and his efforts to track him down. Over a quiet dinner on Sunday he and Sara had discussed the issue at length. Despite Susan's misgivings about it, both he and Sara were determined to press forward, each for their own reasons. The pain of the killer's actions still festered inside him and he knew it wouldn't go away until the man was caught and punished. And Sara wanted the story he knew, even though she didn't come out and admit it. She was involved now, and wanted to help him, and Susan, for personal reasons. But it was her job to find big stories, and she couldn't hide her professional ambition regarding the prospects of the case. He couldn't blame her for that though, and maybe she could help.

He felt himself dozing off, despite all the thoughts swirling through his head. He swung his legs down, got up, and paced across the carpeted office. He stopped in front of an oak bookcase and gazed at a picture of Mom and Susan taken in Crested Butte a few winters ago at a friend's house. They looked so happy, and he felt a twinge of loss again. It was so beautiful there, he should take Sara he thought. He suddenly remembered it was only a week ago that he had been trying to figure out vacation plans, wondering where to go and who to spend some time with. Well he had taken time off he thought, that's for sure, and maybe a few more days away from Denver would help finalize things. He made a mental note to call his buddy and see if the place was open this weekend.

And then there was Will. The detective had called him first thing Monday morning under the pretext of thanking him for dinner Saturday night, but the conversation had quickly reverted to the airline records. Will asked if he could provide him with the details for the computer search, and Marsh suspected there had been renewed interest at the Police Department about the case. He of course had been happy to oblige and he wondered how long it would take the airlines to do the data extraction.

There was a soft, almost imperceptible knock on the door. He glanced at his watch, and realized that a half-hour had slipped away. He walked to the door and opened it to see Mary standing there, a guilty look on her face.

"Yes Mary?"

"I know you didn't want me to bother you Marsh, but Detective Smith is on the line. He said it was important."

"It's all right Mary," he said, a trace of forgiveness in his voice. "Give me one minute, then transfer it in."

She nodded and walked away quickly, obviously relieved.

He closed the door and walked back to his desk, his stomach knotted in anticipation. So soon? Somebody must have lit a fire under this he thought. The phone rang after a few seconds and he put it on speaker.

"Marsh, it's Will," the voice echoed in the room.

He tried to calm himself. "What's up Will?" he replied, talking at the phone.

"Believe it or not I have some information from the airlines, or at least from United, USAir and American. We are still trying with some of the others. Apparently this is not an unusual request from law enforcement agencies."

Marsh's heart skipped a beat. "That's great news Will, unexpected so quickly, but great. When do we get it?"

"They are Fed-Exing it over today. I should have it by tomorrow morning."

"Wonderful. I'll send someone over to pick it up, alright?"

"That won't be necessary Marsh, I'll just bring it over as soon as I get it," Will said.

Marsh smiled at the phone. "Why that's very generous of you detective. Has this case been suddenly elevated in priority?"

"Let's just say that the Captain has given me new instructions regarding the situation."

"You are a master at subtlety Will. I'll have my people get right on it. And thanks again."

"My thanks to you Marsh, and I mean that. I hope we both find what we are looking for. I'll call you in the morning as soon as I get it.

"I'll be waiting. Take care Will,"

Marsh was excited, things were happening. He thought about calling Susan, but nixed that idea immediately, not wanting to stir up any emotional responses until they knew more. He picked up the handset and instead dialed Sara's cell phone. It rang four times before she answered.

"Sara McGloughin."

"Sara, it's me" he said, anxious to fill her in.

"Hi Marsh, I didn't recognize the number. You must be at work."

"Yeah, I am," he started. "Sara, I've got some great news. I just talked to Will and we should have the airline records by tomorrow, or at least some of them anyway."

"Oh my God Marsh, I thought it would take weeks."

"I had no idea what to expect, but somebody in the police department is pulling some strings I think."

"And I have some news for you too. The emails are pouring in from the cities I contacted. I'm building up a huge the profile on this guy. He seems to be quite successful at what he does."

Marsh noted the excitement in her voice. "Putting together a story?"

There was silence at the other end of the phone. "That's not fair Marsh. You asked me to get involved in this, remember?"

He immediately felt bad for the remark. "Sara, I'm sorry. I didn't mean it that way."

She didn't say anything.

"Really, I was just thinking about it a little while ago. I think it would be great if we could solve this thing, together. I would like nothing more than for you to make a big splash with the story."

"Are you sure Marsh?"

"Absolutely, I really mean it. By the way, how about you and I getting away together this weekend, just the two of us. I know a great little place in Crested Butte."

"Mmm, all weekend? Well if you insist," she replied. "And what about tonight?"

"I've got a few things to take care of here. Oh shit, I forgot, I'm having dinner with Lebida tonight."

"A date?"

"Hardly. It seems I promised to take her to dinner for helping us out."

"That's good actually. I should probably see if my condo is still there. Behave yourself alright?"

"What?" he asked surprised. "Oh right. Strictly business."

"Call me later."

"When I get home"

He hung up the phone. A touch of concern passed over him. Lebida had been extremely friendly the last few days, and he wondered what she was thinking. Since she had been with the company she hadn't said ten words to him outside work, and now they were having dinner. He would never understand women he thought.

Susan didn't know what to think. She had been confused since she got back, and couldn't shake the feeling of guilt that had been building up inside her. Fred had picked her up at the airport, meeting her just outside security. He had hugged her and kissed her passionately, and told her how much he missed her. She had hurt his feelings she thought, when she didn't respond in kind. She blamed it on the hangover, and described the celebration they had been through on Saturday. He thought it was funny and didn't give it a second thought, taking her back to his car and driving her home, chattering non-stop along the way about the stock market, the heat, humidity and mosquitoes. He briefly mentioned making some plans about the marriage, which surprised her. No, disturbed her she remembered. He went on and on about how much he loved Colorado, hinting that he could live there. She couldn't talk about it.

He wanted to spend the night together, but she refused, using the excuse of needing to get home to readjust and get ready for work the next day. They had almost gotten into a fight over it, something she couldn't recall ever happening. She had tried to sooth things over by having dinner with him, but she hadn't been very good company. She tried to blame everything on the stress-filled week, and emphasized the need to get home by herself for at least one good night of sleep. Finally he agreed, but was obviously disappointed.

The office bustled around her, but she just sat at her desk and thought. She had hoped that immersing herself in her work on Monday would straighten things out, and she would get back to normal. Everyone had been so happy to have her back, showering her with condolences and sympathy. There were two arrangements of flowers on her desk, one from her co-workers and one from the President of the company. She was touched when she saw them and had broken into tears. Her friends had assumed it was grief, but she knew it wasn't.

Fred had called yesterday, again wanting to get together, saying something about having to leave town on Wednesday. She put him off with an excuse of having too much work to do. He said he understood and she hated herself for lying to him. What was happening to her? Just a few days ago she had been madly in love with him, not wanting to spend a minute apart. She remembered her elation when Marsh had told her about Dallas, and how she had partied all night, so happy. But ever since then she couldn't get the old woman out of her mind. She even dreamt of her last night, a nightmare that had caused her to jump up in her bed, shaking.

She pushed a few papers around on her desk and tried to look busy. Luckily her cubicle faced the window, and few of her co-workers passed by. Outside it was dreary and rainy. She missed Colorado already.

The dream scared her. She was walking in an alley, when she was knocked over by a running man. He fell on top of her and when she looked up it was Fred, disguised in a wig and moustache, the birthmark huge and covering half of his neck. He just laughed at her and she snapped. There was a brick laying beside her and she grabbed it, then slammed it into the side of his head. She was sure she had killed him. The old woman was there, watching the whole thing. She could still hear the voice ringing in her ears, shouting PO-lice, PO-lice! Chills ran through her, her hands wet and clammy.

Get a grip girl, she said to herself. She knew what was wrong. She had to tell him. The guilt and suspicion was tearing her apart and if she didn't let it go she would go crazy. God she wanted so much to feel like she did on Saturday. She remembered the rock in the park, where he had proposed and they had brazenly made love in the open air. Everything seemed so perfect, exactly like she had always dreamed. She wanted that feeling back so badly. I have to tell him she vowed to herself.

The phone rang, and she jumped. She knew it was him and she let it ring a few times. She stared at it and steeled herself for the conversation. Her hands were still sweaty when she picked it up.

"Susan Hawkins."

"Hey babe, it's me."

Her stomach dropped. "Hi," she said, and tried to sound upbeat.

"Is today going any better?"

"Much," she lied.

"Great, I can't wait to see you tonight. I can't believe it has been two days. I miss you."

"I miss you too."

"OK, here's the plan. I have to meet some people at five, and it'll take a couple of hours. Why don't you come over about seven-thirty. I'll pick up some Chinese on the way home and we can just pig-out and spend the night at my place, OK?"

Somehow the thought struck her as funny. "Pig-out?"

"Yeah, chow down," he said. "It's good to hear you laugh babe, I've been worried about you."

"I'm sorry, Fred. I guess I've been a little on edge," she managed to say.

"Well don't worry about it, I understand completely. It's been a tough week. It will all be better tonight I promise. I have a few things to show you, and talk to you about."

Susan was confused. "What things?"

"Not until tonight," he said mysteriously.

She paused for a moment, then let it go. "I have something I want to talk to you about too Fred." The butterflies returned immediately.

"Not bad news is it?" he asked, the cheerfulness still showing through in his voice.

"I hope not," she said. God I hope not she repeated to herself.

"Good, whatever it is. I've got to go to Dallas tomorrow, remember?"

Dallas, she thought, remembering Saturday. "For how long?"

"Just till Friday, short trip this time. I'll see you at seven-thirty." He paused, "I love you."

"I love you too. Bye," she said.

She put the receiver down and tried to cheer herself up. That wasn't so bad she thought. It's a good start.

She had work to do, but decided to leave early anyway. People would understand she thought.

"I'll go over to the lakes and take a walk around," she said, and looked out the window at the rain. "Figure out how to tell him. What to say."

She looked around quickly, wondering if anyone had overheard her. Apparently no one had noticed and she picked up her purse and headed out. She felt a little better already she thought.

Chapter Twenty-Four

Fred sat on the side of the bed, pulled on his boots and tied them slowly. The TV in the room was tuned to CNBC, and the sound of the evening market summary played out into the room. It surprised him that he didn't pay much attention, in fact for two days he had ignored his trading activities completely. He had tried on Monday to get his routine back, made a few trades, but ended up losing a few grand and gave up, his lack of enthusiasm uncharacteristic. Since then he had pretty much just sat in front of the TV, running the plan over and over again. Until now he had avoided mirrors.

He had been worried about Susan. She had been so distant since she came back from Colorado, and he wondered for a moment what she wanted to talk about. He re-laced his left boot and tugged at it. He was anxious to see her tonight and he would show her all his trading secrets, his accounts, everything. He wanted her to understand him he thought. She needed to know the real Fred.

He got up, tucked the checked work shirt into his jeans and walked into the bathroom. He flipped on the light and looked into the mirror. The image stared back at him, then nodded.

"Fred," Stuart said.

"Do you understand the plan?" Fred asked.

"Perfectly."

"Good."

The counter in the bathroom was recessed into the wall, a single sink set in the middle. There were bright spotlights set into the ceiling that shone down and reflected off the marble counter top. There were mirrors on either side of the alcove and Fred turned to his left. The mustache and curled hair reflection looked back at him.

"Kansas City will be difficult," Fred said.

"I know," John replied.

"Not much time to plan this one, but that's all right. I want to leave a trail anyway."

"Not a problem," the image said.

"It will be your last one you know. I'm sorry but that's the way it has to be."

John nodded, not disputing the fact.

"Dude, what about me?" Richard asked.

Fred turned to his right and looked at the rough shaven man.

"No Vegas. Not this time."

"That's bullshit Fred," Richard said, disgusted.

"That's the way it has to be."

"But what about the twins Fred?" The image paused. "It's that fucking Susan isn't it? She's got you all pussy-whipped, like a little school boy."

Fred ignored him and turned back to Stuart. "Ready?"

"Let's do it."

He left the car about two blocks from The Hole, careful to park legally, but where the car wouldn't be noticed. He walked confidently down the street, carrying a small leather briefcase and ignored the rain that splashed down on the sidewalk. He glanced at his watch before opening the door. It was five-fifteen.

He took a deep breath, walked inside, and felt himself change again. He was going to miss this he thought. It was still dark inside the bar and still smelled of stale beer. He glanced around, noticed the place was empty except for two bikers sitting at the far end of the bar, and a lone man in the middle facing away from him. The jukebox was playing country/western this time. He crossed to the bar and stood between two stools and set the briefcase down on top of one. Deke saw him and walked over, still dressed in a t-shirt and jeans. The same t-shirt Stuart said to himself. Some things never change.

"Beer?" Deke asked, then reached down to the cooler without waiting for an answer. He opened it, and set it down with a thud, the foam spilling out over the top and down the side of the bottle. Stuart pulled a fifty from his pocket and dropped it on the bar.

"Over there," Deke pointed with a headshake at the back booth.

Stuart ignored the beer, picked up the briefcase and headed to the back. The booth looked empty until he got there, his contact sitting with his back to the door, hidden by the high wooden seatback. Stuart slid in, but kept the briefcase on the bench beside him.

"You are late," the man articulated.

"It's raining," Stuart said.

"I don't like late."

"I don't like rain."

The man looked at him, and almost smiled.

"Below the table is a briefcase. It contains an untraceable handgun, a nine, and the other device you requested. Included is a telephone number, which when called, will activate the device. Directions are not included."

Stuart stared at the man. It was the most he had ever heard him say at one time. He couldn't tell if the comment about directions had been a joke, and forced himself not to smile.

The man misinterpreted his expression.

"I trust that is satisfactory?"

"Very."

"And you have the amount we agreed on."

"Yes."

"Good. Then our business is concluded." The man smiled this time, just a little.

Stuart turned and unzipped the case, removed a plastic sack, then zipped it up and set it between them. The man took the handle and got out of the booth.

"What about the muscle?" Stuart asked.

The man nodded towards the bar. The lone patron sitting there turned, got off the stool and walked towards them. The resemblance was uncanny.

"Remarkable isn't it?" his contact said.

"Very."

"Hard?"

"And expensive. The remaining arrangements are between you gentlemen." His contact turned and walked away.

Stuart stared as the other man slid into the booth across from him. He wasn't a twin, but close, very close. He lifted a second plastic bag and slid it across the table.

"Ten grand. Twice that when you are done."

"When and where?"

"Denver, on Friday. Inside the bag is a flight number for you to take, E-tickets of course and paid for. Meet me at the Red Carpet Club in the airport, and page me from the desk. I'll be there already. The name to use is with the flight number."

If the double was surprised, he didn't show it.

"Then what?" he asked.

"I'll fill you in on Friday."

The double nodded, grabbed the sack and headed for the door. Stuart waited until he was gone, then reached under the table and retrieved the other briefcase. He didn't say anything to Deke as he walked out, figuring he would never see him again.

Marsh knew he was in trouble ten minutes into dinner. They were at the Great Northern Tavern, a relatively new grill that specialized in North American seafood. Lebida had overdressed Marsh thought, for a casual business evening. Other than the funeral he couldn't ever recall seeing her in something other than jeans or slacks, and some kind of oversized drab shirt. In fact he could barely recall seeing her at all. But this evening she had a blue pleated skirt, and a matching but lighter silk top on, with a silver necklace that hung down from her neck to where the top buttons of the her blouse were undone. His mind drifted while she chattered at him, and he wondered if he should comment on her appearance. He sighed to himself, and took a sip from his scotch. He was making too big of a deal out of this.

She paused for a moment, and he made up his mind. "Did I tell you that you look very nice tonight?"

She looked at him, flustered, then looked down at the table. "No you didn't, but thank you."

"You know," she continued, "I come to work every morning more or less dressed the same way. We sit in our little cubicles all day, and unless we are going to meet with the client, there is not much reason to not wear something comfortable, which in my case is usually pretty drab."

"Well I don't know if I'd go that far," Marsh said, and tried to recall her appearance in one of the project meetings he sat in on. He couldn't.

"Would you like me to change the dress code?" he added.

Lebida's mouth dropped open.

"I, uh…" she stammered. "Jeez I'm sorry Marsh. I didn't mean to say anything bad about work." She looked at him and smiled. "It's just that you are so easy to talk to."

Marsh laughed. "Is there some reason I shouldn't be?"

"Well no, but you're the president of the company, and I'm just a lowly employee."

Marsh sat back for a moment, and tried to be delicate. "Just because

I own the business doesn't mean that I don't have friends Lebida, or did you think I just did power lunches all the time."

"Well, no."

"Good, because I'd like us to be friends Lebida. And I'm very grateful for what you did for me, on the web."

"Friends?" Lebida asked, and pushed a strand of hair from her face.

Marsh looked at her for a moment and felt totally guilty. Jeez he hated to do stuff like this.

"Lebida, I don't know what you were thinking, but this is just dinner. As I said I wanted to thank you for all the hard work the other night."

"Oh I know Marsh," she said and sighed. "I saw the woman you were with at Sheila's house. Is she...?"

Marsh laughed, but felt relieved. "Yes, Sara McGloughin. You could say she is a close friend of mine."

"Everyone at the office always thought that you and Sheila, well, you know..." She sat back and slapped her head. "God I can't believe I just said that."

"It's OK, really." Marsh laughed even louder. "This isn't work, remember?"

The waitress came by, completely frazzled. She stood next to the table, bent her lip, and blew a strand of hair out of her face. She was short, a little stocky and obviously overworked.

"OK folks, what can I get you?" she said as she pulled out a small pad and a golf pencil from her apron.

Marsh glanced at Lebida, who shrugged, then he looked back at the waitress.

"Miss?" he said to her.

"Linda," she said somewhat impatiently.

"Well Linda, I think we would both like to start out with menus."

Linda looked horrified as she glanced around the table, then suddenly dashed off towards the hostess at the front door. She came back quickly, ignoring a man at another table who politely raised a finger at her, and handed them each a folded cardboard menu with a little dark green twisted string running down the spine.

"I'm so sorry," Linda said. "There's a new hostess tonight, and to top it off two of the waiters called in sick."

Marsh smiled. "Don't worry about us, we're having a good time," he turned to Lebida, "Right?"

Lebida smiled at the waitress. "Absolutely."

"Tell you what Linda, give us a few minutes, and if we need another drink I can run over to the bar to get it."

"Oh thank you for understanding," she said and rushed off to another table.

"Is that how you got to be so successful?" Lebida asked after a moment.

"What?"

"By taking control of a situation, and making it right."

"I was just trying to be friendly, and help. No sense unloading on the poor waitress." There was a brief silence before Marsh continued. "Tell me how you managed to find those articles so fast. Will and I were amazed."

"Has he seen them?"

"Yes, and he was very impressed. There is something else, but first tell me how you did it."

Lebida started at the beginning, enjoying the attention as she related each search, the bad results and the final newspaper clue that led her to the list of the largest publications.

"So you really didn't search everywhere?"

"At first I did, but unsuccessfully. Once I knew what I was looking for the only real searches were inside the newspapers archives, so if there was a robbery in that area we would find it. Otherwise we wouldn't."

"And how many cities did you skip?"

"I don't know Marsh," she said, and again pushed a strand of hair back. "I was kind of working off of two lists, the biggest fifty metro areas and the twenty-five largest newspaper publications. I kind of bounced back and forth, but I probably got the top half by population."

"And you found eight, right? Nine including Denver?"

"I guess so. What are you going to do with them anyway?"

Marsh told her the details of the airline records.

"They let you access that information?"

"Not me, the police." He looked at her for a moment, and decided on his approach. "How good are you at database work Lebida?"

She held her hands up. "Not me – I'm strictly a front-end girl - just interfaces."

"OK, then who in the company can I get to crunch the data?"

Lebida thought for a moment. "I presume you just want to brute force this, no fancy reports and no applications. A one time shot?"

"Right,"

"Chun Lee, then. He could do it quickly. He's our DBA on the Oracle side."

"Great, then I need one more favor from you, if I may ask?"

Lebida beamed at him. "Sure Marsh, I'd be glad to help."

"Well Will is coming to the office tomorrow morning to deliver the data. I'm going to be out of the office so if you could meet him?"

"No problem."

"Then get Chun to start on the extract. I'll clear everything with Joe on the project side. I want you to supervise it, and let me know immediately when you come up with something."

She looked pleased. "What are we looking for Marsh?"

He looked at her seriously for a moment.

"Names, Lebida. Take each of the cities, and run a check on anyone who flew in and out the same day for each of the robberies. It doesn't matter where they came from, or where they flew out to. Then run them against each other. We are trying to see if we can get a name for the thief."

Lebida looked at him for a moment, then sat up very straight. "So to summarize, for each of the target cities you want to check all reservation records that match by date, then pull out pairs by passenger name, make sure that flight destination IATA in the set is chronologically before flight origin IATA, bunch those up by each of the eight target cities, cross-reference them and come up with a name that has multiple occurrences, right?"

Marsh looked at her, impressed. "Jesus, is that what I said? What's an IATA?"

Lebida smiled. "It's the transportation industry code for the airport, like DIA. I used to work at Fed-Ex in Colorado Springs. I did the front-end for the track and trace system. We ran queries like this all the time."

Suddenly Marsh felt the data was in very good hands. "I think you get the picture."

Lebida pushed at her hair again, and looked away. "I guess I do."

Fred drove prudently back from The Hole toward his place, the windshield wipers marking time slowly against the increasing rain. There was a small Chinese place that he frequented about a mile from his condo and he made his way there, his thoughts consumed by Susan.

He wondered what she would say when he showed her all of his day-trading activities. He told her last Saturday at breakfast about his money, but couldn't tell how she reacted to the revelation. He had never shared so much about his life with anyone, not even his family. He so much wanted for her to be pleased, and impressed, by how well he had done. The money he thought didn't mean as much to him anymore. He just wanted her to be happy.

He pulled into the strip center and parked directly in front of the restaurant. He opened the door, a small bell hanging in the frame tinkling as he walked in. The place was less than half full and he walked to the back and the small counter, nodding politely at the old Asian woman who as perched behind the register.

"Evening sir," the lady said with a thick accent. "You take out?"

Fred knew what to order. "Chicken lo-mein, beef and broccoli, fried rice and some hot and sour soup."

"You sit," she said and pointed to a booth.

Fred complied, slid onto the seat and fumbled idly with a paper place mat describing Chinese astrology. He looked up the year of his birth, informed he was a rat. Better than a sheep he thought to himself.

He had one last decision to make, regarding the plan, and he had struggled with it for two days. He always flew into Dallas first, and checked into the Adolphus in the morning. But that was when he had more time, and on this trip he had to squeeze a lot into a couple of days. And he was still concerned about flying around with his new equipment; a random baggage scan would certainly cause a problem. Probabilities he thought.

He assumed that Marsh and the detective would be working furiously to check out the airline reservations, and hoped they would get some results. He wasn't counting on it though, the plan didn't depend on it, but it would help if they came up with a name.

An oriental busboy brought him a glass of water and he nodded and took a sip. Suddenly it all became clear, and he wondered why he hadn't thought about it sooner. He would fly into Kansas City first, under his own name. No one would be searching for him anyway. He would spend the day, then catch a flight to Dallas and check into the Adolphus in the afternoon, like most business travelers did. John would get a hotel and a car in Kansas City, and he could leave the gun and the bomb there overnight. It was so simple and he wondered why he hadn't come up with the idea sooner. Then it dawned on him. He was concerned about protecting John's identity, something that was no longer necessary. It would work.

The woman waved at him and pointed to the large brown paper bag on the counter. He nodded and got up to pay for dinner, and suddenly felt much better about everything. He hummed to himself as he left the restaurant and drove home, only a small concern about what Susan wanted to discuss spoiling his otherwise perfect mood.

Fred's condo was in a three-story brick building which until a few years ago had been simple apartments. From the outside it looked plain, but inside it was luxurious, every two of the small units converted into one larger residence. He parked his car in the rebuilt garage and walked across the back yard to the rear entrance of the building. The detached parking was the only thing he didn't like about the place, and every winter he vowed to move into a new place. He hated not being able to park inside his own building.

He walked down the hall, the briefcase in one hand, the Chinese in the other until he reached the door. Inside his place was tastefully furnished but not extravagant. The developers had installed the hardwood floors and he had left them alone, even though he preferred carpeting. He set the food on the coffee table and walked down the hall to one of the bedrooms, which he had converted, into an office. The similarity to Marsh's place struck him for the first time, and he smiled as he opened the closet doors and set the briefcase inside.

Quickly he stripped off Stuart's work clothes and pulled on a pair of nicely creased tan Dockers that hung in the closet then chose a blue striped Polo dress shirt to go with it. He was slipping a belt through the loops on his pants and walking back to the kitchen when he heard a soft knock on the door. His heart jumped, and he rushed over to the door and opened it. Susan looked wet and cold.

"Jesus, what happened to you?" he said, standing aside as she stepped through the door. She was silent as he helped her off with her light jacket, which he shook a little and then hung over the back of a chair at the dining room table. He ignored the droplets that spattered onto the wooden floor.

"I was walking, and thinking."

"In the rain?"

"Around the lakes. You know how much I love it there."

"Do you want some dry clothes? You look like you are freezing," he said and started to walk toward the hall.

She grabbed his arm and stopped him. "No, I want to talk. Now, when everything is fresh in my mind."

He looked at her. Her hair was matted down on her head and over her shoulders, which were damp where the rain had leaked in under her jacket. He felt a stab of anxiety, but took her hand and led her to the couch. They sat down and she was silent for a moment. He waited, and he felt his heart throb.

"What's the matter Susan?"

"I have to tell you something. I didn't want to, but I can't live with it any longer. It's tearing me apart."

"Whatever it is, I'm sure it's OK," he said.

She sat quietly, looking at the floor. Her lower lip trembled before she began talking. "Do you remember Will?"

He was surprised. "Of course, the good detective. What about him?"

"Well, after you left, he came by Marsh's place. He wanted to talk with Marsh and Sara about the accident."

"And?"

She looked at him, her eyes wide and scared. "He had a picture Fred. A picture made by the police sketch artist of the thief. It didn't look like you..." she clenched her fists in her lap, and struggled to speak.

"I wouldn't think so."

"But there was something. A birthmark Will hadn't told anyone about." She reached up and touched his neck. "Like this."

He looked at her, a little stunned, then he smiled. "Go on."

She told him everything, blurting it out and crying. He tried to reach out to her while she talked, but she leaned back away from him, her face ashen. She told him how furious she was, then about the old woman, and how scared she had been.

Fred didn't say anything, but kept smiling, his eyes locked on hers. "And what did you find out about Dallas?"

She was sobbing as she talked her voice clutching. "They checked you out Fred. They called the Adolphus and talked to everyone."

"Good."

"What?"

He reached over again and stroked her shoulder. "Well I would think they would have to. Will seemed like a conscientious detective to me."

She stared at him, but couldn't believe him. "But, but aren't you angry?"

He laughed. "Angry at what? That I have a birthmark? That Will was doing what good cops do?"

"But we all suspected you. I mean no one wanted to but…"

"Mmm… if I had seen the sketch I might have suspected myself."

"But…"

"Well I assume that Drake told you I was in Dallas Monday."

"Drake?"

"Drake the manager, and whoever else they talked to. They seem to all know me. I practically live there you know."

She blinked twice, pushing the tears from her eyes. "Yes, of course they did. We were all so relieved. Even Will was happy it wasn't you. I told you we all went out and celebrated."

"So what's the big deal?" he asked quietly, then reached out and pulled her towards him. This time she didn't resist.

"I felt so guilty Fred, about suspecting you, for not telling you. It was killing me." She sobbed into his shoulder.

"So that's why you have been so distant since you came back. Why didn't you just tell me?"

"Marsh and I talked about it," she said, and lifted her head to look at him. "We all felt so ashamed. I thought I could just forget about it."

Fred smiled at her and stroked her cheek lightly with his fingers. God I love it when a plan comes together he said to himself.

"And how do you feel now?"

"So you're not mad?"

"Susan, the only thing I am disappointed about is that you didn't tell me sooner. It's a coincidence that's all. If I was in Will's shoes I would have done the same thing. It must have been quite a shock to everyone."

She laughed through her tears. "Oh God, you should have seen us. I don't ever want to have go through something like that again."

"I should hope not. I wouldn't want to either," he said. "It's OK, everything works out for the best."

She looked at him, a wave of relief washing over her face

"I'm so sorry babe."

"Don't be. I'm not. Everything is going to be fine now. We're together and I have a lot to show you."

She leaned hard into him, and wrapped her arms around him. "Not yet," she said.

"Not yet?"

"I need to get cleaned up," she said and wiped her streaked face with the back of her hand. "And I'm starved. You said something about pigging-out?"

"Now that's a little better. I'll get the food."

"And I'll change," she said, got off the couch and walked down the hall.

He was arranging the food on the coffee table in front of the couch when she came back, clad only in one of his dress shirts, her slim bare legs sweeping across the floor. Her hair was dry and bounced around her shoulders. He smiled at her, and thought how gorgeous she was.

"Now how are we supposed to talk when you are dressed like that?"

"Just control yourself," she said, and pulled the shirt tails down over her thighs. "First we eat, then we talk. Then if you have been a good boy you might get lucky."

She sat down on the couch and looked at the food. "God I'm starved. I don't think I've eaten much since I got back."

He understood and reached over for her, pulled her close and kissed her. She kissed him back, hard, her hands in his hair and over his back. Then she pushed him away.

"Stop it. Don't try to distract me."

He pulled the table closer to the couch, almost against their legs. She dumped food from both containers onto her plate. He watched her, amazed. He was glad to have her back.

"OK, first things first. He pulled a silver key from his pocket and set it on the table.

"What's that?" she said in between mouthfuls.

"It's a key, to this place."

She smiled. "If you think this means I'm going to be here waiting for you naked every night you are mistaken mister."

"Mmm... naked. Hadn't thought about that."

"Well don't get your hopes up. I'm keeping my place you know."

He picked up a bowl of soup and sipped at it, not using a spoon. "Of course. We can worry about that later. I just wanted you to have one, that's all."

She nodded and kept eating.

He didn't know how to begin. "I told you before, Susan. About my money."

She smiled. "Yes, I know you are rich. Do you think I am sleeping with you for your money?"

"I hope not. But I wanted to show you everything."

She ate while he talked about trading, about his accounts, about the Caymans. She asked a lot of questions, and he was pleasantly surprised. She knew more than he realized and it pleased him. The food was long gone before they stopped.

"You seem surprised," she finally said. "Like I wouldn't understand all this."

"I didn't know. I thought I had been keeping it all to myself."

"I'm no dummy. I don't know if I could do what you do, but I understand the concept. Buy low, sell high. Or sell hi and buy low. How hard is that?" She snuggled in next to him.

"Well when you put it that way, it does seem pretty easy doesn't it?"

She unbuttoned his shirt, her hands playing with his chest. He leaned back and watched her, then pulled her face up and kissed her again. She responded instantly and he could feel her hunger as she climbed on top of him, grinding against his body.

"Wait."

She looked at him, surprised. "Wait? What's the matter?"

"There's one more thing," he said and pulled her up off the couch.

He led her down the hall. She trailed behind him and he held her hand. They stepped into the office and he turned on the light. She let out a gasp of surprise as she looked around the room.

"It's like a damn command center," she said, and tried to comprehend the computer setup. "What the hell do you do with all this stuff."

"I thought you understood?"

"The concept, but not the execution."

She walked over to one of the computers and ran her hand over the top of the monitor.

"I guess I get a little carried away with technology," he said, almost proud.

"Jeez, a boy and his toys. You're not going to give me a computer lesson are you?"

He sat down beside her and moved the mouse a little. The screen saver flicked off and he quickly clicked on an icon on the screen. She watched as the program started.

"I picked this up two days ago," he said as the screen changed. It was an automated will program.

She looked at him, stunned. "What are you doing?" she said, then remembered the conversation at the sidewalk café. "I wasn't serious about that."

"Maybe not, but you were right. I thought about it a lot, and realized that I should have a will. Wouldn't want the government to get all my hard earned money."

She stepped back a little. "You're making me nervous."

A small window popped onto the screen, asking for a password. He typed in slowly, asterisks appearing in the blank field.

"My birthday. I always use it," he said. "Sometimes backwards though. You can't believe how many passwords I have to keep track of."

She watched, disbelieving as he maneuvered through a few pull down menus. Finally a new image filled the screen, the words 'Last Will and Testament' in bold at the top.

"This is it. I left you everything," he said and looked up at her. He clicked on the print icon and the laser printer started to whir. "Do you want to see it?"

She grabbed his hand and pulled him up. Her heart pounded in her chest. She couldn't believe he was showing her this. All that money, she thought, then pushed it away. She didn't need the money she told herself, but it excited her. She pulled him close and moved against him seductively.

"Let's go," she said, face close to his ear. "You've been a good boy."

"You mean I'm going to get lucky?"

"Very," she said and led him away.

Chapter Twenty-Five

As planned, Fred caught the nine-fifteen flight to Kansas City. The plane ascended through the clouds, and for a moment everything outside the window turned gray-white, like being on the inside of a Ping-Pong ball he mused. He found his eyes closing, and didn't fight it. He hadn't gotten much sleep last night, thanks to Susan. She had been wildly passionate in bed, almost insatiable. He wondered about his growing feelings of love for her, and how he now seemed ready to give up everything to make her happy. He knew the revelation of the will had surprised her, as much as it had surprised him that he had made it. In the past he had always been so independent, calculating and intellectually driven to decisions. Now he would get rid of everyone for her, John, Richard, Stuart, all of them. Once Friday was over he would never see any of them again.

He heard the flight attendant speaking softly to the passenger next to him about breakfast, and he opened his eyes and turned his head toward the woman, but declined the service with a brief wave. He'd eaten early that morning with Susan and at one point he thought he might miss his flight. She lingered after they got up, watched him pack, and chattered happily about her week. She now seemed anxious to dive back into her job, which was good. He needed her to be busy for the next few days.

When she finally left he retrieved the case from his contact, opened it on the bed and examined the contents. The gun was a nine-millimeter automatic. He pulled the clip and wrapped both pieces in separate hand towels. The bomb had fascinated him even more. It was about the size of a standard business envelope, only about two inches thick. He held it in his hands and turned it over, surprised at how light it was. Unlike in the movies there was no flashing LCDs or circuitry visible, just a plain green exterior with a recessed red button, a small unlit light, and the word 'ARM' underneath. A phone number was handwritten on a torn piece of paper and taped to the surface. No directions he thought, and remembered the conversation in the bar. The objects were now snugly tucked in his garment bag in the belly of the plane somewhere. He had also removed the plastic bag from the makeup store from his safe, thinking it a good omen that he only had two wigs and moustaches left. Almost late he had tossed the sack into the garbage in the bathroom as he rushed to complete his preparations.

The plane banked a little and he tried to concentrate, and fought off the urge to sleep. When John got off the plane he would rent a car, then find a quiet hotel to check into. He wondered how close Marsh was to finding out the name, a brief twinge of sadness as he thought about sacrificing his friend. John had been good to work with he thought; it was too bad he would be gone soon. He drifted off to sleep, not giving a second thought to the dichotomy of referring to John as his friend and himself.

He awoke with a start as the flight touched down with a heavier than usual bounce, the tires screeching in protest somewhere underneath him. He ignored the activity inside the cabin, and looked out the window as the plane taxied slowly across the tarmac, then settled up to the gate. The clouds that covered Minnesota were gone, and it was sunny and bright outside. The seatbelt sign flashed off with a single ding and he reached down and pulled his case from under the seat, and waited for his turn to disembark.

"It's all yours John," he said.

Several passengers waiting to get off turned and looked at him, but John just smiled, ready.

Will arrived at the office early that morning, anxious to get the information from the airlines, though he knew that his presence wouldn't get it there any faster. It was now just past nine, and he had been waiting to see his boss for over an hour. He could see the Captain through the windows of his office, talking, or shouting on the phone. He walked over to the window and peered in between the Venetian blinds. The Captain looked up and waved him in.

"Jesus what is it Will," the Captain said, voice terse.

"The grocery store robbery."

The Captain glared at him; his red hair looked like it would singe the top of his head. The knot in his tie was pulled down over the open collar of his white shirt. "Not another dead end I hope? You told me Saturday that you had a lead on the suspect. So much for that."

"Well we thought we did, but it didn't pan out. I tried to reach you yesterday with an update but I couldn't find you."

"Fucking Mayor's office," he said, not explaining further.

"I have some information coming, from the airlines. Reservation records for all the cities that have had similar thefts over the last year."

"This is news? You told me Monday that you tracked down these occurrences. And what has changed?"

"The records are coming today. I wanted to let you know that I'm turning them over to the Hawkins guy. He is going to process them somehow to try and come up with a name."

"Hmm," the Captain mumbled, but at least looked interested. "Isn't this something our department can handle? I'm not sure I want confidential information in the hands of civilians."

Will pressed on. "Marsh, Mr. Hawkins, is putting his computer people on it. I think we can get the results faster. Maybe today."

"Then what?"

"Then I need permission to contact the airlines and have them notify us of any air traffic by an individual with the name or names we come up with." He paused for a moment. "Also, we need to do a country-wide search for the individual."

The Captain's eyebrows raised at the statement. "Jesus H. Christ Will, do you know what that takes? How much it costs? To say nothing about invasion of privacy."

"Yes sir I understand the implications."

Will's phone rang in his pocket and he pulled it out and glanced at the number. "It's here."

The Captain looked at him but Will couldn't tell what he was thinking.

"Whatever you find out, it better be fucking good."

Will took that as a dismissal and left quickly, closed the door behind him and took the elevator to the ground floor. He was excited at the prospects as he walked down the drab cement hallway to the mail office at the back of the building. He stepped up to the counter and waited for the uniformed man to notice him.

"I'm Carter," he said, unfamiliar with the routine. He didn't often get packages in the mail, and when he did they were usually delivered to his desk.

The man turned and smiled a little. "So you're the guy," the attendant said. "This must be important." He reached down behind the counter and pulled two Fed-Ex packages out and handed them to Will.

"Only two?" Will said, surprised and disappointed.

The cop looked at him. "How many did you expect?"

"Three. Are you sure there isn't one more?"

"That's it Detective, but the Post Office express deliveries are always late."

"Right," Will said and started to leave.

"Whatcha got in there anyway?" the man asked.

"A thief I hope," he said as he walked away. Two would have to do for now.

John checked into the LaQuinta, located just down Interstate 29 from the airport. He used his platinum Visa both at the rental car counter and the hotel, comfortable in the fact that even if they knew his name now, they wouldn't know where to start with it. The detective would notify the airlines of course, and that is what he wanted. But tracing a Visa card through the millions of transactions all over the country was a nearly impossible task. Of course maybe he was giving them more credit than was due. It didn't matter to his plans of course, but it would be a plus if they identified him in the next day or so.

The room was like a thousand other ones he had stayed in; two double beds, a dresser and a TV. The garment bag was open, and stretched out on the bed. He removed the canvas bag and looked at it. He had used the same bag on each of his appointments, and though he wasn't really superstitious, it comforted him a little. He carefully tucked the three towels, with the gun, the clip and the bomb inside and walked over to the closet, and placed them on the shelf. He zipped the bag back up and got ready to leave, then as an afterthought he turned the TV on, volume low, and messed up the bed a little. The 'Do Not Disturb' sign snapped at the door as he grabbed the garment bag and walked out.

He left through the back door to avoid the desk clerk, and walked to the car. It was hot and muggy, and he was sweating when he put the bag into the trunk with his computer. He got in the car and started it, turned the air conditioner on full and drove from the hotel, back on I29 heading south. It was early afternoon, and he wanted to get out of Kansas City in a few hours.

The office and industrial flavor of the area gave way to a more residential look as he drove, and after a few miles he randomly chose an exit and headed west. He had picked two communities from a map on the web, Weatherby Lake and Platte Woods, both suburbs of the Kansas side of Kansas City. He was a little concerned about the limited amount of time he had allotted to pick a target, usually spending a couple of days scouting out a location for his appointments. The busy street was filled with businesses and small office buildings and he proceeded slowly, stoplights and busy intersections impeding his progress every few blocks.

He passed a large mall on his right and his hopes lifted for a moment. This was the type of neighborhood he wanted. The traffic was heavy, late afternoon crowds, he thought as he drove on, then spotted to his left what he had been searching for. He changed lanes carefully and pulled to a stop, then waited for the green arrow to allow him to turn across the street. He looked over the strip center, and was satisfied with what he saw. The grocery store, a ValuMart he noticed, was set in the middle of the shopping center with smaller stores on either side. It wasn't a huge store but big enough for what he needed. The lot was over half full, a good sign of the high activity.

He parked well away from the grocery store, the noon sun baked down on him as he surveyed the location. There was nothing remarkable about the location; it was like a dozen others he had been in. He walked across the lot and looked at the businesses on either side, then smiled as he noticed a Radio Shack two stores down from the supermarket.

It was cool in the electronics store, and devoid of customers. He walked around inside for a moment, glanced at the telephones, then the cables and computer accessories. There was an older man behind the counter, who was trying to fix the printer attached to the cash register, but John ignored him, and conjured up a story. He spotted the games section and walked over to it, picked up a Gameboy and looked it over, then waited. After a moment the man noticed him and walked over.

"Can I help you sir?" the man said.

He had a white shirt and black pants on, his hair thin and gray. His nametag said 'David - One Year of Quality Service'. John smiled.

"Yes David," he said, holding up the device. "This is what the kids are playing with these days isn't it?"

"One of our best selling models," David replied. "Everybody has one."

John wondered briefly if the man had ever held one in his hands, let alone turned one on. "My son's birthday. It's all he talks about."

"It's on special," David replied, hopeful for a sale.

"Great, but I can't get it today. My son is outside and I want to make sure I surprise him."

David looked disappointed.

"I'll be back in tomorrow though," he said, "You'll be here won't you?"

"Of course sir. Do you want me to hold it for you?"

John looked down at the display. "You seem to have plenty, and I need to talk to my daughter - to make sure I get the right one."

"Sure, no problem."

"David," John said, "I need a favor. Do you have a back door? I don't want my son to see me coming out of the store."

If David was surprised he didn't show it. He pointed past the counter and around the corner. "Sure, right there. Just close the door tightly. Air conditioning you know."

John started off, then turned back. "See you tomorrow," he said.

He headed out the back and into the alley, and turned to memorize the exit. He laughed to himself as he read the store name in red letters painted on the door, then walked quickly to his left and looked around. It wasn't really an alley; there was an open space behind the shopping center that was already being dug up to be developed. A chain link fence separated the store backs from the dusty field. He had to walk around a semi-trailer that backed into a large opening; the metal door rolled up to allow the contents to be unloaded. There was a back door to the grocery store, unmarked this time and he walked over to it. The silver doorknob was hot in his hands as he grasped it, and locked. He looked around and moved toward the far end of the center, and walked all the way to the front and the parking lots.

"So far so good," he said to the grocery store wall.

The front of the grocery store protruded onto the sidewalk, with automatic glass doors on either end. Inside the checkout counters were to the left, about ten of them and they were busy. The store was older, with low ceilings and harsh fluorescent lights. It was more crowded than he hoped for, but that couldn't be helped at this point. He picked an aisle at random, and walked down it to the back, dismayed when he got there. To the far left was the dairy section, then a small bakery. The deli and meat section covered the rest of the back of the store. Not good he said to himself as he scanned up and down, and looked for a hallway that would lead to the back door. He found it after a moment, somewhat hidden next to a display of cakes. The sign above it indicated the restrooms and he walked over and looked down the hall. Where's the office he asked himself.

He debated about looking for a different location as he started back across the store, past four aisles until he reached the far side. The customer service counter was centered there, and he walked up to it and stood behind an old woman who was returning a bunch of bruised bananas. He took the opportunity to look around, and noticed another clerk who emerged from a metal door behind the counter, carrying a tray for a cash register. The office was set back into the wall, but the counter was open on either end. The old woman walked away muttering and he stepped up and pulled a hundred dollar bill from his pocket.

"Can you change this for me please?" he said to the young clerk.

"Of course," she said, and took the bill and moved to the back register.

An older male employee walked behind the counter and John watched him carefully. He pulled a key hung from an extendible cable on his belt, and stretched it toward the lock, then inserted it and opened the door. John couldn't see inside, but could imagine what was in there. The clerk spoke to him again and he looked back at her.

"How did you want that sir?"

"Uh, twenties is fine," John said, eyes still locked on the door behind her.

She nodded and slipped the hundred underneath the register tray and counted out five twenties for him.

"Thanks a lot."

"You're very welcome sir."

He pocketed the bills and walked back to the front of the store. It wasn't ideal, but it would work he thought. He was concerned about getting into the office in plain view of everyone, then having to run through the store to get out the back. He planned on causing a commotion, but wondered if this was too much. Once again he thought about a different site, but disregarded it immediately. He could be looking all day he thought and he didn't have the time. This would have to do.

The sun was still beating down as he left the store and returned to his car. He was already rehearsing tomorrow as he drove away, and headed for the airport. It wasn't a long drive, just as he wanted, and it only took about thirty minutes to find the short term parking lot and head for the terminal. He'd catch whatever the next flight was to Dallas.

Lebida dropped everything to work on the project. The detective arrived at the office about ten, and delivered the Fed-Ex envelopes. He hadn't opened them yet and she was surprised. She felt a considerable amount of responsibility after Marsh had put her in charge, so she opened them in front of Will, and made sure he was aware of the contents. The first one was from American, the only item inside the cardboard envelope was a DAT tape with no information to describe the contents. The other package contained a disk for a zip-drive from United, again with no documentation.

The Detective had made no attempt to leave so she spoke to him politely. "This is going to take a while. I'll call you when we get some results."

He agreed, but left disappointed. Chun Lee was sitting in his cubicle when she walked over, face close to the terminal. She handed him the tape and the disk.

"Format?" he asked.

"I don't know, just dump it off and we'll take a look at it. I'll tell you what to do from there."

"Can't do here," he said, took the material and walked away.

She pulled a chair over from an empty cube next door and sat down to wait. She was thumbing through an HTML manual absently when he came back about ten minutes later. He sat down at the keyboard and fired up an editor. The screen filled with characters. She moved closer, and pushed him aside as she stared at the screen. It was in ASCII she determined, comma separated fields. It took a while but she finally figured out the contents. It was sorted by flight number, with origin and destination IATA's and times. The last entry in each record appeared to be a passenger name. Arriving flights were at the front of the file, departing ones last.

"Which file is this?" she asked Chun.

"File one, DAT tape," he replied.

American she thought, not that it made any difference.

"Show me the other one."

He typed a few keystrokes and the screen refreshed. It was similar, but not exactly like the other one. The data was the same but in a different order.

"OK, we need a temp database, one table." She stood up and leaned over to a white board on the wall of the cubicle, picked up a marker and wrote the names of the fields for him. "Load it like this, all TEXT fields, got it? Call me when you are done."

He nodded and she left him to get to work.

Three hours later she went back, impatient.

"What's taking so long Chun?"

"Very busy," he said. "Many database problems."

"When will you get it loaded?" she asked.

"It's loaded now."

"Why didn't you call me then?" she shouted at him.

"Many other database problems," he said, and shrugged.

She sighed, and wished she knew enough about the query language to do this herself. "OK, let's get started. Can you construct a query that shows if the same name comes up in each of the origin IATAs?"

"Which field?"

She pointed to the name on the board.

"Values?"

"Shit, I don't know them off the top of my head. Bring up the files again. I'll be right back."

She walked back to her cubicle and got the list of cities from her notes. When she got back she grabbed a pad of paper from his desk and scribbled 'DIA' at the top. She knew that one. She pushed him aside again and took over the keyboard, and scrolled through the data. 'ORD' she wrote again, recognizing Chicago. It took a few minutes to get all off them, and she realized that she had nine entries, not eight. Of course she thought after a moment, Reagan and Dulles, and silently thanked the airlines for their foresight.

"Use all of these except Reagan," she told him, and pointed to the pad.

It took him a moment to type in the query statement. He submitted it with no results.

"Damn," she said. OK, we don't have every airline here, she thought. She wished she traveled enough to know off the top of her head which airlines were the most popular in which city.

"OK, try it again but leave out Sacramento and San Jose," she said, tossing out the west coast cities.

The query returned nothing.

She sighed, "OK, now put those back in, but leave out Boston, Dulles, Philadelphia, Orlando and St. Louis."

He changed the query and submitted it again. She froze as she looked at the screen. Her heart raced.

"JOHN ANDERSON" the screen displayed.

"Put Boston back in," she said, and tried to keep her voice calm.

"JOHN ANDERSON"

"Now Philadelphia."

"JOHN ANDERSON"

"St. Louis."

The screen remained blank.

"OK, take out St. Louis and put in Orlando," she urged.

"JOHN ANDERSON"

She sat back, amazed. It was so quick and easy she thought. She didn't have all the cities, but that could be because she also didn't have all the airlines. She was totally pumped.

"OK, one more query, please Chun."

"Very busy."

She ignored the remark. "Show me, and print out all the records for John Anderson."

She watched as the results filled the screen and scrolled many more records than she was expecting. Of course she said to herself, a common name.

"Sorry, all records for Anderson arriving and leaving on the same day for each of the IATA's," she added quickly.

The result list shrunk to sixteen flights. "Bingo. Thanks Chun, nice work," she said and rushed away to call Marsh.

Marsh couldn't leave the conference when his cell phone vibrated in his coat pocket. He was meeting with senior executives from a local telecommunications firm to lay the groundwork for future business opportunities. The first part of the meeting had gone slowly, the executives leery of his company's small size. Lunch had been more of a social affair than a business meeting. In the afternoon he had met with three different departments, giving the same presentation over and over again. He was exhausted.

He listened to his voicemail from the parking lot of the glass office building, and skipped through a few messages until he got to Lebida's.

"Marsh, its Lebida. I've got it. I've found a name. Call me as soon as you can."

He jumped into the car and drove off quickly. He wasn't far, just on the southern outskirts of Denver where development had spilled over from the Tech Center. He drove quickly while he dialed the Mary's direct line.

"Hey Marsh, how did it go?"

"Fine," he said with little enthusiasm. "But right now I need to talk to Lebida."

"You got it boss."

He waited for a moment, trying to concentrate on the road. The afternoon traffic was terrible, as usual, and he took the back way, avoiding the mess on I25.

"Marsh?" Lebida said after a moment.

"Hey, I got your message. What…"

She interrupted him, excited. "I found it Marsh, I got a name. I ran through all the records and got matches for eight cities. I can't believe how easy it was."

"Whoa, slow down," he said, and tried to figure out what to do. "OK, get Will on the phone and see if he can meet us at the office. You can tell me everything when I get there." He pulled to a stop and waited for a light to change. "I should be there in fifteen minutes."

"Super," she said. "I'll see you then. This is good news right?"

"Very good, and thanks."

Marsh hung up the phone and called Sara. "Sara, it's me. Can you get down to my office? Where are you anyway?"

"I'm downtown Marsh, what's wrong?"

"Nothing is wrong. Lebida ran the records, we got a name."

"Who is it?" she asked quickly. "It's not…"

Marsh understood the question. "Shit I didn't ask. I assume not though."

"OK, it's going to take me a while to get there though, traffic is the pits coming from downtown."

"Well get there as soon as you can. And what about this weekend? Can you get away early Friday?"

"About noon I think. This is great news. We can celebrate."

"All weekend," he said. "Bye."

It seemed to take forever to get back to the office.

Marsh parked the car and ran across the lot, skipped the sidewalk and cut across the grass. He punched the up button on the elevator eight times while he waited, and drubbed his fingers on the granite wall. Finally the door opened and he jumped in, then paced inside the car until it stopped on his floor. He ran down the hall and pushed open the oak office door and spotted Will sitting on the couch in the reception area.

"Will, great, you're here."

Will got up and shook his hand. "Of course Marsh, Lebida called me. Good news already I hope."

"Let's go into my office."

They walked first to Mary's cubicle. She was busy on the phone, but Marsh interrupted anyway.

"Mary, get Lebida for me... in there" he said, and gestured toward his office with a nod of his head.

"Right," she said as if expecting the intrusion.

"Oh, and when Sara McGloughin gets here, show her in please."

Will and Marsh stepped into the office. Will looked around and admired the room. "Nicer than my office."

"Its just work Will."

Lebida came in after them, carried a single sheet of paper and looked proud.

"Give us the details please Lebida," Marsh said, unable to wait any longer.

She handed Marsh the paper and let him peruse at it for a moment. Marsh looked it over carefully and handed it to Will.

"John Anderson?" Marsh asked Lebida.

"Yup, in eight of the nine cities including Denver. We only had records from American and United so it's not complete. But I think it tells the story."

"Common name," Will said and handed the paper back to Marsh. "Probably an alias."

"Is that a problem?" Marsh asked.

"Don't know, but it's a start. There will be an ID trail at least. I'll see what the airlines can do about it."

"How long will that take?"

"I don't know Marsh, but I'll talk with the liaison at United and American and see what they suggest. They must have done this before."

Will looked up as Sara knocked on the open door to the office.

"Am I interrupting?" she asked.

Marsh walked quickly across the room and hugged her. Lebida's smile dipped.

"John Anderson," he said, full of excitement. "Eight times that match cities that we are looking for."

"Oh my God," Sara exclaimed. "Great work Lebida, and so soon!"

The smile returned to Lebida's face. "It wasn't hard once we had the data."

Marsh looked at her. "I can't thank you enough Lebida, really."

"I need to get back Marsh," Will said. "I've got work to do."

"Me too," Lebida said, but hoped they would ask her to stay. They didn't say anything about it.

Will walked to the door, and Lebida reluctantly followed behind him. She wanted to stay and talk longer, but got the feeling that her job was done. Marsh was lost in conversation with Sara as she left the office. She hoped Marsh would remember what a good job she had done, she thought as she walked down the hall. She was already back in her cubicle when she realized she had forgotten to point out something in the data they might have missed. There was a pattern in the flights, and she hoped Marsh and Will had seen it. For the first few trips by date, John Anderson had started and ended up in Minneapolis. Then for some reason he had switched to Dallas for the rest. Probably not important, she thought, and went back to work.

Fred checked into the Adolphus later than expected, a combination of a delayed flight and the Dallas rush hour traffic. He was tired when he finally got to his room, and just wanted to relax and call Susan. He unlocked the door and walked in, the familiar mini-suite cool from the air conditioner. He couldn't believe it was only a week ago Monday that his whole life had changed the trip to Denver triggering so many events. Good changes he thought, it's brought Susan and I so much closer together.

He ignored his belongings for a moment, sat on the couch and pulled his wallet out of his pocket. He found the claim check and called the bellman, relayed his room number and asked that his garment bag be delivered to his room. He turned the TV on, switched the channel to CNBC and sat back to wait. He was still watching ticker move ten minutes later when there was a knock on the door.

He got up and walked across the room and opened the door. The bellman had his black garment bag in hand, and he handed the young man the claim check and five dollars. The bellman thanked him and left quickly.

Fred carried the bag to the bed and opened it up, then pulled out the fake Glock he had left in one of the custom pockets. He would need to get rid of this he thought, now that he had the nine. He would dump it somewhere on the way to dinner. He crossed back to the couch, anxious to talk to Susan. It was six-thirty and she should be home by now. He dialed and hoped she was there, then relaxed when she answered. "Hey babe, how was your day?" he said when she answered.

"Intense, but good. It was nice to get back into the swing of things. I miss you though."

"I miss you too."

"How's Dallas?"

"Hot and muggy. I've got to stop coming here in the summer."

"Are you at the Adolphus? Jesus, I almost forgot. I just got off the phone with Marsh. You won't believe it."

Fred perked up. "Did he find something?"

"Apparently your little idea about the airline reservations hit pay dirt. They have a guy, or a name at least."

"It's not me is it?"

"Of course not silly. Don't remind me of that. It's some guy named John Anderson." Fred smiled. The timing was perfect.

"Sounds like a villain. Did they arrest him?"

"No, but Will is working on it."

"Marsh and Sara must be pleased. How are they anyway?"

"Wonderful. I can't believe Marsh is falling for her so fast."

"Don't you like her?"

"Oh no, I think she's great. It's just not like Marsh to get so tied up so quickly."

"She could tie me up."

"Any more remarks like that babe and I'll tie you up, then shoot you."

"Ouch. Point taken"

"They are going up to Crested Butte this weekend."

The remark caught Fred off guard and he had to think for a moment.

"You there?" Susan asked.

"Oh yeah, just thinking. Where's Crested Butte?"

"It's out west, about four hours across the mountains. It's a gorgeous drive. We should do it sometime."

"I'd love to. Where do you go?"

"Well you head west out of Denver on a highway, but I can't remember the number. You go about three hours and then up over the high mountains. In the winter you have to use Monarch Pass because of the snow. But in the summer you can use Cottonwood Pass, and it's spectacular. Tiny winding road running along sheer cliffs."

"Sounds dangerous to me," he said and imagined the scene. "Is it crowded?"

"What do you mean crowded? It's in the middle of nowhere."

"I just wondered if there would be a place by the side of the road where we could stop, and uh, picnic."

"Mmm... I see your point. Keep that thought," she said with a touch of lust in her voice, then hesitated for a moment. "Well better go. The girls from the office are taking me out tonight. Kind of a welcome back dinner."

"Have fun. I love you Susan."

"I love you too. When are you coming back?"

"Friday night, but I don't know when. I'll call you tomorrow OK?"

He hung up the phone and sat for a moment and considered the possibilities. This was better than he could hope for. He quickly unpacked his briefcase and got out his laptop, plugged the modem cable into the phone jack and booted the computer. Winding roads, sheer cliffs he thought. It was perfect. He fired up his connection to the web and brought up a map of Colorado. I love it when a plan comes together he thought.

Chapter Twenty-Six

Marsh woke up by himself Thursday morning, not quite sure if he was lonely or relieved. He stretched himself under the sheets, then put his right arm on top of the pillow, underneath his head and stared at the ceiling. It had been the most unbelievable ten days of his life he thought. It's not that he didn't want Sara in his bed anymore, but he needed at least a one day alone. His life had been an incredible roller coaster of emotions, first with his mother, then Susan and now Sara. For the last three years work and his company had consumed him. Now it seemed like he was the center point of activity, so many different lives revolving around his. He needed a vacation he chuckled to himself, and remembered that this was exactly where he started a week and a half ago.

He climbed out of bed and pulled on his workout clothes, brushed his teeth and walked slowly to his office, stretching. He needed a good workout. He turned the TV to channel 9. It was early, and the local news on before whatever national morning news program aired. The events that had transpired had caused him to change his preference in TV channels he thought, and he wondered what Sara was doing right now.

After a moment he mentally tuned out the news and increased the speed of the running machine, then selected a program that simulated a course with shallow hills. His feet pounded into the black belt with satisfying intensity, and his thoughts returned to Sara. He couldn't help thinking that their torrid relationship had been built on a shaky foundation - his intense emotional reaction to his mother's death, her desire for a story, and his need to find the thief. Risky, he thought, but that was life. But somehow he didn't see any need to worry about the future and where their relationship was going.

He ran for forty-five minutes. The sweat dripped off his face and his t-shirt was soaked when he finally shut down the machine. He walked back to the bathroom and stripped off his clothes, turning the shower on very hot. He was still breathing hard, but felt completely alive, better than he had felt for a long time. He had a long day at the office planned, to get things back to normal. Well not normal, he thought. His time away had shown him that the company could now manage quite well without his constant attention to every detail. Another plus of the whole deal he thought, and he now had bigger plans. He would concentrate more on strategic issues, maybe an expansion into other cities. He found himself excited to get to work, confident that he had set the wheels in motion on the hunt for the thief, and that Will would take things over from here.

Sara couldn't help wondering where her relationship with Marsh was going. She sat at her desk at the station, distracted for about the tenth time that morning with thoughts about him. A week ago she hadn't been interested in commitments to any man, and now she was more involved with one since her failed marriage. He had simply swept her off her feet she thought, totally blindsided.
"Christ you were in bed with him within twenty-four hours," she said out loud.
She smiled at the thought, and remembered how she had seduced him, and led him back to her place after dinner. It had been so easy. She knew he had been attracted to her, but then again so many men always were. Marsh seemed to need her and she wondered if she had exploited his vulnerability.
She picked up her coffee and sipped at it, the sudden thought that she had been using him for a story unnerving her. It couldn't be, she rationalized, there hadn't been any story at the time. She had been genuinely attracted to him, starting at lunch that day, and she tried to push away the feelings of guilt.
"Let's not ruin a good thing," she said out loud again, but wondered again where it would all lead.
No one noticed that she was talking to herself. The station room was almost empty that early in the morning and she forced herself back to work. Her desk was covered with printouts of news stories she had amassed, separated chronologically into piles that detailed the exploits of the thief by city. Her eyes shifted back to her monitor, the outline of the story displayed in the word processing window. She had the mechanics, but needed more psychological background she thought, her journalism training kicking in again. She caught herself.
"What I need is an ending."
She was talking to herself again.
She had made several attempts to write the story, each time thwarted

by not being able to get the right reader involvement angle. Is it a psychological profile of a serial thief - someone who coldly walks into grocery stores and makes off with someone else's money? Or is it a tragedy, the tale of a man who inadvertently shatters the lives of innocent people. She needed to know who the man was, why he was driven, and why he became a thief. It was in Will's hands now.

Her thoughts turned back to Marsh. He had told her he wanted her to work on the story, but she wasn't so sure. It was her job to write about this - it was what she did - her life. She hoped he understood. They could talk about it in Crested Butte, alone together, away from everyone else involved. She felt a twinge of excitement at the prospect of a weekend away.

"Can you step into my office please?"

The voice startled her, and she looked up to see her boss standing across the way, and he didn't look very happy.

"Good morning Howard." She had expected this.

He beckoned toward her, his palm upward, and curled his pointer finger slowly. She grabbed her cup and followed him down the hall to his office, and closed the door behind her as she watched him settle into his chair. She sat down, prepared.

"How's the story going?"

"And what story is that?" she replied and shot him her best smile.

"Cut the crap Sara, it's my job to know what's going on around here."

"It needs an ending."

He looked at her for a minute without saying anything. "It seems to me last week I instructed you to forget about this story."

She kept smiling. "I do recall that conversation, yes."

"And yet you persist?"

"Persist? I like that. But I think investigate is more apropos. Maybe even doggedly pursue."

"And what the hell is it you have been investigating?" he said, the tone in his voice drifted toward anger.

She knew she had him. "How about the story of a serial thief, eluding apprehension around the country, whose exploits end right here in Denver with a horrible family tragedy?"

He leaned back and took a breath, eyebrows raised. "That would be good, if true."

"Not only true Howard, but real-life goddamned news."

He pondered the idea some more. "OK, what can we air now?"
"Nothing."
"Nothing?"
She was ready for this. "Howard, I can give you facts on robberies all over the country. Chicago, DC, San Jose, all perpetrated by the same guy. But what good would that do? There is no resolution. No resolution, no story."
"Mmm... I see your point. But we could use what you have as a teaser."
"A teaser is only good if you follow it up quickly with the ending."
"And you need an ending."
"Right. Look, the police are getting closer. We have a name. They are tracing it. Give me some time on this."
"How much time?"
"Hell I don't know. It could be tomorrow for Christ's sake, or next month." She paused, then played her trump card. "Howard, no one else knows anything about this. It's exclusively ours. If it breaks it's a huge story. It will get played out all over the country. Big publicity for us in all the major markets."
He thought about it for a moment. "Get on it then."
"I'll do that," she replied and waltzed out of the office.

Will was completely frustrated again. He slammed down the phone, cut off again after being on hold for twenty-fucking minutes. He had spent more time with the phone in his ear the last few days than he had in the last month, and it pissed him off.

He had left Marsh's office yesterday elated, finally having something concrete to work with. But by the time he had fought the traffic and returned to his desk it was after hours in Chicago and Dallas, the liaison offices of United and American closed for the day. He had left voice messages of course, and pleaded his case on the urgency of the situation. He had come in early again, to compensate for the time difference, and hoped he would get a quick reply. He had squat.

The captain at least was pleased, well not disagreeable anyway. Will had called him from his car and related the information they had uncovered. The captain had given him the green-light to follow up with whatever means was necessary, and Will had sent email bulletins to every police department in the cities they had confirmation that the thief had visited. He hadn't received any replies yet, but he was hopeful.

He pressed the speaker button and hit redial, and tried United again. He leaned back in his chair, ready to wait through the God-awful elevator music he knew was coming.

"United Airlines Liaison office, Maria speaking," the voice echoed out of the speaker.

"Jesus Christ," he said, sat straight up and almost dropped the phone as he grabbed it from the cradle. "Maria, hi, don't hang up."

"Excuse me sir? Do you have the right number?"

"God I hope so," he said, then composed himself. "This is Detective Will Carter of the Denver Police Department."

"Yes Detective, how can we help you?"

"I'm not sure Maria, so let me explain the situation first. I need to trace a passenger. He is a suspect in a series of robberies around the country, and he has been using United, or American, to make his, getaways."

"Do you wish a list of reservation records sir?"

"No, you already provided us with his flight history, and thank you by the way. What we need to know is the next time he gets on a flight. Is that possible?"

"I'm not sure what you mean Detective, can you be more specific?"

Will thought for a moment. "Well if I give you a name, can't you stop the man when he checks in?"

"No sir, we can't do that."

"Why not? Can't you just put it in your computer somewhere?"

"Detective, we have millions of passengers flying with our airline every day. Without positive identification we can't possibly inconvenience our customers by detaining someone who happens to have the name you are looking for. It would not only be unethical, but a serious invasion of privacy."

"I understand," he said, getting the point. "What can you do then?"

"With the proper paperwork and authorization, we can notify you, confidentially of course, of reservations and movements of passengers within our system."

"Paperwork?"

"I can send you the form Detective."

"Isn't there someway we could do this a little quicker?"

"It can be emailed to us, but only by a senior officer of your department."

"Would a captain do? Or do I need the Mayor?"

"A captain would be sufficient detective. If you give me your email address I can send you the appropriate information, then have your department return it to me as soon as possible."

Will slowly dictated his address, having her repeat it back to make sure it was correct. "Is that all you need?"

"That's it."

"Thank you so much for your assistance Maria, you've been a great help here."

"My pleasure sir."

"Oh," he remembered, "how long will it take?"

"Assuming you get the form back to us immediately, only a few hours, late this afternoon probably. We do try and cooperate you know."

"I understand, and I appreciate that. How will I be notified?"

"In the form you specify a phone contact number. Day or night."

"Right, thank you so much ma'am."

"You are very welcome Detective, have a good day."

He hung up the phone and headed off quickly towards the Captain's office.

Fred packed carefully. It wasn't too hard, since the dangerous items had all been left in Kansas City. He was down to one garment bag, again his custom designed one. The other, bag, and the Glock, he had dropped into a dumpster last night, cutting through the alley on the way to dinner. He finished, looked around the room, grabbed the garment bag and his briefcase and headed downstairs to check out. He left the door open and the TV on.

He waited in line for a moment at the front desk, waved at a bellman who was standing close, and asked for a limo to the airport. When it was his turn he stepped up to the counter and smiled politely at the woman standing there.

"Checking out so soon Mr. Hawkins?" she asked.

He recognized her, but didn't remember her name until he looked at her nametag. "Yes Diane, short trip this time."

She smiled back and pulled up his record on the computer. "I hope everything was to your satisfaction during your stay with us," she said as she worked.

DECEPTION ON MARGIN

"Just fine, as usual."

The printer spit out his record, the paper quite short for a change. She tore off part of it, then handed it over for his review.

"I'm sure it's fine," he said, and barely glanced at it.

She filled in the totals on his credit card slip and he signed it quickly. She tore off his copy and stapled it to his other record. "Have a good day then sir, and thank you for staying with us."

He nodded and picked up his computer, turned and walked toward the revolving doors. The bellman met him, opened the door and pointed to the black Towncar.

"This one's yours sir."

Fred nodded and walked over to the car, but didn't tip the bellman. He opened the door and slid into the back, placing his bags on the seat beside him. He wanted as little contact as possible with anyone that day. The limo driver knew where they were going, and he didn't say anything to him.

Fred leaned back in his seat. This was the only flaw in his plan, at least the only one he could think of. He had debated about not checking out, setting up his computer to make calls, and performing the same routine as always when he left for his appointments. But this time was different - he wouldn't be coming back that night – or maybe not even at all. Besides, a cover shouldn't be necessary by then, the suspicion long since diverted elsewhere.

He tried to relax all the way to the airport, but couldn't stop reviewing the plan. There wasn't much he could do about anything now though, each component already in motion. He arrived at the airport without incident, checked in for the flight as John Anderson, and only wondered for a moment if they would be tracking him.

Susan was at her desk early, and raring to go. She was thankful that the dinner with her friends didn't turn into another celebration like it had in Denver. She hadn't told anyone about the thief. In fact, she left the details of her mother's death out of all the conversations. And for sure she didn't tell anyone about that horrible Saturday and the old woman at the homeless shelter. That was an incident that she never wanted to think about again.

But she did tell them about Fred, and their engagement. That had floored her friends. Where's the ring everyone had asked, and she had been a little embarrassed, that not so insignificant detail completely slipping her mind. She blamed it on the suddenness of the event, and everything else that had happened in Colorado. But now she was a little saddened. Men, she thought. She hoped she wouldn't have to remind him about it.

She was busy, but took a moment to look out the window and wondered what Fred was doing. It wasn't sunny, but the forecast for the weekend was good and she tried to plan something fun for them to do. Maybe a little shopping, and thought of the ring again. She wanted to call him on his cell phone and drop a few hints, but decided against it. He was busy she was sure, and didn't need the interruption. Besides, she wanted him to think about it on his own, maybe even surprise her if he could.

He would be home tomorrow night and everything would be better. She would wait for him at his apartment, maybe greet him naked at the door. That would get his attention. The idea intrigued her, but she decided against it. It turned her on more when he undressed her slowly.

"Stop it girl," she said to herself, "you'll get your panties in a knicker."

She went back to work and hoped the time would go by quickly.

The rental car was right where he left it in the Kansas City International airport short-term parking lot. He unlocked it and tossed his bags into the back seat. It was hot and muggy again, so he leaned in and started the car, letting the air conditioner run for a moment with the doors open. He stood quietly, sunglasses shading his eyes from the brightness and wondered what Susan was doing. He hoped she was happy.

It only took him twenty minutes to get to the LaQuinta, and he parked his car in the back again, then took his garment bag to the room. He opened the door with more than a little apprehension, and was immediately relieved when it looked exactly as he left it - bed unmade the TV on. He had plenty of time, in fact he wasn't on any schedule at all, but he was anxious to get the rest of the plan in motion. He knew that the detective would have contacted the airlines by now, but he wasn't sure how long it would take to set up whatever monitoring process they used. The sooner he got out of town the better.

He crossed to the closet, retrieved his canvas bag and spread the contents over the bed. He opened his garment bag, moved aside the single suit he had packed and carefully slid the bomb into one of the zippered pockets. He then unwrapped the gun and the clip, slipped the clip in the handle and snapped it tight. Just like in the movies he thought. He made sure the safety was on and placed the nine in the bottom of the canvas sack, then covered it with one of the towels. He then set one of the wigs and moustaches in the other towel and slid it into another of the pockets of his garment bag. The other wig and moustache he put in the sack on top of the towel.

One last thing he said to himself and looked around for a phone book, finding it at last in one of the dresser drawers under the TV. He quickly flipped through the yellow pages until he found the listings for taxis and memorized the number. He walked back to the bed, zipped up the garment bag and glanced around, double-checking everything. He grabbed both bags and left the room, left the door open and the TV on.

Ten minutes later he was calm as he drove the few miles down to the shopping center, humming softly to himself. In fact he was so relaxed he almost missed the exit and had to change lanes quickly to get off the freeway. It had been only twenty-four hours since he was there, but it seemed longer. He turned into the shopping center, the Westside Plaza he noted from the large white sign, through the same entrance he used the day before. He drove down past the first barrier and parked the car in the back of the lot where few cars were parked. He left the car running and kept the air on for a moment.

He reached over the seat and got his briefcase, straining as he lifted it over. He punched it open and slid his hand inside, then pulled out his cell phone. He dialed the number for the cab company and waited.

"Yellow Cab," the woman's voice answered after two rings.

"Yes, I need a cab please."

"Phone number," the woman said, almost demanding.

"I only have a cell phone," he said, "and my car broke down, in the Westside Plaza."

"On Westside Avenue?"

He refrained from making a smart comment. "That's it. I'm in the lot by the ValuMart. It's a green Pontiac. I'll raise the hood."

"A car will be there soon."

He put the phone back in his briefcase, then reached into the canvas sack. He took the towel out and carefully wiped down the steering wheel, the control panel, and anything else he had touched. He leaned down and yanked the release lever under the steering wheel with the towel; the hood thumped as it sprung free. He shut off the car, grabbed the keys, got out of the car and lifted hood, then propped it open with the bar inside. Then he pulled his bags from the car and set them on the pavement, and tossed the keys across the lot. He wiped off the outside of the car, dropped the towel back over the gun and stood in the sun and waited.

The taxi pulled up about twenty minutes later, just as he was thinking about calling the cab company back. An older man with a potbelly and stretching red suspenders got out of the cab and walked over to him. He looked like a farmer.

"Having some problems?"

He tried to look frantic. "Yes, damn it all. Stupid thing just quit on me," he said, and waved his hand at the car.

"Want me to have a look?" the cabby said and walked to the front of the car.

"No, don't bother - it's a rental. I'll let them deal with it. Unfortunately I've got bigger problems," he said.

"What's that son?" the man said, tipped his head to one side and stepped a closer.

Fred glanced at his watch nervously. "Believe it or not my computer is also on the fritz. I need to get some parts from that Radio Shack over there, and I've only got a few minutes before my flight."

"The airport's not far."

"That's good to hear, I can't miss this plane. I've got to get to Chicago."

"What can I do to help?" the old man asked.

Fred pulled a fifty from his pocket and handed it to him. "Take this, load up my bags and wait here. Hopefully I won't be more than ten minutes."

"You don't need to do that mister," he said, but turned the bill over in his hands.

"If it makes you feel better, think of it as a deposit."

"OK son. You hurry on, and I'll be waiting and ready to go."

Fred grabbed the canvas sack and walked quickly away from the cab and across the parking lot toward the supermarket. His heart beat faster, and he tried to calm himself as he approached the doors, waiting for a moment as a woman with a small child in a stroller to exit. He looked at no one as he walked quickly though the soup aisle to the back of the store and the restrooms. He pushed the door open and surveyed the small men's room, relieved that it was empty. He entered the lone stall and took out the moustache and wig and donned them, then stepped out and looked in the mirror. John stared back and nodded. He took a deep breath and left the restroom.

The store was not as crowded as yesterday, and he walked purposefully toward the customer service counter at the side of the store. He noticed a different clerk behind the counter as he approached, an older heavyset woman, deep in conversation with a customer. He moved to the end of the counter, waited, and pretended to look at some bargain hunter newspapers. He held the canvas sack by the handles in one hand.

It didn't take long. The same male clerk he observed yesterday brushed past him, pulled out his key and moved toward the office door. John waited until he reached it, then stepped behind the counter, walking boldly, as if he belonged there. The female clerk at the front, still busy with a customer, didn't notice as he moved past her. The man opened the door and started inside. John paused briefly until the door began to shut, then pushed it open and stepped inside the office. John leaned his back against the door, closed it and pulled out the gun. The man's jaw dropped open.

"OK, you don't want to get hurt, do you?" John said, and moved directly in front of him.

The man stammered gurgling sounds emitting from deep in his throat.

"Where's the money?"

The manager's face was white and he looked involuntarily toward the safe. It was closed and presumably locked.

"Open it," John said, moved closer and put the barrel of the nine directly on the man's forehead.

"Don't hurt me," he mumbled.

"Open it, NOW!"

The clerk moved to the safe, his hands shaking so much he could barely lift them to the combination dial. John pushed the gun into his back and tilted his head towards the door, expecting to hear someone any minute. The man turned the dial several times, then yanked on the handle. It was still locked, and the man froze.

"Do it carefully this time," John said, pressed again with the gun, not at all surprised that the man didn't get it right the first time.

The man tried again, this time the handle pulled up in his hands.

"On the floor, face down," John yelled.

The clerk slowly moved aside and dropped to his knees then used his arms to let himself down on his stomach. John pulled the towel from the bottom of the sack, used it to open the door, then flipped it over his shoulder. With his gun hand he scooped piles of bills into the sack, more concerned about the time than how much money he took. He glanced down at the man who was shaking on the floor; satisfied he wasn't going anywhere. He filled the sack half full, more than enough he thought, and left most of the money in the safe.

"Don't move," he said sternly, and placed his foot on the man's back. He pulled the towel off his shoulder, wrapped it around the nine tightly, then squeezed off two shots into the ceiling. The towel muffled the explosions. The man screamed under his foot.

"Stay there, or that will happen to you."

He put the nine back in the bag, covered it and the cash with the smoking towel, walked to the door, and listened for a moment. Finally he yanked it open and stepped out side.

The female clerk stared open mouthed at him as he walked out of the room.

"Don't move," he said, glared at her, and walked quickly past the other side of the counter toward the back of the store.

He walked as fast as he could without appearing to run, ears open and trying to focus behind him to catch any commotion or alarms being raised. By the time he got to the back hallway he still hadn't heard anything, so he broke into a jog, bashed the back door open with his shoulder and ran out into the sunlight. He turned right, running faster, the canvas sack heavy with the weight of the money and the gun upsetting his balance a little. With his other hand he ripped off the wig and the mustache and shoved them into the bag. He geared down as he approached the back door of the Radio Shack, then slowed to a walk and tried to control his heavy breathing. He smoothed his hair, and pulled open the door, then walked directly towards the front of the store. David, the salesman looked up, surprised to see him come from the rear.

"Oh, come back to get the Gameboy?" he asked.

"Yes sir," John said, and waved enthusiastically at the display without slowing down. "Just let me go get my daughter and you've got a sale."

"I'll be here," David said, beaming and taking up a position next to the electronics.

John pushed open the front door of the store and stepped back out into the bright sunlight. He started across the sidewalk and scanned the lot for the taxi. The cab almost hit him as it pulled up.

"Hop in son. I've been watching for you," the cabby said through the open window.

John grinned broadly as he opened the back door and climbed in. "I can't tell you what a life-saver you are Mr…"

The cabby leaned over the seat. "Just call me Barney. Most folks do around these parts."

"Well if we hurry Barney, I might just make that flight."

"Don't worry son, I'll get you there – twenty-five minutes tops," Barney said and looked out the front window as he pulled away. John looked over at the grocery store. There were a few people in front of the store chatting excitedly. John leaned back into his seat and set the canvas sack on the floor where it wouldn't be seen.

True to his word, Barney drove fast, but not recklessly, and got John there in twenty-three minutes. He pulled up to the United unloading zone and eased his way out of the cab to the trunk. John slid out the back door with the canvas sack and watch as Barney pulled out his bags.

"What do I owe you Barney?"

"Nothin', son, in fact I should give you some change back."

Fred smiled and picked up his bags, "Keep it friend, and thanks," he said as he walked into the terminal.

Three minutes later he had found a restroom where he transferred the cash and gun into his garment bag, and the moustache and wig into his briefcase. Six minutes after that he was back in line at the United counter, looking anxiously up at the departing flights list, and hoped he could make the two p.m. flight. Five minutes after that he had checked his bag and headed for the gate. Two hours and one time zone change after that he was safely back in Denver.

John waited for his garment bag among the dozens of other passengers standing around the long oval luggage claim area inside the DIA terminal. This was the only part of his assignments he didn't like much, waiting for the bag, the gun, and in this case the bomb to show up. He wondered what could be taking so long. It had been almost thirty minutes since they arrived at the gate.

He had already been to the car rental counter and reserved a car, an SUV actually. After taking the train back from the concourse, he had slipped into another restroom, put the wig and moustache back on and picked a car company at random. He had requested a larger vehicle, something with power that would take him up over the mountains easily, and was supplied with a Ford Expedition.

His scalp sweated under the wig, and he wanted to get out of the airport quickly. He didn't think he really needed the disguise again, but figured the good detective was close and didn't want to take any chances. Probabilities. He had dumped the wig and moustache in the nearest garbage can as soon as he left the counter, and nodded a silent goodbye to his friend.

Finally the carousel began to squeak and turn and fortunately his bag was one of the first ones out, due to his last minute boarding of the plane no doubt. He had to wait another five minutes for the shuttle bus, which dropped him off directly by his car. It was dark green, and huge.

He was tired now, not so much from lack of sleep, but from all the mental energy he had used in the last twenty-four hours. He drove quickly out of the lot and onto Pena Boulevard and headed out of DIA. He stopped at the first hotel he saw, which was more than ten miles away and almost back to I70. He checked in as Stuart Jones and dragged his bags immediately up to the room.

He unlocked it and looked around, finding it exactly like all the others he had lately stayed in. He was getting tired of hotel rooms he thought. He closed the door and dropped his bags on one bed, then sat down on the other, weary even though it was not even evening yet. He wanted to call Susan, to hear her voice, but it was still too early. He had another call to make anyway.

He found the phone book in the dresser under the TV, and thought again about the similarities of hotel rooms. He turned to the business section and looked up the number for KDEN-TV. He paused for a moment and considered the possibilities. By now the airlines had John, which means Will had him. They probably even knew he was in Denver by now, but that wasn't enough. He needed them to really want to go after John, and Sara was the only way. He thought of the trail he had left them - the abandoned car, the LaQuinta, the theft. Using a real gun instead of the fake Glock was a nice touch he thought. The rounds fired into the ceiling should ensure that the story made a big splash. Of course they would be confused at the flight dates, since he had rented the car and the room the day before he flew in. That would convince them he was even

DECEPTION ON MARGIN

more devious, and make them feel all the more clever for tracking him down. He picked up the phone and dialed the number, and decided.

"KDEN-TV, may I help you?" the woman's voice said.

"I'd like to leave a message for Sara McGloughin please."

"Would you like her voicemail?"

"No, can you just write it down and give it to her?"

"Yes sir, of course. What is it?"

"Look to Kansas City," he said.

"Excuse me?" came to bewildered voice.

"Four words. Look-to-Kansas-City."

"I'll see that she gets it."

He hung up the phone and crossed to the TV, turned it on and found CNBC. He wasn't even paying attention as he flopped back on the bed and fell asleep.

Will sat in his living room, watching the Rockies lose to the Giants and having a beer when his cell phone rang. He cursed softly, walked over to the table to pick it up, but kept his eye on the TV. It was a five run game but anything could happen at Coors Field. He didn't recognize the number on the display, and he hoped it wasn't bad news.

"Carter," he said, and walked back to his easy chair. He sat down and picked his beer back up.

"Detective Carter. This is the United Liaison office calling with your evening report."

Will glanced at the clock. It was eight o'clock. His interest piqued.

"Sure, thanks... how do I get it?" he asked.

"It's already been emailed, but you requested periodic phone calls sir."

Will wanted to know now what kind of information he was getting. "Can you summarize it for me?"

"Sure, flights today for John Anderson through eight p.m. CDT: twenty-seven. Reservations today for John Anderson made by eight p.m. CDT: two hundred and thirty three."

"That many?" Will asked, stunned. "Well sir, it is a common name and we accept reservations up to three years in advance."

"Right, and the thirty-seven flights, those were today?"

"Yes sir,"

"I don't suppose you could read them quickly could you?" Will asked, a little embarrassed.

"No problem sir, if I can abbreviate the information." He sounded like it was a common request.

"Shoot," Will said.

"Flights today for John Anderson, all times CDT: 12:12am Chicago – Philadelphia, 12:36am Newark – Miami, 1:47am San Jose – Salt Lake City. 3:15am Salt Lake City – Chicago..."

The voice droned on. Will was beginning to have second thoughts about this. He was about to thank the man for his time, and wait for the morning when something caught his attention.

"Can you repeat that?" he said, sitting up quickly.

"8:45am Dallas to Kansas City."

"Any flights out of KC back to Dallas?" he asked.

"No sir, but one later, a 3pm to Denver."

"Can you tell if it was the same John Anderson?"

There was a pause and Will could hear keystrokes. "Yes sir, same John Anderson."

"Thank you very much. I can wait for the report tomorrow."

"Good night," the man said.

Will was disturbed. Dallas again he thought, but the man didn't fly back there, he came here for some reason. He wondered if it was a coincidence, some sales guy on the road. It was the second time Dallas came up and he hated coincidences.

Sara checked voicemail three times after four o'clock, but didn't get anything interesting. Marsh was working late and she wanted to begin writing, something she found it hard to do at the office. She went straight home with her laptop and settled in for a long night at her desk. She never made it back to the station that afternoon, and wouldn't get any written messages until the morning.

Chapter Twenty-Seven

Fred pretty much slept in his clothes all night. He had left his belongings on one bed, then collapsed on the other after calling Susan. He was more tired than he had ever been in his life.

The TV had been on all night, but he hadn't heard it. Sometime around midnight CNBC had changed its programming to infomercials, being two am on the east coast, and no self respecting investor would be watching anyway. Fred slept through them and woke up to the regular broadcast schedule. He thought it was the program Market Watch as he rolled off the bed and stumbled into the bathroom, mentally working through the time zone changes to get an approximation of the time. He needed to get going.

He started the shower and stripped out of his clothes, then realized all his toiletries were still somewhere in his garment bag. He fetched them and brushed his teeth. The long hot shower revived him, and gave him time to review his plans over and over again. When he was finished he padded barefoot back into the room, disappointed that in his hurry to find a place to stay he had neglected to check into a hotel with room service. No matter he thought. He could get to the Red Carpet Club early, and try and relax. There would be breakfast there.

He opened up his bag and removed his clothes for the day, jeans and a work shirt. He hadn't taken his work boots since Susan had watched while he packed, but it didn't make any difference. After today it wouldn't make any difference how he dressed at all. He felt better as he slipped into the clean clothes.

He hummed as he began his preparations, the execution of the plan calming him. The ticker that ran across the bottom of the TV showed pre-market trades through Instinet, but he avoided looking at it and tried to stay focused on the business at hand. He took the canvas sack and emptied it on the bed, the gun, towel, and all the cash spilling out over the spread. He sorted the cash quickly, starting with the hundreds, most still packed in bundles of fifty from the store. He set aside ten thousand in hundreds then stacked the rest, turning to the other bed every once in a while to stuff them into the zippered pockets in his garment bag. He didn't count the cash, and kept a few hundred in fifties and twenties for pocket change.

He then picked up the nine, looking at it as he turned it over in his hands. He hadn't decided yet if he should dispose of it now. He didn't really need it any more, just like the Glock he had dumped in Dallas, but it felt comforting somehow. He remembered the kick it had delivered when he shot it through the ceiling, the brief feeling of power. He made up his mind and pushed it into another one of the pockets.

He looked around the room carefully, then walked to the bathroom and picked up his clothes and dop kit, which he stored inside the main compartment of the bag, then folded the flap with the pockets back over it. Finally he reached for the bomb and pulled it out.

He found himself somewhat curious as to how it was put together, and what was inside that would make such a large fire. He could have asked for explosives of course, but an incendiary device burned so much hotter and more efficiently, destroying all traces of what it consumed. He set it down on the bed gingerly, then reached for a pad and pen that had been conveniently left for him by the hotel next to the phone. He double-checked the number on the top of the bomb as he wrote it down, and left the pad by the side of the bed. Then he walked to the closet and got a plastic laundry bag, which he carried back to the bed and filled with the ten grand in cash. He slid the bomb in on top of it.

Finally, he opened his briefcase and put the sack in, then got the last wig and moustache from the garment bag and added them, checking to make sure his cell phone was also inside. Satisfied he got up, took the briefcase and left the room. The TV was still on as he put the 'Do Not Disturb' sign on the door and walked away.

The green Expedition glowed in the morning sunlight as he opened the door and set his briefcase inside. It was another clear morning, perfect for a drive he thought. He stood by the side of the car, leaned down and looked under the front seat. The springs were low to the carpet, but there was plenty of room. He re-opened his case, pulled out the bomb and set it on the floor then hesitated. He held his breath and pushed the red button. There was a slight click and the red light came on. He was still holding his breath as he slid it under the seat, wedged below the springs to make sure it wouldn't slide forward. He let his breath out, and wondered why the light didn't flash, like in the movies.

He got in the car, shoved his briefcase over and started the engine. One more check he said to himself as he pulled the cell phone from the dash and dialed his own number. After a moment he heard his own cell phone ring softly inside his briefcase.

He smiled, hung up the phone, and started back to the airport, not at all concerned about sitting on top of an armed explosive device.

'Look to Kansas City' the message said. It was hand written on a light blue and white piece of paper about the size of a dollar bill that had been torn out of an office 'While You Were Out' message pad. In the corner was also written a date and time - yesterday at three forty-five she read. It was on her chair when she came in.

"What the hell does that mean?" she said out loud, holding the slip of paper between her fingers. She looked around the office to see if any of her coworkers were standing back, watching her and laughing. It wouldn't be the first time they had played a practical joke on her, but no one was paying any attention.

She sat down in her chair and turned the note over and over in her hand as if she might discover something else from it. Who did she know in Kansas City? She couldn't remember ever being in the town, or the state for that matter. She racked her brain for a few minutes and tried to make sense of the cryptic message. She put the paper down on her desk and picked up the phone, then dialed the company receptionist.

"Hi, this is Sara McGloughin in News. I have a message here, from yesterday it appears. Do you know anything about it?"

"Uh, a message Sara?"

"From yesterday afternoon. You know, one of those old-fashioned paper jobbies you tear out?"

"Oh, sure," the woman said, apparently comprehending. "I remember. Someone called in with the message. He didn't ask for you, or want your voice mail. He just wanted to leave the message."

"He?"

"It was a guy."

"That's it?" she asked, hoping for more.

"Sorry, that's all he said."

"Thanks," she said and hung up.

She was confused, and a little pissed at the caller. If this was so important, why not leave a voice mail? She wanted to dismiss it as a prank, but something inside told her not too. Instincts she said to herself.

She stood up and looked around. "Anybody know anything about Kansas City this morning?" she practically yelled across the room. Several people looked up, but shook their heads.

She sighed and sat back down, thinking she could check the news wires. She turned to her computer and used the mouse to click on the UPI icon, then scrolled through the morning's stories. There was nothing of note, then an idea occurred to her. She stood up again.

"Anybody know the name of the newspaper in Kansas City?" she shouted again.

"The News?" a young man sitting a few desks away asked.

"No, it's the Star. I grew up there," one of the other reporters corrected.

"Thanks," she said and sat down.

She clicked on her web icon and waited for the browser, and thought about Lebida. OK, what would she do? She moved the cursor to the address window and typed in 'www.kansascitystar.com'. She was amazed when the browser displayed the Star's home page. She only had to scroll down a little before the story was revealed.

'Gunman Robs West Side Supermarket in Broad Daylight' the banner read. She froze, and stared at the link.

"Oh my God."

She clicked on the link and watched as the full story displayed.

Gunman Robs West Side Supermarket

In a daring noontime theft yesterday, a lone gunman walked into the offices of the crowded ValuMart just outside Weatherby Lake yesterday and held the store manager at gunpoint as he robbed the store of thousands of dollars in cash.

No one was hurt in the incident, although the thief fired two shots. Bill Parsers, the manager of the store was visibly shaken when questioned after the theft.

"He just followed me into the office and stucka gun in my face." Parsers related. "He forced me to open the safe and made me lay down on the floor."

DECEPTION ON MARGIN

The thief described by Parsers as a white male, in his mid-thirty's with curly brown hair and a moustache took an undisclosed amount of money.

Kansas City Police have been called in to aid in the investigation....

Sara was stunned. She read the story three times, still not believing it as she tried to figure out what to do next. Her heart pounded and her thoughts raced. Damn it, she thought, why didn't I get this yesterday? She wanted to follow up as quickly as possible - to get as much information as she could for her story. She changed her mind and picked up the phone to call Marsh. He answered his cell phone after a couple of rings.

"Marsh, it's me."

"Sara, hi," he said. "All set for today?"

"Marsh, listen. There was another robbery yesterday, in Kansas City. Same story line."

"What?" he interrupted.

"I just found out about it," she replied. "I got a message yesterday from somebody, telling me to look to Kansas City. Unfortunately I didn't get the message until this morning. I can't believe it."

"Did you call Will yet?"

"No, I wanted to tell you first. Isn't it amazing? I mean who would tell me?"

"I have no idea," he said, then hesitated. "Do you want to cancel this weekend?"

The implication struck her. Damn she said to herself. The reporter in her wanted to dive into this, find out everything she could. The woman in her wanted to go. She felt excited, and totally guilty.

"I take it that's a yes," Marsh said. "Look, that's OK. I want to follow up on this too. We must be getting closer somehow."

She glanced at her watch. "No, Marsh. I've got a few hours to find out what I can. I'll call Will and tell him to get on it. There isn't much else for us to do anyway. They do have phones in Crested Butte, don't they?"

Marsh laughed. "I assume so. Are you sure you want to still go? There are lots of other weekends. Maybe we should wait..."

"Yes I am. I want to go. Once we get Will involved we can let him handle it. I'll just bring my laptop and we can get to the web for anything else."

"If you say so, though I wasn't planning on working much this weekend."

She felt another pang of guilt. "Only if we have too..."

"Right. I'll be at your place at noon, OK?"

"Can't wait. I gotta run. See ya," she said quickly, and hoped she was doing the right thing as she pressed another outside line and called Will.

For the third straight day Will was at his desk going over the details of the case, wondering if he was on a wild goose chase. He had the list of the twenty-seven trips that the many John Anderson's had made across the country yesterday in front of him, by way of United and American Airlines. He still hadn't heard back from USAir, or any other airline, but he had the feeling that it would just be information overload.

He looked over each of the records carefully and tried to find a pattern. He had highlighted in yellow pairs of records where one of the Johns had made trips in and out of a city, but had since crossed all but one of them off, realizing they were probably just connections made when changing planes. The Kansas City one was the only set left. He was thinking about it when the phone rang.

"Detective Carter," he said automatically.

"Will, it's Sara," she said quickly. "I've got something for you... another robbery."

He perked up immediately. "When Sara, where?"

"Yesterday, in Kansas City. You can get the details from the Kansas City Star's web site."

He interrupted her immediately. "Sara, hold it. Did you say Kansas City, and yesterday?"

She sounded exasperated. "Yes Will, I said Kansas City. And if you would let me finish I can give you the details. It's our man again."

"Just tell me about what time it was first."

"The paper said noon, why?"

"Hang on a sec, OK?"

He looked back at the list, ran his finger down it the two highlighted reservations, and verified what he already knew. Dallas to KC at eight forty-five, out of KC to Denver at two. Jesus.

"Will, are you still there?" he heard Sara ask from the phone.

"Yeah, sure. Did you tell Marsh about this?"

"Of course, right before I called you. Why?"

"I've got the airline records right in front of me. I know his flights."

"That's great news Will. We were hoping you could find out, but I didn't expect it so fast."

"Good news and bad news again."

"Why, what's the matter?"

He hesitated, and pondered how much to reveal. He had made this mistake once before.

"Well the first flight into KC was from Dallas," he said, waiting.

"Oh my God."

"Yeah, my thoughts exactly. But it gets worse. He didn't go back to Dallas, Sara. He flew to Denver yesterday afternoon at two. He's here."

There was a long silence at the other end of the phone. Finally she said, "We've got to tell Marsh."

He couldn't argue. "I know, and talk to Susan. I hate to say this but we need to find out where Fred is."

"Oh Will, do you think we should? Susan's been through so much all ready. And we know Fred was in Dallas last week, when it happened here."

"Too many coincidences though," he answered. "I have to find out."

"I suppose you are right. It's just I feel so sorry for Susan all of a sudden. How the hell can we put her through this again?"

"It has to be done."

"OK, let me call Marsh and tell him. I'll get Susan's number and call you back. We were going to go to Crested Butte this weekend you know."

"No reason not to. In fact it might be better if you left town. I don't understand why he's here. Why not go back to Dallas again?"

"I don't know, but I'll call you right back."

Marsh had been at the office for a couple of hours already, trying to clean up as many loose ends as possible before the weekend getaway. He had been in a great mood, but the news about Kansas City had shaken him. He felt guilty about leaving. Sara was right he supposed, there wasn't much they could do. He was startled when his cell phone rang on the desk next to him.

"Hello?" he said, and didn't recognize the number on the display.

"Marsh, it's me again. I just talked to Will."

"So fast? Had he heard about Kansas City before?"

"Not exactly."

He let the phone drift away from his ear a little. What the hell did that mean?

"Marsh," Sara continued. "When I told Will about the robbery in Kansas City, he already had the flight information for John Anderson's from yesterday."

"That's good, and?"

She hesitated for a moment, her stomach churning. "And, there is a pair of flights that match the time, starting in Dallas yesterday morning."

It only took a second for that to register. "Jesus."

"Yes. The only problem is that Anderson didn't fly back to Dallas. He flew here afterward, to Denver. Will wants to talk to Susan, Marsh, to find out where Fred is."

Any further thoughts Marsh had about a good morning vanished out the window.

"I can tell him where Fred is. He's in Dallas, or at least he was. Susan was just about to call him when I talked to her the other night."

Sara was silent.

"This has to be a coincidence again Sara, just like the last time. For all we know the killer lives in Dallas and flies in and out of there all the time."

"Then why did he come to Denver Marsh?"

"I have no idea. Maybe he left the money here from last time, and is coming back to pick it up. There could be a thousand reasons. I just don't want to jump to any conclusions again."

"Maybe you're right. What do you want to do about Will?"

"I'll talk to Susan, then call Will." He thought for a moment. "Do you want to cancel this weekend now?"

"No, Marsh. I don't see any reason too."

"Good. I'm sure I can clear this up in a minute. You just be ready at noon, and I'll take care of everything else, I promise."

"Are you sure?" she asked.

"Positive. The more I think about it, the less I want to think about it. Let's just go."

"Alright," she said. "Works for me."

"I'll see you soon... bye."

He set the phone down, then pulled his Rolodex up on his computer. He was thinking about what to say while he scanned for Susan's work number. He had that feeling of dread again and he was sick of it. He suddenly wanted all of this to be over. He found the number and called it.

"Susan Hawkins," she answered cheerfully.

"Suse, it's me," he said, and tried to sound just as cheerful.

"Hey big brother. I thought you and Sara where going to sneak away this weekend."

"We are, in a few hours. I need to talk to Fred though, do you know where he is?"

"He's in Dallas again, why?"

He tried not to lie. "I had a question about the search we did, on the airline reservations."

"Oh Marsh, still?" She didn't sound happy and he felt even worse.

"I just need his advice. Is he at the same hotel?"

"The Adolphus? He was, but I'm sure he's checked out by now."

"How about his cell phone. It's kind of important Suse."

She gave him the number reluctantly. "He doesn't always answer though, if he's in a meeting or something."

"I'll keep trying. What are your plans this weekend?" he asked, to change the subject.

"Oh I don't know. I was kind of hoping that Fred and I would go shopping."

"Shopping? That's plans?" he asked, a little confused.

"You men are all alike. My left hand is a little bare right now."

It took a moment but he finally got the picture. "Oh, right. A ring." Another pang of guilt shot through him. "Maybe I'll drop a few hints."

"Don't you dare. He better think of this on his own."

"OK, OK. Well you two have fun. I'll talk to you soon."

"You too. Say hi to Sara for me. I've got to go to a meeting, so later alright?"

"OK, by Suse. I love you."

"You too, bye."

He hung up the phone. It had to be another mistake. He reluctantly dialed Fred's cell phone but it just rang until the message service kicked in. He couldn't figure out a message and hung up, then found Will's number and dialed.

"Will Carter."

"Will, it's Marsh. I heard about everything. I just talked to Susan and Fred's in Dallas again."

"Did Sara tell you about Kansas City - the flight in from Dallas?"

"Yeah, it has to be another coincidence."

"I'm beginning to hate coincidences, Marsh."

"Look Will, I can't put Suse through this again. Let me try and reach Fred and straighten this all out."

"I don't know if I can do that," Will said ominously.

The intercom buzzed. "Can you hang on a second?"

"Sure," Will replied.

Marsh hit the hold button, then the intercom. "What is it Mary?"

"Marsh, there's a Mr. Coffman on the line, from the Colorado Internet Society. Do you want to take it?"

Marsh had never heard of either of them. "Can you take a message?"

"He wants to talk to you personally. I told him you were busy. When are you leaving?"

"About eleven thirty. Tell him to call back later OK?"

"You got it boss," she said and clicked off.

"Will?" Marsh said, getting the detective back on the line.

"Still here."

"Will, you find out everything you can, but let me handle Susan and Fred, alright?"

"I don't like it Marsh, but alright. When are you leaving town?"

"What? Oh, Sara told you. I'm picking her up around noon, why?"

"Do it, and take your cell phone."

Ominous again Marsh thought. "OK detective. I'll call you later."

"Stay in touch. Goodbye Marsh."

Marsh hung up the phone again and wondered what the hell was going on.

Fred sat alone in a somewhat secluded part of the Red Carpet Club, a space set up for quiet business meetings. There was a half-empty pot of coffee on the table in front of him, and the crumbs from several Danish and a banana peel on a plate beside it. The only other items on the table were a road map of Colorado and a black magic marker that he purchased at a newsstand when he arrived at the airport. His cell phone had beeped with another call while he was using it, posing as a Mr. Coffman, trying to reach Marsh at the office. Marsh hadn't taken the call, but he had been successful in finding out what he needed to know. He would be at the office until late that morning.

Fred was relaxed and ready. He wondered if it was Susan who had called a moment ago and felt guilty about not taking the call. He wanted to talk to her again, to let her know everything was going fine and he would see her soon. He picked up his cell again, brought up the missed call list and checked the number. He was surprised to see it was a 303 area code - Colorado - Marsh, or maybe even the good detective he surmised, smiling a little. They were looking for him. He was about to set the phone down when it rang in his hand again.

Susan was already a few minutes late for her meeting and couldn't decide what to do. Marsh had worried her with that phone call, though she didn't know why. She wished that he would just drop this whole investigation thing - she wanted to get on with her life.

She decided quickly, picked up the phone and dialed Fred's cell phone. He picked it up almost immediately and she felt a surge of relief.

"Fred?"

"Hey babe, what's up? I thought you were busy today."

"I am, very. In fact I'm late for a meeting right now," she said. "I just wanted to talk to you, that's all."

"Well I'm always available. Is anything wrong?"

"No, not really. I just miss you," she said almost sadly. "Did Marsh get in touch with you?"

"Marsh?" Fred said, connecting it to the phone number on his call list. "No, but I was in a meeting and missed a call, why?"

"I don't know. He said he had some questions about the airlines. I wish you two would stop all this. It worries me."

"I'm sorry babe. I'm sorry I started the whole thing. I was just trying to help."

"I know. When are you coming home?"

"Tonight sometime. Depends on when I get a flight."

"Can't you come sooner?"

"No, I'm in Ft. Worth. I checked out of the Adolphus the other morning. I had to come over here for a meeting I wasn't expecting," he said, and felt guilty about the lie. "I'm very busy today, but I'll call Marsh when I can. Or he can try me later this afternoon if he wants. I'll try and put this whole thing to rest alright?"

"OK... I miss you. Come home soon."

"Goodbye babe, I love you."

"I love you too."

She hung up the phone and glanced at her watch again. She didn't care about the meeting anymore and called Marsh's office. Mary answered.

"Mary, its Susan. I need to talk with Marsh right away. Is he still there?"

"Oh, hi Susan, of course. Let me get him."

She waited during the silence, anxious. She started talking as soon as she heard him pick up.

"Marsh, I just talked to Fred. He's in Ft. Worth."

"Oh, I tried to call him but he didn't answer."

"I know, he said he's sorry he missed your call but he's very busy. He said to call back this afternoon, alright?"

"What's he doing in Ft. Worth?"

"I have no idea, more meetings I guess. Who knows what he does down there. He said he checked out of the Adolphus yesterday. Look I've really got to run. Have a good weekend."

"Bye Suse."

She was a little nervous about being late, but felt much better after the call.

Fred walked across the club to the men's room and glanced at the digital clock above the bar. It was time, the red numbered display informed him. He pushed open the door to the restroom and walked over to two wide sinks. White hand towels and toiletries where thoughtfully located on either wall. He splashed cold water over his face and grabbed a towel, then looked up into the mirror. Stuart was there.

"Are you ready?" Fred asked.

Stuart was a man of few words. "Let's go," he replied.

He walked back through the club and sat down, opened the map and spread it over the table. He looked at it, and chewed on the cap of the magic marker. He reviewed the route over and over again. A few minutes later a soft woman's voice spoke over the speakers hidden somewhere in the ceiling.

"Mr. Simpson, you have a visitor at the front desk."

The club was mostly empty as he walked back to the front doors and opened them. The double waited in front of the desk. Stuart beckoned and held the door open as the man walked in. "Follow me."

They walked back to the couch without saying anything. The double noticed the map on the table as he sat down. "Am I going on another trip?"

Stuart looked at the double. He was still amazed by the resemblance. The man had on jeans, and a blue sweatshirt without any markings on it. A white t-shirt was barely visible under the collar.

"You didn't tell me it was going to be warm here," the double said. "I thought it was cold and snowy in Colorado."

"Where you're going you'll be fine."

The double nodded and looked at the map again.

"I want you to follow a man and a woman," Stuart began slowly.

"Then what?"

"Just listen, and you can ask questions when I'm done."

The double nodded again, not saying anything more.

"South of here is an area called the Tech Center. There is a man in an office there. I want you to follow him."

Stuart opened his briefcase, took out a piece of paper and handed it to the double.

"The address, company name and phone number. Don't call there unless there is a problem. Also my cell phone number. I want you to be in constant contact with me."

The double didn't look surprised at the instructions. Stuart continued.

"He will be leaving the office sometime after eleven this morning, in a black Lexus. He will probably be alone, and drive downtown to pick up a woman."

"Good looking?" the double asked.

"Very," Stuart said, irritated at the interruption. "They will drive west, into the mountains. I can give you the most likely route, but you may have to improvise. Don't lose them."

"I won't. Are they supposed to know I'm following?"

Stuart looked at him. "Not at first, but later, yes. With the route you are taking it will be hard for them not to see you."

The double leaned over the map, interested. Stuart picked up the marker, leaned over and pointed. "This is downtown, where he will pick up the woman. From here you will head south to 285, then go west into the mountains."

"Sounds like a nice drive."

Stuart ignored him and traced the route. "If they stop along the way just stay back. Don't lose them by taking a leak somewhere."

The double grinned.

"285 runs into 24 here," Stuart said and pointed to the map again, "then intersects with 291 here. They will head north at that point."

"Sure about that?"

"Relatively. If they don't call me."

"Right."

"24 goes through a town called Buena Vista. Just outside they will turn on a small highway, 306, and go west. 306 goes up over the mountains. Cottonwood Pass. The road will climb to around 12,000 feet to get over the mountains. It will turn into switchbacks as it goes up, big drops off the side."

"Sounds dangerous."

"So I'm told. There won't be anyone else up there probably."

They were silent for a moment, and Stuart leaned back. "Got it?"

"Can I take the map?"

"Yes."

The double folded up the map and waited.

"I want you to stalk them. You can occasionally let them see you on the way up. Make them worry a bit but don't get too close."

"Then what."

"When you get onto pass, move in. Play with them, but don't let them stop. Force them up into the top of the pass. Get close, I want them to see you."

"What the fuck? Why?"

Stuart took the wig and moustache out of the briefcase and handed it to the double. "Here's your disguise."

The double took them and laughed. "You're kidding right?"

Stuart glared at him. "You want your money? Go put them on."

The double hesitated, then realized Stuart was serious. He left for the restrooms and came back a few minutes later. He was almost perfect. Stuart pulled John Anderson's driver's license from his briefcase and handed it to him.

"Cover."

The double looked at it and laughed. "Nice likeness."

"One more detail. Give me your neck."

The double looked at Stuart's neck and nodded. "Anything for twenty grand," he said as he turned.

Stuart took the magic marker and slowly drew an oval on the side of the double's neck, then filled it in.

"What happens at the top?"

"Up to you. Let's just say I don't want any witnesses. Like I said the woman is very beautiful."

"My kind of job. Vehicle?"

Stuart handed him the keys. "Green Expedition. West lot, level one, section C about half way down on the left. You can't miss it."

"Nice wheels."

"Very. There's a cell phone inside. Use it."

The double nodded. "How about the cash?"

Stuart pulled the plastic sack from his briefcase and handed it over. "Ten grand. Another ten when you get back. Maybe even a bonus if you do it right. Wouldn't want you to run on me now."

The double glanced in the bag, then closed it. "Wouldn't want to miss out on all the fun," he said with a smile. "Where do we meet?"

"Just call me when you're finished with the job."

"Right," the double said, and grabbed the map and the bag.

Stuart didn't say anything and watched him leave. It wouldn't be long now he thought. He waited a few minutes then caught a cab back to the hotel.

Chapter Twenty-Eight

The parking lot wrapped around the four story brick and glass building on the west and south sides. The dark green Expedition was parked around the corner from the front door of the building on the south side, and faced north to keep the sun off the windshield and, Lexus in plain sight.

All he had to do now was wait. Not that he minded though, it was part of the job. He patted the plastic sack with his hand gently, the cash partially showing through the open top. Ten grand before, ten grand now, and ten grand when he was done – it was the most money he'd made in a long time – and he'd barely had the chance to spend some of it before coming to Colorado. The glass doors opened and two more people came out of the building; a man and a woman who didn't even walk into the lot. He had the right Lexus, was anxious to get going, and wanted to see what the chick looked like.

He opened the box of Marlboros and pulled a smoke out between his thumb and forefinger, tapped it a couple of times on the steering wheel to pack it, then lit it with his new lighter. He held the smoke for a minute, then in a long stream blew it towards the lower front corner of the windshield and the little decal showing a cigarette with a red circle and a line through it. "Fuckin' A," he said.

He had taken the wig and the mustache off despite what the man had told him, his head itching from the damn thing. He wasn't supposed to let them see him yet anyway, so what the fuck he thought. He would put it on later when it mattered. He glanced at his watch. It was well past eleven, almost eleven-thirty. He thought about calling the office number to ask for the man, but changed his mind immediately. The fucking car was right there he said to himself, and he had already called once for directions. He hit the window button and tossed the cigarette out without finishing it, suddenly remembering the man's joke at the airport. He should take a leak now, while he had the chance. He hopped out of the truck quickly, left the engine running and jogged across the lot toward the front door.

Marsh was trying to keep busy, but doing a lousy job at it. At least earlier, before Sara had called with the news, he had waded through all his emails. Now he just flipped through a few of the many computer magazines he tried to keep up with. He was still unsure about the decision to go to Crested Butte, and wanted to stay in town and keep in touch with Will. If he could think of just one helpful thing to do he would stay he thought, but he couldn't.

He looked at his watch. It was almost eleven-thirty and time to go. He shut down his computer and wondered about taking it along. Dumb idea he said to himself, but grabbed his cell phone and the charger and tossed them in his briefcase. He switched off the lights and closed the door as he left.

"I'm outta here Mary," he said as he walked by her cubicle.

"Have a great weekend Marsh." She smiled up at him from her chair.

"You too. Got any big plans?"

"Nope, same old stuff. Hey, you weren't expecting anyone today were you?"

"No, I hope not, why?"

"I got a call earlier, some guy asking directions from the airport."

"To here?"

"Yeah, I gave them to him."

Marsh worried for a moment, and hoped that he hadn't forgotten some meeting or a business acquaintance that was passing through town.

"That's fine. Well, unfortunately I've got my cell phone, Mary," he said and patted his briefcase. "But try not to bother me OK?"

"Yes, sir." She saluted with her hand. "Have fun, and I'll see you on Monday."

He was still worried about a forgotten visitor while he rode the elevator down to the first floor and stepped out into the lobby. He didn't pay much attention until he noticed the man who came in the front doors and walked across the far side of the lobby, and down the short hall to the restrooms. Jeez that guy looks like Fred he said to himself. He started to laugh. He better get out of town he thought, and get away from all this. The obsession of finding the thief was beginning to get to him.

He walked quickly across the empty lobby, opened the front doors and stepped into the sunlight, fresh air filling his lungs. Will can handle it he thought as he headed towards his car.

The double pulled the men's room door open and walked back to the lobby, squinting at the sunlight as he headed back to the truck. He just stepped outside when he noticed the Lexus back out of the parking lot.

He sprinted across the lot for the truck, trying to run forward and look sideways at the same time. He couldn't remember if there was an exit on the other side of the building, and was relieved as he saw the Lexus stop, back up, then pull away from him, and move through the driveway just past his truck. He slowed down, not wanting to run directly behind the car, then walked quickly as he watched it stop at the exit from the lot. He got into the truck and waited until the Lexus pulled out into the street, then followed it.

"Fucking A," he said and reached for his Marlboros again. He was still breathing hard from sprinting, and hacked at the cigarette when he lit it. He waited for his lungs to clear, then picked up the phone, and rummaged around in the mess on the seat next to him for the paper with the telephone number. He had the steering wheel with one hand, the other held the phone directly in front of his face, and punched the numbers with his thumb. He wasn't going to lose the guy again he thought. The phone rang three times.

"Yes."

"I got him."

"Good, don't let him see you yet, not until they are way out of town."

"No problem. Hey what should I call you anyway?"

There was a slight hesitation. "Stuart," the voice said.

"That's not the name at the airport," the double said.

"That's not my name. Call me when he gets the woman."

The double laughed. "No problem." He couldn't wait.

"And just when do you plan on getting some closure on this fucking thing?" the Captain asked point plank.

It was just after noon and Will was hungry, and tired of sitting on his butt at his desk with the phone in his ear. The attitude from the Captain wasn't helping any.

"Captain, the guy is in Denver, or at least he was yesterday. We're sure of that. I've got notifications out to all the hotels and car rental agencies checking for anyone registering under the name John Anderson."

The Captain shook his head slowly. "And what about the guy you thought you had last weekend. Did you check on him?"

Will squirmed in his chair. "He had a rock solid alibi sir. He was in Dallas at the time."

"But that's where the perp came from again wasn't it? And where is he now?"

"As far as we know, he's in Dallas," Will said, now very uncomfortable with the conversation.

"Dallas? What the fuck Detective. Why haven't you tracked him down?"

"Captain, he's the future brother-in-law of Marsh Hawkins, the man we are working with. It was his idea to start this whole search. If it wasn't for him we wouldn't even have the leads."

"So?"

"So when we suspected the other guy last time, it nearly tore Marsh and his sister apart. I didn't feel it appropriate to do that again until we had more facts."

"I'm not sure I agree with that reasoning."

"The most important thing is to find the perp. If it turns out to be the fiancé, fine. If not even better. Besides, I know where to find him. He's not going anywhere that we wouldn't know about."

"I hope so detective. I hope so. I've haven't informed the Mayor on this, but I would like to. This would be fine press for the Department you know."

"I know, and I'll find him. I promise."

Marsh pulled up to Sara's condo a few minutes early and parked illegally in a loading zone. He called on her cell phone when he was about ten minutes away, and she was just finishing packing. Fifteen minutes she had said, and to wait on the street. He waited, stood close to the car and watched the front door of the building. She came out as promised after fifteen minutes, and carried a garment bag in one hand and a small overnight case in the other. Her purse dangled from her shoulder, and it slipped a little as she walked. Marsh left the car and rushed over to help her.

"Jesus Sara, I did say just for the weekend right?" he said, and hefted the bag up.

"Well I don't recall you giving me the itinerary, and a girl has to be prepared," she said with a smile.

She was gorgeous he thought, dressed in short shorts and a tight red tank top. Her hair was pulled back in a matching crinkle, the pony tail fell over her shoulders and just down over her back. It was the first time he had seen her dressed like this - she was normally so conservative - or naked he thought. He pushed the bags to the ground, grabbed her and kissed her.

"Mmm... what's that for," she said and kissed him back.

He looked her over from head to toe. "Couldn't help myself."

"Don't get any ideas," she laughed. "Let's get out of here."

She stood by the car as he slammed the trunk and stepped over to open the door for her.

"My, what a gentlemen," she said as she slid gracefully into the front seat, her legs long and bare.

"You may think so now."

She looked up at him. "Promises, promises."

He walked back around to his side and got in, forgetting everything, and thinking four or five hours was too long to get there.

The Expedition was only about a hundred yards away, backed into a driveway. The double lit another cigarette while he watched his target get out of the car. It was a piece of cake to follow the Lexus; shit there must be a thousand four-wheel drive trucks like his on the road. He could have been on the car's bumper and he doubted if the target would have noticed. He had stayed a few cars back anyway, usually in another lane on the freeway, then followed closer as they came into downtown. He almost had to run one red light, but other than that there were no problems.

She came out after a while and he rolled down the window to get a better look. Great tits, he said to himself as he watched her get into the car. He was beginning to like this more and more. Stuart was right about one thing she was good looking. Up until now he hadn't given too much thought about what to do up on the mountain, but now that he knew what she looked like a plan formed in his mind. He lit another Marlboro and drove out slowly as the Lexus pulled back into traffic. No witnesses the man had said.

Fred sat on the side of the bed, looked out the sliding glass door into the parking lot and wondered what to do with the time on his hands. The double had just called again, checking in as requested with news that Marsh had picked up Sara and they were heading west. His fears that the double would just split with the money no longer troubled him, and now all he had to do was wait. He had picked up another map on the way out of the terminal, and he spread it over the second bed and checked the route again. He took the magic marker and drew a thick line from downtown to 285. So far, so good.

After a few minutes he unpacked his computer, and thought he could kill some time online. In the last week he had spent little time trading and that troubled him. For so long it was his passion, the other activities simply a diversion. But now he had Susan and the thrill of it seemed to have gone away. It was ironic he thought, that it was his association with John, Richard and Stuart that had brought him so much closer to her, and now he would be happy to get rid of all of them.

He walked over, opened the sliding door and let the breeze flow into the room. There was a Denny's across the way and he thought about getting some lunch - just a burger or something to bring back to the room. He had a while before he expected the double to check back in, and it would be nice to get some fresh air. He picked up his cell phone from the bed and thought about calling Susan again, missing her. He decided against it though, it wouldn't be routine. He glanced at his watch as he left the room. Only a few more hours he said to himself.

US 285 wound up out of Denver into the Front Range, south of Evergreen and through Connifer, communities that used to be small mountain towns, but were now being built up by big money, and the people who didn't mind the hour commute back and forth to the city. The two-lane highway had been widened as the city's influence spread west, newer shopping centers and fast food joints that blended badly with older log cabin like architecture. Sara and Marsh hadn't said much on the drive, content to ride and be with each other.

"Having second thoughts about leaving?" Marsh finally asked, and looked over at her.

She smiled. "Not really. In fact I had forgotten about everything for a while. Just enjoying the drive."

Marsh pulled up to a stop light and braked easily. One of the last few lights he thought to himself, and noticed the Friday afternoon traffic was still heavy, even this far out of town. The road seemed to be full of SUV's he thought. After a minute he drove on.

"So what have you been thinking about?"

She laughed. "I was just trying to remember where I was two weeks ago today."

"And?"

"And I couldn't. Another boring Friday night I suppose, with nothing to look forward to but work."

They continued out of the city limits, and Marsh sped up to sixty-five and set the cruise control. "What? Pretty girl like you and no hot date?"

"Let's just say I didn't want a lot of commitments."

"I see. And now?"

A more serious look settled over her face, and she looked forward out the window as she talked. "And now I don't know what to think. So much has happened so fast."

"Any regrets?"

She reached over and touched his arm lightly. "None at all," she said, then hesitated. "Where do you think it will all end, Marsh?"

"How about the cops get the bad guy, the girl gets the story, the boy gets the girl?"

She smiled again. "Mmm, sounds nice. Does it bother you?"

"What?"

"The story. The fact that I'm still working on it."

He thought for a moment, but wanted to answer truthfully. "I don't think so. After all it is your job. And as you pointed out the other day I did drag you into this."

"Yes, but that was before... before us."

"It was at that," he said, then looked over at her. "I want the thief to be caught Sara, that's all I really care about. If you get a big story out of it so much the better."

"You sure?"

"Yes, I am."

He waited a moment, then turned and leered at her. "Beside, I've always wanted to sleep with a Pulitzer Prize winning journalist."

She stared at him, then shook her hair provocatively. "And what makes you think I will let you sleep?"

"Hold that thought," he said.

The double braked the Expedition at the edge of the city limits with the other cars on the highway. The Lexus was still ahead of him, beyond an old VW camper and another four-wheeled drive. He kept well back, presumably still out of sight even though they were in the high country now, long flat valleys with the mountains on either side in the distance. He picked up the box of Marlboros, then tossed it aside when he noticed it was empty. He grabbed another pack from the ripped apart carton and opened it, and added the cellophane and foil to the growing collection on the floor. He lit one, and let the cigarette dangle between his lips as he picked up the phone and pressed the talk button, the number re-dialing itself.

"It's been a while," Stuart said from the other end of the connection.
"Not much to report, unless you want to hear about horses and cows."
"Where are you?"
"Some thriving fucking metropolis called Fairplay I think."
"Have they seen you yet?"
"Maybe yes, maybe no. Not a lot of traffic out here." He pulled the smoke from his mouth and flicked the ashes on the floor next to him.
"Call me back then, when you get to Buena Vista."
"Where the fuck is that?"
"About an hour, hour and a half. The last big town before you head for the pass. It's north on 24. Don't you have the map?"
"Of course I've got the map, but I'm just following these assholes. What the fuck do I need a map for?"
"Call me from Buena Vista."
"Right," he said, rolled down the window and tossed the cigarette out. "Fuckin A."

Will set the phone down, excited. He looked at the hastily scribbled note he had made with the information from the rental car agency and called the day room. "This is Detective Carter. I need an APB on a green two thousand-two Ford Expedition. Colorado License PZR-5546. Probably driven by a white male, mid-thirties. I want this car stopped and the driver detained, got it?"

He put down the phone without waiting for a reply. "Finally a break," he said to himself.

He thought about calling Marsh, then decided against it. No need to ruin the trip yet he thought.

Marsh glanced into the rear-view mirror for the fifth time in as many minutes, and looked at the cars following them. The traffic had bunched up as they slowed down at the city limits, the speed limit dropping to 35, then 25 as the Buena Vista spread out along the highway. There were a number of tourist shops and roadside restaurants lining the way, all busy with the summer season. The green SUV had been with them for a long time he thought, but then so had the yellow VW bus. He looked for somewhere to stop.

Sara had dozed off, her seat reclined and the visor pulled down to keep out the sun. He reached over and shook her arm a little.

"Hey sleepy, how about a snack?"

She smiled and sat up, then adjusted her seat upright to look out the window. "I was not sleeping. Just journalistically examining the inside of my eyelids."

"I see. Are you hungry?"

"I could use a potty break."

"I know just the place."

He looked ahead and over to the right at a small but busy drive-in. He steered the car slowly in that direction, then turned into the lot and next to a weather worn wooden post that held up a flat sheet metal canopy. The brief feeling of paranoia fled as he watched the green SUV keep going in the mirror.

"Quaint," Sara said and looked around.

"I want a greasy burger and a chocolate shake," he said, turning toward her. "How about you?"

"A shake sounds good. Do you think they have any onion rings?"

Marsh rolled down the window and killed the engine, then stretched in his seat. His pants stuck to the leather, and he realized he should've changed into shorts earlier. A young girl, who was probably barely into high school walked up to the window, holding a paper note pad and a pencil.

"Take your order?" the freckled face asked.

"A burger, onion rings and two chocolate shakes."

"You got it," she said and bounced away.

Sara opened the other door and got out, then leaned back in the window. "I'll be right back."

Marsh nodded and settled back in his seat, then craned his neck around and looked over the parked cars in the area. He didn't see the VW or the truck. He scolded himself, then he thought about the office and the man who had called for directions. Jesus, get a grip he thought, they were hours from Denver. He relaxed again, and felt the cool breeze float in through the open window.

Sara returned in a moment and got back in the car. "Did I sleep long?" she asked.

"Oh I don't know, about forty-five minutes probably. I didn't want to disturb you."

She smiled at him. "Sorry about that."

"I didn't mind, I was just thinking, and enjoying the drive."

Freckle face returned with a green rubber-coated wire tray, the food on top and stood patiently outside the door. It took Marsh a second to realize what she wanted, then he started the car and slid the window up a little. She set the hooks on the bottom of the tray on the glass.

"Enjoy," she said and scampered away again.

"Wow, I haven't done this since high school."

"I bet all the guys took you to the drive-ins," Marsh replied, and reached out for the onion rings.

"Of course. Say, you aren't going to try and get me into the back seat later are you?"

"Hadn't thought of that, but probably."

She took the rings from him and munched on one. "Promises, promises," she said.

The double slowed the truck as they pulled into the drive-in, then kept going towards a McDonalds a hundred yards down the road. It was busy, and totally out of place among the little businesses lining the highway. He drove past the drive-through lane and around the back, then pulled to the front and waited for a station wagon to back out of a spot before he maneuvered the Expedition in. He got out of the truck, stretched, and looked down the road at the Lexus. He had a few minutes he thought and walked quickly into the McDonalds to take another leak. When he came back they were still there, eating.

He was getting excited now, anxious to get things going. He had spent the last hour thinking what he might do to her, and how to get rid of the guy first. He got back into the car and checked the map. They were in Buena Vista, and he should call Stuart, or whatever his name was. He picked up the cell phone again, dialed and waited for an answer.

"Where are you?" Stuart's said without a greeting. He must have been sitting on top of the phone.

"Buena Vista of course. Stopping for a little snackie-poo."

"It's time. Let them see you when you get out of town. Call me again at the top when you begin your move. I want to hear all the details."

"Right," he said and hung up the phone.

The guy is fucking crazy he thought. Like some kind of voyeur. If he wanted the details why the hell didn't he do it himself? He lit another smoke and waited. The Lexus was still sitting there when he was done with it. He slid down the window and tossed it out, then took the wig and moustache and put them back on, adjusting them in the rear-view mirror.

"Fuckin' A," he said.

Fred put the cell phone back on the bed and looked at the map again. He took the magic marker and traced a line along the highway, west along 285 to 24, then north. He continued on through Buena Vista and west again on 306, then stopped after another inch where the line became dotted. He drew an 'X' there and set the marker down.

"Not long now," he said to himself.

There was an old deserted drive-in movie theater a mile or so west out of Buena Vista, but Marsh didn't make a cute comment about it. Sara relaxed and looked at the scenery, and he didn't want to alarm her. It was a small two-lane blacktop highway, with painted double yellow lines down the middle and there were no cars on it, except for his and the green SUV a ways behind him. He was worried again, but tried not to be. He was just being paranoid he thought to himself.

"How much longer?" Sara asked, turning in her seat towards him.

Marsh pushed the thought away. "An hour and a half, maybe two depending on how fast we go. It's not quick when we get up on the pass."

"You know I've never been over Cottonwood," she said. "The only time I've been to Crested Butte was to ski, and we always took Monarch pass."

"Cottonwood is closed in the winter. In a few months this highway will be too hard to keep open in the snow."

She was quiet for a moment, and stared out the window. They climbed slowly, nothing but pine trees and rocks lining either side of the road.

"So what is this place, a condo?"

"Actually it's a house, about two miles outside of town. A friend of mine built it with his wife, on some acreage he and some friends bought along the Slate River."

"He doesn't live there any more?"

"Not really. He started his own company, computers of course. Now he's wildly successful and hardly has time to get up here at all."

"Too bad, it's so nice up here. So peaceful. It's nice of him to let us use it though."

"Yes, it is," Marsh said, then glanced in the mirror again. The green SUV was back again. A sinking feeling settled in, but he kept going anyway and didn't say anything to Sara.

They drove up into the mountains, after a while passing through a large iron gate that was pushed to the side of the road. He wondered if this was a good idea. He looked over at Sara, who was oblivious to his misgivings. The road was still paved, but climbed steeper into the mountains, winding more as they went up. They were surrounded on all in the distance sides by high peaks.

"God, it's beautiful Marsh. Have you ever thought about living up here?"

"Not really. I love it too, but I'm too much of a city boy."

"All work and no play?"

"Something like that," he replied, distracted again by the sight in the rearview mirror of the SUV rounding another corner behind them.

"What's wrong," she said, and finally noticed the concerned look on his face

"Nothing probably. It's just that it seems like that SUV back there has been with us the whole trip."

She turned her head and looked back over the seat. The truck was there.

"That's not unusual is it? I mean lot's of people come up into the mountains on Friday afternoon."

"I guess so. It's just that something else happened today, and now I'm worried about it."

"What?" she said, then pulled her leg under her and turned on the seat toward him.

"Somebody called the office today, and asked for directions from the airport. Mary gave them to him."

"That could have been anybody Marsh - you have lot's of people working for your company."

Marsh pushed harder on the gas pedal, and steered carefully with both hands around the ever tightening turns in the road.

"I know, but remember what Will said? He thinks Anderson is in Denver now. Why would he be here?"

"I have no idea," she said, and a frown etched into her face.

"My cell phone is in the trunk, do you have yours?"

She stared at him, face ashen. In my purse."

"Get it out, we may need it."

He watched her lean back over the seat, and didn't notice her slim form at all. She grabbed her purse and sat back down.

"He's getting closer."

Marsh accelerated a little more. "I know."

The double was enjoying this. Each time the Lexus sped up he did, slowly getting closer. The Expedition responded like a sports car, plenty of power and handled the curves perfectly despite its size. He drove with one hand as he reached back over the seat, pushed the top of the cooler off and dug in for one of the cans. He found one with his fingers and pulled it from the plastic rings, settling back in his seat. When the road straightened out he steered with the top of his thighs, and popped open the beer. It foamed as the top snapped down, then he lifted it to his lips and drank most of it. Time to get a little buzz he thought. He went around another tight corner, then drained the rest and tossed it on the floor.

"Fucking A" he said, thoroughly enjoying the chase.

The trees thinned as they went up, more open space and rocks along the road. He didn't notice the scenery though, and concentrated on driving. He pushed harder on the gas pedal, speeding up in the straight sections, getting very close, then dropped back in the curves. Cat and mouse he said to himself. He thought about the woman again, and wondered if she was getting scared now. He liked them scared.

The road went into a straight steep climb and he reached back for another beer, the truck responding obediently underneath him. Just like her he imagined.

Sara was scared now, half sitting in her seat as she looked out the back window. The car suddenly left the blacktop behind, the road turning into compressed dirt and gravel. The rocks smashed into the side of the car loudly as Marsh sped on.

"Don't you think you should slow down a little?" A slight tremble crept into her voice.

Marsh didn't look at her and stared ahead, his eyes locked on the road. "I can't, he's right behind us."

The Lexus was sliding now has he negotiated each corner, the wheels making grinding noises over the stones.

"I think you better sit down. Make sure your seat belt is tight," he said.

"Oh my God," she exclaimed and sat down quickly.

"And you better call Will."

She had the cell phone on her lap and picked it up. "Shit, do you know his number?"

He tried to recall it. He had dialed it enough over the last few days but was having trouble thinking. There was a steep switchback ahead and he turned the wheel hard, cut across the small road and made the 180-degree turn without slowing down much, rocks flying.

"Don't you have it?" he said, a little frustrated.

"I've got his card in my purse somewhere," she remembered, and grabbed it from the floor.

"You better hurry," he said and slammed the car into another corner.

The SUV wasn't losing any ground he thought, and he wished they were on a straighter road where his car could just accelerate away. He cursed himself for not stopping earlier, when he had first noticed the truck behind him.

"Got it!" she exclaimed and tried to steady the card in front of her in the shaking car. She dialed quickly.

"Will," she shouted into the phone after a minute. "He's right behind us." She pressed the phone into her ear, and tried to keep out the noise from the road. "Who the hell do you think?"

Marsh could only hear one side of the conversation, and concentrated on driving. The road narrowed, with bigger drop-offs on the lower side.

"What? Christ Will he's practically on top of us…"

Marsh rammed the gas pedal down on a small straightaway, then just as quickly hit the brake as he turned, the rear end sliding again.

"Yes, a green Expedition," she yelled, and looked over at Marsh. He didn't look back.

"Christ we can't pull over," she screamed into the phone. "We are on top of the fucking mountain!"

"Tell him Cottonwood," Marsh yelled as he yanked the car into another turn.

"Cottonwood Pass, Will, outside of Buena Vista," she screamed over the sound of the engine whining and the rocks flying against the side of the car.

"Right," she said and dropped the phone.

"Well?" Marsh yelled, and risked a quick glance towards her.

"He's coming Marsh, somehow," she yelled. "He said to drive carefully."

"Yeah right," Marsh said and whipped into another turn.

He let the Lexus pull ahead a little, and quickly grabbed another beer. The truck swerved across the narrow road as he leaned back. He popped the top and drank the whole thing before the next corner. The liquid spilled out of the side of his mouth and dripped on his sweatshirt.

"Ahh," he said as he dropped the can and powered into the corner. He wanted another cigarette but passed on it, the beer starting to buzz in his head. "Great truck... Got to get me one."

He jammed the accelerator down again, and the rear wheels spun as the motor gunned.

"Shit, what am I thinking?" he said and pulled his foot off the gas, then hit the button on the dash for four-wheeled drive. There was a clunk underneath him as the transmission complained about the sudden change. Suddenly the truck pulled straight and sure in his hands.

"Fuckin' A." He hit the gas again.

The view was spectacular as both cars went into a long slow climbing turn around the side of the mountain, but he didn't pay any attention to it. The Lexus took advantage of the relatively straight road and he pressed harder on the gas, the huge engine roaring loudly in front of him. He caught them as they slowed for the next sharp turn, then pulled in close and rammed the back of the Lexus with the front bumper. It was higher than the Lexus, and the right taillight shattered under the impact. The Lexus careened, but the truck remained solidly on the road.

"Whooop. Rid'em cowboy!"

He pulled closer again, and tried to peer into the back window. He hoped he would get a glimpse of the woman. The cars smacked together with a loud thud and he accelerated a little more, practically pushing the Lexus along. He laughed and could see the woman turn in the seat and look back. He waved quickly.

"Hello darlin'. Havin' some fun now."

Suddenly he remembered and slowed a bit, then grabbed the cell phone. He punched the talk button. After a minute Stuart answered, but it was hard to hear over the noise.

"Whoooeee," he yelled into the phone. "You should see this shit."

"Where are you?" Stuart asked.

"Top of the world baby, got them in my sights."

"Keep me on the line. I want to hear what's going on."

"You are a weird mother-fucker Stuart," the double said into the phone, then dropped it on the seat. He pulled up again and rammed the back of the Lexus as the road straightened and widened a little as they approached the summit.

Sara screamed, and covered her ears at the sound of the crash at the back of the car. Marsh struggled to hold the Lexus steady, fully aware of the steep cliff that was first on one side of the road, then the other as they turned back and forth up the mountain. He gripped the wheel tightly, his hands sweaty and slick. He couldn't believe this was happening.

The truck came up close again and rammed, and pushed him as he tried to steer away from the impact. He was fighting a losing the battle he thought. Sara turned quickly and looked back for a moment at the truck that was on top of them.

"It's him," she screamed. "I can see him."

"Sara, sit down," he yelled and she obeyed immediately, and shoved her hands on the dashboard in front of her. She was too scared to say anything else.

Fred sat on the bed and held the phone to his ear. He could barely hear the double shouting into the phone, then could only make out the loud sound of the engine and what he thought was rocks flying. He moved closer to the table between the two beds and glanced at the dialing instructions for the phone. Dial eight for long distance it said. He looked at the number on the pad for a moment, then put the phone back to his ear and listened.

"We're almost to the top," Marsh yelled. "Maybe I can lose him on the way down."

DECEPTION ON MARGIN

Sara screamed again as the truck slammed into them. Marsh yanked the wheel hard, swerved dangerously close to the far side of the road, then back again as the wheels gripped a smooth part of the road and the car snapped back straight again.

The fear that started slowly in his stomach had grown now gripped his spine as he tried hard to concentrate. There was another 180-degree turn coming up, and he tried to cut it short as it turned up to the left, thankful that there was terra-firma, not cliff, on the inside of the road.

The truck slammed into him again hard as he started the turn and slid the back of the car around. He yanked the wheel hard into the spin, the front wheels digging into the loose dirt, pulling to the left. He hit the gas again and the wheels spun, the car sliding the other way.

"Shit," he yelled as he noticed the large boulder buried in the shoulder. The side of the Lexus slammed into it, and rocked them sideways, the car stopping abruptly. The dust flew around them. Marsh jammed the accelerator down, but the wheels just spun. He could see the truck coming up below them.

"Shit!" he yelled, and pressed his foot harder into the pedal.

The double watched as the Lexus hit the rock and he had to swerve to avoid crashing into them. He slowed and drove past them, and looked out the side of the window and waved as he went by. The woman really was beautiful he thought as he finally saw her up close for the first time. This was going to be fun as he looked ahead for a place to turn around.

Fred heard the ruckus drop a little, and wondered what was going on. Then the double came back on the line.

"Got'em now," he screamed over the truck noise. "They're stuck in the ditch. Any last requests?"

Fred looked at the number on the pad, '6125555284' and smiled.

"Do what you want," he said with no emotion.

"Fuckin' A," he heard from the phone.

Fred picked up the receiver and dialed eight, then listened again for the dial tone. He set the phone down on the table, then pressed '1', then '6-1-2' and waited.

Sara screamed as the truck went by, the man leering at her. She could see him plainly now, even through the dust on the window. He had curly hair, a moustache, and she could see the birthmark on the side of his neck.

"It's him Marsh," she yelled.

"Get out of the car now!" he screamed back.

The truck motored away as she yanked on the handle, the door pressing down on her from the tilting car. Marsh was out first and ran around and pulled it open.

"RUN!" he yelled and grabbed her arm. They slipped on the stones as they crossed the road and headed for the side of the hill. Sara tripped on the side of the hill, and her knee scraped against a rock.

"Where are we going?" she yelled as he pulled her.

"Up, away from the road," Marsh yelled back, and watched as the truck turned at the top of the pass. He wanted to get as far away from the cliff as possible.

Fred waited patiently, though he found himself a little excited. He pressed the cell phone hard into his ear.

"Turning around now," the double said. "Right at the top of the fucking mountain."

Fred pressed '5-5-5' deliberately.

"You want to hear all this?" the double asked.

"Just a little more."

"Fucking A, weird," the double said, the excitement obvious in his voice. "Coming back down now, two more turns. I think they are getting out of the car."

'5-2' Fred pressed.

"You were right about one thing Stuart my man..."

'8-4'.

"She sure is fucking beau..." then the line went dead.

They were trying to scramble up the hill before they realized that the truck was above them, coming back down. They stopped, not knowing what else to do. The truck came around with one last corner to go, and Fred could see the man through the window, talking on a cell phone.

"What the hell?" he yelled.

"What?" Sara screamed back.

The truck came faster, approached the last turn, when suddenly there was a bright flash. The impact hit them a split second later.

WHUMP, they heard and felt, and it almost knocked them over. They both threw their arms in front of their faces and watched as the inside of the truck was filled with bright orange flames, seeing it only briefly before it slid across the road and disappeared over the cliff.

"What the hell?" Marsh exclaimed, bending over and breathing hard. "What happened?"

Sara was stunned and dropped to her knees. She stared out at the empty road, but couldn't believe her eyes. Suddenly they heard another crash, then a series of them as the truck bounced along the side of the cliff below them and out of sight. The smoke drifted up from the side of the road.

Marsh grabbed her hand and they slid back down the hill, then crossed to the side of the road and peered over. The wreckage was hundreds of feet below them, the truck crushed and upside down, the tires barely visible through the flames and smoke.

Sara grabbed him hard and hugged him. She was crying. Marsh suddenly felt weak, and he was shaking. The adrenaline pounded through him and he ached all over. They both sat down, and tried to figure out what had happened.

Fred clicked the end button on the phone, then flipped through the menu until he found Susan's work number. He glanced at his watch. It was four-thirty in Minneapolis and he hoped she was still at work. She answered after one ring.

"Hey babe. How's your Friday?" he said, thinking of her only.

"Hey yourself. Long of course. When are you getting back?"

"Depends on what flight I get on. Its Friday you know."

"Well hurry," Susan said. "How was your day? Everything go all right?" she asked.

"Wonderful. Just finished up the last loose end a moment ago."

"Great. Can't wait to see you."

"Me too. I love you," he said.

"Love you too. I'll be waiting."

"Bye," he said and hung up the phone. Time to change he thought and stripped off the jeans and work shirt, then put on something a little more appropriate for Susan. He tossed the old clothes in the closet and left them there as he packed up his things and called a cab for the airport.

Chapter Twenty-Nine

Sara sat in the back seat of the crashed Lexus and sobbed softly. It was a cool at twelve thousand feet, and she had found a sweater in her garment bag and slipped it on, much to the disappointment of the two sheriffs standing across the road. She had been in the car for some time, still unable to control her shaking. She certainly didn't feel like a Pulitzer Prize winning journalist now, she just wanted to get off the damn mountain.

She had no idea how long they sat on the ground after the SUV had plunged over the cliff. Finally Marsh had walked her back to the Lexus and tried to soothe her, looking remarkably calm despite what had just happened. She had refused to get into the car though, unable to forget the terror from before. Finally with the sun sinking lower and the temperature dropping she had agreed, especially when the men began arriving at the scene.

There were two police vehicles parked along the road now, facing each other, their flashing blue and red lights doing nothing to relieve the throbbing in her head. The cops weren't doing much however, mostly just standing around and talking, occasionally looking over the side of the cliff. The smoke from the wreck was almost gone, what was left drifted up from below, the wind pushing it to the south as it swept into the pass. One of the sheriffs got off his cell phone, and Marsh looked over at him as he approached, his black boots crunching on the stones

"How long do we have to stay here?" Marsh asked, impatient. "It's been almost an hour now. Can't someone give us a lift, at least down to Buena Vista?"

The sheriff was apologetic. "I'm sorry sir, I'm afraid this is a cross-jurisdictional thing. There is a little confusion on who is supposed to handle it."

"Can't we figure that out somewhere else?" Marsh pleaded, then looked over at the Lexus and Sara.

"It should only be a few more minutes sir. There's a copter coming up from Denver by the way. They requested that you stay here until then anyway."

Marsh shrugged and turned away, frustrated. He walked back into the Lexus and knocked on the window softly, then opened the door and knelt down beside the car.

"Hey, how are you doing?" he said with a smile. "I told you I'd get you in the back seat."

Sara looked at him managed a grin through the sobs. She looked a little disheveled Marsh thought, but still beautiful.

"You did, but I kind of expected you to be here with me."

"Mmm, good point. Soon OK? Apparently there is a helicopter coming in a few minutes. Hopefully we can get out of here."

She reached out, took his hand and squeezed it hard. "I was so scared Marsh."

"You think I wasn't? I don't know what I would have done if I hadn't had to concentrate on driving."

She looked deep into his eyes and spoke softly. "Thank you Marsh."

"For dragging you into this? I'm not sure I deserve that."

"No, for saving my life."

He squeezed her hand back and leaned in and kissed her. "Our lives Sara, and I couldn't have done it without you." They looked at each other for a moment, then he continued. "I do have a couple of questions though."

"What?"

"Well now that you have an ending, when's the story coming out?"

She laughed this time, but didn't answer the query. "And the other question?"

"If you have your story, you aren't going to dump me are you?"

She looked at him, amazed, then grabbed him and hugged him, practically pulling him into the car.

"Probably not," she said into his shoulder, and suddenly felt a lot better.

"I'm going to call Suse. I want to tell her what happened. That it's all over."

"Help me out."

He reached down, took her arm, pulled her up the slope and out of the car. She stood up straight and tall.

"Well I'm kind of a mess," she said a fussed with her hair a little. "But I think I'll just go and interview those two officers over there for a little background. Tell Susan hi for me."

"That's my girl."

Fred got the last seat on the four twenty-five flight to Minneapolis, checked his garment bag and rushed off to the gate. He was in a great mood and couldn't wait to get back to Susan. It seemed like a huge weight had been lifted from his shoulders, and for a change he had been impatient to get on the plane. He pulled out his cell phone and called Susan.

"Hey there," she answered quickly. "Where are you?"

"At the airport. If my flight isn't delayed I should land about seven thirty."

"Why so late?"

"I thought I could catch an earlier flight, but it was full," he said, lying this time and realized he didn't like it. "I guess I should start planning better."

"I would think so. Do you want me to pick you up?"

"No, my car's at the airport. How about you just meet me at my place and we can think of something to do."

"I'm sure we can," she agreed. "Well, some of the girls wanted to go out for drinks anyway. The Friday night singles crowd you know. I told them no, but since you won't be back until later maybe I will."

"Singles?"

"Just think of me as the designated engagee."

"Is that a word?"

Fred looked up as the passengers were beginning to line up around the door. "Look's like we are boarding. I'll see you in a couple of hours, OK?"

"Can't wait."

"Bye, I love you" he added but she was already gone.

Susan had left work a little early, it being a summer Friday, and was at her house when Fred had called. She briefly wished he had phoned earlier so she could have gone straight to the bar with her friends, then realized she didn't really want to go anyway. Suddenly the idea of hanging out in a singles place didn't appeal to her. It was a warm cloudless evening, and she thought maybe a walk around the lakes would be nice instead. She was about to change clothes when her cell phone rang again. She wondered if it was a problem with his flight, then looked at the number. It was Marsh.

"Hey big brother," she answered, "I thought you'd be in Crested Butte by now."

"Suse, it's all over."

He sounded a bit distraught and she immediately thought of Sara, and wondered what had happened. Jeez did they have some sort of a fight already? "What?" she asked, concerned.

"The thief. We've got him!" he said, charged. "In fact he's dead."

She was stunned and sat down hard onto the couch. "Marsh, what are you talking about? What's going on?"

She sat there, riveted to the couch while he told her the whole story. She couldn't believe it, and didn't know what to say.

"Are you OK, Marsh," she said finally. "And Sara?"

"We're both fine, or will be once we get off this rock. We're going back to Denver I hope. The Lexus is toast."

"Oh my God Marsh, I can't believe it. It's really true?"

"Absolutely."

"I can't wait to tell Fred. He'll be so happy."

"And we owe it all to him. Where is he anyway?"

"I just talked to him. He's on a plane coming home. He should be here in a few hours."

"That's great," he said and she thought he sounded relieved. "Tell him thanks for me alright?"

"Of course, and give Sara a hug for me."

"I better go. I'll call you this weekend. I love you Suse."

"I love you too. Call me," she said and hung up.

She jumped up and stretched her arms to the ceiling. "Yes," she screamed. It's all over she thought. She couldn't wait for Fred to get home and to tell him. They would be together forever now with no worries. In fact they were rich. She was surprised at the thought and how it suddenly excited her.

They heard the helicopter long before they saw it, the sound beginning with a low thump, thump somewhere in the distance. They looked up, scanned the sky, guessing which direction it would come from. Marsh was relieved that the ordeal was finally ending, and he spotted it first, coming in low from the east. It was a beautiful sight he thought as it swooped in over the slope, hanging in the sky over the area for a minute before it began to settle down. After a moment he realized the only place to land was up the mountain a ways, at the top of the pass, so he grabbed Sara's hand and they walked up the road that the SUV had come down after them. They just reached the last switchback when they saw Will jump out, ducking underneath the whirling blades, looking for them. He was dressed impeccably as usual and looked out of place in the mountains as he strode confidently towards them.

"Thanks for coming Will," Marsh said and shook his hand. "Nice ride you have there."

"Seemed like the quickest way to get here." He looked down the mountain to the gathering below and the car in the ditch. "I see you ignored my advice."

"What's that?"

"About driving carefully. Looks like you kind of wrecked the Lexus."

"I was thinking about getting a new car anyway," Marsh said and smiled.

"Not an Expedition I hope," Will replied, a smile bending the corner of his lips. He looked at Sara. "You OK too?"

"I'm much better now you that are here detective, thank you," she said, but leaned a little closer to Marsh.

Will just nodded and smiled again.

"When can we get out of here Will?" Marsh asked.

"In a minute," he replied. "I better go on and talk to the boys down there. Why don't you wait here - I shouldn't be too long. You can give me the whole story on the way back to Denver."

He started to walk away, and Marsh began to follow. Will looked at him, questioning.

"All our stuff is down there Will."

"I'll get someone to bring it up. Give them something useful to do."

"That would be nice Will, thanks."

Will nodded and trudged off. They watched him for a moment then walked toward the helicopter. It was big Marsh noticed, room for four passengers behind the cockpit. They scrambled inside behind the pilot and settled down into a soft seat thankfully. Sara sat very close to Marsh as they buckled in.

"I've never been in a helicopter," Marsh said after a minute.

Sara was surprised. "You're kidding. I fly in them all the time."

"I must be in the wrong profession," Marsh said.

She smiled and leaned her head on his shoulder.

The few minutes turned out to be almost a half-hour, but Marsh waited patiently, happy to be off the road. He thought Sara was sleeping on his arm when Will finally jumped back in, then leaned up to the pilot and said something. The pilot flicked a few switches and the rotors began to turn slowly, a high pitched whine filling the inside of the cabin. Sara sat up next to him and looked out the window.

"Got your stuff," Will shouted at them over the noise. "A tow truck is coming for the car."

Marsh just nodded. It was too loud to talk any further, in fact they weren't able to hold any sort of conversation on the trip back. Marsh was content to look out the window and admire the scenery, not really wanting to talk anyway. Sara was silent also, her hand tight in his.

It was after six by the time they got back to the station and Will's desk. Not even three hours had passed since the chase but to Marsh it seemed like days.

"I know you have both been through a lot, and are tired and want to get out of here, but I need to understand what really happened," Will said.

Marsh was weary, but understood. Sara nodded in agreement.

Marsh related the whole incident again, with much greater detail than he had told Susan. Sara helped out, her reporter's instincts adding many things that Marsh had forgotten. She seemed totally recovered now, and was almost enthused as they talked. Building the story Marsh thought to himself, but didn't say anything.

"So you think it was Anderson that called the office for directions?" Will asked.

"I'm positive. In fact I saw someone that I remember looked like Fred just as I was leaving the office. I thought I was seeing things."

"Did he have the birthmark?" Will asked.

"He was too far away. I couldn't tell."

Sara leaned forward. "I'll never forget that face Will, as he drove by the car. He definitely had the birthmark on his neck."

Will thought for a moment, and reviewed the story in his head. "But Marsh, you said he looked like Fred, and you Sara, said he had curly hair and a moustache."

"But we know the wig and the moustache are a disguise Will," Sara reminded him.

"I realize that, but it seems like he went to a lot of trouble to let you see his face. You did say he drove past you and up the mountain before coming back right?"

"I guess he needed to turn around," Marsh said, and suddenly wondered himself.

"Could be. Has anyone talked to Fred since this happened?"

"Suse has," Marsh said quickly. "I called her from the pass. He was on a plane home."

"Home from where?" Will inquired.

"Ft. Worth I suppose, why?" His stomach wrenched at the thought but he didn't tell them.

"Let's get back to the SUV," Will said, and changed the subject. "It was coming back down the mountain after turning around, right?"

Sara and Marsh just nodded.

"And you two were running from the car and saw the driver again, and he was talking on a cell phone?" Will asked as if he didn't believe it the first time.

"I think so. It sure looked like it."

"I fell. I didn't see anything at that point," Sara added.

"Don't you find that a bit curious? I mean if he's trying to kill you, why the hell is he talking on a phone?"

"I have no idea Will."

"And then the Expedition just blew up? Before it went off the cliff?"

"Definitely before it went off the cliff. The inside of the truck filled with a bright orange light, then the sound and shock wave hit us."

"Damn strange," Will said.

"Well he had been ramming us all the way up the mountain. Maybe his fuel line broke or something," Marsh offered.

"Maybe," Will added, his face blank and unreadable, then looked at his watch. "Look, it's past six thirty and you guys are probably dying to get out of here. We can finish this up tomorrow. I'll get a car to drive you home."

"That would be a relief," Sara said and rose quickly from her chair.

"So what happens now Will?" Marsh asked, and wondered about some sort of closure on the whole ordeal.

"Well, we've got eyewitnesses, yourselves included, from the robbery in KC, and here. We've got the plane reservations and the car rental records. We've got a wrecked car and a body probably burned beyond recognition. Kind of wraps up the case."

"But?" Sara asked, sensing the hesitation.

"But we still don't know who the guy was, or is," Will said, the pensive look on his face again. "One thing still bother's me though."

"What's that Will?" Sara asked for the both of them.

"This Anderson guy. How did he know to come after you two?"

Susan was just about to unlock the door to Fred's place when her phone rang in her purse. She stopped in the hall to answer it and looked at the time on the display. It was past seven thirty and she hoped he wasn't going to be late.

"Hi," she said cheerfully.

"I'm back," Fred said. "We were a little early but I had to wait for my bag. I'm almost at the car and should be home soon. Should I stop along the way for some dinner?"

"No, just come right here. We can figure out something later," she said. "And hurry."

"OK, see you in a few minutes."

"Bye," she said and put the phone back in her purse.

The condo was dark when she walked in, so she hit the switch by the door. The hall light was harsh as she closed the door, so she walked over to the couch and turned on the floor lamp behind it for a little better mood, then turned the hall light off again. There was an antique mirror on the wall toward the kitchen, out of place she thought, and she caught her reflection in it for a moment. She looked around and surveyed the place. Needs a woman's touch she thought, then her thoughts drifted to where they would live. Her house was just a rental, and this place seemed so bachelor like. Maybe someplace around the lakes. It doesn't have to be big, and they could certainly afford it. Her stomach flipped a little as she thought about the money. She walked into the kitchen and began to snoop around, for the first time really looking at his belongings. Typical male she said to herself, not much warmth here.

She walked down the hallway toward the bedroom and nosed through everything. The walls were basically bare and lifeless. She definitely didn't want to live here she decided quickly as she entered the bathroom and turned on the light. At least it's clean she said to herself, no hair in the corners or anything. She was about to continue snooping when she noticed the small garbage can was full. She bent down, thinking she would empty it when she saw the label on the plastic bag shoved inside.

'Mefisto's House of Disguises' the banner read as she unfolded it. 'Costumes, Wigs, and Makeup For All Occasions', it said below. She held it in her hands, then looked in the bag. There was a slip of paper inside and she pulled it out, wondering what Fred could have possibly purchased at such a place. It was a computer receipt, like from a department store. She froze as she read it, and couldn't believe what she saw.

"Twelve wigs and twelve moustaches," she said out loud. She stood there, paralyzed. Suddenly the dream she had with the old woman and Fred came crashing back down on her. A wig and a moustache she thought.

"Oh my God, it can't be," she exclaimed. Her heart pounded in her chest. She was close to panicking, but had to find out more. She ran into the bedroom, started opening drawers and dug through his clothes. She had no idea what she was looking for, but needed something, anything, to get rid of the terrible feeling growing inside her. She looked at her watch. Christ he'll be here any minute she thought, and ran to the closet and threw the doors open. She pawed through his suits quickly, not finding anything, then looked on the shelf above. She tossed his sweaters down to the floor.

"Get a grip girl," she said suddenly and stood up straight amidst the piles of clothes. "There has to be some sort of an explanation."

She tried to convince herself as she ran out of the room, into the office and looked around. She walked over and hit the power buttons on the computer and monitor and wondered what the hell she would look for.

She turned in a circle, looked around desperately, and felt helpless, her heart still racing in her chest. Then she noticed the paper on the printer. She picked it up and stared at it. "Fuck the will," she said, then tossed it to the floor.

It slipped out of her hand and drifted through the air toward the closet. She watched it, then saw the safe barely visible behind the door. She reached over and threw the closet door open, practically ripping it off the hinge. The safe was locked, the red digital display confirming it. She dropped to her knees in front of it and yanked on the handle anyway. How much time? She looked at her watch again. Five minutes, ten? Get out of there, her mind was shouting, but she couldn't force herself to get up. She wanted to know.

She stared at the keypad, the numbers on little white buttons like a telephone. The combination? What would the combination be? GET OUT OF THERE!

"Calm down!" she yelled, and it helped a little.

The will was lying on the floor next to her and she picked it up and stared at it again. When they had talked about it, he wanted to tell her everything he had said. What was it? She suddenly remembered the scene vivid in her mind. She could hear his voice echoing in her mind.

"My birthday, I always use it," he had said. "Sometimes backwards though. You can't believe how many passwords I have to keep track of."

"Birthdays…"

She tried to steady her hand as she reached over and punched in his birthday. The numbers appeared one at a time in red in the display. Nothing happened as she yanked on the handle again.

"Shit," she said and tugged at it.

How much time? She glanced at her watch again, but that was useless. He could be here any minute. GET OUT OF THERE!

"Backwards, try backwards."

She tried again, patiently reversing the digits. After the last number she heard a slight click and the display changed to 'OPEN'.

She yanked on the handle again and pulled the door, amazed despite the fear that ripped her stomach apart. There were bundles of cash stacked inside, thousands of dollars she thought. My God, what has he done? There was a single sheet of paper lying on the bottom shelf that looked like a printout from a spreadsheet. She picked it up. Her hands shook as she read it.

"Chicago, Boston, D.C., Philadelphia, St. Louis…" she recited, then looked at the totals. Hundreds of thousands of dollars. She sat there, finally comprehending everything. GET OUT OF THERE! She was still arguing with herself as she got up.

"You've got to tell Marsh," she said as she ran out of the room.

Her phone was in her purse and she looked around, finally locating it on the kitchen counter. How much time? Call him from the car girl! Get out now while you can. She clutched the paper in one hand and ripped her phone out of her purse and hit the speed dial for Marsh's cell phone. "Answer, damn it!" she yelled at it.

DECEPTION ON MARGIN

Marsh and Sara were at the elevator getting ready to leave the station, anxious to get going when his cell phone rang. Will had escorted them out and was about to head back to his desk.

"Now what?" he said to Sara.

"Whoever it is, you can call them back," Sara said wearily. "Let's go home."

Marsh agreed. "Let me just check to see who it is," he said as he pulled the phone from his pocket and looked at the display. "It's Suse, I wonder what she wants now?"

Will touched his arm slightly, enough to stop him. "Answer it Marsh, quickly."

Marsh and Sara both stared at Will, unsure at what he meant. The phone kept ringing.

"Damn it Marsh, answer it or I will."

Marsh pressed the talk button and held the phone to his ear, suddenly dreading the call.

"Susan?" he said, nervous.

"Marsh it's Fred! It's been Fred all along!" she shouted in his ear.

He looked at Sara, then Will.

"What are you talking about Suse? What about Fred?"

Will reached over and grabbed the phone from Marsh. "Susan, its Will. Calm down and talk to me," he said, his voice commanding

"Will, listen. I'm at Fred's place. I found a bag with a receipt for wigs and moustaches. I opened the safe, and there is all this cash inside..."

"Where's Fred?" Will asked, still calm.

Sara and Marsh stared at him, wondering what was going on.

"On his way here. There's a printout, with cities and totals. All the robbery cities Will!"

"Susan, you need to get out of there now. Do you hear me?"

"Yes, OK."

"Are you on your cell phone?"

"Yes,"

"Call 911 now, while you are leaving. Tell them there is someone in the house, and you think he's armed, you got that?"

"What's going on Will?" Marsh shouted, wanting the phone back. "What's wrong with Susan?"

"Oh my God," Sara said, comprehending everything. "Fred." She moved over and grabbed Marsh's arm. Her fingernails dug into his arm.

415

"Do it now Susan," Will said, his voice still steady. "Call me right back when you get out of there."

But she never did.

Will's voice calmed her a little and she disconnected, then grabbed for her purse as she dialed 911.

"Come on," she said as the phone rang.

"911 Emergency," the voice finally came.

"There's someone in the house. He's got a gun," she shouted into the phone, freezing in her tracks to talk. GET OUT! The voice in her head insisted but she didn't move.

"Are you on a cell phone ma'am?" the voice said patiently.

"Yes, yes," she replied quickly, still shouting.

"I need the address please."

Fucking polite aren't you? She thought, and tried to remember. "2134 S. 22nd street."

"Minneapolis?"

"Of course Minneapolis! Apartment 1C. Can't you hurry?"

"Please stay calm and stay on the line. I'm sending a car over now. Is someone inside the apartment with you?"

"No!" she yelled, then thought better of it. "Yes. YES! I've got to get out of here."

"Please ma'am…"

She cut off the phone and headed for the door, trying to call Marsh back at the same time. She had to stop to look at the phone to bring the speed dial up again when she heard the bags drop in the hall and the key in the door.

"Shit!" she said, dropped the phone and looked around frantically.

She backed slowly into the kitchen and held her breath. She didn't know what to do. She could fake it she thought pretend she didn't know and sneak out when he was in the bathroom or something. She told herself to calm down over and over as the door slowly swung open.

"I can't," she whispered.

"Susan?" she heard Fred say as he stepped inside, the open door between them. She stepped back further, almost to the stove, then noticed a wooden cutlery block with knives stuck in it on the counter. She quietly slid the biggest one out and held it in her hand behind her back, quickly discarding her plan to get away.

"Susan? Are you here?" he said, walked in and kicked the door shut with his foot.

She stayed in the corner of the dimly lit kitchen and watched. He tossed his bags on the couch and looked around, not yet seeing her. GET OUT the voice said again, but the rage in her had taken control, the knife solid in her hand.

"Are you hiding from me Susan?"

"Why Fred?" she asked from the dimness of the kitchen, her voice suddenly steady and ice cold despite the pounding in her chest. "How could you lie to me?"

He turned at the sound. "Hey babe, am I glad to see you." He smiled and walked forward like he hadn't heard her.

She stepped towards him slowly, still holding the knife behind her back. "How could you do this to me Fred? Or should I say John..."

He stopped and the smile faded from his face. "What's wrong Susan, what do you mean?"

"You bastard," she said, her voice cutting. But the word was not enough for how she hated him.

He took another step and hesitated, his hands out.

"I loved you, Fred." She glared at him. "You used me. You used all of us. Why?"

His eyes widened, as he understood.

She took another step. "What's in the bag Fred? More blood money from Kansas City? Did you kill somebody's mother there too?" The anger and hate built her confidence.

"No, I..." he stammered and stared at her, then stepped back. "It was all for you," he pleaded. "I'm giving up everything, everyone."

She didn't say anything but moved closer.

He turned, walked back to the couch suddenly and grabbed his garment bag. He opened it quickly and revealed the zippered pockets. He opened all of them, and grabbed a handful of cash and threw it on the floor.

"I don't want any of this anymore. I'm through, don't you see? It's all over. No one will ever know."

"Who was in the truck Fred? Someone else you didn't need?"

"It doesn't matter Susan. We're safe now!"

She stepped closer, looked down and saw the bulge in one of the pockets. She could hear the sirens wailing in the distance.

"A gun? You call that safe? Who's next on your list Fred?"

He took the gun out slowly and turned it over in his hands. "I don't care about this, you can have it if you want..." he said. He took the barrel in his hand and held the handle toward her. The mirror was just to his left, and he glanced at it. The man's hair was unkempt, and face unshaven.

"Shoot her Fred. Remember the twins?" the mirror said.

She hated him she thought. The sirens were getting louder, and closer. She looked at the gun, then pulled the knife from behind her back and slashed his forearm with one clean swipe. His shirt sliced clean through, along with most of his flesh. The blood spurted up from the wound and sprayed both of them.

Susan hesitated in front of him, but he couldn't look at her. The mirror called. "I told you Fred," Richard said, then the image switched.

He glanced at her. "Susan, please." He spoke softly and held his arm out, the blood flowing.

She stepped closer. "That was for me." The sirens were screaming in her ears.

He didn't move but looked back at the mirror. It changed. "Dude, you have to do something," Stuart said. The image switched again.

"God damn it, shoot her Fred!" Richard said.

The image changed again.

"I'll do it Fred," Stuart said, and he switched the gun to his other hand.

Susan stared at Fred, who just stared at the mirror, then saw him put the gun in his other hand and raise it.

"This is for Mom," she said, her voice like ice. She raised the knife and plunged it into his chest, feeling it bounce off his ribs. His eyes opened wide, not fully comprehending what happened.

"Susan..." he gasped.

He collapsed, the knife pulling out as he fell; the gun still locked in his lifeless hand. She watched unemotionally as the red stain covered the front of his shirt. His eyes stared lifelessly at the ceiling. She heard the screech of the cars stopping out front as she dropped the knife beside him

"Bastard," she spat at him. "It's over."

She kept the gun in his hand as she got down on the floor next to him. The blood from his shirt stained her blouse as she maneuvered him into position. She slid the knife close by her side, then grabbed his dead hand, her index finger over his on the trigger.

She waited and listened. It took only a few seconds before she heard the sound of footsteps pounding in the hall. She lifted his arm up and pointed it at the wall behind her. Almost, she thought calmly.

"Police... open up!" she heard, squeezed his hand hard and pulled the trigger

The shot exploded next to her head. Her ears rang and she thought of mom. She set his hand down to the floor carefully, and made sure the gun stayed in it as she heard them try to force the door in. Then she screamed, very loud.

Chapter Thirty

"OK, maybe its not all over," Susan said to the wall. She didn't smile because it wasn't a joke, and it certainly wasn't funny. She was glad there wasn't a mirror in the small room - she could only imagine what she looked like. For about the hundredth time in the last few hours she brushed the front of her blouse with her hands. The caked bloodstains wouldn't go away.

She wasn't quite in jail, but in custody, and she certainly wasn't going anywhere. The room was almost square, about six full steps by seven she had determined long ago. There was a small table in the center, with a couple of wooden chairs pushed underneath on either side. The walls were kind a kind of egg-shell white and stained from years without washing. The door was in the center of one of the walls, with a small square window about face high. She had seen rooms like this in dozens of movies and TV shows, but never imagined she would be locked into one.

She couldn't stop wondering what was going to happen to her, and she was so tired. The adrenaline that pumped through her body, first from fear, then from rage had long since been broken down, and left her whole body aching, her head the subject of a dull throbbing action. Her eyes were red and puffy from crying earlier, and now they were dry and stung.

There was one additional item in the room, the cause of all her current problems. She looked over at the papers, and glared at the top page of the will she had tossed across the floor. She thought back to the breakfast at sidewalk café where she had first brought the subject up and a chill shot through her. It seemed so long ago. She must have been a different person then she thought not to mention the man she had been sitting with. She was having difficulty remembering just exactly who he was, her image of the man she had loved blurred with visions of multiple identities and carefully plotted crimes. She shuddered again.

The police had shattered the door immediately after the gun went off, and flew into the room with their guns drawn. She kept screaming until they had pulled the dead body from next to her. What she remembered most after that was the sight of Fred's lifeless form laying in the middle of the floor - and all the blood. She had sat on the couch as more and more officers had come into the room, doing whatever police do in that situation, and kept to herself by herself on the sofa. No one really talked to her until two plain-clothes detectives, a man and a woman had finally arrived. They had questioned her slowly; almost sympathetic about what had happened.

She had tried to get away she told them, totally scared. She had called Marsh and Will, then 911, then was trying to leave when he came through the door. She hoped she could trick him and get out when he wasn't looking, but had been trapped in the kitchen. She had no idea why she grabbed the knife. They had argued and he pulled the gun from the garment bag. She had panicked and tried to get away when he pointed the gun at her. They struggled and he shot wildly. She pushed him away and stabbed him in the chest.

Then one of the officers had come from the hall with the will. They looked at it, their expressions changed. They had taken her to the station, for some more details they explained, and where she had been ever since. She couldn't remember how many times she had gone over the story since then. They let her call Marsh, who was frantic, but that was hours ago and other than when she was questioned she had been alone. She had no idea what time it was, or what was going to happen to her.

She pulled a chair out from the table and sat down again. She just wanted to sleep.

The noise of the jet droned monotonously underneath Marsh, who looked at his watch again. It had barely changed since the last time he thought. He picked up the glass from the armrest at his side and took a sip of what used to be scotch over ice, but was now a scotch and warm water. He sipped it anyway and wished it would calm him down. The other glass was empty. Will had finished his a while ago. Marsh looked over at the detective, who had his eyes closed and his head back against the seat. Marsh wondered if he was sleeping. It had been Will's suggestion to get the drinks. Hey they're free he joked, and Marsh knew he was just trying to get him to relax a little.

"No, I'm not," Will said. His didn't head move and his eyes didn't open.

"Not what?"

"Sleeping."

"Oh."

The plane flew on, the cabin quiet. Marsh looked at his watch again. It said it was ten-thirty, but it was eleven thirty in Minneapolis he thought. He set about the task of changing his watch to the new time zone, and wondered what was happening to Suse. He picked up his glass again and finished off the warm liquid.

"If you don't stop fidgeting I may have to arrest you," Will said, still not opening his eyes.

"Sorry."

Marsh looked out the window, but it was totally black. He tried to figure out where they were. Iowa or South Dakota maybe. He could check the map he thought, then decided it was silly.

The three of them were frantic when Susan didn't call back - well at least he and Sara had been. Will had simply gone into action. He had dragged them back to his desk after waiting for five minutes, then shoved the phone back into Marsh's hand.

"Keep calling," he said.

He had picked up his phone and called someone, appeared calm, but deadly serious. Despite their growing fear, Marsh and Sara had been amazed.

"If you don't get me someone in Minneapolis that knows every fucking thing that happens in that town, you will be parking cars in the police lot, understand?" Will had said to whoever it was, then turned to Marsh. "Police procedure," he added.

Marsh kept dialing her number, but the phone wouldn't answer.

Will just waited, his face a study in concentration. Finally he had spoken to Marsh again.

"You are a frequent flyer I presume?"

Marsh had nodded.

"There's a phone over there. Get us on the next flight to Minneapolis."

Marsh didn't question him. He handed the phone to Sara and got up to call United.

"Marsh..." Will had added softly, stopping him. "Not Sara, just us two."

Sara protested strongly, wanting to go too, but Will had been firm.

"I'm sorry Sara, but not this time." He had left little room for argument.

"What do you think is going on?" he asked Will.
Will moved this time, and looked at Marsh. "Here I am, a poor black cop sitting up in First Class, trying to enjoy this luxurious ride and you keep bothering me with questions."
"I'm serious Will. I'm worried about her."
The humor wasn't working Will decided. "OK Marsh, sorry. I'm worried too, but I'm sure she is fine."
"Why are they holding her? Why won't they let her go?"
"Procedure. They have a dead body, and I will put it bluntly, a motive. To be honest, it's what I would do."
The fear shot through Marsh again. How could this be happening again?
"Marsh, it's just routine. Susan was in his apartment, and Fred is dead. She has admitted that she killed him, in self-defense of course, but there is this matter of the will they found. She is the sole beneficiary and that raised some eyebrows. There are a lot of people running around, trying to figure out if they should charge her or not."
"With murder."
"Possibly, but I would think it would be a lesser charge, manslaughter maybe."
"Jesus."
"Don't worry. We'll get it all straightened out. The lawyer will be there when we arrive, and I'll add my two cents worth. It will be fine, trust me."

They had left the station in Will's car, a black BMW. They had two hours before the flight and had driven to Will's place first, for a change of clothes. Then to Marsh's where Sara would stay while they were gone. It was there that Susan had finally reached them.
"Are you OK Suse? Where are you? What happened?" Marsh had said when he answered the phone.
"I'm OK I guess," she sobbed. "I'm at the police station. They are asking me all kinds of questions. I'm so scared Marsh."
"We're coming Suse. We will be there as soon as we can. Hang on OK?"
They didn't let her talk much longer, but Will spoke briefly to the

male detective who was questioning her. He didn't reveal much. It was then he called the contact in Minneapolis. The conversation was long, and Marsh and Sara could only hear one side, mostly Will just acknowledging something after listening in silence. Finally he had hung up the phone.

"They are holding her for a while," Will had told them. "To be honest they don't know what to do at this point. It seems as if Fred left a will. I suggest we get a lawyer down there fast."

Marsh had tracked down Steve Race, and tried to explain the situation as best he could. Then once again Will took over the phone and explained to the lawyer in police terms what was going on. Steve assured them that someone would be there, a friend of his from law school, who was the best. They had left for the airport immediately, promising Sara they would call her when they arrived.

The flight attendants began to move around the cabin again, and prepared for landing. Marsh couldn't wait to get off the plane.

"Are you ready for this?" Will asked, a concerned look on his face.

"I think so."

"Promise me one thing. Stay calm and let me and the legal eagle handle everything. You are there for support, for Susan. I don't want you talking, or getting all emotional on me. Understand?"

"I'll try."

"Fucking civilians," Will said. "I should probably just handcuff you to the car."

Marsh just stared at him.

"Relax Marsh, it's almost over," Will smiled.

They took a cab from the airport downtown to the police station.

The lawyer's name was James Adams, and he met them in the lobby of the station, dressed in jeans and a golf shirt. Marsh was immediately disappointed.

"Marsh?" he said and held out his hand. "Jim Adams. Nice to meet you."

Marsh shook it reluctantly. "Hi, Marsh Hawkins, uh thanks for coming Jim."

"How'd you know it was him?" Will asked.

Jim shook Will's hand next, firmly. "Detective Smith, nice to meet you. Steve filled me in. He said Marsh was shorter and older."

Will smiled. "You'll do. Let's go somewhere to talk."

Marsh couldn't believe they were joking. "Where's Susan? Can we see her?"

"Over here," Jim said, and nodded with his head towards the corner where there was a couch and a couple of chairs."

"First things first Marsh," Will reminded him and they walked over and sat down.

"OK, here's what's going down," Jim started. "As of a half hour ago, when I got here they hadn't charged Susan. But they are still holding her."

"Why?" Marsh asked again.

Will shot another glance at Marsh. "I think we all know that. Let the man talk." He turned to Jim. "The question is, are they going to?"

"I don't think so, at least not tonight. I checked with some people I know here and here's the problem. One of the detectives that brought Susan in is bucking for a promotion, and is a little over zealous so to speak. When Susan explained everything, he realized that this was more than a domestic self-defense incident, and they had an honest to God wanted man in their pocket."

"Shit," Will said. "A fucking cowboy. That's all this is?"

"That about sums it up. If it wasn't late on a Friday night somebody would have stepped up to the plate already and let her go - at least until Monday when I presume this whole thing will be straightened out."

"I'm still confused," Marsh admitted.

"It's pretty simple Marsh," Will explained. "The people in charge have found out about Fred, who he is and what he's done. Susan is a ticket to instant recognition. They play up the fact that they have resolved a series of previously unsolved robberies, and wrap it up nicely with a potential murder. Makes great press. Sara should be here, she would understand."

Marsh couldn't believe it. "All at Susan's expense?" he said, incredulous.

"I'm afraid that's the way it works Marsh. I'm sorry," Jim said, face solemn.

"So what do we do now?"

"Well to be honest, I've been waiting for you," Jim said.

"Why?" Marsh said, demanding.

"Marsh, when I found out you would be here about the same time as I would, I decided to wait," he said, an apologetic look on his face.

"You let her stay in there? Alone?"

Jim looked at Will, nodded, and allowed the detective to continue the explanation.

"He was right Marsh. Susan needs somebody now, trust me. A half-hour is not all that long and she is a strong woman. Imagine what it would be like to be released to this," Will said and waved his hand to the empty room, "with no one to meet her - to be with her."

Marsh understood, but reluctantly. "Maybe you are right..."

Will turned to Jim again. "I suggest you go work some lawyer magic."

Jim got up, nodding. Marsh started to get up also, but Will put a strong hand on his shoulder and pushed him back into his seat. "Not you," he said.

Jim walked away and they waited.

It was over an hour before Susan came out. She spotted Marsh and ran across the tiled floor, her flat heels echoed in the empty hall. Marsh jumped up and ran towards her and grabbed her hard. They hugged for a long time without saying anything.

The lawyer followed behind and smiled. Will walked over and shook his hand.

"Sorry it took so long. They were... reluctant," Jim said.

"I can imagine. Nice work though," Will said.

Susan cried hard into Marsh's shoulder. Finally they parted a little and walked over to Will and Jim.

"I don't know how to thank you," Marsh said, his arm around Susan.

"Not a problem, glad to do it," Jim responded

"Yes, thank you," Susan said, her face streaked with tears. "I don't even know you..."

"Sure you do. You'll find out next winter when I want to go skiing," he said with a smile. "By the way, you have two rooms reserved at the Marriott City Center. Thought you might need someplace to stay."

"But how?" Marsh stammered.

"I had a half hour to kill remember? I'll call you tomorrow." The lawyer walked away and left them alone.

"Well I think that about wraps up the legal shit," Will said. "Do you suppose the rooms at the Marriott have a mini-bar?"

Susan stared at him for a minute, then ran over and hugged him, not saying anything. Finally she pulled back and held both his hands in hers.

"What would we have done without you Will?"

"Struggled along I suppose. Shall we go?"

"Yes we shall," she said.

Will left the next afternoon, after a long and leisurely lunch. He had detective shit to do he explained. Marsh stayed in Minneapolis through Monday afternoon, and made sure that all the legal issues were completely resolved. Susan was cleared of all charges, though there was still a big splash in the papers on Sunday. Sara had wanted to fly in, but Marsh told her not to, he wanted to be alone with Susan for a day. She claimed that she was missing out on a big story, much to Susan's amusement. Marsh didn't think it was very funny.

"So what are you going to do now?" Marsh asked.

They were having a drink at the airport before his flight back to Denver. He had avoided the subject up until then.

"I'm going to take some time off," she said, almost reluctantly. "I called in and resigned as soon as we got the word this afternoon. I don't know why but I couldn't really face going back to work… and the people there."

"It wasn't your fault Suse."

"I know, but I feel like a notorious woman, because of the papers and everything. I don't know how any of my friends would be able to look at me and not remember what happened."

"Like a celebrity?"

"A fallen one. I don't want to be famous Marsh, I just want to be me."

He smiled, and thought this was the right time. "What about coming back to Colorado? You could be you there."

"I'll think about it," she said, "Really."

They were both quiet, the sounds of the airport busy around them.

"What about you?" Susan asked.

"What do you mean?"

"Well, you and Sara for one thing."

"Ahhh, a girl question."

"Yes, a girl question." She said and smiled.

"I don't know. It's been an amazing few weeks. She is working on her story, and I have a business to run."

"Now that's a typical male response. How romantic."
"We both will give it some time," he said.

Epilogue

The sun was warm on her back as Susan walked from the bar by the pool, the sand hot on her feet, the margarita cold in her hand. She had a large sun hat on, and the yellow thong bikini she had gotten from what's his name ages ago. She ignored the stares from the three young men playing catch with a football, even though they stopped throwing it around as she went by. She looked instead toward the beachside cabanas and wondered who was staying in each one as she passed it. Hers was the fourth one down from the pool, and she skipped quickly over the last few yards. She opened the waist high wooden gate and stepped onto the carpeted sitting area and set her drink down on the table under the huge umbrella next to her computer.

She looked at the long phone cord that snaked across the floor back into the cabana and sighed, knowing she had a little more work to do. She sat down in the high-backed padded chair, took a sip of her drink and looked out over the Caribbean. It was late afternoon - well after five she thought - and she deserved a break and a cocktail. The sun danced off the tops of the gentle waves, and a slight breeze drifted over her. She watched for a moment and thought how beautiful it was before she turned back to her computer.

The next email from Steve Race, now her attorney, was marked urgent as usual. He was complaining again, how she wasn't paying proper attention to the tax implication of her inheritance. She paused for a moment and thought how ridiculous that sounded. Inheritance didn't seem to fit she thought. She had retained Steve at Marsh's insistence even though at first she didn't want the money. The computerized will had taken several months to prove valid, much to the objection of Fred's relatives. A quarter of a million dollars had convinced them not to fight it.

She was suddenly rich, and a good conversationalist she thought, and at first didn't know what to do with the money. She had taken care of two things immediately however. First, she paid back every one of the grocery stores, with interest of course, of all the money that had been stolen. Then she set up a small trust fund for Liza and moved her into a managed care facility in Denver. She had done it anonymously, but had visited her several times over the summer. It had been the first big step in her recovery.

The last mail was the formal notification of the Board of Directors meeting for the company. She had invested a million dollars in Marsh's firm, allowing him to begin to expand into other cities. She was a silent partner, but Marsh insisted she be installed on the Board, and she couldn't believe what a hassle it was. She sighed again and sipped at her drink. Big business, who would have thought?

Then there was a note from Sara, reminding her to get the current issue of Time, where the story would be printed. She had already approved it of course, well before it was published. She thought it was a little too personal, but didn't want to say anything. It was news after all - old news anyway. She sent back a quick reply, and asked again when the wedding would be. It was a personal joke between them but she hoped someday to get a response.

The rest of the messages were from her bots, and she ignored them. She had done enough trading for the day. Lebida would get copies anyway, and if there was something urgent she would handle it. Susan thought for a moment, and wondered if Marsh was really mad at her for stealing the resourceful young woman away to be her ace researcher on the Web.

She got up and walked to the railing, then looked out towards the sea again. The Grand Cayman Islands was a magical place she thought, and she had kept the largest account there just to have an excuse to come down. It was Thursday, and she had to leave on Monday to close on the house in Wash Park, very close to Sheila's it turned out. She wished she could stay longer. She walked back and glanced at the clock on the computer. It was still early afternoon in Denver, and she wondered when Will would call.

She had invited him down for the weekend.

He said he would think about it.

Printed in the United States
1062200002B/232-246